Together by Christmas

Karen Swan is the *Sunday Times* top three bestselling author of nineteen books and her novels sell all over the world. She writes two books each year – one for the summer period and one for the Christmas season. Previous winter titles include *Christmas at Tiffany's*, *The Christmas Lights* and *The Christmas Party*, and for summer, *The Greek Escape*, *The Spanish Promise* and *The Hidden Beach*.

Her books are known for their evocative locations and Karen sees travel as vital research for each story. She loves to set deep, complicated love stories within twisty plots, sometimes telling two stories in the same book.

Previously a fashion editor, she lives in Sussex with her husband, three children and two dogs.

Visit Karen's author page on Facebook, follow her on Twitter @KarenSwan1, on Instagram @swannywrites, and on her website www.karenswan.com.

Also by Karen Swan

Together by
Christmas

KAREN SWAN

PAN BOOKS

First published 2020 by Macmillan

This edition first published 2020 by Pan Books
an imprint of Pan Macmillan
The Smithson, 6 Briset Street, London EC1M 5NR
Associated companies throughout the world
www.panmacmillan.com

ISBN 978-1-5290-0610-0

1 3 5 7 9 8 6 4 2

A CIP catalogue record for this book is available from the British Library.

Typeset in Palatino by Palimpsest Book Production Ltd, Falkirk, Stirlingshire
Printed and bound by CPI Group (UK) Ltd, Croydon, CR0 4YY

Visit **www.panmacmillan.com** to read more about all our books
and to buy them. You will also find features, author interviews and
news of any author events, and you can sign up for e-newsletters
so that you're always first to hear about our new releases.

For Helen Fearn.
Another strong mama.

Prologue

Turkish–Syrian border, 2014

'I can't believe you got a car.' Lee looked around the spartan interior of the old Toyota Hilux, impressed.

'Of course I got a car.' Cunningham looked across at her and winked, the hot wind blowing his dark hair back, his eyes hidden behind his aviators.

She shook her head with a sigh. He could charm the devil. 'How'd you do it?'

'Fifty bucks and all my smokes.'

She arched an eyebrow. 'All of them?'

'Well, maybe not quite all.' He grinned, reaching into the pocket of his flak jacket and handing some over.

She shook her head.

'You quit?' He sounded incredulous. Cigarettes and whisky were some of the only pleasures to be had out here.

'Trying to. Those things will kill you, you know.'

He threw his head back and laughed, replacing the cigarettes in his jacket pocket. 'Yeah, right – it's the cigarettes that'll get me.'

She smiled too, dropping her head onto the armrest, feeling happy to be back. The windows were open – the air con had died in this car long before war had broken out – and she could feel the sun beating ferociously on her arm as it lay flat on the ledge.

Her camera lay on her lap, ever-ready, but for once she didn't pick it up. She wasn't working yet and her eyes grazed the empty landscape, looking for beauty – a green tree, a high-flying bird, cattle grazing, some flowers. Instead, they were amid an unbroken panorama of red, baked earth, mountains at their backs, the mighty Euphrates a few miles south. Every so often, they passed a stray coil of barbed wire twisted on the ground, a deep gash in the ground where an IED had gone off, tumbling concrete ruins of what had once been villages, plumes of dust in the sky from not-so-distant gunfire and mortar attacks.

She closed her eyes, enjoying the feeling of her blonde hair tickling her face in the breeze, trying to resist sleep. She had only been back out here for three days but those three days had been spent on the road trying to catch up with Cunningham since her flight into the military airbase in Hama, the region where they were supposed to have met up. She had gone home for six weeks for a badly needed break but Cunningham hadn't stopped moving in that time: she had left him in Raqqa, he'd journeyed through Hama – seemingly without stopping – and now, here they were in Aleppo province, nudging the Turkish border.

To Lee – momentarily softened again by her retreat to the land of electricity and hot running water, of luxury cars and feathered beds – it felt like standing on the knife-edge of the world, the horizon found and captured with nothing else beyond. The colours, the heat, the noise – everything was raw here. Conditions seemed to have deteriorated in the time she'd been gone; she wouldn't have thought that was possible after Homs, but somehow the level for rock bottom kept dropping down.

The road was in desperately poor condition, deep potholes and ruts bouncing them around alarmingly; it seemed unlikely the old Toyota's suspension could take it, and yet somehow the little car kept motoring along, blooms of dust in their wake.

'I saw you hooked up with Schneider.' She arched an eyebrow.

He looked across at her and gave a bemused laugh. 'Now don't you get jealous. I had to use someone. I didn't know if you were even gonna come back.'

'I said I would, didn't I?'

He gave her one of his looks, the ones that went where words wouldn't. They both knew how she'd been when she'd left here. Homs had been brutal, a relentless, pounding bombardment that had pulled the marrow from the bones of even the most seasoned reporters.

'He's not a patch on you, Fitch, and you know it.' He gave her one of his famous grins and she couldn't help but grin back – she did know it – both of them feeling the adrenaline surge that came from doing this job. By any normal definition of the word, they were mad, driving headlong into a conflict zone and actively looking forward to it.

How many assignments had they been on together now? Eleven, twelve? Pretty impressive given the areas they'd worked, given this had been an accidental partnership in the first place. But Homs had been a pivot for them both. She'd thought she'd seen the worst there was to see, she'd thought barbarity had lost its shock value for her and no depravities remained to break her heart. Until the barrel bombs had started falling from the skies. Even now, the sight of a helicopter, the sound of its distinctive drone, made her blood stand still in her veins.

And what was it for? Why did she and Cunningham put themselves through this, dismantling their own souls, putting their lives on the line when it didn't change anything? Words on the front page of a newspaper weren't enough; a photo of a child's terror, a mother's desperation, wasn't enough to stop those bombs from falling, because still they fell, and harder than ever. But she was drawn back here – against her better judgement, against all reason – for *the very simple reason that if not her, then who? People only believed what they could see; she had to be their eyes. These stories had to be told. These people had no one else. And neither did she.*

Cunningham reached over and squeezed her thigh. 'It's good to have you back, Fitch. I missed you.'

'Yeah, I guess I missed your ugly mug too. Although I'd have appreciated you telling me to meet you here, instead of a hundred miles away,' she said with a sarcastic smile. 'That was three nights' sleep I'll never get back.'

He chuckled, his fingers tapping lightly on the top of the steering wheel. 'Gotta go where the stories are, Fitch.'

'There's stories all over this hellhole. You can't move for stories. There's not a person in this country who doesn't have a story.'

He looked across and winked. 'Not like this one.'

Something in his body language caught her attention and made her antennae twitch. 'Oh God,' she groaned. She had seen that look only a handful times over the course of their partnership but she knew exactly what it meant. 'What have you got?'

'A tip-off.'

'Uh-huh,' she mumbled, waiting for more. Cunningham prided himself on his network of contacts; it ran across the country, criss-crossing regions like a gossamer spider's web, unseen but for a tiny vibration in the wind.

'There's a small village, Khrah Eshek, eight miles west of here. There's a guy there I want to talk to. Name of Moussef. I helped his cousin, Abbad, in Raqqa—'

She watched him as he talked, seeing how burnt his skin was, the dust in his hair, fatigue as worn upon his body as that shirt. Did he even notice any more? She had only been gone six weeks but her perspective was fresh again. She saw this place with new eyes.

'—get his three kids out of their house when it took a direct hit.

His little girl was pinned beneath a lintel. We managed to get her free but both her legs were crushed.'

'How old was she?' She winced, already seeing it clearly in her mind's eye. How many other little girls had she photographed in the same anguish?

He shrugged but she saw the little ball pulse in the corner of his jaw. 'Six?'

'Will she walk again?'

'She'll walk. But she'll never be a dancer.'

Lee inhaled sharply, looking back out of the window. No one danced here anyway. It was almost perverse to think of music and laughter and dancing when the sky was bright with fires, the country burning.

'Anyway, that's background,' he said tightly, not wanting to dwell on what the little girl had lost; she was alive – that was all that mattered. 'Moussef, like I said, is his cousin. The village has been overrun with people escaping Kobanî. You've no doubt heard ISIL have been ramping up the number of attacks there recently.'

Of course she'd heard, and Lee squeezed her jaw in anger, already knowing the stories she and Cunningham would hear when they got there, already knowing how this would play out; the jihadists' strategic aim wasn't just about gaining control of the city, but the entire canton. They had overrun the region in recent weeks and had already taken control of hundreds of villages. Nowhere was safe. With the city under siege – there were reports of the electricity and water supplies already being cut off – it was no better on the outside either for the tens of thousands of displaced citizens fleeing from one toppled village to the next, straight into the arms of their enemy.

Hadn't these people been through enough? When would it end? There were already no more houses to live in, no shops to shop in, no people to rule – millions of Syrians had been displaced by this war already. What were they even fighting for any more? Dust?

'But that's not the story,' he whispered, leaning towards her.

Being first in on an ISIL insurgence wasn't the story? She arched an eyebrow in surprise, seeing his excitement fizzing below the surface, his eyes burning. Instinctively, she picked up the camera and snapped him. In his element. She rarely took pictures of him, scarcely ever recorded the fleeting moments of brightness, but occasionally those moments felt as necessary as the dark ones, and right now, more than ever, she felt impelled to grab it, to remind herself that life was about more than just staying alive. She didn't need to check the viewfinder to know she'd nailed the shot.

'You remember those two teenage girls who left Lyons to become jihadi brides – about two years ago?'

She watched him, waiting for the reveal. '. . . Vaguely.'

'According to Abbad, they've fled ISIL and are hiding out in Khrah Eshek, trying to get to the border. Their husbands were killed in a drone strike; one of them's got a kid, the other's pregnant. They're trying to get back to France but getting to the border camps is risky – ISIL have put a high price on their heads and they're paranoid as hell they're going to be sold out.'

'That's not paranoia. They will be.'

He nodded.

She frowned. 'How does Abbad know this if he's almost a hundred miles away?'

'Moussef is helping them.' Cunningham's eyes glittered as his plan became clear. 'Abbad thinks I could help swing the international spotlight on them. He's offered Moussef to be our guide, and translator, if needed.'

'Oh, I see. You can help get those girls out of there – and you also get a world exclusive?' A sardonic note coloured her words.

He shrugged, not denying it. 'We get a world exclusive. An

insider's view of life within ISIL? It'll be the pinnacle of both our careers.' He glanced over, eyes shining, his body already primed with adrenaline, and she knew that whatever his motivations – glory, compassion or common, decent humanity – he never felt more alive than this. *'You speak French, don't you?'*

'Un peu.' She sounded like she was spitting out a fly.

'Good. Could be useful.'

'I doubt it,' she scoffed. *'Unless they're giving me directions to the bakery to buy two baguettes and a croissant. Or need to know the time. Or my daily routine when I was at school.'*

The first faint signs of the destroyed city that was Kobanî emerged on the horizon and they both flinched as a mortar flew out across the sky, miles from here, and yet close enough for them to feel the vibration in the ground as another building was levelled. More lives lost.

Lee saw his grip tighten around the wheel. *'And you're sure you can trust him, this Moussef guy?'*

'I saved his family, Fitch.' He stared dead ahead at a horizon that had, somewhere along it, two terrified young women, far from home. Being hunted by some of the most dangerous individuals on the planet, they couldn't know that right now their tickets to safety were hurtling towards them in a clapped-out pale-blue Toyota with a Canon 5D Mark III as their only defensive weapon. *'. . . We're going to do some good in this godforsaken hellhole today,'* he murmured, although whether for her benefit or his, she wasn't sure.

'Right.' Lee shifted position, feeling the old familiar fear begin to pitch in her stomach as they drew ever closer to the red zone. She had hoped there would be some time at least before they ran headlong into the maws of war, even if it was just twenty minutes in a room with her feet on the ground, instead of endlessly bumping along hard, stony roads.

He glanced over again. He could read her better than any other *person on this planet. He instinctively knew when she was uncertain, afraid, unsure. 'Hey, you trust me, don't you?'*

She stared back at her old friend and sighed, her hands on the camera, all ready to lift and point. 'God only knows why I do.'

He grinned his prize-winning grin again. 'Then what could possibly go wrong?'

Chapter One

Bloemgracht, Amsterdam, 14 November 2020

'I can see him!'

'Really? Yay!' Thank God. Lee shifted her weight against the railing as Jasper wriggled on her shoulders, barely able to contain his delight. The parade was now coming into view, the growing cacophony of the crowd and the increasing din of a brass band telling her the great moment was finally upon them. Every under-ten in the city had been waiting for this moment all year, although she had begun praying hard for it herself about twenty minutes earlier – her neck was stiff from being bent forwards and her shoulders were screaming for relief from her beloved son's jiggling, kicking weight as they stood awaiting Sinterklaas's triumphant arrival in the city. Not to mention it was f-f-f-freezing. She had spent the past few minutes watching her own breath make lacy patterns in the air.

'There's Zwarte Piet!' Jasper yelled, waving a red plastic flag excitedly above his head as the first boat in the flotilla passed by. It was laden with bewigged men and women dressed in brightly coloured velvet costumes, with puff sleeves and ruff collars, tossing sweets and gingerbread to the children on the banks. Their very presence here marked the start of the festive season and every child along this canal's edge believed that, as of now, they – Sinterklaas's helpers – would be scooting down their chimneys each night for the next few weeks, leaving small gifts for the good and well-behaved, in the build-up to Pakjesavond (or 'present-giving evening') on the 5th of December and St Nicholas' Day on the 6th, the highlight of the Dutch festive calendar. Christmas came a distant second here, although having an English mother meant Jasper reaped the benefits of visits from both Sinterklaas and Santa Claus.

'He saw me! He waved at me!' Jasper yelled, drumming his heels painfully against her chest, utterly oblivious to her discomfort.

'Stop kicking, Jazz,' she called up, squeezing his shin to get him to calm down.

'But he looked straight at me and gave me the thumbs up! He's going to visit, mama. I've been good, I've been good!'

She couldn't help but smile. 'Of course you have. You're the best little boy in the city, I keep telling you that.'

'There he is!' Jasper's voice rose three octaves and the heel-drumming began again as Sinterklaas's barge glided past them. The great man had a flowing white beard, was dressed in a red-and-white robe with matching mitre, and was carrying a hooked staff. He was waving beatifically to the great crowds gathered for him, knowing that as he disembarked a few hundred yards further up, ready to ride his white horse, Amerigo, through the streets, they would follow him too. There would be almost half a million out today, joining in the start of the festivities. 'Let's follow him!'

'Okay then.' She turned away from the water and moved uncertainly through the jostling crowd, her hands gripping Jasper's skinny calves. He wouldn't give her his hands, too busy waving frenetically and pointing at all the presents piled atop the barges as the Christmas convoy sailed into town. She slowly climbed the short slope to the humped bridge but it was like wading through treacle, prams and buggies not helping the sluggish flow as parents battled to keep their children both close and under control.

Everyone had come out, it seemed, a carnival atmosphere permeating the cold streets, trumpets blaring intermittently and whistles blowing; even those without kids were leaning from their windows, watching the festivities with beers in their hands, music drifting from narrow apartments in the handsome seventeenth-century black-bricked buildings hooded with white gables.

The congestion eased somewhat as they moved above the water, crossing the bridge. They had to walk down the very centre of it; there was no chance of getting near the edges with these numbers, not with that vantage point. From the sudden cheer, she could tell the boat had docked ahead and that Sinterklaas was disembarking.

'Can you see him?' she asked Jasper, who was still wriggling and twisting on her shoulders like she was a swivel seat.

'He's getting on Amerigo!' he pointed, oblivious to the fact that she couldn't see over most people's shoulders. Being almost five foot ten didn't mean much when everyone else was that – or taller – too.

'Great!' she cried back, wondering if this would mean they could wrap it up now and go get a hot chocolate with marshmallows somewhere. She was beginning to lose feeling in her fingers and toes. 'Well, listen—'

But he knew her tone of voice too well. 'I want to see him on the horse!'

She squeezed his leg again, still unable to see Sinterklaas

directly. 'But that's probably as good as it's going to get, Jazz. He's got all the other kids to see now, hasn't he? And you said Zwarte Piet saw you, right? So we're good for him coming over. So why don't we—?'

The sound ripped through the crowd – sharp, shocking. They startled as one, the collective gasp like a muscular contraction, everyone looking left and right for the source of the noise. Everyone except her. In one fluid movement, with a strength she didn't know she possessed, Lee had Jasper off her shoulders and in her arms and she was running. Sprinting, in fact. Pushing through the crowds, her arms over her child's head, she cut a line through the bodies that only moments before had seemed so impossible to navigate. She heard words carry through the air but she didn't stop.

'Mama, wait! Stop!' Jasper cried, his voice muffled against her coat as she kept on going, turning off the main drag onto the smaller side streets, one, two, three back . . . Within minutes they were alone, just a dog walker and a couple of cyclists either side of a small canal, chatting away easily with that relaxed stance that marked out the locals from the tourists.

Lee put her son down on the cobbles and looked him over, her eyes frantically roaming for blood, dust, signs of injury . . . He blinked back at her, still, silent, trembling, as she realized she had a stitch. As she realized he looked frightened. As she finally processed what the man beside her had said to his wife in the moment immediately after the 'bang'.

'It's just a groundcracker.'

Chapter Two

Thursday, 26 November 2020

'I love you.'

'I love you, mama.'

'Give me a kiss.' He reached up with a rosy pucker and planted a kiss on her lips. Her hands clasped his face for a moment, her gaze raking over its lusciousness: those plump cheeks, the thickly fringed long lashes, glossy chocolate-brown eyes. He was such an utterly perfect miniature human, even after five years she still couldn't quite believe that he was real – well, until she saw the state of his bedroom every morning. 'Now run along. And when you go for your walk later, try not to send any more cyclists into the canal, please. Pigeons aren't actually that exciting when you catch them, and I can't afford the dry-cleaning bills.'

'Okay,' he sighed, looking despondent at the prospect of good behaviour.

'Hmm,' she replied, staring into those eyes for another moment, before pinching his chin lovingly and straightening up. 'Off you go, then. I'll see you later.'

Jasper turned without further prompting and ran up the steps into the kindergarten building, his backpack jostling up and down on his narrow shoulders, his jeans rolled up at the ankles, flashing his Spider-Man socks.

She stood there for another moment after he had disappeared inside, just in case he popped his head back around the corner again – even though he never did – and after another pause, she turned and walked back to the bike she'd left propped against the railings. It always felt strange getting back on it without his bulk and weight on the passenger seat in front of her, the whistling emptiness between her arms as she began pedalling reminding her of life before him. Her life *before*.

She cycled with her usual lackadaisical manner, rolling languidly over the small humpback bridges and giving way to the trams but not the tourists. The city was still teeming with visitors, none of them yet put off by the cold wind and icy cobbles when there were illuminated Christmas trees, festive shop windows and pretty lights to admire. She almost looked forward to those first bruisingly cold, bitterly bleak months of the new year. It was the only time, it felt, when the locals briefly had their town to themselves again, before spring washed in the first influxes and the tourist cycle geared up again. Amsterdam was beginning to sink under their numbers, that much was certain. Just like the city's seventeenth-century Golden Age, there were too many people and not enough terra firma to go round. The new mayor was making noises about turning the city car-free, but as far as Lee was concerned, it wasn't cars that were the problem. The locals hardly used their vehicles in town anyway, everyone by far preferring to get around on foot or by bike or boat. No, it was the tourists and the Instagrammers, all idly walking around down the middle of the cobbled streets, with no concept of moving traffic heading towards them, that drove her mad.

People didn't walk down the middle of Bond Street or the Champs-Élysées or Via Montenapoleone, expecting the traffic to swerve around them, did they? The self-absorption was incredible, the desire for a good selfie overriding even personal safety. Was this a new mutation in human behaviour, she wondered, was it where the human race was heading – the glorification of the ego, the adoration of the 'I' transcending everything else? Not for the first time, she figured peace had a lot to answer for. From what she had seen, it bred insularity, selfishness, contempt for community . . .

She tugged her hat down over her ears and tightened her scarf around her neck, feeling the first drops of sleet that were trying to be something more. It was still only November but they were into a hard winter already, with a wet, windy autumn succeeded by a succession of hoar frosts, and there were already reports of first snows falling in the countryside. The canals were beginning to look ever more sluggish and thick as the temperatures stayed low, the trees bare-armed against the northerly winds, and she knew it wouldn't be long before the sea ice crept through the city too, like mercury bleeding through veins.

She wheeled around the myriad narrow streets, ringing her bell authoritatively at anyone stepping into her path – she had right of way and she would use it – gliding past the handsome black-bricked townhouses whose large square windows still glowed with breakfasting lights, people moving within them like puppet vignettes. Like the tourists, she couldn't help but glance in. It was one of the city's quirks that its inhabitants never drew their curtains, living their lives in plain, unabashed view of the neighbours, and this had been one of the hardest things for her to adjust to when she had first come back here. The instinct to scurry and hide, to tunnel down for safety, had become so ingrained that it had felt provocative and downright perverse to just . . . live freely and openly. In plain view. After five years here, she still couldn't do it.

Her studio was only an eight-minute commute from Jasper's kindergarten and she hopped off the bike with easy grace, triple-locking it securely through the back wheel and rear triangle against the stands opposite. This was her third bike already this year, and she now approached bike security like Bear Grylls on a picnic.

'Lee!' her assistant Bart said with evident relief when she tumbled through the door a few minutes later, shaking out her long, autumn-blonde hair as she pulled off her slouchy black woolly hat. Jasper had chosen it for her for Mother's Day last year (aided by his overindulgent godfather, Noah) and now she refused to wear any other. It had little black cat ears on it and often prompted amused looks from the tourists as she cycled past, but she couldn't care less; besides, it was hardly the most eccentric artistic expression in this city. 'It's the gallery,' he said, the phone in his hand, his palm blocking the receiver. 'Wondering if you've reconsidered on the guest list? They're getting a lot of calls from management agents; the interest is there, Lee—'

'We've already discussed this. It's still no,' she said in brusque Dutch – she made a point of only speaking English with Jasper, although most of the city was bilingual anyway and sometimes they all drifted into a form of 'Dutlish' (sentences in half-English, half Dutch) without even noticing. She shrugged off her thick dark-green-and-black tartan coat and unwound the navy scarf that was double-wrapped around her neck.

'But the exposure would be off the scale—'

'Yes, but for all the wrong reasons. I already told you, I don't want a bunch of C-list celebrities piggybacking the show just to get their faces in the social pages and further their careers. It goes against everything this exhibition is about – authenticity, resilience, truth.'

Bart gave one of his dramatic groans and she looked back at him, tall and rangy with bulging blue eyes behind round-rimmed glasses, once-red hair that had been bleached to the colour of pale swede. She hung up her coat on the hook. They argued the way most people chatted; sometimes she wondered if he even remembered she was technically the boss. '*I* know that, but don't you think it could all come off as a little . . . dry? Those images are so powerful, nothing's going to dilute the message. It wouldn't undermine what you're trying to say just because there's a few celebs in pretty dresses milling about.'

She pinned him with a withering stare. 'Bart, please don't be suggesting that people can only understand the horrors of assault and battery if Helena Christensen stands beside the pictures of it.'

'I'm *not* saying that,' he protested. 'I'm suggesting the chances of people getting to know they have an opportunity to understand the horrors of violence will be markedly increased if someone like Helena can bring a spotlight to it.'

She shook her head wearily. 'So we can't process grit without glamour? Is war going to need celebrity endorsement too? What the hell is wrong with this society? Don't you see what's happening to us? If even war can be trivialized, human suffering diminished . . .' Talent she respected, but vacuous celebrity, fame for fame's sake, made her shake with frustration.

'Lee, you know I admire your principles, but we'll be

suffering too if we can't pay our bills and afford to eat. You do actually need to sell the images too, as well as exhibit them.'

She stared back at him.

'A few famous faces would just help with word of mouth and raising the show's profile. It's about getting punters through the door, not cheapening your message.'

'You just said the interest's already there.'

'Ugh.' He rolled his eyes as she tripped him up with his own words.

'The answer's no, Bart.' As far as she was concerned, the conversation was over. She walked over to the coffee machine and pressed the buttons with practised familiarity, closing her eyes as she waited for the tiny cup to fill, trying to ignore the fatigue that feathered her consciousness after another night of only four hours' sleep. She could only ever sleep in short blocks of oblivion before one horror or another reached out from the past and crept into her dreams.

'It's a maybe. I'll call you back,' she heard Bart murmur into the phone.

She pretended she hadn't heard, too tired to take him to task further. She always needed a double dose of caffeine before her day could begin. Even the strongest coffee she had been able to find here couldn't give her the hit she was used to; she'd spent too many years drinking coffee that could have powered tanks to scale back to the mild blandness of the domestic stuff.

She downed the coffee in a single gulp, pressing the back of her hand to her mouth for a moment, as though feeling her life force gather, before turning back to the room. It was a vast space, with thick timbered beams and a concrete floor. Light poured in through the south-facing windows, creating pools of brightness when the skies were clear. Not today, though. The sky was thick with tumbling clouds, muffling the light; it was like peering through a gauze veil, everything softened and diffused.

Bart walked over to her officiously. 'While I remember, I've booked the car to collect you for the opening night from your place at eight.'

'Okay.'

'And ditto for the Hot dinner two weeks Friday.'

'Okay,' she mumbled.

'. . . Are you even listening?'

She was looking around flatly at the space, the centre of her working life now, so different from the landscapes she used to work in. A charcoal linen sofa and a rustic wooden coffee table were set by the far wall and a bolt of black canvas was draped from an overhead arm in the middle of the space, creating a mobile backdrop; a three-legged bar stool was set in the centre. Everything was light, bright, minimal – architect friends called it 'urban', but urban to her was rubble, a sink-hole and twisted metal.

She narrowed her eyes slightly, falling into concentration (and a numb despair) about the day ahead of her. For the past two weeks and into the next, she was shooting a select number of assorted new stars who had broken through this year to the upper ranks of stardom, for cult magazine *Black Dot*'s Hot List. It was considered *the* touchpaper to the zeitgeist, the kingmaker, and everyone who wanted to be Someone wanted to be in it. Forget running through Sniper Alley in Beirut, *this* was nearer her idea of hell, but it was a prestigious gig and they paid her an obscene sum to do it. She had sworn this year would be her last time at the helm – but then she'd said the same thing last year and the year before that too, and Bart had taken to teasing her that she was 'pulling a Daniel Craig' – feeling tainted by her association with something so unashamedly commercial, but not quite able to turn down the money . . .

She felt a disdain for her subjects, all chasing fame as though it meant a damned thing – popularity, talent, success – when in fact it was pure vanity and ego. None of the stars sitting for her even objected to being cast as a redux of someone else already famous and so far she'd done the 'new Naomi', the 'new Tarantino', the 'new Ronaldo', the 'new Ellen', the 'new Trudeau' . . . Today they had the 'new Kit Harrington', though she didn't go in much for TV herself. What was his name? Max something . . .

Whatever, she already knew today was going to require juggling his ego (her role) and his PR's nerves (Bart's). A high-profile shoot like this, for a publication like *Black Dot* . . . these were his first steps into the big time and he was going to want the fantasy – the fawning, the prepping, the flirting. They all did. Her only nod to that was getting Bart to buy the king-size, traditionally baked *stroopwafels* from the Lanskroon Bakery on his way in.

'So remind me – this guy we've got today . . .' she asked Bart, walking over to the set and picking up a speck of lint that would glow like a firefly against the black drapes.

'Matteo Hofhuis.'

'Hofhuis, right.' She clicked a finger as though in recognition, though her eyes remained blank. A frown developed. 'And who is he again? Why do we care?'

'Played the lead in the Netflix series *Liar Liar* and now the object of housewife fantasy across Europe. Supposedly Barbara Broccoli's eyeing him as the new Bond.'

Lee emitted a small groan.

'And he's just been announced as a new Unicef ambassador.'

She rolled her eyes. 'Oh God, *of course* he has,' she muttered.

'Bills, Lee.' Bart gave a shrug every bit as cynical as her words. Lee walked back over to the two-metre-long workbench where she saw he had left Matteo's file open. She grabbed her heavy-rimmed glasses and studied the headshots again – black-and-whites, slumped on a chair, muscular legs long and splayed, his shirt half-open to reveal gym-honed muscles, aggressive eye contact with the camera. He was good-looking and he knew it. She looked at the other images. Tuxedo looks. Barefoot in jeans with a chunky jumper. So far, so clichéd. He was the handsome stranger, the boy next door . . . She glanced across at the rail of clothes the stylist had sent over – some well-cut suits, crisp shirts, an overcoat, a fine roll-neck sweater. Everything was manicured, precise, so very tasteful and safe. His managers clearly wanted her to stay on message.

The sound of voices in the hall made her and Bart both look up. They could hear the PR's shrill voice as she issued directives. He was here already? He was twenty minutes early. Christ, he really was keen. The rest of her own team – hair and make-up – wasn't even here yet.

'Pastries?'

'Done,' Bart murmured, jerking his head in the direction of the Sub Zero fridge just as the door burst open and a young twenty-something redhead in black skinnies, boots and a grey blazer led the charge.

'Hi! Lee?' she asked, almost breaking into a run at the sight of her standing by the bench.

Lee shook her hand, forgetting to smile for a moment. 'Hey.' She pushed her glasses further up her nose, feeling extra tall and mannish in her battered boyfriend jeans, slouchy polo neck and hi-tops compared to this petite waif. It wasn't a particularly unusual feeling for her, nor an unwelcome one.

'I'm Claudia, Matt's PR.'

'Hi, Claudia. Lee.'

'We're so pleased this was booked. It's been a personal ambition of Matt's to work with you. He's a huge fan of your work.'

'Oh. How kind.' Lee knew the 'work' in question was her commercial stuff, the images where she was paid to flatter, not reveal.

'No, really – he says you're a visionary. That your eye is completely unsurpassed. He says no other photographer—'

'—can get to the essence of someone the way you do.'

She looked up to find the man himself standing there. His hair was longer than in his photographs, a five-day beard getting to the point where it was soft and not scratchy (Lee knew beards). Only his eyes remained true to the pictures she had seen – beautiful, arrogant, imperious. She was expected to fall in love with him, she already knew, even though he had to be eight, ten years younger than her.

As he came over with his hand outstretched, she saw him realize he was only an inch or so taller than her. They stood toe to toe, almost eye to eye, hands clasped. 'It's a real pleasure to finally meet you, Lee.'

'And you, Matteo.'

'Matt, please.' He made a move to say something else and she guessed he'd reflexively been about to ask whether she'd seen the show – it would be all anyone ever talked about to him, she knew, his standard patter; but from the way he deflated fractionally again, she could tell he sensed she hadn't, that she wasn't one of the housewives he'd left in a flutter.

He dropped her hand, breaking the gaze and casting a curious eye around the space, catching sight of the rail of sober clothes nearby. 'So, what are we doing today?'

'Well, as you can see . . .' She paused, not quite able to suppress the boredom in her voice.

Did he pick up on it? His gaze came back to her again. 'I am happy to put myself completely in your hands. I'll submit to your vision, whatever that may be.'

Claudia gave a small startled sound that quickly became strangled under one of Bart's delighted, arched-eyebrow looks.

Lee shifted her weight as she stared back at her subject, a small light climbing into her eyes, though it was scarcely visible behind the reflection of her glasses. 'Really? . . . Are you quite sure about that?'

Chapter Three

'They're going to hit the roof,' Bart said as she shrugged on her coat, her eyes on the clock. Their guests had just left and she had fifteen minutes to collect Jasper.

'Good. Reaction is the whole point, isn't it?'

'Yes, but there are still protocols to observe, as well you know. You didn't use a single item of clothing they sent over. Couldn't you at least have put him in a pair of trousers? I mean, they're a magazine, Lee, they need to keep their advertisers happy—'

'That's their problem, not mine. I did my job and got the shot. That shoot will make the cover and the cover will sell out the issue and that'll make the advertisers happy instead.' She wound her scarf around her neck and pulled her hat on over her hair, making sure the little ears were on straight. She leaned over Bart as he sat on the high stool, resting her chin on his shoulder; he was looking at the images on the contact sheets on screen and she felt another small thrill of professional achievement, so rare these days. Matteo Hofhuis was utterly transformed from the cookie-cutter heartthrob who'd walked through the doors seven hours earlier. The beard was still there, but the hair was not (Lee always kept a pair of clippers in her props bag for just such moments as these) and his bare, tanned skin had been blackened, daubed and smeared with mud Bart had had to quickly gather from the pot plants in the lobby, mixing soil and water to her desired consistency. She had been adamant he had to look like a rough sleeper, a soldier, someone living by instinct, opportunity. She wanted to scrub off the starry artifice that was already layering upon him like a golden glow, to show him stripped back and raw.

The nudity hadn't bothered him either. He looked good walking around with a tiny towel between shots and he was at that point in his career when he'd do anything to prove 'artistic integrity'. It helped that Lee took a matter-of-fact approach to these things, offering to close the set for him – but it was only her, Bart and Claudia anyway, as she had sent away both the hair and make-up artists upon their arrival.

Claudia hadn't realized the full extent of what was happening with her client until it was too late, Bart getting out the king-size *stroopwafels* at the pertinent point when Lee had brought out the clippers. She had started the shoot gently, taking the stool away and standing him in the black space in the very clothes he'd arrived in, getting him used to the camera as she prowled around him like a cat, changing height, perspective, coming in tight, pulling away, insisting he keep his eye locked on the lens at all times. She had got Bart to turn up the thermostat and as the studio warmed and his layers came off, as the minutes ticked past, she had seen the change happen in him that she'd been gently prodding for – the studied poses and eager willingness to perform for her gradually yielding to something less contrived and conscious, the novelty beginning to pall, boredom to surface, until the camera was no longer something to play to but to endure. The eyes had flattened, becoming harder, the jaw had relaxed, and steadily the act, the public persona, had fallen away until it was just her and him, even the camera being forgotten. They had been connected by the lens, divided by it, as he fell back into being the man of his private moments when he moved unobserved. Unjudged. It had been like watching a wax figure melt, blue-eyed chiselled distinction blurred out so that only the core remained. It was the moment she always strove for – naked truth. Basic humanity. Shared experience. Equality.

Lee had taken this box-fresh housewife's hero and recast him into something so much more than a stud in a suit. If he wanted Bond, this was his golden ticket. Or Hamlet. Or Atticus Finch. Or Mr Darcy. Doors were going to open on the strength of these images.

'Hmm,' she said with a pleased nod, straightening up and walking briskly towards the door. 'Not a bad day's work. Who've we got next?'

'The last one, you'll be pleased to hear. An author. He's the new . . . hmm.' Bart thought for a moment, trying to pigeon-hole their next subject. 'A. A. Milne meets Eckhart Tolle.'

'*Who?*'

'Mindfulness, Lee – gratitude, acceptance, kindness. It's a thing,' he said wryly.

She rolled her eyes, not needing to be told. She'd seen quite enough of the schmaltzy quotes being passed off as deep insight on social media to know what he was referring to. Insta-wisdom.

'So he's on Monday morning, ten o'clock start; then you're done – unless they want a re-shoot of Haven, the "new Billie Eilish" girl. I know there's not supposed to be any editorial interference but her management can be *very* tricky . . .' He pulled a face.

'Ugh.' She used to creep through jungles and over burnt-out cars to show the world images that mattered. How had she ended up pandering to the ego of an eighteen-year-old singer who hadn't even been alive when she'd bought her coat?

'Bills, Lee,' Bart murmured, reading her mind.

'. . . Yeah.' She sighed and turned away again.

'Talking of which—'

'No!' she called over her shoulder, knowing exactly what he was going to say: the gallery again. She was in a good mood, but not *that* good. 'See you tomorrow, Bart.'

The doors closed behind her and she stepped back outside. It was dark already, the city lamplit to an amber glow and looking postcard-perfect in its night-time guise. It always fascinated her how the city, with such a mannered masculinity by day – all lean lines and sombre colours – switched to a more expansive mood by night: lights glowing on the water, threaded through the trees, arching with the bridges and pooling on the cobblestones, the famous narrow, multi-windowed buildings now as pretty as gingerbread houses.

She unlocked her bike, giving her daily prayer of thanks to the Bike Gods that it was still there, and pushed off over the cobbles. The air was crisp, the first notes of a frost beginning to lace her breaths, and she felt her cheeks grow pink, her good mood bloom further as she pedalled. The cold was still something of a novelty for her and maybe always would be; it had been one of the things she had missed most in her old life and part of why she'd been drawn back here. She had swapped red dust for rain and slush, quite deliberately. She had wanted an opposite existence to her old life.

She glided past the townhouses' overly large windows like a shadow, silent but for the whirr of her wheels, feeling lighter than she had on her way in this morning. It was a struggle for her to feel accomplishment after these intense days in the studio, to feel that any of this glossy, airbrushed reality she helped create actually mattered. Today had been different though; she had captured something real through her lens and made contact – a transitory but honest connection – with another human. It wouldn't change the world but it had shifted hers, just a little.

She smiled, the gold streamers Jasper had begged her to buy at a Christmas market last year fluttering and flapping from the handlebars like a cheerleader's ribbons as she rode with her usual languid grace and unflinching aggression, using her voice and not her bell, cheerfully shouting at people to 'Move!' as she approached. She would not be made late for her child by 'influencers' trying to get a shot.

Twenty minutes later, she and Jasper were home again and she closed the front door behind them with a sigh of relief. Another day was done. Jasper gave a shout of joy to be home – she felt much the same herself – and, throwing his bag down, he pulled off his shoes and tore up the stairs to the open-plan kitchen and living area on the first floor. Lee put on the three bolts and two chains on the door and carefully slid his little trainers to the wall, out of the way, hearing his socked feet pounding on the wooden floors above her and echoing through the three-storey house. Going straight into the utility room at the back of the house, she switched this morning's laundry load from the washing machine into the tumble dryer and double-checked the back door was locked. The guest bedroom was across the hall from the bottom of the stairs and she stopped in the doorway, as she always did, checking there were no signs of disturbance.

The curtains were drawn, naturally – she would never subscribe to the Dutch preference for unobscured windows; she rated privacy (and security) above light – and she switched on the light, trying to appraise the room with fresh eyes. She rarely actually came in here, but she knew it wasn't the most successful space – the double bed was fitted without a head-board, the lamp shade was a cheap Ikea rattan number that looked more like a lobster pot and the pillows were different thicknesses so the turquoise kantha quilt lay on a slope. Still, she had painted the walls a rich blackish-green, which felt luxurious, and a thick creamy imitation Moroccan rug felt good underfoot.

She turned out the light again and pulled the bedroom door to, and was about to walk up the stairs when someone rang the bell. She turned and stared at it in shock. It was half past five. She'd said eight. Surely—? She stood there for several moments more – it could just be kids messing about, tourists wanting directions, someone with the wrong address . . . She walked over, but just as she was about to look through the spyhole, she heard a cough.

It stopped her in her tracks, her heart rate accelerating into a gallop. She would have known that sound anywhere. She didn't need to look through the spyhole to know what she would see: a square-jawed face, possibly getting a little jowly now, salt-and-pepper hair, expansive ever-smiling mouth and dark, soulful eyes pleading for forgiveness.

She froze, not daring to move, willing him to go away.

'Fitch, I just saw the light go off. I know you're there!' he called after another few moments, making her jump again.

Oh God, Jasper. The neighbours. Jasper. She didn't want him hearing any of this.

She took a step back, onto a cracked floorboard. It creaked. She froze. He couldn't have heard that.

But an immediate soft sound against the door, a hand perhaps on the wood, told her otherwise. 'I know you're there, Fitch.' His voice was low, quieter, closer. He was talking straight through the door to her. So close. 'Please. Please just open the door.'

Her heart pounded as she continued staring at the door, feeling rooted to the spot, flooded with panic. With his voice came so many other sounds, so many memories. She put her hands over her ears but it was no good. She couldn't block them – him – out. They lived inside her head.

'I just want to talk to you.'

She scrunched her eyes shut, willing him to go away. Just turn around and leave. She had made her feelings perfectly clear. She ignored every letter, every card, every text. He knew she would never open the door, she never did.

'*Please*, Fitch. You can't keep ignoring me for ever.'

But she could. She had done it for six years and she would do it for six more. And then the six after that, and the six after that . . . She waited, forcing herself to breathe deeply and slowly. He would go. Eventually. He'd have to. The freezing temperatures would drive him away, if nothing else.

'Fine, then. I'll do it here.' She heard his sigh through the thick wood. 'There's something I have to tell you.'

She didn't care. She didn't care. She didn't care—

'Gisele's pregnant.'

Lee's hands dropped down from her ears, her eyes wide. She felt the floor tilt beneath her feet as the words settled like rocks in her stomach. Gisele was pregnant. She was surprised – and she wasn't. This day had been bound to come. They had been married three years now; she was young. It made sense she'd want to start a family, to have his child.

Did he really think she cared? Was that what had prompted him to come and stand on her doorstep in these temperatures? Did he think it somehow made him a better human being, now that he was going to be a father? Wasn't it rather too late for that? She felt herself harden, wet clay to concrete, anger to action. She turned away and walked back up the hall, up the stairs, his voice receding at her back, her heart hammering in her chest.

'Please, Fitch, just let me come in. Five minutes, that's all I'm asking . . .'

She walked into the vast open-plan kitchen and living area, drenched in light and sound. She turned down the dimmers slightly. Jasper was on his hands and knees on the floor, playing with the remote-control car his godfather Noah had given him, 'just because', a few weeks earlier. *Star Wars* was playing on the TV in the background, thankfully throwing out enough galactic noise to drown out Cunningham's mournful pleas.

'Hungry?' she asked, walking to the cupboard and hoping a dinner she'd forgotten to buy ingredients for would miraculously emerge before her. She was what she called a cupboard cook, using whatever happened to be on the shelf – nothing was ever planned, rarely was it successful, but somehow she and Jasper got by on her strange concoctions. Jasper's favourite was her sausage noodle bake, which never tasted the same, no matter how often she cooked it.

'*Star*ving!' Jasper proclaimed dramatically.

'Okay, well . . .' she said, staring into the fridge like it was a maths equation. There had to be an answer in there somewhere. It might be only just after five thirty, but it was supper time, and their lives ran according to the clock of Jasper's stomach. 'Spaghetti arrabbiata?'

'We had pasta at lunch.'

'Oh well, that's a first-world problem, my darling,' she shrugged, reaching for the diced pancetta. 'There are worse things than having pasta twice in one day.'

She put on a pan of water, rummaging in the cupboards

for a ready-made tomato sauce and hoping she wouldn't have to water down some ketchup like last time. Whilst the pasta cooked, she lit a fire in the baroque marble fireplace, and when dinner was ready, they went straight into a spaghetti-sucking contest. Afterwards, they shared a bath and then flopped on the sofa for some telly-watching before bed and a story. It was their usual Thursday night routine, and identical to the Monday, Tuesday, Wednesday and Friday routines too. Nothing ever changed in their lives because there was no need for it to. That in itself was a luxury, she knew. There were no potential ambushes to outfox on the way home; no bombs tearing through the sky as they cycled to the shops. Life here was quiet, repetitive and predictable. It was safe. It was everything she had promised to give him.

'I love you, Jazz.'

'I love you, mama,' he said, the duvet tucked all the way up under his chin.

She stroked his cheek, feeling its padded velvety softness against her own skin, which felt so rough by comparison; she had spent too many years scrabbling through rubble to ever have the soft hands of TV advert mothers. 'Give me a kiss.' He puckered up his rosy lips and she planted a kiss on them. Her hands clasped his face for a moment as she marvelled at the miracle of him. He was the image of his father. 'Sleep tight, little man.'

'You too, mama,' he said, his eyes burning intensely, anxiously.

'I will, darling. Don't worry.' She tapped the end of his nose with her index finger and winked.

She navigated her way expertly over the scattered Lego – her newly domestic equivalent of crossing a minefield – and closed the door softly behind her. She stood there for a few moments, hearing him shift position onto his side and say something quietly to Ducky, his beloved cloth toy, before walking down the hall to her own bedroom. The bed was still unmade from the usual rush this morning but she didn't bother making it now. What was the point, when she'd only be getting back into it to sleep again in a short while anyway?

She stepped out of her bathrobe and pulled on a pair of black loose trousers and a black jumper with a deep V; there was no point in putting on underwear at this time of night either. Twisting her damp hair into a rough bun, she padded barefoot back down to the first floor that housed her enormous kitchen and lounge. If the space was extravagant, its furnishings were not. She had spent most of her savings on the construction work when she had first moved back – the timber piles supporting the house had rotted and needed to be replaced with concrete ones, which had also meant replacing the lower-ground-floor parquet; and converting the first floor into one giant room across the front section of the house had been fiddly, ergo expensive, as the builders had had to take extraordinary care not to damage the intricate rococo plasterwork that trailed on the panelled walls and ceilings.

With the bones of the house intact, she had kept everything else simple – white walls, black free-standing kitchen units made for her by a carpenter friend of a friend. Mila called it 'classic', but it wasn't her style that was questioned, just the scarcity of it. She didn't have *enough* furniture, apparently; friends kept telling her she needed to get more *stuff*, but it struck her as somewhat grotesque to have extra possessions purely for the purpose of filling a space. She had sufficient chairs for friends to sit on, a large enough table for them to eat and drink at, beds for her, Jasper and mythical guests who never came to stay, a couple of sofas, some bookcases . . .

really, what more did they need? They had 'enough' and she had lived for too long in too many places in the world where enough counted as a feast.

. . . *Gisele's pregnant.*

The fact of it came back to her again, ignored but not forgotten. She went to the larder cupboard and pulled down her favourite bottle of whisky from the top shelf. She poured herself a snifter in an eggcup – an old habit that wouldn't die – and knocked it back, closing her eyes as the burn hit the back of her throat, liking it – liking it for the memories it triggered of a life when everything had been more intense, when the things she did had mattered, when nothing had existed beyond Now, when life had made sense precisely because it was framed by death. She was safe now but sometimes she felt it was this domestic version of living – so cocooned and soft and dulled – that left her feeling bewildered and lost.

She wanted another but she made herself put the bottle back and reached into the fridge for some beers instead; she considered glasses too, but thought better of it. She padded down to the ground floor and set the beer bottles on the bedside table, switching on the floor lamp in the far corner and smoothing the wrinkles off the bedspread. She looked around at the little scene just as she heard the knock at the door – not the bell, just like she'd said. She didn't want Jasper to be disturbed.

She checked the time. It wasn't yet eight. She went through to the hall and pulled back the bolts and locks and chains.

'That's some security you've got going on there.' Matteo Hofhuis grinned as she finally opened the door to him.

'You can never be too careful, in my experience,' she said. 'And you're early. Again.'

He smiled back at her unapologetically and she could see the shadow already darkening on his shaved head – the memento of their day together, the token of his trust, the reason Claudia had fled the studio in tears. He shrugged, those famous blue eyes set to full smoulder and working their magic, even on her. 'I couldn't wait a minute more. Giving you three hours has been bad enough.'

She felt a small part of herself come alive again, knowing she needed this. It was something to grab onto, at least for a little while. She held the door a little wider. 'Well, I guess you'd better come in then.'

Chapter Four

'Hurry-hurry,' she said brightly, waiting by the front door as Jasper wriggled into his padded coat and fiddled with the buttons. She looked out at the world hurrying about its business too, commuters walking briskly, dog-walkers idling as their pets sniffed at trees and lamp posts, a jogger in gloves and hat labouring on the other side of the canal. She could see the water had begun to finally freeze on the surface. It had been coming on for the past week, the cold days clobbered by plummeting temperatures at night, and now looping swirls curled in the fragile ice, the water caught mid-twist, dead leaves and the small wooden boats tethered along the canal walls held in a tightening grip.

She hoped it would hold, that the freeze would deepen and the city would become white. She loved how it became a negative of itself in the winter – the characteristic black bricks of the buildings and the black water of the canals becoming bright and light . . .

'Please Jazz, we're going to be late,' she sighed, gesturing with her arms for him to exit the building.

'But—' He stared at her nervously, his coat finally done up.

'What now?'

'I've left my water on the table.'

She groaned. 'Oh, honestly! You would forget your head if it wasn't screwed on!'

Big brown eyes blinked back at her, making it impossible to be cross. She ruffled his hair with a grin. 'Hurry up there, then. I'm going to unlock the bike. I'll take your bag so just pull the door closed behind you.'

He scampered up the stairs again as she jogged down the stone steps and crossed the cobbled street to her bike. Fiddling with the lock keys, she went to swing the little rucksack into the large basket at the front when she noticed something was already in there. She frowned, pulling out a tall, slim hardback book.

Odd.

It was entitled *If* and on the cover was an illustration of a flock of sheep in the rain, one standing alone and forlorn; it was simply drawn and undeniably charming, washed over with deeply tinted watercolours. But what was it doing here? In her basket?

'Mama?'

She looked up to find Jasper waiting obediently on the pavement opposite, his water bottle in his hand. She startled, frightened that her attention had been so fully engaged else-where, away from him. She looked left and right. 'Okay, you can cross.'

He ran over to her and held up the bottle for her to put in the side pocket of his rucksack. 'What's that?' He stared at the book in her hands.

'It's a book,' she said, handing it to him so she could lift him up and strap him into his seat. 'I found it in the basket.'

'Why is it in the basket?'

She shrugged, clicking him in and reaching for his helmet. 'I don't know. Someone must have lost it, I guess.'

He peered closer at the cover, pressing a finger to the illustration as she pushed his hair back from his eyes. He needed a haircut – another one; she had never known anyone grow hair as quickly as this child. 'He's getting wet.'

'Yes.'

'He looks cold.'

'Mm-hmm,' she hummed, bending slightly to fasten the clasp beneath his chin.

He carried on looking at the picture. 'He should stand with the others to be warm.'

Lee pulled back and looked at him with a small smile. *If.* If we stand together . . . ? 'I guess that's the moral of the picture, yes.'

'What's a moral?'

'The right thing to do.'

'Moral,' he repeated, as though trying out the word for size; it was accentless in his little bilingual voice. 'I like this book,' he said decisively. 'Can we keep it?'

'I don't see why not – it's not like we can give it back to the person it belongs to, is it? We don't know who it belongs to and there's a lot of people living here.' She quickly fastened her own helmet. 'Okay. Now hold tight, we're already wildly late. I don't know *what* your teachers are going to say.'

'They say—'

'No, no! Don't tell me!' she insisted with a laugh, as she swung her leg over the top tube and began pedalling. Her day had started on a good note; she wanted it to stay that way.

She walked into the studio twenty minutes later, unwinding her scarf and pulling off her kitten hat. 'Morning!'

Bart looked startled. 'You're bright today.'

She arched an eyebrow. 'And you can tell that from a single word?'

'It was the way you said it. All bouncy.'

'*Bouncy?*' She tutted as she hung up her coat and headed for the coffee machine. She had never been called 'bouncy' in her life, and she wasn't sure she liked it. Nevertheless, she was in a good mood this morning, she couldn't deny it. Last night had done what she'd needed – given her a brief escape. 'Want one?'

'Got one, thanks,' he said, watching her suspiciously. '. . . Anything you want to share?'

'I'm not giving you *my* coffee. I just offered you one.'

'No, I meant – agh, forget it.' He gave up, knowing perfectly well she was being obtuse. She knocked back the coffee shot and took a moment to enjoy the hit before walking over to him. 'Okay, so where are we at?'

'Well, I think you'll be pleased.' Bart took a folder from the top of his paperwork pile and slid it along the bench to her. 'Which is not the same thing as saying the client's management will be. Apparently he's just signed as the lead in some Viking epic, and hair – preferably long hair – was taken as a given.'

'Why? Were there never any bald Vikings?' she grinned. 'Relax. It'll have grown back in a couple of months. When are they beginning shooting?'

'Next month.'

'Huh. Well, he should have said, then.' She opened up the file and stared into the eyes that had been locked onto hers only a few hours previously in her spare room. Echoes of the connection that had tugged between them through the lens yesterday vibrated through her again now. The electricity crackled on the page; it was what gave the images their vibrancy, magnetism. But though she could read it, she no longer felt it. Like the diminishing toots of a stream train puffing out of sight, the feeling was distant already. He had been precisely what she had needed – but she had only needed it for a few hours.

'Mmm . . . The lighting's a bit sharp in this sequence,' she murmured, putting on her eye loupe and scoring out three whole rows of images with a red cross. 'And I don't like the angle in these here, do you?'

It was a rhetorical question. Bart knew Lee never doubted her instincts on her own work. She could ruthlessly edit herself without any need for input from anyone else, and had many times thrown out entire shoots, refusing to hand over the images to the client if she wasn't absolutely happy with them. It made her a nightmare to work with but it was also what made her desirable; no one had higher expectations of her than she did of herself and her very perfectionism and uncompromising vision was the reason the bookings kept coming.

She went through the contact sheets with brisk efficiency, eliminating scores of images (mainly the early ones) on account of an awkward pose, a forced look, a 'too perfect' symmetry, so that by the time she'd finished, they had perhaps a dozen left from an initial count of one hundred and eighty.

'Yes.' She stepped back, looking at the survivors with a critical hawk-eye. She famously never retouched her images and it was in her contract that her clients were forbidden to alter her work in any way. 'Give them those. I reckon there's a good three cover options there if they want them. That I'd choose, anyway.'

'Yep.' Bart nodded in agreement. It wasn't unknown for the publications to go out with multiple covers in limited-edition runs when she'd spoilt them for choice like this. He shuffled the edit into a new pile and took them back to his desk.

She sank onto her high stool, flicked quickly through the post and checked her emails. It was the usual depressing mix of marketing spam and domestic miscellanea – her studio insurance was coming up for renewal, her *Life* magazine subscription was about to expire, a dispatch note for the new inner tubes she'd bought for her bike.

'So are you going to call him, then?' Bart asked from across the space, his eyes on his screen.

She clicked on an email for dinner arrangements at her place with Noah, Liam and Mila tomorrow night. 'Who?'

'Matteo!' He swivelled around on his chair, pointing a finger at her. 'And don't even try to deny it! It was pretty damn obvious there was something between you. I can always tell with you.'

She gave a groan. 'He's an *actor*, Bart. Easy on the eye, perhaps, but—'

'He's never going to save the world?' he finished for her, knowing her too well. 'But does he need to? You don't need to marry him, you know. You could still go on a date with the guy, just have a few drinks.'

'I have a five-year-old. I don't have time for dating. I barely have time to sleep,' she muttered.

'Lunch then. You've gotta eat.'

She peered over her glasses as him. 'Bart, it's sweet of you to worry about the abysmal state of my love life but I'm honestly more concerned about who's going to win *The X Factor*.'

'You don't watch *The X Factor*.'

'Precisely. You know, sometimes I think you forget Happily Ever After only exists in *fairy tales*.' She flashed him a sarcastic smile.

'So cynical. So sad,' he tutted dramatically, just as the phone rang. 'Oh, and before I forget, Dita called. She's getting on a plane now,' he said as he picked it up, 'but-says-she's-going-to-be-in-town-next-week, most-likely-Wednesday-but-could-be-sooner, and-are-you-free-for-brunch? Hello, Fitch Studios,' he said all in one breath.

Dita?

Lee felt her laissez-faire mood seep away like water into sand, the past dragging down her spine like a sharp red fingernail. Her former boss was a hard woman to pin down these days and hearing from her was like getting a call from the White House. She'd been like Lee and Cunningham and Schneider and all the others once too. It had taken being ambushed by Tamil Tigers to make *her* step back from working in the field; her daughter had been three at the time. But unlike Lee, she hadn't turned her back on that world altogether and, as the Reuters bureau chief in London, her voice down the line – too often heard when Lee had been dialling in from some godforsaken, drought-addled war zone – had represented safety. Civilization. The land of bubble baths and coffee machines. More than once she had talked Lee down from rising panic as mortars had been shelled over her head. More than once she'd arranged a pickup to get Lee out of a 'sticky situation', as she'd called extracting her from Tahrir Square in 2011 when the protests quickly became riots and no woman was safe; and rescuing her when Lee found herself in the maze of Gaza tunnels as Israel began its aerial bombardment of the West Bank in the summer of 2014. Dita had a reputation amongst the men they worked with for being an uncompromising and un-scrupulous hard-ass, but to Lee, she was a gravel-voiced, dirty-laughing surrogate mother.

Lee dialled her number but it went to voicemail. 'Dita, I

got your message. Text me where you're staying when you get here. Don't worry, I'll make sure I see you.'

They never bothered with pleasantries. Their phone calls had always had to be punchy and to the point when a line could be cut at any moment. Still, Lee wondered what she was doing over here. Dita usually transferred flights through Paris. Why was she going to be in Amsterdam?

'That was Julia from the gallery,' Bart said, intruding on her thoughts. 'The painting is all done. They're ready when you are.'

'Great. Did you collect the prints?'

'Of course,' Bart said, leading her over to the workbench and whisking away a long sheet that had been draped over the top. 'Ta-da!'

'Oooh!' She stepped back, taking in the large five-foot images that were now mounted and framed to her exact specifications. He had set them out along the table in a double line and she looked at them in pairs, front and then back, working her way along the row as Bart watched on, nervously biting his nails. 'Yes,' she hissed under her breath with a feeling of satisfaction – and relief. 'They look great, better than I'd even hoped,' she murmured, peering at one of the images more closely – a thin, dark-haired woman with her hair twisted up in a chignon, pearls at her throat. She had her back to the camera and was wearing a pale-grey taffeta Dior evening gown, her face turned in profile. 'God, you really wouldn't know, would you?'

'I know,' Bart agreed, standing beside her, his arms hugging his torso as they both stared at the images of soignée perfection. 'It's really powerful, Lee. You've done it.'

She turned to face him. 'Do you honestly think so?'

'I know so. You're amazing.'

She raised an eyebrow and jogged him with her elbow. 'Even without *celebs* at the party?'

'Fuck 'em!'

She chuckled, but her smile quickly faded. 'I just hope the colour turns out the way I wanted,' she said nervously.

'They sent over a couple of snapshots last night, if you want a quick look,' he said, bringing them up on his phone to show her. Lee squinted. The gallery's previously standard white walls had been painted a deep, lustrous plum colour and lacquered to a glossy finish. It was a rich, opulent shade, but with an old-world glamour too, matching the Belle Époque formality of the ballgowns the women were wearing in the images.

'Yes,' she said again, feeling pleased. 'I love that. The white would just have been too stark, don't you think? I really want these images to be treated and hung like paintings. I wanted them to feel grand and formal and enduring.'

'Well, you've done that all right. If John Singer Sargent was alive now, he'd have a camera in his hand and be shooting portraits just like that.'

For different reasons, though, Lee thought to herself; she wasn't in the flattery game. They rose to standing again. 'Okay, well, if they're ready for us, let's load these up and get over there. I've done the running order on a flat plan, so once we're happy it works, I'll leave you and Julia to the installation.'

'Why? Where are you going?' he asked, watching as she picked up her faithful Hasselblad 501C. It was an entirely different beast to the Nikon Nikkormat, which had been her first ever camera and remained her favourite even now. She'd never shot another image with the Canon 5D since that last day in Syria; she'd bought the Hassy just a few months after arriving in the city, a token of her fresh start. She zipped it into its bag, checking the correct lenses were packed and slinging the strap across her body.

'To the hospital. Sinterklaas is visiting the wards today, remember?' She gave a rueful grin. 'Honestly, spending an afternoon with a bunch of overexcited kids and a man in fancy dress? Give me the Taliban any day. And I'm not even getting paid for it! I must be mad.'

'You must be nice.'

She winked at him as she pulled her hat onto her head, making sure her cat ears were straight, and they walked out of the studio. 'Yeah, well – don't tell anybody.'

The light was always tricky here. Strip lighting did no one any favours, much less those battling diseases that ravaged their immune systems.

'Is this one your favourite?' Lee asked, picking a small furry tiger from the assorted collection of toys on the bed. She was sitting on a chair to the side, trying not to be overwhelmed by the number of tubes coming out of the child's body, fretting that with every move she might pinch or dislodge one.

'This one,' little Amelie said, holding up a pig. It had a beanbag body and weighted trotters. 'I like how it feels when I go to sleep,' she said in a small, weak voice, carefully arranging the toy across her chest in a demonstration.

Lee smiled, knowing just what she meant. 'It makes you feel held?'

The little girl nodded.

'Yeah, I like that too. It's a nice feeling.' She wondered when the poor mite had last had a 'nice feeling'. Lee hadn't seen her on the ward before and one of the nurses had said she'd been transferred from Rotterdam, awaiting a new heart. 'Are you excited about seeing Sinterklaas?'

She nodded again. Talking was clearly tiring for her.

'What do you hope he'll bring you?'

'Some cat socks.'

'Cat socks? That's it?' Lee wrinkled her nose. 'I think you should be thinking a whole lot bigger than just cat socks.'

'They've got pictures of *my* cat on them. She had to go live with my granny because her fur makes me too sick. Granny sends me videos of her, but I miss her.'

Lee's heart broke a little. 'Oh, well, that's different then – socks with *your* cat on them would be pretty cool. What's your cat called?'

'Nibbles.'

She grinned. 'Cute. Did you name her?'

Amelie nodded. 'When she was a kitten, she would take these tiny little bites of her dinner and her nose would twitch.'

'What a character—' She looked up as one of the nurses came through, clapping her hands excitedly.

'Hey kids, guess who's come to see you all today?'

Lee looked back at Amelie with excited eyes, giving her a wink. She rose and readied her camera as the children all sat up in their beds expectantly. The doors swung open and Sinterklaas came through, carrying his signature big book of names and followed by a procession of kids in wheelchairs and on crutches, plastered limbs jutting out at right angles.

Lee immediately began clicking, not shots of the great man, but of the children as they gathered around him, touching and admiring his red velvet robe and mitred hat, his sceptre, the bushy white eyebrows and long, flowing white beard, which was matched by equally long, crimped hair. The commitment to the costume was a significant step-up from the rather feeble Father Christmas outfits she had seen growing up in England, where a pillow was stuffed under a thin red velveteen jacket and the straggly white beard was attached by elastic ear loops.

She saw the wonder in the children's eyes as he began talking to them all, asking whether they'd been good, and she worked quickly – glad she was forgotten now, a background figure, able to get the images she wanted – capturing spontaneous laughs, eyes that shone, heads that were raised.

He went over to the boy in the first bed and sat on the edge of it, carefully holding open his large book. 'Now then. Tomasz—'

The little boy's mouth opened in amazement that Sinterklaas knew his name without having to ask.

'—have you been a good boy this year?' The bushy white eyebrows rose up questioningly.

Tomasz nodded.

'Well, let us see.' Sinter ran his finger down the page, stopping a third from the bottom. There was a short pause. 'Hmm. It says here you painted your father's car.'

'Because it had scratches from when mama hit a bollard in the car park.'

'I see.' Sinter looked at Tomasz from the depths of his snowy white hair. 'Well then, that was kind of you to try to colour it in.'

Tomasz nodded earnestly.

Sinter read some more. The eyebrows went up again. 'And I see you let your sister's rabbit out of its hutch.'

'It wanted to run around the garden. It was bored.'

Lee had to suppress a bark of laughter, but she wasn't entirely successful and Sinter's eyes swivelled towards her briefly. She remained hidden behind her camera but she saw, through the crystalline clarity of her 35mm lens, the eyes of a man significantly younger than the plumes of white hair suggested.

'Yes, well, again, that's very . . . kind of you, Tomasz. I can see that you're a caring boy. That's why you're on my list of Good Children.'

'I am?' Tomasz breathed a sigh of relief.

'And because you're such a good boy—' Sinter turned the page on his ledger to a large blank sheet of paper and, with a navy felt-tip pen, drew in the space of a few brushstrokes an image of a rabbit with enormous, outsized twitchy ears. Across the bottom, he wrote: *Kindness echoes.* 'That's for you. To remember to keep being kind.'

Lee clicked away, both impressed and intrigued. She hadn't realized Sinterklaas did party tricks! Nor that he had such sexy eyes. Who knew?

'Oh sorry, I thought this was the ladies,' she said, stopping in the doorway, one hand still on the door.

'Unisex,' the man replied, glancing at her in the mirror. He was stuffing something into a bag.

'Oh.'

'. . . I'm leaving anyway,' he added, seeing how she still hesitated. He shrugged on a coat, his eyes grazing questioningly over her inert reflection, catching sight of the bag slung across her body. He turned suddenly, looking at her more closely, as though she had just come into focus. 'Wait – aren't you the photographer?'

Her gaze fell in turn to the large bag on the floor beside him. A tuft of snowy-white hair was tickling out the top. 'You're *Sinter*?' she gasped.

The man stopped moving and looked guilty, as though he'd been caught red-handed doing something he shouldn't. 'Don't tell me you still believe?' he asked slowly.

Lee laughed at his joke, walking in and letting the door

close slowly behind her. 'I'm English, I only believe in Santa Claus!' she quipped. 'I just can't believe *you're* Sinter. You're like . . . a baby!' He couldn't be more than . . . thirty-ish?

'They're what do it.' He waggled his eyebrows, even though they were no longer white. He watched her scrutinize him, trying to marry the image of the dark-haired, dark-eyed man in here with the hirsute septuagenarian from the children's ward. The scarlet robes had been swapped for dark jeans and boots; he had artfully scruffy, loosely curly chestnut-brown hair, with exceptionally round and dark eyes. His skin was olive, but pale at this time of year, a prickle of stubble along his jaw. Nonetheless, there was a certain porcelain-like quality to him, a generous Renaissance beauty in his features. He would be able to walk out of here, through a crowd of the very children he had just delighted and enchanted, and not one of them would be able to guess his alter ego. 'I'm Sam, by the way.'

'Hi, Lee.' They shook hands and she felt an instant spark of attraction leap between them.

He smiled. 'I'm amazed *I* recognized *you*. You may not have been in costume but you practically wore that camera like a mask.'

'Just how I like it,' she conceded. 'It's like my very own invisibility cloak.'

'You didn't lower the camera once, from what I saw.'

'Got to be ready. Can't miss the shot.' She shrugged.

'Do you do this regularly then?'

'Photographing the kids?' She stuck her hands in her pockets. 'Not really, just at this time of year. I offer my services in the run-up to St Nicholas' Day. It's nice to try and get some happy photos of the kids, you know? For them and their families. It must be so hard for them being in a place like this at this time of year.'

'That's really kind of you.'

There was a pause as they both remembered Tomasz. They grinned. 'Are you going to draw a rabbit for me too?' she chuckled.

'If you'd like.' His eyes shone with amusement as he watched her and she felt the spark ignite into a small flame.

She ran her hands through her hair. '. . . So are you an artist then?'

He nodded. 'Full-time artist. Very occasional Sinter.'

'Do you do Santa Claus too?'

'Actually I do,' he grinned. 'But not the Easter Bunny. Every self-respecting man's got to draw the line somewhere.'

'Of course. The Easter Bunny's the line, everyone knows that,' she said, aware she was grinning madly too. She needed to stop grinning.

But his smile had crept into his eyes and curled his mouth into a curve so that for a few moments more they stood there, two strangers grinning inanely in the toilets.

She heard a silence start up as their smiles lingered and she realized the conversation would now have to turn into something more consciously sustained than just passing chit-chat, or dwindle out altogether.

'Well, I . . . I'll leave you in peace,' he said reluctantly, gauging the same dilemma. He lifted the bag and walked around her. 'It was nice meeting you, Lee.'

'Yeah—' She was scanning her brain, trying to think of something to say, something to keep him from leaving, something that didn't sound completely desperate. But he was at the door already. 'Hey, Sam.'

He turned.

'You don't do . . . house visits, do you?' She smiled, knowing her cheeks were flaming.

'House visits?' He looked confused but definitely interested, the spark still flickering between them.

'Yeah. Uh, my little boy is five—'

'Oh.' She saw the fire die in his eyes.

She swallowed hard again, wanting to tell him right here, right now, that he had nothing to worry about, that she was *not* looking for a father for her kid. But she couldn't tell him yet what she *was* looking for either. That would be premature, precocious, and they were, after all, still just two strangers making small talk in a unisex hospital toilet. 'I'm a . . . single mum, so he never really has anyone to do the Sinter thing with. His godfather has dressed up a few times, but the costumes are so bad I worry he'll *stop* him believing!'

Sam watched her for a moment, digesting the information she'd just given him. Mother. But single. The ball was in his court . . . 'Well, the costume's borrowed,' he said after a moment. 'But I reckon I could get them to let me hold onto it for a bit longer.'

'Really?'

'Yeah, although I'm not looking forward to having to rip those eyebrows off again. I feel like I waxed myself.' He checked his eyebrows' appearance in the mirror quickly, dabbing them gently. They were still slightly red.

Lee chuckled. 'That would be amazing. I can't tell you how much he'd love it.'

'He's five, you said?'

'Yes, his name's Jasper.'

He walked back towards her and put the bag down, taking out his phone. 'Well, if you can write a short list of some of the good and naughty things he's done this year, and give it to me when I turn up, I'll put it in the *book of shame* . . .' he said in a funny Halloween voice, looking up at her from beneath his lowered lashes and making her stomach somersault.

'Okay,' she grinned, feeling girlish. She never felt girlish. 'We've got a potted bay tree on the top step. What if I put it in there for you so you've already got it before we come to the door?'

'You've done this before, I can tell,' he teased, standing close enough that she could smell his scent. 'So . . . what's your address?'

Their eyes caught as she gave it to him and a tiny, distant voice was telling her she was crazy to be giving her home address to a complete stranger. This was not the sort of thing she did. But he was a stranger who dressed up as Sinter for the kids in hospital. And he was an artist. Artists never turned out to be axe murderers.

'. . . Bloemgracht's great, I love the Jordaan district,' he murmured, tapping it in. He looked back at her, locking eyes again, sending the flame between them flickering wildly, as though someone had just opened a door. 'So when were you thinking?'

She shrugged, trying not to look as startled by his presence as she felt. 'When's best for you? We're always around.'

'Well, I've got stuff on for the rest of the day and this evening. How about tomorrow night?'

'Oh. We can't tomorrow.' She gave an apologetic shrug. 'But other than *that*, we're always around.'

He grinned. 'Sunday then? Seven-ish?'

'That would be great. And I'll pay you, obviously. I mean, I don't expect you to . . . just do this out of the kindness of your heart.'

'Why not?'

She was surprised by the question. 'Because people . . . don't?'

He was looking at her still; he had a way of regarding her, as though he was intending to draw her, observing her mannerisms and funny, nervous tics. She felt him absorbing her. She felt sucked in, magnetically drawn to him.

'*Or*, how about a glass of wine afterwards instead?'

'Wine . . . wine would be good,' she smiled, feeling her heart rate go into overdrive.

'Great.' He picked up his bag again. 'So then I'll see you on Sunday. I'll turn up in the costume, just in case Jasper answers the door. It should be a *great* look on my cycle over.' He rolled his eyes.

She laughed. 'You might be mobbed.'

'I'll just have to cycle fast then. See you Sunday.'

'Yeah, see you.' She watched the door swing closed behind him and gave a small squeal of excitement. Had that really just happened? She sank against the basin and bit her thumbnail excitedly. Roll on Sunday.

Chapter Five

Lee sat on the refectory table, elbows on her knees and hunched over, as Mila moved around the kitchen like it was her own. Mila was dressed in a frilly blue gingham apron with cherries embroidered on it, which had been intended as an ironic birthday present for Lee several years back from her friend Noah, but which Mila wore in all seriousness. She knew far better than Lee where Lee's own colander was kept and that she actually had paprika (expiry date November 2014) in her spice rack.

'I really think it suits you,' Lee nodded, watching her friend chop some pak choi.

'Yeah?' Mila put a hand to her sleek, dark-haired head. The move from 'student long' to 'elfin crop' had been dramatic, but then so had her recent break-up with yet another man who'd forgotten to mention he had a wife.

'It's a good sign – indicative of changes for the better. Not to mention,' Lee said, earnestly stabbing the air with a finger, 'quicker in the mornings.'

'Well, so long as it's efficient,' Mila quipped.

They heard heavy footsteps on the stairs and looked towards the door. Lee had deliberately left the door on the latch for her friends – it looked fully closed from the street but nonetheless it left her jumpy and she didn't take her eyes from the doorway until she saw her friend's large bulk emerge.

'Noah! Did you bring the beef?' Mila asked with obvious relief. 'Please say you got my text?'

'Of course.' He held up a bag and handed the swag over to her as she reached on tiptoe to kiss his cheek.

'You are a star. Cheers,' she added in English.

'It will never cease to amaze me how coming to dinner at yours . . .' Noah said, bending down to wrap Lee in a bear hug. His strawberry-blonde beard tickled her skin, his sudden warmth like a tranquilizer shot. '. . . Means we supply the food *and* cook it!'

Lee gave him a sweeter-than-sweet smile. 'Excuse me. I'm providing the space and the booze and the cute kid. None of you has one of those, and they're expensive to hire.'

'Well, we can't be sure Liam's not got a few dotted around the city. The way he gets around,' Mila tutted.

Lee and Noah swapped amused looks. It appeared to be evident to all but Mila that she was wildly in love with their raffish friend.

'He *is* coming tonight, right?' Lee asked, having another sip of her drink. 'I've not heard otherwise.'

'Yeah, he's on his way. He said he was stopping in at some drinks thing first, on the way over,' Noah replied.

'Well, so long as we're not cramping his style,' Mila said, sipping her drink too.

'And where is my handsome god-thing?' Noah asked, looking around the huge space.

Noah was her son's second favourite person in the world and Lee smiled, watching and waiting for his joyous welcome. Sure enough, a second later, his cheeky face appeared around the back of the sofa. 'Here I am!'

'Jazz King!'

Lee watched as her son raced across the floor and into Noah's outstretched arms. He was a bear of a man even to her; she could only imagine how gigantic he seemed to Jasper. Noah swung him around, his little feet flying high through the air (this was another valid reason why *not too much stuff* was a good option for them – less to knock over).

'How's my main man?'

'I knocked a cyclist into the canal.'

'No way?' Noah exclaimed, bursting out laughing and holding up his hand for a high five. 'Ten points!'

'Not helpful!' Lee groaned, chuckling too.

'You've grown again. Let me see how tall you're getting.'

Jasper went and stood beside Noah, stretching himself as tall as he could. The top of his head came to Noah's thigh. 'Very good. You were down here last time,' Noah said solemnly, dropping his hand an inch, even though they'd seen each other only last week. 'Sinterklaas will be pleased with you. You're obviously eating your dinners and going to sleep on time. Have you had any visits from Zwarte Piet?'

'Yes. He's brought me *pepernoten* and chocolate letters,' Jasper said, pointing to the tiny clog left out by the fire. It already had tonight's offering of a carrot and a handwritten poem in it.

'Huh. I think I know someone who can go one better on *pepernoten* and chocolate letters . . .' Noah arched an eyebrow as Jasper began jumping up and down excitedly. Slowly he reached into his coat pocket and drew out a slim package.

'A lightsaber!' the child cried as he tore off the packaging. Noah shrugged off his coat and sank onto one of the bar stools, watching on with a pleased smile.

'You are spoiling him,' Lee said sternly, getting up and

planting a kiss on his forehead. He was the best father surrogate she could have hoped for in her son's life and every day
she was more glad she'd had the foresight to ask him to play
this role. They had first met when she had just arrived in the
country with her newborn, knowing no one but Mila. While
she was escaping the rain one day, on one of her endless long
walks trying to get Jasper to sleep, Noah – as a driver on one
of the city's hop-on/hop-off canal-boat tours – had let her
stay on his boat for seven full circuits of the city. The gentle
movement of the boat had helped Jasper settle, so she had
gone back the next day too, as eager for adult conversation
as for the baby to nap. Within two days, she knew Noah's
patter to the tourists off by heart and within the week, his
life story. He was one of the dearest people in her life; the
brother she had never had. 'You're undoing all my hard
work.'

'That's precisely the point of godfathers.'

'You won't say that when he becomes a teenager and I send
him to go and live with you.' She walked over to the bar area
– a small console set up with various spirits and mixers. 'We
thought we'd try gin and Dubonnet tonight. Good for you?'

'God yeah.' He sank deeper into the stool. 'Make mine a
double.'

'Tough day?'

'Oh man.' He dropped his head, looking worn out. He'd
been made a manager in the summer, a job far more perilous
than it ought to have been. 'We had a stag party from Berlin
booked in for a private cruise today. Three got so drunk they
jumped into the Herengracht canal and the driver, in trying
to fish them out, ended up crashing into the side of 7 Ponti
Bridge.'

'Oh no!' Mila winced.

'Oh yes. Structurally it's fine but it's more paperwork to deal with. Not to mention, one of the idiots who jumped is now threatening to sue us.'

'For *what*?' Mila cried, outraged.

Noah gave a weary shrug. 'Reckless endangerment? Negligence? Whatever a lawyer thinks they'll be able to get away with.'

Lee handed him his drink. 'Fuckers,' she said sympathetically.

'Yeah.'

She went back to her spot on the kitchen table, watching Mila chop. Jasper was jumping around the sofas, swishing his lightsaber dramatically with his shadow.

'Anyway, how about *you*, busy lady?' Noah asked her. 'I've been seeing posters for your upcoming exhibition everywhere.'

'Have you?' She felt another spike of nerves.

'Yeah, me too,' Mila chipped in. 'There's one outside the office.'

'It's next week!' Noah said, incredulous. 'Aren't you supposed to be flat out and frantic with last-minute preparations? I'm feeling deeply honoured you're hosting us tonight.'

'Well, clearly I'm a woman of limitless capabilities and abundant energy,' Lee quipped, giving a lackadaisical shrug from her spot rooted on the table. 'Mila, are you sure I can't do something?'

Mila shot her a wry look. They all knew Lee's idea of 'help' was to open another bottle.

The sound of the front door slamming shut made them all jump. 'Relax! I'm here!' a voice called from downstairs. Lee and Noah both looked over at Mila, who had dropped her knife and was checking under her eyes for smudged mascara.

A moment later, Liam's handsome face appeared. Blessed with a boyish look, he was tall and lean, with soft light-brown foppish hair and backlit blue eyes; he looked as good in trackies as in a narrow suit and cashmere scarf, and he couldn't walk down a street without women stopping to turn and stare. He was too pretty for Lee's tastes but Mila practically wilted in his presence, although thankfully Liam appeared to be unaware of his effect upon their friend. 'How are we all?' he grinned, clearly already loosened with a few drinks.

'Ready to kick off now you're here,' Lee replied with a smile. Things were always amusing when Liam was drunk. He had an enviable contacts book and a taste for gossip. As Lee was constantly trying to tell Mila, it was far better being his friend than girlfriend.

'You look stunning tonight, Mils,' she heard him saying with a note of surprise. 'That colour really suits you . . . No, wait – is it the make-up? What've you done that's different?'

Mila tucked her hair behind her ear, blushing madly as Liam scrutinized her, trying to pinpoint the change.

'Haircut,' Lee said, putting them all out of their misery.

'. . . Oh yeah!' Liam said brightly, before realizing what a dramatic haircut usually signified; God only knew, he'd been behind enough such makeovers himself. 'Oh Mils, I'm sorry. What was it this time?'

'A wife.'

'Ah, babe,' he said, sweeping her up in a tight platonic hug. 'He's a tool not to see what a good thing he had with you. You're an amazing girl. The best.'

Lee and Noah glanced at each other.

'He'll be sorry once he sees that new look on you, I guarantee it.' Liam put her back down again and looked at the others. On to the next thing. 'So – who do I have to sleep with to get a drink round here?'

'That would be me, you lucky sod,' Noah drawled, getting up to pour him a drink before Mila could offer.

'Hi Jazz!' Liam waved at the little boy. 'Cool saber!'

'So how was your drinks party?' Mila asked, looking almost trepidatious to hear the answer.

'It was good, actually,' he said, taking the stool next to Noah and swinging idly in it, his long legs outstretched. 'I'm glad I looked in. It was an old uni friend's thing – a bit of a reunion. Ten years, I think. Saw lots of old faces I'd not seen in years.' He chuckled. 'No one's doing what you thought they would – this one guy, who was top scholar, primed and schooled his whole life to take on his father's company, jacked it all in and is now working as a potter. A potter!' he laughed, genuinely amused. 'And another guy who literally didn't attend a lecture in four years is now a bestselling author. His book's sold, like, two million copies.'

'Oh, talking of books, I had a funny thing happen this week,' Lee said as Noah handed Liam his drink. She noticed Jasper climb onto the sofa and curl up in the cushions. His lightsaber was still in his grasp but tiredness was beginning to catch up with him; he'd stayed up late to see everybody, but she'd need to put him to bed shortly. 'Jazz and I were heading off to kindergarten yesterday morning and we found a book in the basket of my bike. A brand new book, just sitting there. How weird is that?'

'Yes! That's his book! That's my mate!' Liam said excitedly.

'I haven't told you which book it is.'

'I already know which book it is! It's got the sheep on it.'

Her eyes widened in surprise. 'How'd you know that?' she chuckled, amazed. 'Oh, wait – did *you* put it in my basket?'

'No! They've got this mad marketing campaign going – he was telling me all about it: they're just leaving signed copies of the book in random places about the city.'

Lee frowned. 'Why?'

Liam struggled to remember why. 'I think because it's a . . . nice surprise? Something about . . . paying it forward?' It was clear he had no idea what was being paid forward. Liam worked in finance, so had no concept of anything ever being free.

'Well, next time you see him, you can tell him your friend got one of them.' Lee shrugged.

'I'll introduce you to him and you can tell him yourself.'

Lee was bemused. 'I think you're overestimating my excitement about it.' She glanced over at Jasper, his head on the cushions, eyelids drooping . . . 'Come on, Jazz: time for bed, bud. Come and say goodnight to everyone.'

'No seriously, I'm thinking about having a Christmas party,' Liam continued as she got off the table. 'I'll introduce you.'

'Yes! Get in!' Noah cheered. 'A party! New women! Thank *God!* I'm in severe drought over here. I've not had a whisker of action for months now.'

'*Months*? Oof.' Liam gave a pained look that suggested he never went more than days if he didn't want to. Mila's face fell.

Jasper came over and they all sank to their knees in turn to give him goodnight hugs and kisses. 'Goodnight, buddy,' Liam said, giving him a high-five.

'Don't let the bed bugs bite, little dude,' Mila whispered, kissing his cheek.

'You keep sleeping tight and you'll be as big as me before you know it,' Noah said, wrapping him close to him so that all Lee could see, for a few moments, was the top of Jasper's head.

'Up you go,' Lee said as Jasper passed her. 'Brush your teeth, I'll be right there to tuck you in.'

She watched him climb the stairs, his lightsaber banging against the treads.

'I'll tell you who *has* been getting some action, though,' Liam said in his most gossipy voice. He looked across at her again, not missing a beat. 'Your old friend Harry Cunningham. His wife's pregnant!'

Lee felt her body go very still as three pairs of eyes settled upon her. 'Yes, I know.'

Liam deflated again at her apparent boredom on the issue. 'Oh. The way they said it, I thought it was a big deal.'

'Why? How did they say it?' Mila asked, her eyes flitting over to Lee.

'Well, I got the impression they must have been trying for ages and that's why they kept the pregnancy so hush-hush for so long. Harry's getting on, let's be honest.'

'Mmm.' Lee nodded noncommittally but her mind was racing. They'd kept it quiet? How far along was Gisele, then? Lee had assumed just a few months at most. 'How did you hear about it?'

'One of the guys at the party just now goes to the same gym as her. *Don't* tell Harry, but I think he's always had something of a thing for her. Anyway, he said he hadn't seen her around for months and then bumped into her in the street sporting this massive bump.'

'Right.' Lee sincerely doubted anything about Gisele was massive. From what she remembered, the woman was a doll. 'And how did *you* and he get onto the topic of Gisele being pregnant? She didn't go to university with you, did she?' Lee knew she was six years younger than them, for a start.

Liam thought back for a moment, trying to recall the flow

of conversation. 'Oh. It's because I said I was coming on here, to yours. And Viktor recognized your name of course, because of you and Harry winning the Pulitz—'

'Right,' she said brusquely, cutting him off. She couldn't even bear to hear it said out loud.

'Anyway,' Liam continued, already well oiled with drinks and oblivious to her stony stare. 'She's in bits, apparently.'

'Why?'

'Well, why go to all those lengths to have a baby – for him to just bugger off to Syria with a few weeks to go?'

'What?' It was Mila who cried the word, but Lee felt the colour draining from her cheeks, the blood pooling in her feet. 'Syria?'

Liam looked across at Mila. 'Yes, Harry's gone jungle again.'

Lee reached for the door frame, needing to feel connected to something. It felt like the world was tipping on its side, everything sliding off. 'But he's injured,' she said slowly, as though self-control would somehow make this okay. 'His leg . . .'

Liam frowned as he saw how pale she had grown. 'Didn't you know? I just assumed—'

She ignored the question. She couldn't believe what she was hearing. There had to be a mistake. 'You're sure he's gone to Syria?'

'Yes.'

'Where in Syria – Homs? Damascus? Aleppo? Raqqa?'

'I don't know. Syria's just . . . Syria, isn't it? There's no good places there.'

It was the sort of comment that made her want to scream, the sort of comment that made her feel it had all been for nothing. People still knew nothing. They were ignorant. They didn't care.

She walked over to the table and knocked back the rest of her drink, needing something to take the edge off her nerves; they felt aflame. Cunningham was back in Syria. That was why he'd really come over the other day, she realized. It wasn't just to tell her about the pregnancy – he knew she wouldn't care about that; his happy personal life was none of her concern. But he'd been to Afghanistan and the Rohingya region and Iran since she'd quit and he hadn't notified her of his movements then. So why now? Why come over to tell her he was going back *there*?

She closed her eyes, remembering how they'd first met in Sirte, when Colonel Gaddafi's grip was failing. She'd been a freelance rookie desperate to make her name, he was the senior correspondent for the *Washington Post*, both of them choosing the same small pile of sandbags to hide behind as sniper bullets zipped past their heads. Later, when they'd escaped, both shaking like tambourines, he'd taken her to a hotel bar where whisky was served in eggcups, and he'd introduced her to all the other reporters and journalists out there. He'd taken her under his wing and it had been like a sparrow being sheltered by an eagle; at twenty-one years older than her and a living legend in the war-reporting community, he knew everyone, and that meant that pretty soon they all knew her. Friendships formed fast in situations like that, becoming at once both deep and yet also transitory – your life might rest in that person's hands the very next day, hour, minute. On the other hand, people did die every day, hour, minute and you somehow had to keep going; there was no time for grief. Not getting shot whilst getting the shot was all that mattered.

She was brave, he was experienced and something about them just clicked. People were constantly moving about, losing track of one another for weeks, even months at a time, but always somehow converging again in unexpected predicaments, meeting by chance in the most unlikely scenarios; she always remembered Cunningham telling her how he had once met a woman he'd photographed in Bosnia – weeping by the bodies of her father, uncle, two brothers and teenage son – crossing the road seven years later in London with Sainsbury's shopping bags. That was how it had been for the two of them, meeting time and again in random coincidences until finally he had asked her to be his exclusive photographer – no more freelancing, hawking her images to the highest bidder. They had officially become a team.

The last time she had worked with him had been in Syria, six years ago; but the last time she had actually seen him had been here in Amsterdam a few years later, when she'd seen him walking with his pretty soon-to-be wife, Gisele. She had tried to cross the street but it was too late by the time she saw them, Cunningham already breaking away and jogging ahead to catch her attention. She had spent several minutes engaged in polite small talk in which she revealed nothing at all about her life and gave all her attention to Gisele, sensing his growing dismay as she covered her contempt with a smooth, bulletproof politeness; it was the kind of 'bullshittery' – his favourite word – that he had always deplored, which had given her some satisfaction, at least.

She had learnt that Gisele was six years younger even than her, but it hadn't surprised her: he had always attracted younger mates – though weathered from hard years of living in conflict zones, Cunningham had somehow retained a vigour for life that knocked decades off his actual age. His easy, cavalier manner and the half-smile permanently on his lips were juxtaposed with eyes that had seen death too many times, in too many ways, and the fracture this drew through him was intoxicating – men saw the heroic crusader, women the wounded soldier.

He'd invited her to their wedding a few months later but Lee had ignored it, as he had probably known she would; every letter, text and call went unanswered. They had only had one true conversation since Syria and it had been terminal. He knew perfectly well why: he knew what he had done. There was no going back and she had seen the pain in his eyes on the cobbles that day. It gave her a boost if ever she was feeling low.

From what Dita had told her, he'd been back from his most recent trip – to Tehran – maybe ten, eleven months. It was the longest anyone had ever known him be out of the field and she'd assumed, like everyone else, that this was his life now. Semi-retired, he had a beautiful wife, a baby on the way, responsibilities, people who loved and needed him. Why risk that?

He had been badly injured by shrapnel from a drone strike and had had to be airlifted out with a US marine unit, his left leg held together by a splintered floorboard and tied on with the rags of his own trousers. Dita had told her, without being asked, that it had been months before he could walk on it unaided and he might always have a limp now; he certainly couldn't run about a war zone yet.

And if he couldn't run, then how could he be safe?

And if he couldn't be safe, what good was he dead?

He knew all this. He had taught her this. So what the hell was he up to?

Chapter Six

They lay sprawled on the sofa, Lee curled around Jasper, the fire flickering away. They were watching *Return of the Jedi* and only a few hard kernels of popcorn were left in the bowl on the floor; the lightsaber Noah had bought him was lying on the ground too, ready to be picked up and intergalactic fighting continued the moment the film finished. To the casual observer, this was just another lazy Sunday in their household, but Lee had been hard at work behind the scenes – she had *hoovered*; she had stripped, washed and ironed the spare bedroom sheets; she had washed her hair; she had used her most expensive body lotion (her only extravagance: clean, scented skin was the truest luxury after years of no bathing and rubble dust); and under her boyfriend jeans and black cashmere sloppy joe, she was wearing her best lingerie.

She was lying still, Jasper nestled in the crook of her arm, but really she was watching the minutes tick past. She had timed everything to perfection. The film was 136 minutes long – she knew that because she had watched it with Jasper nine times now – so she had ensured they began watching at twenty to five to guarantee a finish just before seven. The last thing she wanted was a meltdown because they received a visitor with twenty minutes of the film left.

The credits began to roll and Lee felt the butterflies take wing in her stomach. She had been unaccountably excited all day. She gave a stretch. 'Hot chocolate?' she asked, tickling him in the ribs to get him to move.

'Only if I can toast marshmallows.'

'Oh, all right then,' she grinned, amused that he considered *he* was doing *her* the favour.

She got up and began heating the milk in her coffee machine frother when the doorbell rang. Perfectly on time. She swallowed, falling still for a second. This was it, then.

'Oh, I wonder who that could be?' she asked aloud, sounding as wooden as a spoon. 'Jazz, do you want to get that for me?'

He stopped a saber swipe mid-pose and looked at her in surprise. 'But I'm not allowed to open the door.'

'It's okay just this once. I don't want to burn the milk. You go down, I'll listen out for you. Go on.' She watched him run uncertainly out of the room and down the stairs; she had undone all the chains and deadbolts earlier, when she'd put the list out, so that all he had to do was turn the lock.

Putting down the milk, she tiptoed to the top of the stairs, hearing the audible gasp as her child saw who was standing on the doorstep.

'Well, hello there. You must be Jasper,' she heard Sam say in an altered voice.

She bit her lip, feeling a peak of hysteria that he was actually here, a rush of affection for his kindness. She couldn't believe he was doing this for her.

'May I come in?'

'Mama!' Jasper called excitedly, his voice bubbling with undisguised joy. 'It's Sinterklaas! Sinterklaas is here!'

Fleeing back to the hot milk on her tiptoes, tiny giggles

escaping her too, she was stirring the hot chocolate when they both emerged a few moments later. 'Hmm?' she asked distractedly. 'Who is it?'

'It's Sinterklaas!'

'No, it can't be, darling.' She looked up casually, feeling her heart somersault at the sight of Sam standing there, disguised again – robe, mitre, sceptre, big book; white beard, white eyebrows, white wig. Only his hands and those eyes revealed the younger man in disguise, but they weren't the sort of finer details five-year-olds clocked. 'Oh! Sinter!' she exclaimed in fake astonishment.

'Good evening. You must be Jasper's mama.'

She went over to him, clearly able to see the laughter in his eyes too as she drew closer. 'Yes, I am.' She placed a hand on Jasper's shoulder. 'How good of you to visit us.'

'Well, I'm seeing all the children on Bloemgracht today.' He looked down at Jasper again. 'I've got my book here to tell me who's been good and who's been naughty. Have you been a good boy, Jasper?'

Jasper nodded with the same awed solemnity Lee had seen in Tomasz.

'Shall we have a look then?'

Jasper nodded again.

'Please, take a seat,' Lee said, ushering them towards the armchair. The sofa cushions were crushed from where she and Jasper had been lying watching the film. She picked up the remote and turned off the TV; the credits were *still* rolling. 'Before you begin, Sinter, would you like a drink? A cold glass of milk, perhaps?'

Sam's head turned and he pinned her with a bemused gaze. It was all either of them could do not to burst out laughing. 'No, thank you. I just had some milk in the last house.'

'I've already put my carrots out for Amerigo,' Jasper said, pointing to the tiny filled clog by the fireside.

'And he's been enjoying those very much, Jasper, thank you. He does get very tired leaping from roof to roof each night. It's not easy when you have to stay so quiet.'

Jasper nodded, sympathetically. Horse hooves were clippity-cloppity at the best of times.

'So, let's see what we have here,' Sam said, heaving open the book. 'Jasper, Jasper, Jasper . . . ah yes, here we go.' He read the sheet of paper Lee had left out for him. The crinkles appearing at the edges of his eyes told her he was trying not to laugh again. 'Right. So, I see you chased a cyclist into the canal.'

'No, I was chasing the pigeon,' Jasper said earnestly. 'The man got in the way.'

'Oh.' Sam looked up at him from beneath his fluffy eyebrows, laughter evident in his eyes. 'Well, that was very silly of him.'

'I just wanted to stroke the pigeon. It had velvety fur.'

'Feathers,' Lee corrected gently.

'It sounds like you're a loving boy, then,' Sam said, looking back at the sheet. 'What else? Hmm, and you – oh, you turned your mama's hair blue?'

'I was making magic potions . . .' He glanced at Lee worriedly. 'But I forgot to tell mama I used her shampoo.'

Sam looked at her, almost shaking with laughter.

'It was fine. Nothing an emergency trip to the hairdresser couldn't sort out.' Lee grinned, ruffling Jasper's hair and trying not to burst into hysterics too.

'But I'm a good boy, I am,' he said worriedly. 'I climb into bed with mama every night and hold her hand when she has the nightmares.'

Lee's smile faded.

Sam's shaking stopped too as he looked across at her. 'Oh. Well then . . .'

'And I never cross the road without her and I always wear my helmet and I don't run whilst I'm eating because I mustn't die. It's very important that I don't. I'm her whole world and she's seen too many dead people.'

No one said anything. Lee stared at the floor, feeling mortified. She hadn't anticipated Jasper going solo.

Sam shut the book firmly. '. . . Well, that's it then. Not only do I know for certain that you are a good boy, Jasper; now I know that you are the *best* boy. The best boy in all of Amsterdam.'

'Really?' Jasper gasped, his dark eyes shining.

'I've seen them all and there's no doubt in my mind – you are the best.' He looked at Jasper closely. 'Tell me, if you were an animal, which would you be?'

Jasper looked up at Lee, confused. She forced a smile and nodded encouragingly.

'A bear.'

'A bear? And why do you say that?'

'Because I like honey and I like sleeping and mama says I'm cuddly but also brave.'

Sam's gaze met hers again briefly, his eyes loaded with questions. 'Yes, I can see that about you.' He reached inside the cover of the book and pulled out a slip of paper, Lee and Jasper watching on as he quickly began to draw. It was more an elegant assortment of penstrokes than a consciously worked image and yet it captured the very essence of a slumbering bear, a tiny kitten curled up between its paws.

'This is for you,' Sam said, holding out the sheet. 'For being a brave, kind *and* gentle boy. Your mama must be very proud of you.'

Jasper took it with wide eyes.

'What do you say?' Lee prompted him, seeing how he was shocked into silence.

'Thank you, Sinter,' Jasper whispered, his gaze travelling over the plush white beard, eyebrows, mitre . . .

Sam rose from the chair. 'Well, I must get going. There are still plenty of other boys and girls to see this evening, but it has been a pleasure meeting you, Jasper.'

'Jazz, you run along upstairs now and start getting ready for bed,' Lee said. 'I'll see Sinterklaas out.'

Jasper stared at him for another moment. 'Goodbye, Sinter.'

'Goodbye, Jasper.'

Jasper ran from the room – the hot chocolate completely forgotten – and sprinted up the stairs, his drawing rustling loudly in his hand, as together Sam and Lee walked down to the ground floor.

'It was very kind of you to visit us this evening, Sinter,' Lee said loudly, for her son's benefit.

They got to the hallway. 'Oh my God, you were amazing,' she whispered excitedly. 'He just loved that!'

'He's a great little boy,' Sam said, seeing how her hands were pressed together in front of her mouth, her eyes shining.

They stared at each other, reminding themselves of one another from their fleeting encounter in the hospital toilet, and a small silence bloomed as she felt the atmosphere shift between them, one reason for coming here being replaced by another.

'If you get changed in here,' she whispered, opening the door to the spare bedroom. 'I'll just get him into bed and then we can have that glass of wine.'

A small smile came onto his lips. 'Okay, great.'

'I'll just—' She went over to the front door and opened it.

'Goodbye, Sinter!' she said loudly, before closing the door again with a slam. She winked at him as she passed. 'I won't be long. Give me five minutes.'

She shut Jasper's bedroom door softly and jogged down the stairs to the kitchen; she needed a box of matches for the scented candle she'd bought for the guest room.

'Oh!' she said, drawing up short as she saw Sam standing by the island on his phone, the bottle of red she had left out and two large glasses in front of him. 'You're in here.'

He looked up with a surprised grin. 'Yes. Where else would I be?'

She shrugged – she had expected him to stay downstairs – but she was happy to see him looking like himself again; it was deeply disconcerting being attracted to a white-bearded old man. He was wearing jeans and an ivory chunky ribbed sweater, his skin still a little pink from where he'd had to peel off the beard and eyebrow glue again.

'Pinot Noir?'

'Great,' she said. She was used to other people hosting in her kitchen.

He poured and held out a glass for her. Lee took it, feeling the charge between them surge now they were alone again. It had been instantaneous on Friday and she felt it again now, a powerful attraction neither one of them was trying to hide. 'To good deeds,' he said.

'To good deeds,' she murmured, already anticipating naughty ones.

They both took a sip, feeling the evening settle into its second act. She had been waiting for this all weekend. Their first meeting on Friday had left her frustrated and impatient for this as it was, but last night's news about Cunningham had only compounded her need for an escape. She needed to think about something other than him for a while.

'So you think he enjoyed that, then?' Sam asked, sinking slightly against the unit.

'It was everything to him! His eyes were just . . .' She tried to find the right word. '. . . ablaze when I was tucking him in just now. He's at that age where it's all still so real for him.' She paused for a moment, trying to imagine a world like that, one full of magic and hope and good things. 'I just hope he'll be able to sleep tonight. I don't think he can believe what just happened.'

'Then I'm glad to have been of service.'

'Oh, trust me, that's going to keep him going for a full year.' She chuckled. 'God only knows what we'll do next year to top it!'

He shrugged. 'Well, I can always come back and do it again.'

Her eyes flashed towards him, her heart stuttering and missing a beat, panic pinballing through her. *Next* year? He was just being polite, right? 'That sketch was beautiful,' she said instead. 'You're very good. And so fast! I can hardly draw a stick man.'

'Oh, I'm sure you could. It's just a matter of confidence and finding your style. I spent years trying to master oils and gouache, only to realize that my preparatory paper sketches in pencil, ink and charcoal were far better than anything on the canvas. It was a bruise to my ego at first, it felt like I wasn't a proper artist.'

'Does it relax you, drawing?'

'Yes. It's almost like a meditation sometimes.'

'You make it look so easy.'

'Well, I could say the same about you.'

'Ha. Anyone can point and click a camera,' she said dismissively.

'That's true, but in the way that anyone can also put a pen on paper and draw a shape. There are levels, aren't there?' He took another sip of wine, his lips becoming gently stained. 'What's your bread-and-butter work? You said you were just volunteering the other day?'

'Oh, mainly editorial for magazines – features, occasionally fashion shoots.' She rolled her eyes in disdain. 'But I only do studio stories. I won't go on location.'

'Because of Jasper?'

'Yes. He's in kindergarten. I have to keep a routine for him.'

'Sure. And do you have a nanny, or . . . ?'

'No, it's just the two of us.' He nodded and she knew what he wanted to ask her next – what about his father? – but she closed the door on that opportunity. 'But we like it like that.'

'Right.' He was watching her closely, studying her almost, and she felt he could see more than she was giving, as though he could read her regardless of what she showed. 'And you said you're English?'

She nodded. 'But I lived here for five years when I was a teenager, which is why my Dutch is passable. My father was a diplomat, so we were stationed here when I was thirteen.'

'Are your family still here?'

'No. My parents moved back to the UK when Dad retired, but they're both dead now. Passed away within eighteen months of each other.'

'Oh. I'm sorry.'

'Yeah, me too.' She gave a small smile; the pain of being an orphan, alone in the world, was still as undimmed as the day of her mother's funeral. 'Still, I've got Jasper and he's all I need.'

'No other family? Brothers, sisters?'

'Nope. But I do have a small circle of very good friends who are like surrogate aunts and uncles to him, so they're our family now.'

'It sounds good, maybe I'll do that. I'm not sure I'd choose certain members of my family,' he quipped.

She chuckled. He was easy to talk to as well as easy on the eye.

'So what are you doing here in Amsterdam? Why not the UK?' he asked.

'Umm, well, I guess it was because of Mila, really; she was my best friend when we were living here. We'd done so much travelling over the years for Dad's job that the UK didn't really feel like home. Especially after they died.' She sighed. 'So when I was coming back and needed to put down roots, this seemed as good a place as any. She was my only friend in the world at that point.'

He sipped his drink. 'Where were you coming back from?'

So many questions. She watched his mouth as he talked, just wanting to kiss it, just wanting to get on with what they both knew he'd come over for . . . Did they really have to know each other's life stories? 'Huh?'

'You said when you were coming back, you needed to put down roots. Had you been abroad?'

'Oh.' Dammit. She hadn't wanted to stray onto this. It invariably opened up a litany of questions and it wasn't talking she wanted to do. 'Um, yes. I . . . travelled a lot in my previous job.'

'Like where?' he grinned, having to pull it out of her.

'Middle East mainly, but parts of Asia and North Africa too.'

He looked intrigued, which was not what she'd wanted.

She didn't want to waste time talking about this stuff. 'Wow. What were you doing out there?'

She inhaled, knowing there was no way around it. 'Actually, I was a war photographer.'

Sam's mouth dropped open, his glass moving back to the countertop. *'What?'*

'Yes. I was freelance to begin with, then worked for the *Washington Post.*'

'God, I wasn't expecting that,' he replied and she could see he was reframing her – she was no longer the anonymous, slightly kooky blonde woman from the hospital loos, but a GI Jane with a camera. He looked around the large space with fresh curiosity. 'You haven't got any of your work up on the walls.' They were enlivened only by a yellow neon sign that said 'Sunshine Days' in slanting script.

'No. I have a young child,' she reminded him. 'I don't want him thinking about suicide bombers over his breakfast. There's no benefit to him being exposed to those horrors at his age. He'd never sleep again.'

'Is that why you don't?'

She looked up at him questioningly. How did he know how she slept?

'Jasper mentioned your nightmares. He said he holds your hand.'

'Oh . . .' She looked away, feeling panicked again. 'Well, he didn't mean that literally. He was exaggerating for your benefit,' she lied.

But Sam was still watching her closely. 'It must have been intense.'

'Intense,' she repeated. 'Yes, I guess you could say that.'

'Do you miss it?'

She laughed. 'Nobody misses—' Her voice cut off suddenly

as the memories came unbidden: ruined buildings, blazing cars, people screaming, the rat-a-tat-tat of gunfire like background radios.

She felt something warm on her hand and looked down to find he had covered it with his own, a look of concern in his eyes. She smiled, forcing back the memories that crawled over her like shadows. 'I'll tell you one thing I miss about it – living in places like that makes you appreciate the moment. When you have to live by the minute, you don't waste time dwelling on the past or worrying about the future. All you have is the here and now, and that's liberating. No one plays games, there's no bullshit. There's an integrity that's missing here. In the field, the best way from A to B is always the shortest way.'

He was watching her like she was a unicorn – something magical and beautiful and rare – and she took a step closer to him, knowing this was the moment. The magnetism between them was undeniable. She turned her hand over, still in his, clasping his fingers. 'Out there, no one makes things harder than they need to be,' she murmured, letting her gaze roam him freely before reaching up and boldly, provocatively, kissing him lightly on the lips.

She felt his lips yield slightly to hers, accepting the kiss. But where she had anticipated passion, there was hesitation. She pulled back. He was staring at her, his brown eyes inscrutable now – the veneer of mannered politeness was gone and his gaze kept falling to her lips. He wanted her, she could see that. Her smile grew again, a suggestive light gleaming in her eyes—

'Why don't we sit down?' He glanced over to the sofas.

She put her hand to his chest, able to feel the steady, distant pound of his heart beneath her palm. 'Or we could just go downstairs.'

'What's downstairs?'

She laughed. 'My spare bedroom? Where you got changed earlier?' She plucked suggestively at one of the ribs on his sweater.

He watched her fingers work, before placing his hand over her own. It was heavy and warm and firm. '. . . How about we take our time getting to know each other first?'

She stared at him in bafflement. *Huh?* 'Why?'

It was his turn to laugh. 'Because you intrigue me. I want to know more. I don't want to mess things up by rushing in too fast.'

Oh God, he was a gentleman. 'The thing is, Sam, time is something I don't have with a five-year-old. I don't "do" dating and I'm not looking for a relationship.' She sighed, moving into him again, getting in his personal space, reaching an arm up and running a hand through his hair. 'This can just be easy and fun,' she whispered, seeing how his eyes dilated at her touch.

For several long seconds, they stood there, eyes locked, feeling the energy flow between them. Then she stood on tiptoe and kissed him again, once, twice, feeling his lips respond, his barriers weakening, chivalry collapsing . . . His hands gripped her arms, pinning her to him as the kiss became deeper and more involved and she felt that rush of freedom and abandon come into her body, as it always did when she could lose herself like this.

They pulled apart, his eyes burning with a heat that had been on a gentle simmer since their first meeting. It took the breath from her now. 'So you're saying it's this or nothing?' he asked, both of them breathless. 'You want me to just fuck you and then leave?'

'If you wouldn't mind,' she smiled, pressing herself to him again, eyes hooded with desire.

He looked back at her, emotions raging behind his eyes, his hands still on her arms, before he carefully stepped her back, out of his orbit. '. . . Then I'll go.'

She gave an astonished laugh. 'What?' He had to be joking, of course, but when he didn't smile back . . . 'Sam? What's the problem? We both want this, don't we? We're consenting adults.'

He stepped away from her again, as though establishing a safety zone. 'This wasn't what I came over for.'

'What are you . . . ? Of course it was!' she scoffed, disbelief turning into panic now. Humiliation. Anger. 'Okay, fine, I get you may have expected a little more . . . conversation. Perhaps some food. But what's the point in delaying? We both knew where tonight was going to end up.'

'No. I was hoping for more than that.'

'More than . . . ?' She was confused. What was more than a night of no-strings passion?

He stared at her for a moment, an entire monologue left unsaid in the air as words were tried and discarded in his head. 'Goodnight, Lee.'

'This is ridiculous!' she cried as he walked over to the kitchen table and retrieved his phone. 'Sam, you're not seriously—'

But he slipped from the room without looking back, his feet heavy but quick on the stairs, the click of the front door telling her he was deadly serious.

He had gone.

Chapter Seven

Lee stood on the street, staring up at the door. It had taken her by surprise. Of all the doors she might have expected him to have, this was not what she would have chosen. It was a super gloss blackish-green. It was panelled. It was double-width with bronze mask-head knockers. It was pristine.

He had never been pristine in his life.

She wasn't quite sure what she was doing here. She certainly hadn't consciously made the left turn onto Prinsengracht on her way to the studio; she hadn't dropped Jasper at nursery with the intention of coming on here. And yet here she was. Outside his door. His home. A home he had left. A home she had had the address for, for five years, and never once visited before today.

This was ridiculous. She needed to get out of here before someone saw her. He wasn't even in there. What was she *doing* here?

'Lee?'

She turned, startled at the sound of her name. 'Oh shit,' she hissed to herself, not moving her lips, as Gisele drew nearer, pedalling in easy loops, her long light-brown hair tied in a loose plait, her cheeks stung pink by the breathtaking cold. She had freckles and milky skin, a face that echoed with smiles, coltish legs emphasized by clumpy Balenciaga boots.

'I thought it was you!'

Gisele stared at her uncertainly for a moment, then jumped off the bike and they air-kissed like the old friends they weren't. Lee felt mannish and oversized as her hands folded over the bony nub of Gisele's shoulders; everything about her was delicate.

'Gisele, how funny, I was just about to knock.' Lee smiled awkwardly at the lie. Had Gisele seen her standing there, staring up at the door like a crazy woman, as she'd glided the length of the straight long street? She could hardly have missed her. 'I just . . . I just heard about Cunningham.'

Gisele started at the unfamiliar sound of her husband being called by his last name, but then her smile froze on her pretty face and an unassailable sadness flooded her eyes. 'Yes, he's . . . he's gone to . . .' The words trailed off, seemingly unsayable, as her shoulders heaved once, twice, and she struggled to hold back tears that Lee could see were ever-present. '. . . I'm sorry. Would you like to come in?'

Lee wanted nothing of the sort but it was clear she couldn't let the poor woman cry on her own doorstep. '. . . Sure. Thanks.'

Gisele rolled her bike up the narrow ramp beside the steps and slid her key into the lock of the pristine door. Lee followed her into the smart hallway that was the opposite of her own. Dusty, creaky floorboards had been replaced with smart stone flags, a huge Christmas tree was already set up at the far end by the whorl at the bottom of the spiral staircase. And on the walls were beautifully framed images that sucked the air from the space and punched her in the guts. *Her* images. Tripoli. Gaza. Kabul . . . Moments captured from each. They were printed in black and white but she had personally lived through them in full colour, and it was that full palette in which she saw them now.

82

Gisele walked past unseeingly and took off her coat as Lee followed, dragging her gaze over each picture and hearing the whistling bullets, rumbling tanks and booming explosions which had accompanied those very moments that now hung in perfect monochromatic stillness and silence. In peace. Did Cunningham just breeze past them too – surely familiarity bred blindness – or did they take him straight back to those places, those moments?

Like her own house, the main living areas were on the first floor and they climbed the stairs to the kitchen. It was high-ceilinged and bright, an expensive mélange of pale grey-veined marble surfaces and white bespoke cabinets where everything was hidden behind smooth, push-release doors. Cunningham must hate it, Lee thought to herself; he was a fan of a sturdy doorknob. 'When you need a door to open, you just need it to damn well open; I don't want to have to hunt the damn thing down,' he'd said once as they'd tried to find the concealed fridge in an apartment the *Post* had rented for them during an assignment in Tel Aviv.

'Coffee?' Gisele had recovered enough of her composure to force a smile again.

'Love one, thanks,' Lee replied, her gaze falling inevitably to the tight drum of Gisele's stomach. She was carrying high and in front. Lee couldn't remember what that signified. Boy? Girl? One of the two, anyway. 'Congratulations, by the way! I heard the news. You must be so thrilled.'

Gisele looked down at her cylindrical belly, as though still surprised it was there. 'Yes. Thank you, we are.'

We are. There was something territorial in the phrase.

'So, how are you feeling? 'Cause you're looking *great*.' Lee gave a grimace at the forced jollity in her tone, well able to imagine the look Cunningham would have been shooting her, were he here. But he wasn't, of course. He was 2,500 miles away.

'You're sweet to say that,' Gisele smiled, glancing back at her as she popped a pod in the coffee machine. 'But I'm like a water balloon. By the end of the day, my feet and ankles are like—' She blew out her cheeks, trying to indicate grotesque oedema but only managing to look cute, like a kid holding their breath driving through a tunnel. 'And then I'm getting restless legs at night. Sometimes I have to get up and just pace and pace. Which I suppose is easier in some respects, now Harry's not here. He's not a great sleeper at the best of times and I would worry about disturbing him—'

'Yeah,' Lee smiled politely, remembering how he had once fallen asleep standing up in the queue for a meal at a US military base in Raqqa.

'—other hand, I'm up in the night and all on my own, so . . .' She gave a tiny, vulnerable shrug.

'Right, right,' Lee nodded, only half hearing her. She was looking for a sign of him, her former friend, something in his own house that would remind her of his presence. But everything was so neat and tidy and white and *pristine*. There was almost no sign that he lived here – no jumper dropped on the bench in the window, no packet of B&H on the worktop, no whiff of cordite in the sofas, no muddy combat boots by the door – only a picture of him on the wall, so very different to the ones downstairs. It was of the two of them, him and Gisele, their cheeks pressed together, the wind blowing against them, eyes slitted and mouths spread in breathless laughter. They were on a beach somewhere, the sort that had never hosted a mass evacuation. She sank into a high bar stool, gazing at his image, drinking it in – his now fully grey hair, which suited him better than when it had been brown, perma-tanned skin, deep-set eyes that saw everything and missed nothing.

Almost nothing.

'Uh . . . so how far along are you now?' she asked, suddenly realizing Gisele had stopped talking and was pouring a froth of hot milk into her coffee. It was too late to say she liked it black.

'Thirty-two weeks.'

'Wow. Pretty far, then.'

'Yes. She's viable now, which is something. I've been so worried about every little ache and pain.'

Lee swallowed. She? 'You know you're having a girl?'

'That's what they said.' Gisele nodded. 'I was just happy to make out the head.' She smiled happily and Lee forced one back. Cunningham was going to have a daughter.

'We kept the pregnancy a secret for as long as we could. There've been a few complications, shall we say. Not to mention—' She shot Lee a look. 'Well, it's taken Harry a while to get his head around it.' She handed over the coffee. 'When I first met Harry, he told me he didn't want kids.'

Lee nodded. 'Yeah, right, I thought—' But she couldn't finish the sentence, the words drifting from her like a candle blown out by stray winds.

'He was upfront about it from the start. When things started getting serious between us, he told me to find someone else, a younger guy who would give me a family. He was adamant that with his job, it just wouldn't be fair – well, as *you* know, of course,' she said, remembering to whom she was talking. 'I mean, you know better than anyone what it is he goes through out there.'

'Mmm.' Lee forced herself to drink some of the milky coffee, refusing to remember.

'But then when he came back from Tehran, I don't know, he seemed different. The injury really shook him. I think he finally came face to face with his own mortality. He talked about walking away from it all, committing properly to our life together here.' She shrugged. 'So we started trying.' She bit her lip. 'I think we both just assumed it would happen immediately, but when it didn't . . .' She gave a wry smile. 'Typical Harry, never taking "no" for an answer. It seemed to make him want the baby even more. He became desperate to be a father.'

Lee felt her smile become more strained. This was way more information than she needed. Or wanted. 'So then . . . why Syria?'

Gisele looked up at her through her long eyelashes again, but this time, there was no amusement in her eyes. Just a veil of tears. Her pretty face crumpled a little, and Lee understood why Cunningham would have denied her nothing. She was exquisite. 'I was hoping you could tell me.'

'*Me?*'

'You know him better than anyone. You're his best friend. You know what that world's like and the risks he'll face.'

Lee stared back at her. 'Gisele, Cunningham and I . . . we've barely seen each other. In years. We're not . . . close any more. I had no idea he was going back.' This couldn't be a surprise to her, surely? What had Cunningham told her about them, about why she'd cut him off?

Gisele sighed unhappily. 'Neither did I. He only told me the morning he went.'

Lee was shocked. Had Cunningham really just dumped the news he was leaving for a war zone on his heavily pregnant wife, the morning he went?

Gisele must have seen the look on her face because she

added, 'I don't think he wanted me to worry any longer than was necessary.'

'Did he say *why* he was going?'

'Just that he had something he needed to do before the baby was born.'

'Like what?'

Gisele shrugged helplessly. Hopelessly. 'He wouldn't say.'

Lee felt her heart race. Something he *needed* to do? Not an assignment. Not an exclusive. Something *he* needed to do?

She realized Gisele was waiting for her to say something, to offer some crumbs of comfort. She cleared her throat. 'He'll be back, Gisele, don't worry about that. Cunningham knows the risks; he won't do anything stupid. Not now. You're his world, he won't leave you and the baby alone.' But even as she said it, Lee knew her words were hollow. He wasn't fighting fit; he was lame still. Compromised.

'So then, why did he go? Why now, when the baby's almost here?'

Lee's mouth opened but for a moment nothing came out. What could she say? 'I don't know. Perhaps he felt this was his last chance to do the only thing he's ever known? Because everything will change once the baby's here. It always does.'

It certainly had for her. She had known she couldn't be a mother and expose herself to that life. Jasper had no one in the world but her; she had a responsibility to keep herself safe, for his sake.

'But he's spent thirty years putting his neck on the line. He told me he'd quit and that he'd turned his back on that world, that all he wanted now was to be a father. So why go back to it? This makes no sense.' She stared straight at Lee. 'I need someone to explain it to me. Someone who understands.'

Lee stared back into her coffee. It was an almost impossible thing to explain. There were lots of stock answers she could give – that he was driven by a need to show unspeakable truths, reveal genocides hidden behind government propaganda, to bring justice to people robbed of liberty, human rights and basic dignity? For all the journalists out there, faces down in the dirt every day, those were certainly the motivations that had propelled them to pick up their cameras and voice recorders and run onto military planes in the first place. But there was a darker truth too. How could she explain that somehow you felt most alive when you were surrounded by death? That you felt the intensity of life pulse through your veins when the ground shook beneath your feet? It was selfish. Reckless. Vainglorious. Cunningham had been doing this for too long to be able to settle in a picture-postcard city, pushing a pram along a canal. She knew it now, just like she had always known it, but how could she tell that to his doll-like wife, the one who thought she'd tamed him?

'What he does out there . . .' She faltered. 'It's more than running through rubble, interviewing casualties and witnesses. It's not just been his life's work, it's been his life's purpose. He knows a new chapter is coming; he's got a baby on the way, he's got you. But I guess he must have felt he just had to . . . do a farewell lap. Goodbye to all that, you know?'

Gisele nodded, trying to believe, to understand, but Lee could read her easily – she felt inadequate, not enough. She hadn't been enough to stop him from going, in the end.

'Have you heard from him since he went?' Lee sipped the frothy coffee again. It was like drinking foam.

'Saturday night. He'd landed and checked into the hotel.'

Hotel? Lee felt her antennae twitch. There were precious few hotels in Syria any more. She cleared her throat. 'Where is he exactly?' The question was casual but she felt her body stiffen, an automatic bracing of her muscles.

'Palmyra.'

She closed her eyes for a moment. 'Right.'

'Do you know it? Is that bad?'

Lee forced a smile. 'No worse than anywhere else. If I had to choose between a package holiday there, streaking down the Gaza Strip or a night out in Magaluf? Tough call, they're all strong choices.'

Gisele gave a frozen smile, not quite getting her humour. Then again, not many did. 'I know he was sorry to miss you before he went. He said he was going to drop by your house.'

Lee felt a twist in her guts. 'Oh. I must have missed him. It would have been—' The lie died in her mouth. She had left him standing on her doorstep, and not for the first time. 'Did he say when he'd be back?'

Another shake of the head. 'Not specifically, but before the baby comes, definitely. He said it would depend on who he could find.'

Who he could find. Lee mulled on the words. Was he gathering material for a story after all? Was he finally going to write the memoir that publishing company in New York had been pushing him for? It would be a big-money deal, as she recalled.

'If he rings again, I'll tell him you were here,' Gisele said. 'It would mean a lot to him to know that you came over. He really misses you.'

Lee heard the plea – and accusation – in her words. She had finished her coffee (thank God). 'I should get going,' Lee said, pushing back her stool and standing up. 'I didn't mean to take up your time. I just wanted to . . .' Why had she come here? She still didn't know. Having coffee with Cunningham's perfect wife had not be high on her to-do list.' . . . check you were okay. I know it's often hardest on those who are left behind.'

'Thanks, Lee,' Gisele said, looking surprised, and Lee wondered what Cunningham had told his wife about her – how he had explained their estrangement and yet called her his best friend.

They walked down the stairs again, Lee buttoning up her coat. The high pressure that had stalled over the country for the past week was showing no signs of moving and the clear skies meant biting temperatures.

'You know, if you don't mind me saying – you're different to how I thought you'd be.' Gisele stopped behind her.

'Oh? How did you think I'd be?' Lee asked, turning back to her on the doorstep.

Gisele shrugged. 'Tough? Scary? Harry always says you're the bravest person he's ever met – man or woman.'

Lee looked away, feeling her throat close up. 'Well, Cunningham is prone to exaggeration. You haven't seen me trapped in a bathroom with a spider.' Gisele laughed and Lee felt her constriction ease. 'He'll be okay, Gisele. Cunningham's a pro. He knows what he's doing.'

'I hope so.' Gisele nodded, closing the door softly with a smile.

The door clicked and Lee's smile disappeared as she stood on the step, the echoes of words running through her head. *Palmyra . . . Hotel . . . Something he needed to do.* In spite of her encouraging words to his wife, something wasn't right about this, she could sense it.

She went slowly down the steps and stopped again, her

heart pounding as her mind strained for reasons, connections and clues, while her eyes slowly refocused on her surroundings, telling her something else was wrong.

It was another moment before she realized her bike had gone.

'I'm here, I'm here!' she proclaimed, knocking back the doors so hard they banged against the walls. 'Sorry!'

Bart peered around the black curtain re-rigged for the set, his eyes wild with barely contained panic. He ran over. 'Oh my God, where the hell have you been? I've been trying you all morning! I was about to start calling the hospitals.'

She gave him a withering look. 'My bike was nicked. I had to get another one.'

'*Right now?* They've been waiting for over an hour!' Bart hissed, gesturing towards the back of the set. Music was playing and she could hear low voices on the other side of the curved curtain, a young blonde woman pacing in and out of view, arms crossed over her chest and a finger pressed to her lips in thought. She was wearing cream heeled knee boots and a navy mid-length skirt with a polo neck. She looked put-together, composed, chic. Everything Lee, right at this moment, was not. 'Did you even remember this was on?' he demanded, trying to keep his voice down.

Oh damn.

'Of course I did,' she lied. She had cycled to Cunningham's house without any conscious thought, drawn there as though on a pulley, needing answers, finding none. 'But I had to get it sorted, otherwise how will I get Jasper later?'

'Uh – a cab?' he replied sarcastically.

'Duh! It's not that easy – his bike seat is a special order now he's so big. It'll take four days to come in as it is. I had to get it ordered this morning. I mean, really, he wants his own bike but I'm still not sure he's ready yet, you kno—?'

'No, I don't know, Lee, and right now, nor do I care. You should have rung, or texted, to let me know.'

'I'm sorry, I'm sorry. I just . . .' She flapped her hands around her head, feeling uncharacteristically overwhelmed. 'I've just got a lot going on at the moment. None of it any good.' She tried not to think about last night's fiasco. 'Anyway, I'm here now. Just remind me who . . .' Her gaze flicked towards the set again. The blonde had stopped pacing and was glancing over. She wasn't looking happy.

'Jesus, Lee!' he whispered, almost buckling at the knees in exasperation. 'I know you don't rate these people. They're not saving the world, why are we lauding them? But at least bother to know their names! Today's the "new Eckhart Tolle", remember—?'

'And how are we doing? All ready to go now?' the blonde asked, striding over suddenly and clearly out of patience.

'Ah, Jacintha, good. Come and meet Lee. Her bike was stolen again this morning, hence . . .' Bart waved his arms around in a vague manner. 'Jacintha is Mr Meyer's publicity agent.'

'I'm sorry about your bike,' Jacintha replied coolly, not looking at all sympathetic as they shook hands.

'Mmm, seventh this year,' Lee lied, taking an instant dislike to her. She lived and died by making snap judgements and there was a passive-aggressive edge to Jacintha's words she didn't like. 'I'm sick of it.'

'Where did it happen?'

'On Prinsengracht.'

'Really? I thought thefts were relatively low there.'

'My luck,' Lee shrugged. 'Anyway, I'm sorry for the wait

but Bart's got everything set up, haven't you?' Her trusty assistant gave a reluctant nod. 'So we're good to go. No more time to waste.'

'What were you doing on Prinsengracht?' Bart whispered as they walked towards the set.

'Shuddup,' she muttered. 'And turn that music up, will you? Did you stop at the bakery?'

They rounded the curtain and the 'new Eckhart Tolle' looked up from his phone.

Lee froze mid-step. 'Sam?!'

Bart looked impressed (and relieved) that she knew his name. Then suspicious.

'Lee.' Sam's expression matched hers, she imagined – namely, horrified. He was wearing a casual unlined black blazer, jeans and white shirt. 'I didn't . . .' He looked to Bart and Jacintha. 'I didn't know it was y—'

'You two know each other?' Bart asked, his mischief antennae already up and scanning as he took in Lee's stunned face and deep blush.

'Uh, we met last week,' Sam said, recovering first. 'At the hospital.' He looked across at Jacintha.

'Oh yes, the Sinterklaas visit,' the PR said after a momentary blankness. 'That was very well received, by the way. The kids loved it. They've booked you back in for Christmas too.' She looked over at Bart. 'Really great for tapping into the whole family-gifting vibe.'

Lee looked away, trying to compose herself. How could it be him? Bart hadn't told her Sam's name – had he? No, he would have known she'd have forgotten it by this morning. And she would have remembered on Friday when she met him, she would have made the connection. Surely?

'What were you doing there, Lee?' Jacintha asked her.

Lee flicked her eyes over and away again. 'I do some volunteer work there at this time of year. I covered Sam's visit.' She looked back at Sam. 'Although you told me you were an artist, not an author.' Her expression was determinedly benign, but there was accusation in her voice.

He blinked and she could see the tension in his face too. 'I am. I've been a properly struggling, impoverished artist for the past decade. But then I produced a picture book that's done quite well.'

'*Quite* well?' Jacintha laughed. 'Honestly, if only all my authors were this modest! Sam's book has sold over two million copies.'

Lee stared at him, not hearing, not caring. How could this be happening? The one person in the city she had hoped never to see again was standing in her set . . . ?

Wait. Two million?

'But of course, you'll have seen it, of course you will. The details were in the press pack sent over to you.' Jacintha cast a concerned look in Bart's direction as if it was his fault his boss hadn't prepped for her client's shoot. 'It's been in the charts for sixty-three weeks already.'

Lee nodded dumbly. 'Of course I've seen it – it's called *If* and it's got sheep on the front,' she mumbled, saving Bart. He gave a wholly audible sigh of relief.

But Lee couldn't take her eyes off Sam. That was his book? The one that had been put in her basket? The one that Liam had told her about? *He* was Liam's friend? Oh God, the connections came thick and fast. If any of what had happened (or rather, not happened) last night got back to Liam, her humiliation would be complete.

'You told me she was a news journalist,' Sam said to Jacintha in a low voice.

'She is. Was. Well, it was more war correspondence than . . . plain old news.'

Lee's eyes met Sam's again momentarily, startling them both, it seemed. He clearly didn't want to be here any more than she wanted him here. Lee tried to think of a reason to cancel the shoot – setting off the fire alarms, perhaps, or breaking a leg. But she knew it would only delay the inevitable. This was the last portrait for the feature, it had to be done. As Bart was forever saying to her: *'Bills, Lee!'*

She saw both Bart and Jacintha were watching them, everyone picking up on the strange tension in the room between the two main players. The only way past this was going to be through it.

'Right. Well,' Lee said, weakly clapping her hands together. 'Shall we get started then? I've already wasted quite enough of your time today. Let's see if we can't get the shot quickly.'

'Here you go.' Bart handed her the camera with a loaded look, but she refused to acknowledge it. Her heart was thudding against her chest so loudly she was convinced everyone could hear. Just point and click, she told herself. Get the shot and get the hell out of here. This could all be behind her in an hour if she was lucky, and *then* she'd never have to see him again.

She kicked off her Vans shoes so that she was in just her socks, and walked over to the high stool in the centre of the set. 'Sam, if you'd just like to come over here?'

She pretended to adjust the exposure as he walked over, trying not to replay in her head everything that had happened between them only last night – the way he had tried not to kiss her, and then the way he had, how he had stepped away from her with effort, left without looking back . . .

He instinctively sat with both feet on the foot rail, knees

splayed, hands laced together. It was a confident, relaxed pose. Most of her subjects perched nervously on the stool, one leg on the ground, their hands at a loss for where to be.

'I'm so sorry I was late; did you hear what happened?' she said with an absent-minded faux-cheeriness, loud enough for Bart and Jacintha to hear, as her eyes ran up and down him with a professional, almost doctorly indifference, taking in the composition of his pose, the drape of his clothes. 'My bike was stolen.'

'Oh.' There was a pause as he took in her tone; he knew perfectly well what she was doing, performing an act of civility for the crowd. But he was no actor, his voice sounding awkward and stilted. '. . . Where?'

'Prinsengracht.'

'Bad luck.'

'I know, right? I've had a run of that lately,' she said distractedly, repositioning him slightly so that he wouldn't be so forward-facing to the camera. He didn't say anything, but sat perfectly still as she picked a red thread off the shoulder of his jacket, smoothed a wrinkle in the arm, pushed a stubborn curl back from his forehead that kept trying to fall over his left eye. 'And you didn't want hair and make-up today?'

He didn't move his head but his eyes flicked up to her diagonally. 'No.' He seemed . . . bemused by the suggestion.

'Good,' she said, deliberately tracking her eyes over him busily, not daring to linger anywhere. 'I much prefer shooting people in the raw.'

There was a small pause. 'I hope that's not a euphemism.'

Behind her, Bart spat out his coffee. 'Sorry,' he spluttered, laughing. '. . . Wasn't expecting that.'

Nor was she. Lee was surprised by the flash of humour

too but she didn't acknowledge it. She would not laugh, she would not smile. They were not friends.

'Well, talking of raw, we had an actor in here last week,' Bart said confidingly as Lee made an adjustment to one of the rig lights. 'Big name. Huge heartthrob. And by the end of the shoot, he was in the buff, head shaved and covered in mud.'

'Who was it?' Jacintha asked, when Sam didn't.

'Well, I really shouldn't say . . .' Bart protested feebly. 'But seeing as you no doubt move in the same circles . . . Matteo Hofhuis,' he mouthed.

'Oh, he's *gorgeous*,' Jacintha breathed, losing some of her composure. 'Did you really shave his head?'

Lee shrugged. 'He was game. He had some gumption, unlike a lot of people.'

She felt Sam's gaze flicker towards her briefly but she didn't care if he felt the barb; she put the camera up to her eye and began to walk slowly around him, seeing how he looked in the frame. It never ceased to amaze her how the whole world fell away when she looked through the lens, anything outside the shot cut out so that her focus zeroed in entirely on the subject. Like looking through the crosshairs of a rifle, there was nothing beyond the target. It was as though the world was put on mute.

Unlike Matt, Sam didn't try to engage with the lens; there was no provocative eye contact as she moved slowly – moving the camera up, moving it down, not snapping yet, not committing to an image, but getting a feel for him. Seeing how he moved, how he stayed still. The angle at which he naturally rested his head, the upward tip of his chin, the straight line and then gentle flare of his nose. His really was a face that had been eight hundred years in the making. It was classical, noble . . .

He blinked rapidly, several times, and she realized he was feeling the weight of her scrutiny; in spite of his outwardly relaxed demeanour and loose hands, he either wasn't used to having his photograph taken, or he felt uncomfortable in her gaze.

She was in front of him now and she still hadn't clicked the shutter, not yet taken a single image, unable somehow to commit to the process of capturing him. He was looking into the middle distance ten degrees past her right shoulder, her covered gaze gliding over the sweep of his shoulder, the cut of his jaw, the smooth blow of his cheekbone—

She felt his line of attention shift and found he was looking straight at her. Like faces either side of a window-pane, he filled her field of vision, his gaze directly on hers like a missile on lock. She felt held – caught – as he stared right through the glass to her; right through to her glass heart.

And in that golden silence, the shutter clicked.

Chapter Eight

Her old boss had bagged one of the velvet sofas by the window, the city laid out behind her six storeys below. They had arranged to meet at Soho House – it was suitably central and chic for Dita's needs. After so many years living in war red zones, her tastes now ran to the extravagant, by way of recompense.

She was wearing her usual uniform – a navy tunic with matching wide-legged trousers that she would dress up, when required, with a vibrant scarf. Today's was bunched up in her handbag, a green and orange abstract print that looked like it could (when unfolded) be a Matisse print. To anyone passing by, they would have guessed she was a former art teacher, rather than bureau chief of one of the biggest press agencies in the world.

'How are you, old woman?' Lee asked, coming to stand by the table, Dita engrossed in something on her phone.

'Lee!' Dita looked up with a pleased smile, tossing the phone away casually. 'You made it.'

'Well, it was touch and go, the traffic was a bitch,' she quipped.

Dita laughed and the two women hugged, not in the social air-kissy way, but with pressed fingertips and closed eyes. Their clothes might be freshly laundered and their hair smelling of shampoo today, but they had embraced each other covered in dust and blood before now. They had seen other worlds and lived other lives before this one. They were neither of them fooled by the pretty artifice of their surroundings.

'When did you get in?' Lee asked, sinking into her seat and ordering a black coffee and croissant.

'Knocking on midnight, in the end. Another air traffic control strike. I swear to God, it's easier getting out of Beirut than Paris these days.'

Lee grinned, crossing her legs and sitting back in the chair as Dita cast a critical eye over her. She always did this when they were reunited; at twenty-six years her senior, her old boss was an unspoken mother figure too. 'Hmm, I really thought you'd be fatter by now.'

'Well, what's the culinary equivalent of being green-fingered? Because whatever it is, I *don't* have it.'

'Is it your culinary skills which are to blame – or just a lack of appetite in general?' As ever, Dita had a way of cutting straight to the chase.

Lee smiled, making no comment. They didn't need to extrapolate on the difficulties of adapting to 'civilian' life – it didn't need to be said; rather, it sat as a quiet understanding between them. 'So how long are you in town for?'

'I fly out tomorrow evening. I'm en route to Pyongyang.'

'Wow, lucky you – *you* must have done something right.'

'Yes, I'm in the good books at the moment.' Dita laughed at her sarcasm, a throaty sound that caught the room's attention, and eyes settled upon them, the two thin women with cat-startle reflexes, calloused hands and direct stares. 'And I hear *you've* got an exhibition coming up.'

'Did you? Where did you hear that then?'

'Oh, a little bird told me,' Dita said secretively.

'It's this Thursday,' Lee said with a wry smile. 'I'll get you on the list if you can stay for it.'

'I only wish I could.'

Lee nodded. She knew how it was.

'So what's it about? I'm guessing not a retrospective, or you'd have been in touch with us for archive pics.'

'No. I've been visiting a women's shelter for the past few months.'

'Ha! Of course you have,' Dita laughed, clapping her hands together.

'*Of course* I have?'

Dita held her hands up, indicating their plush surroundings. 'Even somewhere as beautiful and safe as this, you'll manage to find a war on the doorstep.'

'The war *is* on our doorsteps, you know that – refugees, migrant camps, assimilation issues . . . We live side by side with the consequences of war every day. Even here.'

'I know. I just thought you'd turned your back on these harder subjects. No one could say you haven't done your time at the coalface. I thought you were all about the glamour of glossy editorials these days.'

Lee rolled her eyes. 'I'll *never* be about that. But I've got bills to pay and a little boy to take care of now. He comes first.'

'Well, I admire you for it. I know what a sacrifice it is for you.' Dita smiled. 'And how is my godson?'

'Wonderfully wicked, you'll be pleased to hear,' she grinned. 'He sent a cyclist into the water the other week, chasing pigeons.' An echo of Sam's laughter as he had read it out of his book flashed through her mind before she could stop it.

Dita gave one of her signature laughs again too. 'Darling boy! Of course he did! Remind me, how old is he now?'

'Five.'

'Ah yes, well, I must get his Christmas present sorted.'

'Oh don't worry too much about that, you know I don't like to go in for him getting too much *stuff*.'

Dita made a clucking sound. 'What did I always say? You can take the girl out of the war zone . . . You still like to travel light, then?'

'Travel light. Live light.'

'I hope you're not still sleeping on the floor?'

It was Lee's turn to laugh. 'I'll have you know I transitioned back to beds quite a while ago now, thanks.'

There was a small, comfortable silence as the waitress came back with their breakfasts, Dita watching Lee with her keen gaze. 'And no one special's come along?'

'Not that I've noticed.' Lee spread her hands in a bewildered gesture, feeling another inward ripple of humiliation as Sam's face drifted into her mind's eye again and she recalled the shock of finding him in her studio yesterday morning. She smiled harder, banishing him from her thoughts. She would never see him again now. What did it matter?

Dita laughed again, shaking her head as she reached for her cup. 'Oh Lee, you're a tough nut to crack.'

Was she? Lee often felt she was the opposite of that.

'And how's Cunningham? You two talking yet?' Dita asked lightly, sipping her coffee, but from the way her eyes flickered up to gauge Lee's reaction to his name, she knew her old boss wasn't asking after his health. She was digging. She wanted to know if Lee knew he'd gone.

'Actually, I was hoping you could tell me,' she said evenly, sitting back in the chair, elbows splayed over the arms. 'Did you know he was going?'

'Going?'

'To Syria. Did you send him out there?'

Dita looked back at her, seeing that she knew, that bluffing was useless. She sighed. 'No. I didn't send him out there. But he did call me a few weeks ago, asking for me to arrange the paperwork to get him back in.'

Lee felt her heart accelerate, as it did every time it was mentioned. 'And did you?'

'I tried.' Dita shrugged. 'But I couldn't do it in the timeframe he wanted. As you know, he quit almost a year ago, surrendered his visas, permits . . . All the paperwork needed fresh approvals, so . . . these things can't be done overnight.'

'So you didn't get him out there?'

'Well now, I didn't say *that*,' Dita said obliquely. 'Just that I couldn't get the paperwork he wanted arranged in time.'

Lee felt a shot of acid burn her stomach. She knew exactly what this double talk meant. 'Why didn't you tell me?' she demanded.

Dita arched an eyebrow. 'I'm not allowed to mention his name in your presence, but if he's leaving the country you need to be told?'

'It's Syria, Dita. It's not just anywhere. You know that.'

'Look, I didn't think he'd actually do it. When we spoke about it, he was conflicted. He sounded a mess. I think he'd been drinking. He was rambling, making no sense. He's going to be a father soon. I thought the baby would keep him here. That's a big reason to stay.'

Clearly, though, there was a bigger reason to go, Lee mused. And if this trip hadn't been instigated by Dita, then that meant he wasn't out there for a story. So what was he doing over there? The memoirs notion was seeming less credible too: he'd never been motivated by money and he certainly wouldn't prize it over his new little family. 'Do you know where he is out there? I heard Palmyra.'

'Who told you that?'

'His wife.'

'You saw his wife?' Dita looked surprised. 'You *must* be worried.'

Lee ignored the question. 'As far as I'm aware, things are pretty stable in Palmyra at the moment. There's no obvious reason I can see that he would choose to go there. You and I both know that's not where the headlines are.'

Slowly, grimly, Dita nodded. 'He said Palmyra to stop her from panicking. He doesn't want her stressing about him and risking the baby.'

'Okay.' Lee's muscles braced, knowing this meant bad news. If he was giving out false information to stop his pretty young wife from worrying, then clearly there was reason to worry. 'So where is he then?'

'He was smuggled over the Turkish border in an aid convoy.'

Lee's eyes narrowed, her heart giving a small skip of fear. 'Where on the border?'

'Near Jarabulus.'

Lee inhaled sharply. She knew it well – it was in the northern region of the Aleppo province, where the Euphrates flowed in from Turkey. The road came in from Karkamış on the Turkish side and was – as far as she knew – open, controlled by the Syrian National Army.

She felt a kernel of anxiety take root in her stomach. Jarabulus was close, too close to be coincidental . . . She could feel Dita watching her, trying to read her reactions. 'And now? Where is he heading for?'

Dita shrugged. 'I don't know. He's gone off-grid. One of our guys heard he'd hitched a ride with a US unit heading east, but that's all we know.'

He was heading east.

Dita sat forward, her fingers interlaced between her knees. 'You're worried. I'm worried. This isn't like him. Cunningham's a pro. He knows the protocols. Without the right paperwork, he knows there are no back-ups in place if anything goes wrong, he'll have no UN protection.'

'So then why did you help him?'

'He wasn't going to be stopped. If not me, he'd have got someone else to get him out there. This way, at least I knew the drop point.'

Lee blinked, her eyes feeling dry, her breath a rasp. 'It *could* all be perfectly innocent. Perhaps he really does just want one last run before domesticity hits.'

'No.'

'How can you be so sure?'

'Because he left a message on my personal phone once he was over the border, the night he disappeared.'

'Saying what?'

'That he's got some unfinished business to deal with.' She stared directly into Lee's eyes. 'I don't suppose you know what that would be, do you?'

Lee felt her thoughts become jumbled and confused, like they were snow in a snow globe being shaken. 'Why do you think *I'd* know?'

'Because the last thing he said before ringing off was that I was *not* to tell you.'

'You're agitated today,' Dr Hansje said, seeing how her fists clenched and unclenched.

Lee looked down, catching herself, and stretched them out, sliding them slowly down her thighs. 'Sorry. It's been a shit week.' She breathed out through an exaggerated exhale.

'Are you ready to begin?'

Lee closed her eyes, trying to steady her breathing. 'Sure.'

A silence was allowed to breathe and grow, filling the room, and as she found a rhythm in her breath, the world began to fall away, and Lee felt herself become smaller, disappearing into the couch.

'Then let's go back to where we left off last week. You had arrived in the village . . .'

They walked slowly through the streets, aware of the many faces watching them from windows, doorways, around corners. Cunning-ham kept stopping to ask questions, his Arabic better than hers. All she could pick up was Moussef's name, and see the direction in which the men pointed down the narrow streets. She felt their eyes upon her as they walked – westerners in a foreign land, conspicu-ous by their pale skin and light hair – even though she was covered up, her head and shoulders wrapped in the scarf she kept in her bag, and she was careful not to look anyone in the eye too directly.

The village was operating as usual – shops were open, market stalls set up – although some of the buildings had taken hits at some point in the past, heavy artillery shelling having blown out the middles of some of the taller dwellings, collapsing the roofs of others. But there were no burning cars – suicide bombers weren't going to waste their martyrdom on minimal casualties here when there were headline-making numbers to be had in Kobanî. It felt almost normal here.

'What did he say?' Lee murmured, her fingers twitching on the camera slung about her neck, as they walked on from the latest directions.

'Third street on the right,' Cunningham said, staying close to her. It was clear from the looks they were attracting that there were no other reporters here yet. Cunningham was going to get his

exclusive again. She could practically smell the anticipation on him. He was on the hunt.

They turned at the third corner. A heavy, acrid smell hung in the air, the dusty ground volatile and unsettled, their feet kicking up plumes as they walked.

'There.' He stopped walking, pointing fractionally with his finger in the direction of a building with steel rods bent and poking through blasted concrete, a pile of rubble on the ground.

She followed him over, her hands clasping the camera now, ready to shoot. They walked into the lobby of the building but there was no relief to be had, no coolness in the shade. Harry tried the door of the nearest apartment. It was unlocked, the rooms scattered with splintered furniture, dirty mattresses on the floors. Food smells seemed recent, an open bottle of arak attracting flies. She had a sense of missed activity, like walking into a room after a secret was shared.

She began to shoot, adjusting the focus, the zoom—

She heard the click behind her and fell still. Slowly she let go of the camera and raised her hands. Cunningham had heard it too.

'Don't shoot,' he said in Arabic as they both turned slowly. 'Press.'

A man was standing behind them, wearing patched trousers and pointing a rifle at them.

'Press. American,' Cunningham repeated. 'Are you Moussef?' The man said nothing but his surprise at the name indicated familiarity. Recognition. The gun was lowered, the man staring at them both with hard eyes. He looked at her, then said something to Cunningham. She didn't understand but she heard Cunningham say Abbad's name.

He looked at them both again, his eyes particularly hard on her. Then he jerked his head towards the door. 'Follow me.' It was one of the few terms she understood. That and 'prostitute'.

They followed him through the building and out the back.

A cluster of lower dwellings were built in a square, creating a courtyard, some children kicking a ball made of a bunched-up towel knotted with twine. They stopped playing as she and Harry walked through.

The man led them towards a building at the back that was low and narrow. Several women were sitting against the wall in the shade, some holding babies, one washing clothes in a bucket. She smiled at them, trying to establish a connection, but their gazes back were distant and mistrustful. Their guide stopped just inside the doorway and spoke to someone. Lee couldn't see in but the low rumble of a male voice drifted through the open windows. She listened as Cunningham said something, Abbad's name being mentioned several times; then he stepped back.

A man came out into the harsh sunlight. He was large both in height and girth, with a broken nose and a lantern jaw covered in a beard. He looked at them both for a moment, his gaze, of course, sweeping over her like she had two heads. But then he smiled, his teeth looking exceptionally white against his skin as he raised his arms towards them in greeting.

'Welcome, my friends. I have been expecting you. I am Moussef.'

Chapter Nine

'It looks *incredible*,' Mila said firmly, sitting cross-legged on her bed with a glass of champagne in her hand as Lee twisted one way, then the other, in front of the mirror.

'It's not very me,' she said, almost baffled by her own reflection. She was so used to seeing herself in long, floppy layers that enabled her to move easily, get down on the ground, get to the angle she needed for the shot. And black, always black. Not this claret-coloured velvet – it wasn't red exactly, but it sure as hell wasn't black. 'I mean, I don't do dresses or . . . frilly bits.' The sleeve had flounces at the end and she shook her arm, seeing how they rippled as she moved. Sort of intriguing, also highly irritating.

'No, but that doesn't mean you shouldn't. It looks good on you. Feminine. Soft.'

'I am neither of those things.'

'Of course you are. You just try to pretend you aren't. We are all a mix of everything.'

Lee groaned.

'Anyway, tonight is a business function. You have to play the game and that means wearing a nice dress and being *visible*.'

That one sentence summed up everything her old career *hadn't* been about. And why she'd loved it so much.

'I know! What about if I wore this to the Hot dinner?' If she could delay . . .

'The what?'

'You know, the Hot List I'm doing for *Black Dot*. We have a dinner afterwards, all the celebs, editorial staff. Basic hell.'

'You can't have dinner in that dress. You'd be trailing your sleeves in the soup. I'm sorry but no. My answer is final.'

Lee looked back at the black Yohji Yamamoto dress on her bed that Mila had ordered her to take off as she walked in, handing over the 'surprise' hanging bag like it was a holy relic. '*Why* can't I just wear that? It was expensive,' she added, in case that made a difference.

'It's also shapeless, hides your figure and the colour is blah. It won't photograph well, trust me.'

Lee arched an eyebrow. The photographer was being told what would photograph well? Mila sputtered on her champagne as she too realized the irony a moment later. 'I mean, just trust me, because you've never been good at seeing yourself from the outside. You've got no vanity, that's your problem.'

Lee was baffled as to how a lack of vanity could be considered a problem. 'Ugh, whatever,' she said, losing interest and turning away. 'It's not like I*'ve* got to look at myself. But don't think about telling me to wear contacts,' she warned, pushing the heavy black geek frames up her nose. 'My glasses are me. I don't even recognize myself in the mirror without them.'

'You can't see yourself in the mirror without them,' Mila quipped, raising her glass in a little toast to this sartorial victory. She was already wearing her outfit – a flesh-coloured tulle dress with black polka dots that had a Dior New Look vibe – and her shoes were so pointy Lee would have classified them as weapons.

They went down the hall, Lee peering into Jasper's room

as she passed, but he was already fast asleep. Brigit, the babysitter, a twenty-year-old philosophy student at the university, was sitting on the sofa surrounded by files. Lee ran through the drill with her again, lest he should wake up, have a temperature, a nightmare, separation anxiety . . . She saw the babysitter's eyes slide over to Mila once or twice, as if asking for help. Or strength.

The pre-booked cab was already waiting when they went downstairs – Mila had put a veto on cycling over, on account of her hair – and they slid into the back seat together.

'So how are you feeling?' Mila asked her quietly as the car pulled away. 'Feeling okay? Nervous? Anxious?'

'Well, I am now you're banging on about it,' Lee snapped, feeling a sudden spike of both those things.

'It'll all be fine.'

Lee looked across at her bossy, kindly friend, her face barely visible in the dim light. 'But what if no one comes?' The question had nagged at her all day, her nerves growing by the hour.

'Of course they will.'

'But they might not.' Lee could hear the ripple of panic in her own voice. Had she been too quick to judgement, shooting down Bart's pleas to get a celebrity crowd in? She'd been so particular about the guest list, so certain the 'wrong sort' might undermine her message, that she risked an only half-full room even with a 100 per cent acceptance rate of those she had invited.

'How could they not? It's you, Lee Fitchett, Pulitzer-Prize-winning photographer. This is the first exhibition you've put on since you retired from war reporting. It's your first public gig in Amsterdam. Tonight is a big deal. People will be dying to see what you've done.'

'No they won't. They don't want to see what fists can do

to a smaller body than theirs; they don't want scenes of aerial bombings or children bleeding out. They want girls in bikinis with lip fillers, they want free champagne.'

Mila reached for her hand and held it in her own, feeling how it trembled. She squeezed it tighter. 'You're panicking. Just relax. Even if it's just you, me, Liam, Noah and a teenage reporter from the *Metro*, you are going to knock it out of the park. I don't think you realize the impact your images have on people. You're a living legend, Lee.' She smiled. 'Although of course, to me, you'll only ever be the person who made spaghetti Bolognese with lamb mince and who thinks tacos filled with French fries is a balanced meal.'

Lee chuckled, mollified somewhat.

They both stared out into the night, looking at the lights that usually reflected and glowed on the inky water, but the ever-thickening ice absorbed the reflections tonight so they were mere smudges of brightness.

'Do you think it's going to snow?' Lee asked in a murmur, looking skywards.

'Yeah. It can't stay this cold and *not* snow, can it?'

Globes of light picked out the graceful arches of the small bridges, traced the roof lines into peaks, laced the canopies of trees in climbing whorls. Christmas trees were shimmering like grandes dames in the squares. Everywhere felt lit, special. Amber light glowed throughout the city, spilling from the facades of the tall narrow townhouses that stood shoulder to shoulder in elegant rows on the grand Old Town canals; and down the side streets, with the cobbles and straight avenues of trees and smaller canals, there was a toytown charm, as though they were all living in dolls' houses; a living, breathing Lilliput.

The car slowed as the driver looked at the building numbers and Lee leaned forward to show him where to stop.

'It's just up there,' she said, pointing to the gallery up ahead. 'Right by the—'

'Oh my God,' Mila murmured, as the two women looked at each other in alarm, blue lights flashing.

'Are we happy? Are we happy?' Bart asked, his own eyes wide with excitement (and possibly something else) as he successfully pulled them through the crowd. It had been a battle just getting in through the door. They actually had security guards in place, police managing the crowds outside.

Lee wasn't sure she was. Relieved? Yes, but crowds always made her edgy. She looked back at all the bodies still jostling to get in. 'Are they sure they're in the right place?' she asked in disbelief. Surely they had to be mistaken. Perhaps they thought this was someone else's party. Or someone had said there was a free bar.

'Of course they are!' Bart laughed with an energy that told her he was flying.

'Bart, what have you done?' she asked nervously, looking for the rent-a-crowd she had expressly forbidden. But there were no women with hair extensions or gel nails that she could see.

'Lee! What a party, mate!' Ricky Lazell hollered across to her, four people away and unable to get closer, a scrum of people clamouring to talk to him. He was the 'new Ed Sheeran'. She had shot him a few weeks back.

'Rick!' she exclaimed in a voice that wasn't her own. 'Thank you for coming! I'll find you in a bit!' She looked back at Bart pointedly. What was he doing here?

'I know, amazing, right? He's mid-tour too; came back from Oslo to be here. Everyone was *so* keen to support you; they love you, Lee.'

'Who? Who loves me?' she asked, feeling panicky. 'I categorically said no celebrities.'

'No. You said no *C-list* celebrities and no management agencies. I've only asked the certified, *Vanity Fair*-approved A-listers.'

She saw the big-hitting crime author Sean May over by the bar. She'd shot him for the January cover. 'By which you mean, anyone who's been in the studio in the past month?'

He nodded. 'Pretty much, yeah. Isn't it great?'

She looked at him. 'First thing tomorrow, I'm firing you.' It explained the security guards, at least.

He laughed, not remotely perturbed. 'Party first, fire me later. *I* think tomorrow you'll be thanking me. I'll go and get you both a drink.'

Mila stepped in to her. 'You won't fire him, will you?'

'As if,' she muttered. 'He's the only one who can get hold of my contraband coffee.' She scanned the room, feeling overwhelmed but also temporarily anonymous in the cherry velvet; no one had ever seen her in a dress before. 'Is anyone even looking at the photos?' She frowned.

'Give them a chance!' Mila laughed. 'They're all too busy checking each other out. I can't believe you actually know all these celebs.'

'I don't. I shoot them, that's all. It's work.'

'Lee! Lee, I'm here. I know it's me you're looking for!' Noah laughed, squeezing through the crowd to get to her, people stepping aside to the let the big man through. He wrapped his arms around her and she felt her back crack; it always happened with his bear hugs. Instantly, she relaxed a little. 'Well – and to think I thought *we* were doing *you* a favour by coming along tonight! I've just spent the past fifteen minutes talking to the stone-cold fox over there in the green dress.'

Both Lee and Mila glanced over to see a brunette already deep in flirtatious conversation with a man who had to be a model. 'She's been laughing at all my jokes. I reckon I'm in with a chance.'

'You didn't tell her your priest and nun story, did you?' Mila asked.

'Yes. Why?'

Mila patted his arm sympathetically. 'Then you're not in with a chance. No.'

Noah's face fell. 'Is Liam with you?' Lee asked him.

'Not with me, but he's here somewhere,' he said, looking around blankly. It was impossible to see straight through from one side of the gallery to the other; the life-size images were suspended on wires from the ceiling, hanging in pairs like giant mobiles. The point was for the visitor to see the image taken from behind first, then walk around to see the contrast on the front – the show was called 'Back to Front', after all – but no one appeared to be doing much other than talking and drinking. 'I saw him hitting the Moscow Mules with some hottie. Talking of which, why don't *you* have drinks?'

'Don't worry, Bart's gone to get some for us,' Mila said, looking increasingly nervous as people she knew only from flat screens brushed past, scented, glowing, aromatic. Unicorns. They were coming up to Lee and shaking her hand, clasping her shoulders and drawing her in for air kisses. 'Oh my God, is that Matteo Hofhuis?' she gasped, gripping Lee's arm tightly.

'Lee!' A digital recorder was suddenly thrust in front of her as Rosa, the *Vanity Fair* reporter, pushed her way through, an unfortunately short man on her tail holding up a small hand-held digital video camera which was going to result in an unflattering camera angle.

Lee watched the red light flash, trying to keep her cool and not think of sniper dots.

'Daniel's recording for the online footage,' Rosa said dismissively, seeing her apprehensive look. 'Listen, we'd better do this early before you're wheeled off to chat with the great and the good. I can't believe the crowd you've pulled. My editor thought this was just going to be filler, but I reckon she'll go to a full page when she sees who's here.'

'Uh . . .' Lee hesitated. There were so many people looking over at her. Did they really have to do the interview here? But it was hard to move.

'You put your work hat on,' Mila said, squeezing her arm. 'Noah and I are going to actually look at the pictures. We'll catch up with you in a bit.'

Lee felt another twitch of panic as her friends moved away, leaving her in a sea of strangers.

Rosa cleared her throat. 'So Lee, you must be thrilled with the acclaim that has greeted this exhibition. What should people expect if they come to see it?'

She took a deep breath. This was work. 'Well, to be shocked, for one thing. Much like the men who drove these women into the refuge, I haven't pulled my punches,' Lee said briskly, catching sight of the gallery's official photographer across the room; with the camera permanently to his eye, he moved through the gallery unseen, taking shots of the glamorous guests. She wished she could be behind his camera instead of in front of this one; she didn't belong here in the bright lights. She looked back at Rosa.

'And what is the show about?'

'Uh, well, it's called "Back to Front" and, as you can see, we've designed an interactive way to present the exhibition. I wanted to bring attention to domestic violence and how it's happening among us, right here, every single day. Even in an educated, liberal city such as this, daily pain and terror is a reality for tens of thousands of women, and some men too. Statistically speaking, we probably each know someone who has been affected by this abuse, even if we don't know we know it. Now, partly that's because abusers tend to be clever about it, tactical: they know where to hit so the bruises are hidden – the torso, arms, thighs . . . All the women I met at the shelter were able to hide their injuries from their families, friends and colleagues for a very long time. But this issue also goes unnoticed because there's such a stigma around the issue still. Beatings and abuse aren't the preserve of sex workers or addicts; it happens to teachers and vets and office workers. Our neighbours, our friends . . . These women need to be able to feel they can stand up and say, "it happened to me." It can be really hard because, in a lot of cases, these women still love and want to protect the person hurting them. Plus they don't want to be seen as victims—'

Someone reached over and kissed her on the cheek. 'Lee, amazing, darling!' the woman cried as she drifted into the crowd again. Lee was certain she'd never seen her before in her life.

'Uh . . .' She looked back at Rosa again, having lost her thread.

'So tell us why you decided to style these women in couture gowns?' Rosa asked. 'What was the thinking behind that?'

'Well, I wanted to make a statement about the dichotomy between perception and reality – how easy it is for victims to hide painful truths but also how easy it is for us, the unsuspecting public, to see what we want to see. By dressing these women in beautiful gowns and doing their hair and giving them real jewels, we created images of perfection that I then shot from the back. That represents the viewer's gaze – it sets up an assumption which is then dismantled by the full-frontal image—'

'Lee!' someone else trilled, blowing kisses and waving at her. She waved back blankly.

'Uh . . . You'll see we've suspended the images from wires. That's so the viewer can walk around and then be confronted with the brutal reality of what has happened to these women – their cuts, their bruises, their split lips, black eyes, broken clavicles . . . I wanted there to be a shocking contrast between the Front and Back photographs, an extreme made even greater by the juxtaposition of the image that's originally set up. I want people to confront their own assumptions and prejudices, to show that everything's back to front. Our culture is obsessed with images of perfection, of shallow beauty and empty fame, but where are the dialogues about women and children being beaten in their own homes? Where are the resources to give these women proper refuge and shelter? Where are the education initiatives to stop men from using their fists in the first place? The repercussions of this problem are felt *throughout* our society – school truancy, homelessness, drug abuse, prostitution . . . Why are these issues not being treated as the front-line emergencies they are?'

Rosa nodded furiously, holding the recorder right up to her face, but her eyes were tracking someone (clearly famous) over Lee's right shoulder. '. . . And why did you decide to apply an age limit to the exhibition? Aren't you worried that may put some people off?'

'Well, that was down to the gallery, not me, to be honest, but anyone who comes to see this show needs to be prepared to be shocked and even upset – the photographs are unflinching. I haven't edited or retouched the images. We have to make ourselves look at the truth. If we're going to make meaningful change in our society then we can't keep on turning the other cheek.'

'What do you hope to achieve with this exhibition?'

'To spark a dialogue. I hope this show can help turn a conversation into a political and social agenda. Also, I want to raise a ton of money. I've waived my fee for this project and all profits will go directly to the Nest women's shelter.'

'Everyone knows your famous images that won the Pulitzer back in 2015, just as you retired from the war reporting scene. Do you feel that documenting and shining a spotlight on hard-hitting social issues, rather than political ones, will be your new métier?'

Lee shrugged. 'I don't have an agenda as such. Like anyone else, I have bills to pay, so I can't always and only shoot material that appeals to me personally. But I do know that, as a pack race, humans have to see in order to believe and that imbues photographers with both a power and a responsibility to use their craft wisely. Photographs have the power to change the world – they can spark a protest, a riot, a revolution. It is the truth in photography that keeps us all connected, keeps us accountable—'

'Lee, your champagne!' Bart yelled, reaching over the heads of the crowd to pass the flutes over for her and Mila.

'Oh, *that* was well timed,' Lee deadpanned, looking back at the reporter. 'Do you want me to say that last bit again?'

Rosa chuckled. 'No, I think we've got it, that was great, Lee,' she said, turning off her recorder and shaking Lee's hand, her professional duties now completed. From the way her eyes kept boomeranging back to the photogenic crowd, it was clear she was about to make use of the free bar. 'Thanks, we'll let you know when it goes up.'

'But you'll edit that bit, right?' Lee asked as Rosa began to wander off. 'These are important issues. I don't want to come across as some champagne socialist.'

'I don't think anyone could ever accuse you of that!' Rosa laughed again over her shoulder.

Lee felt a tap on her own shoulder. She turned, feeling overwhelmed. So much was happening, and so many people . . .

'This is quite the party. I'm honoured to have made the cut.' Matteo Hofhuis grinned at her, leaning in closer, his breath hot against her neck. 'Although you didn't need to get your *assistant* to call me, you know.' He kissed her on the lips; with his eyes open, it was little more than a peck, yet it was also, clearly, a privilege that would have been afforded only to an intimate. It made a statement to anyone looking on.

'Matt,' she faltered. It was only a week since their shoot – their night together – but his shaved head was already completely covered by a dark fuzz, his blue eyes looking especially bright tonight. He was beautiful – conceited, but beautiful. 'You made it.'

'And I'm so glad I did. I can't take my eyes off you in that dress. You look stunning.'

'What, this old thing?' She held up an arm, regarding the frilled cuff with a quizzical bemusement.

He laughed, seeming to understand she hadn't chosen it. She took a sip of her drink as they looked at each other and she remembered the momentary buzz of their connection, ignited through the lens. It had been a fun night and just what she'd needed – mindless sex, a brief escape from her responsibilities, a sprint out of the clutches of her past – especially after Cunningham had turned up unexpectedly only hours before.

From the way Matt was smiling at her, it was clear he was

keen for a rerun. Would it be such a bad thing, she wondered, breaking her cardinal rule of never going back? If nothing else, her ego could do with the boost. Sam's unequivocal rejection had left her reeling, far more than she might have expected, and things had hardly been helped by having him turn up on her set the *very next day*, like some sort of karmic sick joke.

She had never wrapped up a shoot so quickly. They'd been done within ninety minutes, and where she usually took two hundred shots in a session, she'd taken less than thirty. Somehow, in spite of the barbed-wire-topped walls between them, she had been able to read him, to get what she needed. She remembered how he had tried to talk to her afterwards, how she had used Bart and Jacintha as human shields, hiding behind a fake smile and limp insincerity just as she had that day on the cobbles with Cunningham and his doll-wife. It was amazing how effective manners could be as a deterrent, holding people back behind an invisible line.

She realized Matt had asked her something. 'I'm sorry, what? It's so loud in here.'

'I said, what are you doing after this?' He was grinning confidently. 'We could go on somewhere.'

'Um—'

'I want to see you again, Lee,' he pressed. 'We had fun, didn't we?'

'Yes, the thing is . . .' She became aware of a distant buzzing. She pressed her arm closer to her body, squeezing the bag on her shoulder, and realized it was her phone ringing.

Was it the babysitter? Had something happened with Jasper? 'I've got to take this. I'll catch up with you,' she said, pressing the phone to her ear and turning her back on Matt's puppy-dog eyes. 'Yes, hello?'

'. . . ear me?' The voice was almost indistinct over the noise of the crowd.

'Brigit?'

'. . . you there?'

'Who is this? . . . I'm sorry, I can't hear a thing! . . . Is it you, Brigit? Is Jasper okay?' But it was futile: the ambient noise level in the gallery was just too loud to hear anything. 'Just wait . . . let me move to another room,' she said, pushing through the crowd with apologetic nods and smiles, heading towards the office at the back. 'Don't go . . . Are you there?' She pushed through the doors, but even in the office there was no refuge. The caterers had set up service in there. 'Brigit? Is everything okay?'

'Fitch? It's me.' The voice was suddenly clear in her ear – right there, as though she could reach out and touch him.

'*Cunningham?*' she cried, just as she pushed open the fire door and fell out into the small courtyard at the back. The cold night air hit her like a brick and she gasped at the biting temperature. 'Harry? Are you there?'

The line was bad again, static fading in and out. 'I'm . . . on a . . . in . . . leppo . . .'

She pressed the phone as hard as she could to her ear, not that there was anything to hear. 'Harry? Can you hear me? The line's so bad.'

'. . . my letter . . . Have to know if . . .'

'What letter? . . . Harry, I can't hear what you're saying! You're breaking up!' She pressed the phone harder to her ear and stared up at the moon, willing the satellites somewhere up there beside it to bounce down a better signal. 'Can *you* hear *me*? Harry? . . . Look, just come back, okay? Whatever it is you think you've got to do, just don't. Don't do it. Just come back.'

But he was already gone, the line as fragile as a spiderweb. She stared at the useless phone. *'No!'* she cried, kicking at a stone flower-pot and immediately regretting it in her open-toed heels. 'Fuck! Fuck-fuck-fuck!'

She sank down in a ball, sitting on her heels, her hands scrunched into fists and pushed into her eye sockets. How long had he been trying to get hold of her in there for? How long had the phone been ringing, her talking to journalists and actors and drinking champagne whilst he sat in some rebel stronghold in one of the most volatile and dangerous pockets on earth?

That couldn't be it. She had got nothing from him. Not a location, a reason for being there . . . 'Fuck,' she whispered again, sighing heavily several times and trying to calm herself down. She had to think clearly.

He would call back as soon as he could; she knew that. She'd been on the other side of calls like that enough times to know he would move somewhere with a better signal and try again. She dropped her face in her hands, feeling depleted, wanting to cry, knowing she wouldn't. 'Damn you, Harry,' she whispered to herself, hearing the crack in her voice.

She sat there for several moments more, trying to still her wildly beating heart, knowing she couldn't stay out here, knowing she had to go back in there and deal with all those guests. It was too cold to remain outside, for one thing.

Slowly she rose and turned to go back in. But she hadn't taken a step when she froze.

Sam blinked back at her from his spot, leaning against the wall. '. . . Hi.' He looked awkward.

It was several moments before she could even speak. How long had he been there? She hadn't detected the pitch in sound, hadn't seen the beam of light swing into the courtyard as the door opened.

'What are you doing here?' she demanded, but her voice was pale with shock, humiliation a fresh bloom that gathered again on her pale, cold cheeks. It was all she could think about, every time she saw him – his rejection, over and over again. Him walking out, leaving her.

'I was invited.'

'Not by me.' Bart would be lucky to get away with just being fired tomorrow morning; now she was going to kill him. She could just imagine Jacintha's delight at the invitation, telling her client it would be 'good for his career' to be seen here.

'Liam asked me. I couldn't get out of it. We're going on afterwards, but he wants you and me to meet—'

She swallowed again but understood from his look that he hadn't told their mutual friend they had already met. More than that.

How could this be happening? How hard could it be to avoid one man in a city of almost a million?

'—which is how I came to be hiding out here. I figured I could pretend to him later that we'd talked. I didn't expect you to . . .'

He didn't finish the sentence. He didn't need to. He hadn't expected her to burst out here like a lunatic, trying to have a conversation with a person in a war zone on a satellite call.

A silence sprouted, unfurling its petals like a spring flower, and she became aware of how she held her body in his presence now, tense and stiff, her arms crossed like barriers, the easy manner of their very first meetings now long distant. She thought she saw something in him slacken.

'Look, I had no idea it was going to be you photographing

me on Monday. Jacintha had organized a car to pick me up and it brought me straight to the studio. I paid no attention, my mind wasn't on it. I kept thinking about . . .' He looked straight at her. 'Well, you.' He pushed himself away from the wall but she instinctively stepped back.

He saw the caution in her eyes and stopped where he was, a flicker of concern in his face. 'Lee, I was going to call you. I was hoping we could talk.'

'There's nothing to say.'

'I disagree.'

She felt his eyes catch her but she wriggled free again in the next instant, a worm off the hook. 'I don't want to see you again, Sam. It's done.'

He straightened. 'No. Nothing has been done, that was the point!' He gave a mirthless laugh. 'Jesus, do you really think I'd have left if I thought I was never going to see you again *anyway*?'

'Why? Would you have stayed then? Taken what you could?'

He looked shocked by her provocation, her aggressive words. 'Lee, I left because I saw how it was going to be with you and I wanted more than just a one-time thing. Is that such a bad thing?' He gave her a bewildered look. 'I feel like there's something between us that could be good. And I think you think so too.'

She shook her head, flatly rejecting the idea. 'I've been clear that's not on offer with me. I don't want a relationship. But if that's what you're after, then you'll find plenty of other women on the other side of that door—'

'I'm not interested in other women.'

'Then that's unfortunate, but I can't help.' Her voice was stony and cold, but as his stare lengthened, she was forced to look away. Her ribs felt rigid, her breathing shallow. Something about his gaze made her feel like a cornered animal, trapped, with nowhere to hide.

'This isn't you,' he said after a moment.

She scoffed. 'You don't know me!'

'Don't I? I know what I saw when you were helping those kids in the hospital; I know what it means that you've taken those pictures of the women in there. I know how you were surprising your son on Sunday night. And that woman – big-hearted, loving, kind, compassionate – she wasn't this one. Why are you so threatened by the idea of a relationship?'

'I'm not.'

'Really? So when was your last one, then?'

She felt her heart rate move up a gear. 'I don't need to answer your questions,' she said after a moment, but her voice was thick. She went to walk past him, to walk away. 'Think what you like, it doesn't matter to me.'

'No. Clearly only Harry does.'

The comment was like a punch, a quick one-two knocking her sideways. She turned. '*What?*'

He took a step towards her. 'Who is he? I'd love to meet the guy, see exactly what it is about him that's made the rest of us consolation prizes.'

'You don't know the first thing—'

'I know what I just heard. And saw . . .' He looked at her pityingly. 'He must really be something.'

'Fuck off.' She may as well have slapped him.

He recoiled, looking down at the ground and then back at her again, but his calm had slipped now too; she could see the frustration flash through his eyes, and his voice, when he spoke again, was dangerously low. 'Well, I guess that's something of a move on from what you wanted from me on Sunday.'

Her eyes narrowed and she stepped towards him, only inches away now. 'You know what?' she whispered, a sneer twisting her smile. 'I'm glad you walked out. I'm glad you came away with nothing. It would have been a massive mistake and I would always have regretted it. As it is, I can just forget about you instead. Move on, and pretend we never even met—'

Just then, the gallery door opened and a dazzling cone of light shone into the courtyard, lighting them up like statues.

'Lee? What are you—?' Matt stood darkly silhouetted in the doorway, jolting slightly as he took in the sight of her standing out here in the dark, so close, with Sam. 'Oh, I didn't realize—'

'It's not what you think,' she said, immediately stepping out of Sam's orbit and only serving to make herself look guilty as hell.

'Actually, it's exactly what you think,' Sam contradicted with an almost lackadaisical tone. 'But don't worry, I'm leaving.' He looked back at her, a new coldness in his eyes that she hadn't seen before. 'It looks like you're all sorted for tonight,' he said in a low voice. 'You can get straight on with forgetting me.'

For a moment, their eyes held the conversation in silent abeyance. She had done it – broken the thread he had been determined to keep – but she couldn't reply. Just like at the shoot on Monday, he could undo her with a look, and unsaid words and feelings were tumbling through her, too fast to sort. Harry, Sam, Matt – falling over each other, crowding her. Her usually ordered life was suddenly a mess.

Sam stared at her for another moment in a silent goodbye. Then he walked past her, patting Matt casually on the shoulder as he went by. 'Sorry about that, mate. She's all yours.'

Chapter Ten

'Mama? Mama!' It wasn't so much the words that woke her as the voice – that high pitch, the tone of bewilderment in it, a slant of fear.

She turned with a groan, having to hold an arm over her face as the light assailed her. It took a moment to get her bearings. This wasn't her bedroom. 'Wha—?'

Jasper was standing over her in his pyjamas, his hair standing upright on the back of his head. 'Why are you sleeping down here?'

She looked across the bed in alarm – memories coming back in flashes – but it was empty, her velvet dress a crushed heap on the floor, her shoes toppled onto their sides, facing in opposite directions. 'Oh God!' she said with a start, trying to sit up but being forced back by the pickaxes being swung inside her skull. 'Ow.'

'Are you sick?'

She looked up at him, seeing the two-thirds-empty whisky bottle on the bedside table, the eggcups beside it. He had found that amusing, she recalled. Just the sight of it now made her stomach heave. 'A little bit. But I'll be okay.' She tried moving again, more slowly this time.

What time was it? What day? . . . Oh God, was it Friday? Did she have to be a functioning adult today?

'Are you ready for nursery?' she mumbled, forcing herself to go through the motions, knowing it would mean she had to sit up, move . . . She was the worst mother in the world.

'No. I'm hungry.'

Of course he was. He was five years old, the poor thing. He shouldn't have to make his own breakfast. 'Okay, well, we'll get something sorted.' The effort it took just to speak . . . She swung back the duvet and gingerly rose, reaching for the bathrobe that was hanging on the door and wrapping it around herself. 'Let's see what we've got,' she managed, her voice a half-croak, half-whisper.

His heart-shaped face turned up to her as slowly – so slowly – they climbed the stairs. 'Can I have my chocolate from Zwarte Piet?'

She looked back down at him, knowing he had sensed her weakness, that now was as good a time as any to strike. She couldn't help but smile. 'Well, just this once.' Like she was doing him the favour!

He cheered with delight, running ahead of her into the kitchen. She peered around the door, watching as he raced over to the treats box. There were oranges in the fruit bowl. At the very least she should peel one for him, but even the thought of that was a step too far for her this morning.

'Listen, Jazz, we're very late,' she said haltingly, forcing down the nausea that kept threatening to overwhelm her. 'So while you eat that, I'm going to have a shower and get dressed and put your clothes out. I want you to come up and get dressed as soon as you're done, deal?'

'Okay, mama,' he said distractedly.

She hauled herself up the next flight of stairs with visible effort, automatically stopping in at his bedroom. The curtains were still drawn, his Jedi duvet half on the floor, and she felt a stab of self-loathing that he had been sleeping alone up here all night whilst she had been passed out downstairs. Anything could have happened and she would have been unable to help him – if he'd woken needing the toilet, if the house was on fire, if an intruder had broken in . . . He had been as defenceless and vulnerable as if she'd never bothered coming back at all.

She made his bed (barely) and picked out some clean clothes for him, then continued into her bedroom, stepping straight into the shower. It was a luxury she never took for granted, much like turning on a light and having a fridge. She stood there with the water pouring over her face, trying to remember last night – Matt's distracting kisses, his clever hands, his smouldering eyes, Harry's voice breaking up over thousands of miles. But, to her despair, it wasn't to either one of them that her mind kept returning. Worse, they weren't the reason tears were streaming down her face.

Lee glanced at her friend on the other side of the window as she padlocked her bike. Mila was sitting at the breakfast bar, reading the local paper, a dispatched ginger shot beside her. Always punctual, she looked beautiful in the winter sunshine, her elfin features and shiny dark cropped hair rendering her positively doll-like. She was wearing her yoga kit; they had clearly already had very different mornings.

Mila looked up as the bell rang and Lee shuffled into the coffee shop, her expression changing at the sight of her. 'Oh my God, what happened to you?' she whispered as Lee sank into the chair beside her, which she'd bagged with her coat. 'You weren't that bad when I left last night.'

'Half a bottle of whisky,' she croaked by way of reply.

'After all that champagne?' Mila regarded her with silent

concern, seeing how even her kitten ears were wonky, before putting a worried hand on her arm. 'Black coffee?'

Lee nodded, pulling off the hat. Her hair stood with static. 'Better make it two.'

Mila returned a few moments later with a tray of coffee and tiny slices of ginger cake on the saucers. Wordlessly, Lee put the cakes onto Mila's plate. It was still too early for her to look at food.

Mila watched her closely. 'So, did he go back with you?'

'Who?'

Mila looked around them, to check no one else was listening. 'Matteo Hofhuis. You were all over each other.'

Lee swallowed, staring down into the coffee. 'Oh. Yeah.'

'You don't seem very happy about it.' She leaned in to whisper excitedly. 'He is so *gorgeous*.'

'Also incredibly conceited, shallow, really quite dull and an egomaniac. But yeah, gorgeous.'

'Obviously he didn't stay over?'

'Obviously.'

'And you got Jasper off okay?'

'Eventually – an hour and a half late. Having had chocolate for breakfast. Poor kid having *me* as a mother . . .' She rubbed her face in her hands, feeling her failures writ large.

'He'll cope,' Mila said, barging her affectionately. 'And how about Bart? Did you call him too?'

Mila was always her go-to person for morning-after post-mortems and she was expert in managing Lee out of the door. 'Yep. I told him I was taking a duvet day, like you said.'

Mila grinned, as though the words sounded especially amusing coming from Lee's lips. 'And what did he say to that?'

'Well, once he'd picked himself up off the floor, he sounded relieved. I wasn't the only one caning it last night.' She looked at her friend with a feeble side-eye. 'Talking of which, did *you* have a good time?' As far as she remembered, Mila had left with a blonde chap who kept saying he was 'big in stationery'. Lee had no idea how he had come by an invitation.

'Yeah, it was all going really well,' Mila smiled brightly. 'Till his wife rang.'

'*Another one?*' Lee rubbed her face in her hands again, as though trying to slough off the exhaustion.

'I know. Tell me about it.'

'Why are all men such arses?'

'Not all. Just the ones *I* meet.' Mila sighed, her fingers fiddling with the ginger cake. 'I must have "Mistress" tattooed on my forehead in an invisible ink that only married men can see.'

Lee rested her head against her friend's arm, partly to show support and partly to grab support. 'You're worth so much more than that, Mils,' she mumbled, wishing she could go back to bed.

'I know. But last night . . . No. It was the last straw.' Mila said with a determined voice. 'I've had enough of being Miss Second Best, always the runner-up, the fallback option. I'm not doing it any more.'

'Good for you,' Lee murmured, her eyes closed.

'Which is why I've decided to officially take a sabbatical from relationships. Starting from today I'm going to do a Man Detox and not date for six months.'

'Six months?' Lee's eyes flew open as she saw her own social life contract in sympathy. Mila was her best friend, her partner in crime; when they went bar-hopping, they went together. She couldn't go out with the guys – Liam would abandon her within moments of arriving anywhere and no one would approach her if she was with Noah; he was far too big to risk messing with. 'Now hang on, don't you think that's a bit—?'

'Rational? Yes, I do. I've already deleted all the dating apps from my phone, there will be no more blind dates or speed dates, and if you see me looking like I'm giving my details to a guy at a party, you are to stage an intervention. Promise?'

Lee looked back at her friend, aghast. But Mila seemed calm, logical and absolutely determined, and with the hangover Lee was facing right now, she was in no fit state to fight her on it. '. . . Okay.'

They sank into an easy silence, both watching as a photogenic young family walked past, the husband carrying their baby in a hammock, his wife's hand clasped in his own. They could have been models in a winter catalogue for J. Crew. Life looked easy for them, effortless.

Both Lee and Mila looked away, staring down into their coffee cups instead.

'So are you tempted to see him again?' Mila asked her.

'Who? . . . Oh, you mean Matt?' Lee tutted, already bored of talking about him, and shook her head. 'Don't be daft.'

'You know they're saying he could be the next Bond?'

'Mils, I swear to God I've heard it somewhere that my postie could be the next Bond.'

'But he's so sexy, and he seemed really into you.'

'Yeah, because he knows I'm not that into him. His ego can't believe it. Trust me, he thinks it's a challenge to "break" me now.'

'I wouldn't mind being broken by him,' Mila murmured wistfully.

'Uh, sabbatical?'

Mila's eyes widened in surprise, then she pointed at her. 'Exactly. Thank you. That was a test. You passed.'

Lee's own eyes narrowed, not believing a word of it. 'You've got to stop attaching narrative to everything, Mils. This is not a romantic situation. He doesn't want me to fall in love with him any more than I do – no matter what his ego's telling him. Last night didn't mean *anything*. It was just sex, for both of us.'

'But I don't understand how you can . . . hold back, emotionally I mean, like that. If I like a guy enough to bring him home, then I like him enough to see him again. I just don't get your "love 'em and leave 'em" approach.'

'It's not for everyone,' she conceded. 'I just know the right balance for me – I've got to like the guy, but not so much that I'm actually going to fall for him. One hot night to keep my hormones in check, and then I get to give all my love and attention to Jazzy.'

'But don't you think sometimes it would be nice to have a partner? Someone equal to you, someone you can share things with?'

Lee leaned into her again. 'I've got you for that.'

'Aww,' Mila grinned. 'Maybe I should get a kid, then,' she quipped. 'Although you would think it'd put guys off.'

'Surprisingly, no. That's only if they think you're looking for a surrogate father for them. Most of them can't believe their luck when you tell them it's "thank you, next".'

'That's so depress—' Mila stopped. 'Wait, what do you mean, "most"? Not all?'

'No, apparently not. I had a guy turn me down last weekend – because he wanted more!' She gave a scoffing laugh but it was a thin, brittle sound. 'He wanted to *slow things down*. Can you believe that?'

Mila was quiet for a moment. 'You're telling me this guy wanted more from you than just meaningless sex?'

Lee rolled her eyes wearily in reply. 'I mean, please.'

'What did you say to him?'

'I told him straight – that I'm not in the market for that.'

'. . . And what was his response?'

'He left. Just left me standing there.' She shrugged, picking at a slice of ginger cake herself. 'I mean, what an idiot. No-strings sex is every man's fantasy, right?'

Mila didn't reply.

'Right?' Lee jogged her.

'Well . . .' Mila watched her, her face sliding into an apologetic grimace. 'Is it, though? Or is it just that *you* think it is?'

Lee arched an eyebrow. 'Hello? Earth to Mila? Have you ever met a man?'

'Yes, but Lee, you're this successful, independent, beautiful, strong woman. Men love you, of course they do. But your utter conviction that they want nothing more from you . . . Perhaps you make it so plain to them that nothing more will come of a hook-up that they don't even try.'

'I haven't seen any of them crying on their way out.'

'I doubt you've ever looked.'

'Hey!'

'Am I wrong? Tell me honestly, you can't get them out of there fast enough. You never see anyone twice.'

Lee blanched at her friend's truths. It had been a fatal mistake allowing Matt back again last night. But she'd just been so determined to prove Sam right, to get on with forgetting him. Which she was already doing.

'Lee, has it ever occurred to you that you use Jasper as

an excuse to avoid getting into a relationship? You're always so adamant about having sex without love, no ties, but maybe you're trying to avoid deeper feelings. You're terrified of true intimacy. And before you say it,' she said, holding up a hand as a stop sign, 'no, I have not been reading *Grazia* again.'

Lee stared back through the window at the people on the little humped bridge outside, most of them stopping to look down at the thickening ice or take a selfie. Bikes were stacked four or five deep along the railings. It was perishingly cold, everyone in gloves and hats and bundled up with thick scarves, occasional fat flakes of snow fluttering down from on high. 'Cunningham rang. Last night,' she said after a moment.

'Harry? But that's great!' She saw Lee's expression. 'Isn't it? You were so upset at dinner the other night when you heard he'd left. What did he say?'

Lee sighed. 'Practically nothing. We couldn't manage a conversation. The line was so bad, we'd have had better luck with a piece of string and two plastic cups. I still have no idea of what the hell he's up to.'

'Oh no.' Mila frowned. 'Well, is he going to ring back?'

'Don't know,' Lee shrugged. She had thought she might have heard from him again by now. She kept checking her phone every few minutes for missed calls.

'Well, at least you know he's safe; that's something.'

Lee slid her gaze towards her friend's cup, but no further. There was no point in explaining that safety there was momentary. He had been safe in those few moments as they each shouted down the line, trying to connect, but he could already be dead by now; he could have been dead within a minute of hanging up on her. He could have stepped on an IED. A building could have collapsed on him. A bullet could have ricocheted . . . 'Maybe,' was all she said. She bit her lip. 'He's sent me a letter.'

Mila's eyes widened. 'A letter? Oh my God, that's so old school! What did it say?'

'I don't know. I've not received it yet.'

'Oh. Well, when did he send it?'

Lee shrugged.

'What do you think's in it?'

Lee spread her palms wide. 'I don't know, Mils! That he wants to transition to being a woman? He's gone vegan?' She laughed weakly, but it turned into a sigh. 'Honestly, I've no idea.'

Mila stared at her intently, prompting Lee to arch an eyebrow. 'What?'

'You know what.'

'I don't! All I know is you're staring at me like some kind of mad, crazy woman.'

'What if he's writing to tell you he loves you? That he always has and he always will?'

'His wife is pregnant,' Lee replied in an arch tone. 'It's *not* that.'

'He could realize he's made a terrible mistake?'

'They spent months trying. There's no mistake.'

Mila's face fell. 'I've just always had the feeling about you two that . . . you know, there was more there than just . . . former colleagues. You're like . . . soulmates.'

Lee dropped her head in her hands. 'You're attaching narrative again. We've talked about this.'

'But he followed you to Amsterdam after you moved here! He knocks at your door even though we all know you will never answer it. Lee, *no one* could drive each other as crazy as you two drive each other crazy, without it coming down to either love or hate.'

Lee was silent for several moments. 'It isn't either of those,' she said quietly, her fingers interlacing around her cup. 'I'm afraid it's far worse than that.'

Chapter Eleven

She pulled the Christmas tree up the stairs, backwards, thousands of needles scattering across the treads. It was heavier than it looked.

'Come on, you bastard,' she muttered to herself, heaving it into the living area and over to the window. She would still need to get the stand and decorations down from the loft, for her and Jasper to put up together this weekend. But not now. Not now. Her hangover was getting the better of her again.

Massaging her temples, she went over to the kitchen and made herself a coffee. Her sixth so far today. Now she wasn't sure if it was the caffeine or the whisky giving her the shakes.

'So much for a duvet day,' she thought, reaching for the blanket from the armchair. She was too much of a puritan to spend an entire day doing nothing, even with a cracking hangover, and since getting back from dropping off Jasper and having brunch with Mila, she had done the shopping for tomorrow's Pakjesavond festivities and stripped and washed the bed in the spare room. She had even gone as far as opening the window to air the place. She didn't want a trace of Matt left in her house, not even aftershave molecules lingering in the air. He had followed up already with a text and she had immediately deleted that too.

No more Matt. No more Sam. She'd had quite enough man trouble lately and some peace and quiet was what she craved now. That and a saline drip.

Putting down her coffee, she sank her full height along the length of the sofa with a grateful sigh and pulled the blanket up to her chin, closing her eyes. She needed this. An hour's rest before she had to collect Jasper . . .

Her eyes opened again and she frowned, unable to get comfortable. She fluffed the cushions; they were too flat. Her hand touched something smooth and hard.

'What is tha—?' she asked herself, pulling out a book and falling still. 'Oh, you've got to be kidding me,' she murmured. It was the book she had found in her bike basket. Sam's book. Jasper had asked to keep it and she had forgotten all about it. He must have been reading it, looking at the pictures.

She stared at the cover, at the arresting simplicity of the image, recognizing now his style. She could hate him and still see that it was beautiful. She could admire his book and still want never to see him again, she told herself, as she flicked through the pages. She stopped at one of a koala in a tree, looking down at a kangaroo holding open its pouch. *If you fall* . . .

Two million copies. She kept flicking past the pages. Two million copies had been sold of these pithy, Insta-happy wisdoms and pretty pictures?

'Hallmark, eat your heart out,' she mumbled to herself, nonetheless turning to the next page.

She stopped mid-movement, jolted by what she saw there – a small flyer for her 'Back to Front' exhibition lay loosely against the page. She picked it up. A coincidence? Surely not. She had assumed the book ending up in her basket had been entirely random – first when she'd thought a stranger had dropped it, and latterly, too, when Liam had told her about Sam's publisher's marketing campaign. But the presence of a flyer for her own exhibition suggested otherwise.

Her eyes fell to the open page behind it and she felt herself start at what she saw there: Sam's illustration of a curled-up badger had been overwritten in vivid purple felt tip with a message infinitely less reassuring than his.

She frowned, staring at it for several long moments. Was it a joke? For a moment she thought Jasper might have written it, but the certainty in the line of the letters, the desperate, rushed stab of the pen against the paper, told her not. And besides, they weren't words he would – have cause to – say.

In her old life, she had seen messages written in a hurry, in desperation, before. She had heard these very words count-less times. No, this was no prank. She sat up, flicking through the pages more quickly now, scanning for something else that might give her a clue as to who had written it – a name, an address. But there was nothing, just the plea. A desperate shout in a sea of calm.

HELP ME.

'Bohemian Rhapsody'. She liked the song, but seriously – hearing it all the way through twice, on loop . . . How long did it take a switchboard to find the right number? She had all of twenty minutes left before she needed to collect Jasper from nursery.

'Come on. Come on.' She was sitting on the sill of one of her two large square windows that gave onto the canal, one leg bent as she chewed on a nail. A duck was walking across the thickening ice and she could see the fallen leaves that had become trapped just below the surface.

The song clicked off just as Freddie Mercury became a poor boy.

'Oh hi, yes,' she said, snapping to attention as a voice came onto the line. 'Is that the marketing department for—' She checked the name of the publisher's imprint on the spine; the book rested face down on her thigh. '—Olander Books?'

'Yes.'

'Great. Could I please speak to someone who does the marketing campaign for Sam Meyer? Uh, I mean Samuel Meyer. Samuel. Or Jacintha, if she's there,' she added, remembering the stroppy PR's name.

There was a pause. 'Who is calling, please?'

'Well, my name is . . .' She hesitated. She didn't want this getting back to Sam in any way. 'My name's Ms Van Alstyne.'

Huh? Sometimes she amazed herself.

'With which company?'

'I'm calling as a private individual, actually.'

There was a pause. 'Can I ask what this is concerning?'

'Yes, I need to speak to someone about Mr Meyer's book distribution campaign – you know, the freebies you put around the city?'

There was a longer pause. 'And what is it you need to know?'

Lee rolled her eyes. Great, a jobsworth. 'Well, in the first instance, I'm trying to find out if the number on the top of the title page means anything?'

'*Means* anything?'

'Yeah. I've got one of the books and it's got "276" written in it, in the top right corner of the title page.' She stared at Sam's looping script across the body of the page: *If you find this . . . may it brighten your day.* Well, it hadn't, she thought with some perverse satisfaction. Quite the opposite.

'I see. Well, five hundred copies were distributed, so that would mean yours is number 276 of 500.'

'Okay great, yes, I thought it might be that,' Lee said, feeling a spasm of hope. 'So then my next question was whether, when you handed out those five hundred books, did you have some sort of "plan", like a map of where you were going to leave them? Or was it completely random – you know, an assistant dropping them on park benches on her lunch break?'

There was a stern pause. 'I'm afraid I don't understand. Why do you need to know that?'

She could sense the marketing woman's growing irritation and bafflement. 'Because I need to find out where my issue – number 276 – was left.'

'But surely, if you found the book, it was left where you found it?'

Lee suppressed a sigh of annoyance herself. Did this woman think she was stupid? 'Well, the thing is, I think *someone else* found the book first, and then they put it in my bike basket.'

'Paying it forward, you mean? Well, that's good to hear. It's very much in line with the ethos behind the campaign. Treating each other with kindness. Sam's very—'

'No, no. I think there might have been more to it than that.'

'I don't think so. Someone obviously found it, read it and then they left it for you to have afterwards.'

'No, you really don't understand.' Lee dropped her head into her free hand, massaging her forehead. This headache was a kicker. 'There was a message in it. Written over one of the pages.'

'. . . What sort of message?'

'I'm afraid I can't say. But I really do need to find the person who found it first.'

She heard the woman sigh, out of patience. It would be

143

one of the more bizarre telephone calls she'd have taken this week. 'I'm sorry, Ms Van Alstyne, but I'm afraid we can't help you. The success of the campaign rests on the very notion of anonymity—'

'I understand that, but this really is important. I'm not intending to ask them on a *date* or something. This person needs my help.' There was a long pause and, as Lee replayed her own words over in her head, she knew they sounded mad. *She* sounded mad.

'Even if we knew who had found the book – which we do not – we could not hand out their identity or details to you; that would be a personal data breach. I'm sure you understand.'

'I do. But if you could just give me the place where it was left—'

'I'm sorry, but there's really nothing further I can do. Goodbye.'

And before Lee could get another word out, she had hung up. Lee stared at the phone in disbelief. 'Bitch!'

Chapter Twelve

The queue was snaking back towards the door. Lee twisted round and tried to count the number of people behind them. Twenty-five, thirty maybe? There had been that number in front of them when they'd arrived. She had tried getting to the front of the line with Jasper 'for just one quick question', but the store security guard had sent them packing and they were having to wait with everyone else. The crowds were monstrous. Tonight was Pakjesavond, or present-giving evening, and the Dutch equivalent of Christmas Eve. All the shops would be closing by lunchtime and people were on their final bursts of last-minute shopping; book-buying was seemingly a big part of that.

Jasper was sitting on the floor, cross-legged, by her feet, reading a picture book. Lee clutched her own book more tightly in her hands. The queue was moving quickly at least and they gained another few inches, Jasper bum-shuffling on the floor without looking up.

She dipped to the side, looking up the queue again. There were a lot of women standing in line, she noticed, and more than a few times the words 'handsome' and 'gorgeous' had drifted to her ear. She could see the desk, hear the excited voices of the people at the front as they got what they had come for. But would she?

'Mama, what's that?' Jasper asked her in Dutch.

She looked down at the angelic face peering up at her. He was pointing to an illustration in his dinosaur book. 'A diplodocus, darling,' she replied in English.

'Dip-lo-do-cus,' he repeated in his little voice.

Her eyes grazed the store for the hundredth time as she waited, but she somehow wasn't tiring of it. It had been decorated as a wooded wonderland – a smattering of faux trees with improbably dense, over-arching canopies, spreading and touching tips just below the ceiling. It had been sprayed with a crispy frosting of sparkling snow from cans, and felted woodland creatures were dotted through the branches, peering out of knot holes, carrying through to intermittent nearby shelves. A small family of roe deer, standing on a white, glittering snowy carpet, was positioned by the children's corner, and every time Jasper ran over to get another book, he stopped to stroke them, talking to them as if they were real.

They shuffled forward another few inches again, the voices at the front becoming gradually more distinct. The cash desks had been enveloped by some sort of plaster grotto and covered with fairy lights, and all the shop staff were dressed as elves. It was cheesy, she tutted, but she couldn't ignore the fact it still soothed her. Christmas played a very lowly second fiddle to St Nicholas celebrations for the Dutch and whilst, as an expat, she had embraced her new home's traditions, she still felt a need to mark her own childhood customs. She went in for the full Christmas works – they did the tree, Christmas carols, mince pies, stocking, and in spite of her exceptionally limited culinary skills, she still heroically grappled every year with the smallest turkey she could find (which was unfathomably never less than five kilos).

Almost there.

They were gaining ground incrementally but the queue sometimes lurched forwards, as now, when a group reached the front and then peeled off en masse.

'A gingerbread?' an elf asked her, stopping by her elbow and making her startle. She hadn't noticed him making his way from the back of the line. He was holding out a tray of gingerbread biscuits.

'Thanks.' She took one and Jasper was on his feet in a flash, agonizing over which of the absolutely identical gingerbread men he should choose.

'Excuse me, but is it absolutely necessary for me to queue?' she asked the elf as they waited for Jasper's decision. 'I'm not actually here for the signing. I just need to ask a question.' Just one question and she could go again and pretend this – unwelcome but unavoidable – interlude had never happened. She was very much looking forward to getting on with never having to see him again.

'I'm afraid everyone has to wait in line, madam,' the elf replied, staring pointedly at the copy of the book held in her arms, before wandering off.

'Can I get another book, mama?' Jasper asked, sending crumbs all over the floor.

'Sure,' she sighed. 'But come straight back here. And stay where I can see you.'

She watched as he ran back to the children's corner, having completely forgotten the book he had just been reading. She bent down to pick it up before someone tripped over it. She put the book in her arms with the other three Jasper had picked and, as she straightened up, she saw the woman in front of her was now having her copy signed, Sam's head bent as his pen squiggled across the page. 'I hope you enjoy it. Happy St Nicholas,' he smiled, handing the book back to the reader and his eyes already sliding over to the next cust—

Her.

She saw the smile fade from his face, a flash of panic and then something else – something darker – bloom in his eyes at the sight of her. Did he think she was going to cause a scene and start another argument? Or was he remembering Matt? *She's all yours.* Did he sense what she'd done? Could he guess she'd done it to spite him? Did he even care?

Whatever was going through his head, none of it could account for, or make less confusing, the fact that she was standing here now.

Hesitantly, she stepped forward. 'Hi.'

'Hello,' he said in a short tone, and it was quite apparent from his expression that he had never expected to see her again either. He had closed the door on her and turned the key. 'This is a surprise.'

And not a nice one, clearly. 'Yes, I—'

His eyes fell to her copy of the book in her hands and he reached out for it brusquely, looking away from her. His mouth was set in a grim line. She stepped in closer, pushing the book towards him.

'Look, Sam—'

'At least I don't have to ask your name,' he murmured, flicking for the title page. 'So we can do this quickly.'

'No,' she faltered, watching him, feeling his hostility. 'That's not why I'm here.'

He looked up, pen paused mid-air, one eyebrow arched. 'What?'

'I need to talk to you.'

'You're aware this is a book signing? I'm working. This is

hardly the time.' His words were quiet; to onlookers, they were just having a conversation.

'Sam, I need your help.'

'I *sincerely* doubt that,' he said, going to sign his name and seeing his own handwriting already written across it. One of his free marketing copies.

'I do. I need to find out where this book was left.' She pointed to the number written in the top corner. 'I tried your marketing department but they won't talk to me.'

'You did *what*? You spoke to my mar—' He shook his head as he stared back at her and she felt the invisible thread between them quiver. But he looked away quickly again in the next instant and gave a shrug. Whatever. He didn't care. He wasn't interested, not even interested enough to ask her why she had done such a thing, and she couldn't tell whether he was angry or relieved to learn that she hadn't come here because of *them*. He closed the book without signing it and held it back out to her.

Out of the corner of her eye, she saw the feet of the woman behind her step forward in anticipation. Lee turned her head just enough, in warning, and the feet took a half step back again.

'Please, Sam. You're the only person I can ask. Look.' And she quickly thumbed to the defaced page. She watched as his face changed at the sight of it and he took the book from her again. The desperation in the words was clear to see. This was no hoax, no childish prank. She knew he could see that too.

'I'm going to have to ask you to move along, madam,' an elf said to her, stepping forward from a sentry position behind Sam's left shoulder. 'We have to keep the queue moving.'

Lee looked from him to Sam again, beseeching him with her eyes.

'Mama! I found this one!'

Jasper came careening over with a copy of a Star Wars jigsaw book in his hands. Sam slammed the book shut – hiding the message – as Jasper held up the new book to her expectantly. The fifth one. 'Uh, okay yes, we can get that one too,' she murmured, trying to hold her voice steady.

Jasper stared at Sam. 'I know you,' he said frankly.

'No,' Sam hesitated. 'I don't think we've met.'

'I remember your eyes.'

Sam's gaze slid towards her. 'Oh. Well then, it must be my mistake. What's your name?' he asked quickly.

'Jasper.'

'Hi, Jasper. My name's Sam.'

'This is the Sam who wrote the book, Jazz,' Lee said quietly, trying to gloss over to her child that coming here had been a mistake. Why should Sam have helped her out? He'd already granted her one favour, and that was clearly one too many. It was perfectly evident he regretted ever getting involved with her. 'Remember we wanted to come here to get the sheep book signed?'

Jasper looked back at Sam earnestly. 'I like the koala best.'

Sam smiled, his face lighting up. 'Really? He's my favourite too. Everyone else seems to like the squirrels.'

'Did you sign our book? Mama said we could only read it when you put your writing in it.'

Sam's mouth opened as he glanced across at her. '. . . Well, actually, I was just about to do that, but your copy has a tear in it,' he said, sliding their copy fully out of reach and producing a new one from under the desk. They both knew there was no way they could let Jasper come across that message. 'Shall I address it to you?'

Jasper nodded, not really understanding what that meant. He watched in silence as Sam's hand flew across the page, Lee's attention instead on the nape of his neck, the line of his jaw, the flop of his fallen-out curls . . . *She's all yours* . . .

'The koala.' Jasper's eyes lit up as Sam handed the book back and the child hugged it tightly.

'Ssh, don't tell anyone or I'll have to do it for *everyone*,' Sam whispered, putting a finger to his lips and winking at him.

'Jasper, what do you say?' Lee asked quietly, putting a hand on his shoulder. Sam's kindness to her child didn't mean coming here hadn't been a massive mistake.

'Thank you.'

'It's my pleasure, Jasper,' Sam replied.

'If you could allow the next person to come through now, please.' The elf had stepped forward again. Lee's time was well and truly up.

She nodded, Sam's eyes meeting hers briefly. But his stare was cold and, when he made no attempt to comment further, she had no choice but to move on. She heard the woman behind her start babbling immediately, stepping into the space Lee had left almost before she'd vacated it. She glanced down the queue again. They were through the door now and out onto the street. His adoring fans.

'Right . . . Well, we'd better pay for these,' she said slowly as they moved off, trying to gather herself as her disappointment grew. She felt crushed by his refusal to help, devastated by his scorn.

'And then we can go to Vondelpark?'

'Sure.' They walked over to the cash desk in the fairy-light grotto, Jasper running off to look at some colouring pencils in the nearby display.

'I'll be right with you, I just have to replace the receipt roll,' the sales assistant said as Lee stood at the desk and got out her purse.

'Huh? Oh yes, that's fine,' Lee murmured, her gaze falling to Sam's book on the top of the pile. She opened the front cover to see the special illustration he'd drawn. It was of a koala sleeping, all curled up, and one paw was being held by a much smaller koala. A baby. Beneath it was a message.

To Jasper,
Keep holding your mama's hand.
Sam

The cold had sent the birds down from the trees, scavenging for crumbs on the tabletops and daring to peck beneath the chairs where people sat enjoying the bright sunlight. On days such as this, it felt like the whole city relocated here, everyone swapping the narrow, cobbled water-edged streets for undulating space, tree-dotted lawns and wide, sweeping carriageways where they could run, walk, cycle, skate . . .

Jasper was kneeling on a chair, reaching over the tray for his hot, oozing *bitterballen* and juice. It was their weekend treat to come here. Depending on the weather, they would feed the ducks and go to the playground, before ending up at one of the large cafes for lunch. He loved running about with the other kids, and they would often bump into kinder-garten friends here, Lee always at a loss to remember the mothers' names.

'Are you warm enough?' she asked, reaching for his bare hand and squeezing it. He could never wait to toss away his layers – hats and scarves were torture for five-year-old boys, it seemed.

'I'm boiling.' Chasing pigeons could be an Olympic sport, the way he went at it.

'No, leave your coat on please. You're hot because you've been running around but you'll cool down quickly now we're sitting still. It's December, for heaven's sake, and there's ice on the ground. It's far too cold to sit outside without a coat on.'

'Is it going to snow?'

Lee turned her face up to the sky. 'I don't know. Not today it won't – it's too clear. But soon maybe.'

'I hope it snows. I want to build a snowman.'

'Yes, that would be fun. I should check the forecast . . .'

'We'll need a carrot. For his nose.'

'You're right,' she agreed. 'I'll put carrots on the shopping list.' She heard a familiar sound overhead. 'Oh look!' she said, pointing up to the sky at the small flock of green parakeets flying from one tree to another. They were Jasper's favourite birds and she still got a thrill every time she saw them too, as though Rio had come to town. London had its own wild colony as well.

'Please can we catch one, mama?' Jasper pleaded. 'Please. It can sleep in my room.'

She gave a bemused grin. 'Even if you could catch one, which I'm afraid you definitely couldn't, you'd never sleep. It'd keep you awake all night with its squawking, and you need your sleep so you can grow to be really big and—'

She stopped mid-flow. Sam was standing a table away holding a coffee, his dark hair covered by a black beanie, a thick cashmere scarf at his neck. She imagined she must look as shocked as he had sitting at his table earlier. 'I heard Jasper asking to come here,' he said by way of explanation, looking over at her son and giving him a friendly wave.

'But . . . the queue was onto the street,' she stammered, as if *that* was the pertinent point.

He shrugged. 'The store was closing at one. And I'm heading out to Friesland shortly.'

'Oh . . . You're from there?' she asked blankly, stunned into autopilot politeness.

He nodded. Everyone was travelling, it seemed, to be with their families. Noah and Liam had left the city last night, Mila was celebrating with her brother across town. Only Lee and Jasper were staying put, it felt.

They stared at one another in silence, apparently bewildered that they were both here. She'd gone to him with a begging bowl and he'd all but sent her packing; she couldn't believe he had followed and found them. And neither, seemingly, could he. His gaze was still weighty, laden with an anger and resentment that he wouldn't express – she wouldn't play by his rules and he wouldn't play by hers. For a man she had known a little over a week, they already had a complicated history.

'Do you want to sit down?' she ventured. If nothing else, Jasper's presence meant this would stay civil.

He hesitated and she could see the conflict in him – to go, to stay, to help, to turn away . . . 'Thanks.' He pulled out a chair – scaring off a pigeon that was strutting between its legs – and sat opposite them, warming his hands around his travel cup. His cheeks were flushed from the cold, the tips of his fingers blanched white by contrast. Their eyes alighted and flitted off each other like the sparrows on the empty tables, both aware that the conversation they needed to have wasn't suitable for a young audience.

Jasper was staring at their unexpected guest with guileless scrutiny and Lee knew his little brain was trying to place him, this newly met man with the familiar eyes.

'Hey Jazz, why don't you do some colouring in the new book we bought?' And she reached into her bag and pulled out the animals colouring-in book and pencils.

'Which one shall I do?' Jasper asked, happily distractable as he began flicking through the pages. The tiger? The elephant? The parrot? The butterfly?

'How about the parrot?' she said. 'Seeing as we just saw the parakeets.'

'Okay. But I'm going to make them rainbow colours.'

'Good idea,' she agreed, watching as he got out all the pencils and began shading between the lines.

Lee sat back in her seat, looking over at Sam watching them. 'Thank you for coming,' she said quietly.

Sam half nodded, half shrugged, his eyes darting from her to her son and back again, as though he wasn't sure what – or how much – to say. He cleared his throat. 'I couldn't stop thinking about what you . . . showed me.'

'Yes.' It had troubled her own sleep last night, marbling her usual nightmares with a fresh strand of intrigue.

'Have you shown it to anyone else?' he asked.

'No. Not yet.'

His finger tapped against the cup. 'Do you have any idea who wrote it?'

'No.'

'Where did you find it?'

'In my bike basket, last week. I forgot all about it till yesterday when I found it round the back of the sofa.'

'So, it was just a random drop in your basket?'

'No, I don't think so. It's got a number in the top corner,

suggesting it was part of your publicity campaign, but there was a flyer for my new exhibition in with it. I think whoever left it was showing they wanted *me* to find it. To help them.'

'So why not just ask you for help then? Isn't it . . . complicated, leaving it in your basket like that? Anyone could have taken it.'

'I know.' She shrugged. 'I can't explain it.'

'They obviously didn't feel like they could talk to you directly.'

She flinched at the barb in his words. 'No, obviously not.'

'Unless it's just a coincidence the flyer was in the book too. I mean, how would they have known they were leaving it in *your* bike basket? There are a lot of bikes in Amsterdam.'

'Well, I guess they must know where I live. Or they know me well enough to recognize my bike.' She thought for a moment. 'I always put these gold streamers on the handlebars now, for Jasper, so he can recognize our bike easily.'

Sam's eyebrows shrugged, a sign of acceptance that gold streamers certainly made the bike distinctive. 'Maybe this person is a victim of domestic violence then, and they've somehow . . . found out where you live.'

'Maybe,' she agreed, but she suppressed a shudder of fear at the thought. Security and privacy were one and the same to her. 'But I don't think so. I'm careful about my personal details staying out of the public domain.'

He didn't reply, but the sudden arch to his eyebrow was a clear contradiction and she knew what he was thinking – she had given him, a complete stranger, her address in the hospital toilet, hadn't she?

She looked away quickly. 'But it might not be a domestic violence issue, we can't assume anything. This person might need help in other ways.'

'Like what?'

'I don't know – drug addiction? Gambling debts? A toxic boyfriend? A stalker?'

A young woman edged past their table, holding up a laden tray. Sam glanced up at her, then back at Lee again. 'And what if it is something like that? A stalker. Drugs. Should you really be chasing this stranger down and getting involved? It could be dangerous.'

'Well, luckily I've got previous with that.' She hadn't meant the response to come back as so pithy but she couldn't help it. She didn't need to be patronized about dangerous situations. She'd been in far more than him.

He blinked, seemingly not liking her answer either. 'Why does it have to be you, taking this on?'

'Because *I'm* the one who's been asked. Whoever put that book in my basket targeted me.' She leaned forward, dropping her voice. 'Sam, they need my help.'

'Really? Or do you just always have to be on a crusade?'

She sat back again. There was venom in the words; she wasn't forgiven. She stared back at him levelly, feeling the walls rise higher still between them again.

He looked away, frustrated by her, resentful he was here, his elbows on the arms of the chairs, his fingers loosely interlinked.

Lee's gaze fell to an ink stain on his right-hand fingers, a pressure mark against the skin, and she realized this wasn't his problem. He hadn't asked for any of this. He was just a random guy she'd unwisely drawn into the loop of her chaotic existence. One who'd got away.

She tried softening her approach, knowing she just had to get what she needed from him and set him loose. He didn't deserve the drama that came with getting involved with her.

'Look, I appreciate this all sounds mad and I probably am mad for following up on it. But I'm not asking for you to get involved any further than making a call for me. Just ask your marketing people if they can find out where exactly that book was first dropped – *before* it was put in my basket – and I'll do the rest myself. I promise you'll never hear from me again.'

His eyes whipped up to hers and he said nothing for several moments. 'How will that help, finding out where it was left?'

'Well, follow the chain of events – the books your marketing people sent out would have come direct from the printers, yes? They'd have been sealed, bound and boxed. I think we can safely assume it's unlikely anyone at the printers or your publishers wrote that message – it wasn't some generalized call to arms or a political statement. It's a cry for help, and because it was put in my bike basket, with my gallery flyer inside, it's reasonable to assume that the person who put it there is known to me. That means there has to be a stage missing between the book leaving *your* marketing team's possession and it ending up in *my* bike basket. There's got to be a third party who found the book, wrote in it and left it for me to find. If you can help me discover where it was left, I'll continue from there and I won't bother you again, I promise. No more favours.'

No more favours. She'd invited him into her life for a favour; now she was releasing him with another.

He stared at her and she wished his gaze was less unsettling. 'And what if no one in marketing knows? What if they were scattered around at whim?'

She sighed. 'Then I'll be all out of ideas,' she shrugged. 'There won't be anything further I can do. That'll be it. They'll have to reach out to me again, in a more direct way.'

He stared straight back at her and she felt the silver thread tighten and vibrate again, as it did every time their eyes locked. Even when they were arguing. Even when they were hating each other. She remembered how it had felt to stand in his shadow, knowing she was about to kiss him. If he'd just not been so . . . chivalrous, she'd be over it by now. Over him. He'd have been another ship in the night and they'd be sailing to opposite continents.

He sighed, looking over at her son. 'Jasper, do *you* always do what your mama tells you?'

Jasper broke off from his colouring in. 'Yes,' he said, so solemnly Lee almost choked on her coffee.

Sam laughed, sunlight breaking out from behind the clouds in his eyes. 'Hmm. I'm beginning to think most people do.'

A ripple of hope kicked through her. 'So then, you'll do it?'

'I'll call on Monday and do what I can,' he sighed. 'But I can't make any promises.'

'That's fine,' she said earnestly. 'One call is absolutely all I'm asking for.'

'Yes,' he said with an inscrutable look. 'I know it is.'

Chapter Thirteen

'Higher, I can't reach,' Jasper said, straining towards the branch.

'Oof, that's easy for you to say,' she scoffed, trying to lift him higher. 'Have you been eating rocks?' He placed the bauble on the frond and she put him back on the ground with a groan. 'My poor arms. I'll look like Rocky by the time this is done.'

'Who?'

'Never mind.' She ruffled his hair as they stepped back to look at their efforts. The tree was short but wide, like a hooped skirt, and already decked with several metres of lights. So far, they appeared to have a strong bias towards the bottom left corner.

'I think we need more on this side,' she said, pointing to the right. 'And there's a big gap in the back there. What *will* the neighbours think if they have to look at an empty patch of Christmas tree in the window?'

He looked up at her. 'You're going to have to lift me up again, mama.'

'Or I could do the high up bits and you do the lower bits?' she suggested.

'No, you said *I* could decorate the tree. I want to do all of it.'

'Okay, well, let me get a chair then, because my arms aren't going to be able to do that much heavy lifting. Honestly, who knew I had a tank for a son?'

She walked across to the kitchen and switched on the kettle. 'Do you want a hot chocolate?' she asked as she brought back the chair and positioned it in front of the tree for him. 'This is thirsty work.'

'Yes please, mama. Look, I made this!' He had found the pom-pom robin he had made last year.

'That's one of my favourites,' she said, getting the milk from the fridge and pouring some into a pan. 'Make sure that one goes towards the front where I can see it.'

'Okay,' he replied earnestly, putting it in the very centre.

She watched him, feeling a rush of love for this child who had changed her life so completely. It was impossible to imagine life without him, the person she'd been before she became his mother now just a ghost who moved restlessly through her bones.

She looked down at the day's post; she had picked it up on their way back in from the park and set it down again unthinkingly, her mind still preoccupied with Sam and what it meant that he had followed them to the park and those eyes of his that said different things to his mouth . . . She flicked through the envelopes disinterestedly still, as she stirred the milk; it was just the usual clutch of junk mail, a Christmas card from her aunt living in Wiltshire, a copy of *Life* magazine, an electricity bill. Nothing of interest, no—

She remembered Cunningham's words. His letter.

Still no letter.

She frowned. That call had been two days ago. He must surely have sent it before he left Amsterdam or, at the very latest, when he arrived in Turkey, a week ago? It should be here by now.

Unless . . .

A thought occurred to her. She quickly picked up her phone and found his details, which Dita had insisted on forwarding her when he'd moved here. 'In case of an absolute, end-of-the-world emergency,' she had insisted, when Lee had protested.

She rang the number, her fingers tapping the counter impatiently. Why hadn't she thought of this before?

'Hello?' Gisele's voice was soft down the line.

'Gisele? It's Lee. Fitchett,' she added.

There was a pause. 'Hi Lee! How are you?' Forced jollity.

'Well, thanks. You?'

'Oh, the heartburn has started but' – she forced a smile into her voice – 'that's par for the course, right?'

'Sure, yes. Poor you, though. It's horrid.'

'Yes. Did you have it?'

'Uh, no. But I had everything else – or at least, that was how it felt.'

Gisele chuckled politely. 'Right.'

There was a small pause, both of them exhausted on small talk already, and Lee realized she ought to have taken a breath before she'd picked up the phone, or at least rehearsed in her mind their conversation.

'Um, anyway, look, I don't want to bother you, I'm sure you must be up to your ears getting ready for tonight. I was just wondering if there was a letter there for me? From Cunningham?'

There was a pause. 'A letter? . . . No, I haven't seen one, I'm sorry.'

'Oh.' Disappointment crashed through her, hope snatched away again in an instant. For a moment there, Lee had thought she was close to getting her answer, some kind of clarity on what the hell Cunningham was up to. 'Oh . . . well, never mind.'

'What makes you think there's a letter here?'

'Cunningham asked me whether I'd received it.'

'You've *heard* from him?' Gisele sounded shocked.

'Yes, he rang on Thursday night.'

There was a longer pause. 'What did he say?' Her voice sounded tremulous.

Lee winced. Maybe this hadn't been her most tactful moment? 'Well, the line was so bad, I couldn't make out anything other than that he was asking if I'd received a letter. It's not come by post so I was wondering if he might have left it there instead, that was all.'

'Oh. I see.' There was a long silence. 'No, I . . . I'm sorry but I haven't seen any letter here.'

'Oh well, not to worry.' She inhaled, preparing to say thanks and ring off.

'I . . . I haven't heard from him since he called that first night, after he landed . . . Is he okay? Did he sound okay?'

Lee wasn't sure how to respond; she could hear the hurt in Gisele's voice. 'Well . . . I mean, like I said, I could scarcely hear him. But he didn't *not* sound okay.'

'. . . Right.'

It was hardly a round reassurance. Lee felt a stab of guilt that she had heard from him when his wife had not. 'He probably just wanted to pick my brains about something out there. I know the area quite well, so . . .' She remembered in the nick of time that Gisele thought he was in Palmyra. 'Big place, Palmyra.'

'Oh.'

Lee felt ever more awkward. It would have been better to do this in person; the phone always amplified tension. 'Well, anyway, I'm sorry to have bothered you, I should let you get on. What are you up to tonight?'

'Um, I – I . . .' She sighed. 'Well, nothing, actually.'

Lee couldn't hide her shock. Pakjesavond was the biggest festive celebration of the Dutch year. The entire population was with their loved ones, feasting, celebrating, children waiting impatiently for the gift-giving to begin. Everyone she knew was with their family. It was inconceivable that Gisele wouldn't have someone to spend it with. 'Oh, I'm sorry, I just assumed . . .'

'I'm fine with it, really. Harry and I had planned to have a quiet one, our last one just the two of us. But of course, now he's gone . . . And my brother's skiing with his family and my parents have gone on the holiday of a lifetime in the South Pacific islands before they become grandparents, so . . . But it suits me to have an early night. I'm in bed by eight most nights at the moment.'

'Oh Gisele, you can't spend it alone. You just can't.'

'But I don't mind. Really I don't.'

'No. It's not right. You shouldn't be in that big house all on your own. Come to us.' The words were out before she could stop them; before she'd even known about them.

'. . . What?'

Lee's eyes widened too. Oh God, what had she done? Invited her estranged former colleague's lonely pregnant model wife to spend the biggest evening of the year with them? She swallowed. 'I insist.' Why wouldn't the words stop?

'But—'

'It's not right to be alone at a time like this. It's only Jasper and me here, so we've not got anything big planned, but we've still got more food than we can eat. You'd be helping us out, actually.'

Gisele gave a small laugh. 'Lee, that's just so kind but—'

'No buts. Let me give you our address.'

'Oh, I know it. Bloemgracht, with the dark-red door and the bay tree on the steps.'

'Yes . . .' Lee faltered. How did she know that?

As if reading her mind, Gisele said, 'Harry and I used to walk past all the time. Any chance he got, he'd turn in, always looking up when we passed that house, always trying to see in through the windows even though the blinds were always down. It was a while before I realized it was yours.'

Lee didn't know what to say. 'Oh.' She wondered yet again what Cunningham had told her by way of explanation for their estrangement. Had he told her the truth, as he knew it? Or had he given her a cover story? Was she the bad guy in it? The antagonist? 'Well, that's good you know where we are, then,' she said weakly. 'Shall we say six o'clock?'

Gisele cleared her throat. 'Yes. Six would be great . . . Thanks, Lee. See you then.'

Lee hung up the phone and buried her face in her hands. 'Oh-God-oh-God-oh-God. What did I just do?'

'What's wrong mama?'

'Oh, just your mama speaking before she thinks again,' she muttered, wanting to kick herself. She looked across. Behind him, the tree was almost beginning to lean at an angle, such was the bottom-heavy weight of the decorations on its lower left side. She broke into a grin, shaking her head at the sight of it.

'Do you like it?' he asked excitedly, seeing her face.

'It's just perfect, my little Jazz Man. Absolutely perfect.'

'This is the biggest one I can find!' Jasper said, holding up the carrot and placing it at the end of his nose.

'Oh my goodness,' Lee exclaimed. 'That's got to be one of the longest I've ever seen. Wouldn't you agree, Gisele?'

Gisele, curled up on the sofa, a glass of non-alcoholic wine in her hand, nodded. 'Oh definitely.'

'That's longer than a witch's finger,' Lee added.

'You've never seen a witch's finger,' Jasper admonished, but a tiny question mark hovered in his eyes as he looked at her.

'You'd be amazed at the things I've seen and the people I've met,' she said, watching as he placed the carrot against his own short fingers, trying to imagine the scale of a witch.

He went over to the open fire where one of his little clogs was set back on the hearth – as it had been for the past three weeks. She watched as he positioned the carrot carefully inside the wooden shoe. It also held a rolled-up picture he had drawn for Sinterklaas and there was a glass of cold milk to the side, which for some reason now made her think of laughing eyes from beneath snowy-white eyebrows every time she looked at it.

Some of Jasper's friends liked to put hay for Sinterklaas's horse in with the carrot too, and even though Lee repeatedly explained about the potential fire risks of doing that with an open fire, as opposed to a stove, Jasper looked at her disappointedly; fire risks meant nothing to a child who just wanted to feed the white horse standing on their roof.

They all looked down at the small offering that meant so much – a carrot, some milk and a drawing, in a size 11 clog. 'Sinterklaas will like that,' she said proudly. 'He's left you some pretty nice presents these past few weeks, hasn't he?'

'Sinterklaas came here to meet me,' he said to Gisele. 'He said I'm the best boy in Amsterdam.'

Gisele laughed. 'Oh, wow! Well then, if Sinterklaas says it, it must be true!'

'He drew me a picture. You can see it.' And before Gisele could even reply, he had shot out of the room to get it. It had quickly become his most treasured possession since Sam's visit.

'He's rather overexcited,' Lee said with an awkward smile as the sound of his feet thudded overhead. 'This is the first time we've had anyone over for Pakjesavond.'

'It's so kind of you to have asked me,' Gisele said again. She had arrived laden with gifts – flowers, a bottle of champagne that she couldn't drink, a *Kerstkrans* ring cake in a tin, a wrapped present for Jasper . . . it was gratitude and embarrassment intermingled into overkill; Lee could only imagine what else she might have brought if she'd had more than three hours' notice.

Gisele was wearing a navy knitted mini-dress, black tights and those clumpy boots again, somehow managing to look waifish even with a seven-month bump. Lee was in her usual drapey-jersey trousers and a skinny gassato cashmere roll neck but she had smudged on some make-up and raced around the house in a frenzy after putting down the phone, trying to make everything look extra-festive and perfect for their one guest.

'You really must stop thanking me. It's nice for me to have the adult company, and Jasper gets an audience—'

He came tearing back into the room again. 'Look!' he panted, holding out the image of the bear Sam had drawn him.

'Aah . . .' Gisele's indulgent expression changed to one of genuine amazement. 'Oh my God, that really *is* good!'

'I know,' he beamed.

Gisele looked over at Lee, who just shrugged. 'Hidden talents, Sinterklaas. Who knew he was such an excellent artist?'

'I think Sinterklaas should diversify into doing murals for nurseries.' Gisele laughed, looking over at her pointedly. 'I don't suppose Zwarte Piet left his number on any of his visits, did he?'

'I could always have a look and double-check.' Lee grinned, but she didn't think that, with two million copies of his book sold, Sam would need to diversify into anything. 'So are you almost all set for the baby coming?' She took a sip of her wine again, pleased by the aromas that kept drifting over from the kitchen. Accidentally inviting Gisele over here had forced her to up her game and the results seemed to be encouragingly decent. She was determined that no ketchup was going to be used in the making or eating of this meal.

'Yes, we'd bought all the furniture and the buggy before Harry left. And I've got my hospital bag ready packed; I keep it by the front door, just in case there should be some sort of emergency when I'm on my own.'

Lee frowned, feeling a pang of sympathy for her. 'Oh, but there won't be.'

'I know. I just get a little jumpy sometimes, what with it being my first and no one to tell me when to panic and when not to.' She gave a weak smile. 'But it's really just the nursery left to decorate. We'd been about to start choosing things when Harry upped and went, and now . . .' She wrinkled her pretty nose. 'Well, it doesn't seem right, somehow, to do it without him. Every time I tell myself to go out and just choose a scheme, another voice tells me I should wait.'

'I'm sure Harry wouldn't want you not to do it, though.' Lee sincerely doubted Harry cared about the paint colour on the woodwork or the pictures on the wall. 'It's such an important part of the bonding process, nesting. It gets you ready emotionally, as well as physically. You wouldn't want the baby to come and have to deal with it then, would you?'

'No, I guess not.'

'And if Harry's not given a definite return date . . .' Her voice trailed off. The less they touched on that, the better.

A flash of pain crossed Gisele's symmetrical features. 'You're right. I should just choose and be done with it.'

They were hardly words of excitement. 'Yeah.' Lee smiled, but she felt sad for this beautiful young woman who was supposed to have it all.

'Oh, I'm sorry, just listen to me – you've invited me to share in your special evening and I'm *wallowing* in self-pity.' A flush of shame had spread across her cheeks, one hand pressed to her sternum.

'Gisele, *stop* apologizing. I completely get it. I know exactly how tough it is being pregnant, especially having to do it alone too.'

Gisele looked over at her. 'Was it like that for you?' She blinked nervously, seeing how Lee's expression froze. 'I'm sorry, I don't mean to pry. Harry's never told me what happened with you and Jasper's father,' she said quickly. 'I just assumed . . . I mean, it doesn't seem like he's in your lives, so . . .'

Lee kept her face neutral. She had been asked this question so many times before; she knew how to deal with it, and yet her heart was hammering. She swallowed hard. 'Yes, you're right, he's not in the picture. And I won't lie, the pregnancy was tough. I was very much alone. My parents are dead and I'm an only child, so it was just me and my little Jazz Man.' She got the words out quickly, giving answers to questions before they were asked, controlling the narrative while trying not to actually remember any of it. The pregnancy had been a fog, and the first few weeks after the birth . . . 'But then we moved here and we got lucky with the friends we made and they became our family instead. Somehow, against the odds, it all pretty much worked out.'

'So you don't regret it?'

Lee hesitated. 'Not for a second. I've gone through a lot for my son, but he was worth everything, all of it. I'd walk through fire for him. I *have* walked through fire for him.'

Gisele looked over at Jasper, resting her head in her hand, her eyes soft and hopeful. 'Jasper, what were your best presents from Zwarte Piet?'

'I liked the chocolate J best. It was as big as my arm.' And he traced a line from his wrist to his elbow.

'Wow!'

'We ate it in three days. I had it for breakfast.'

'Breakfast?'

'None of my friends are allowed to have chocolate for breakfast. Their mamas say it's bad for you. They're *boring*.'

Lee gave a tight smile as she heard the sleight of judgement that was passed along in such comments; she could only imagine the arch to the eyebrow as the other mothers heard about her lax parenting style, her son's reprobate breakfast habits. She knew those women already found her 'odd', as though her past life was inked like a tattoo on her face, warning them away. Was she too tough? Rough? *Dusty?* Did she intimidate them? She was never invited to coffee mornings, she wasn't part of the dinner-party circuit. 'Well, it's all about perspective, Jazzy,' she said breezily, drawing herself up and passing Gisele a bowl of olives. 'What if chocolate was all you had to eat? Would it be bad then?'

'No,' he replied earnestly. 'Then it would be good for you.'

'Exactly. And besides, what do we always say?' Lee continued. 'There's no point in delaying good things for later, is there? Later might never come.'

Jasper looked at Gisele. 'Because you could get killed.'

'Oh.'

'Mama says we have to live for every single moment. I could get hit by the tram or fall in the canal and all the chocolate would be wasted.' He looked over at his mother for a moment. 'If I got killed, I'd want you to eat my chocolate.'

Lee smiled, feeling herself softened – rescued – by his words. 'Thank you, my sweet boy. I feel exactly the same.'

'Can we do the poems now?'

Lee groaned. 'Only if I get to go first. I spent ages writing mine.'

Gisele looked embarrassed. 'I'm so sorry, I didn't—'

'Stop,' Lee demurred. The tradition of writing and reciting a tongue-in-cheek poem about the people sharing Pakjesavond with you was a charming one, but time-consuming. 'There is no way we expected you to write poems for us. I need several days to do one as it is, so I certainly didn't attempt another.'

'That's a relief,' Gisele smiled.

Lee pulled the poem from under the chair where she had stowed it for safekeeping earlier. She shook out the piece of paper and peered at Jasper through her thick-rimmed glasses. 'Okay. Ready?'

He nodded excitedly, wanting all the insults.

'Alrighty then,' she sighed with a weary shake of her head before glancing at the sheet and then back at him, over the tops of her glasses.

'He sings like a trapped mosquito.
And his favourite food is a Dorito.
He has never made his bed.
And sometimes he forgets his head.
He loses all his socks.
And cripples his mama with his building blocks.
But his kisses are the best.' She winked at him.
'And he does remember to put on his vest.
So, Sint, please visit this good boy
And be sure to bring his favourite toy.'

Jasper laughed, wriggling into her. 'I've never forgotten my head.'

'Only because I put bolts in your neck when I was making you. See there?' she grinned, tickling his neck and making him squeal.

'Right, now mine,' he shouted excitedly, springing up and tearing out of the room again, his footsteps thundering overhead as he ran into his room, before returning a moment later with a sheet of paper in his hand. He handed it over for her to read with a look of delight and she took it with a wary smile.

'The Sint was just thinking, What for mama he should be gifting . . .' She gave him a wink, knowing this was the kindergarten's stock opening for all the parents' poems. *'She is often—'* She faltered as she saw what was written there, the words immediately blocking her throat, but she made herself go on; it was supposed to be a tease, after all. *'She is often sad. He wants her to be glad. The answer it flew. And then the Sint knew. She does not need a toy! Mama must have another little—'*

She looked up at him, dumbstruck, seeing all the excitement

on his face, and the pride. 'Do you like it, mama? I wrote it nearly all on my own!'

'. . . Jazzy,' she whispered, not sure what to say, painfully aware they had a guest. He had never mentioned anything about having a sibling before. She had thought he was happy, like her, with the way things were. 'You're such a clever boy,' she stammered. 'I can't believe you wrote that nearly all on your own. Your teachers really didn't write it for you?'

He shook his head excitedly, Lee's gaze sad at the happy sight of him.

He wanted a baby brother? They – just the two of them – weren't enough?

'It's wonderful, Jasper,' Gisele said, stepping in and saving her, seeing how she was reading and re-reading the words, falling into regrets about things that could never be. 'You must have spent so long working on it.'

'I did. And my teacher said I was the best at sitting still.'

Gisele shifted position and planted her feet on the ground, sitting erect. 'Show me how. Uncle Harry always says I have ants in my pants—'

Downstairs, there was a hard rap against the door and they all fell quiet. Then Gisele and Jasper looked at Lee, and her gaze fell to the clock, pulling her back into the moment. It was time.

Jasper knew it too, his body going rigid with excitement. Lee watched, seeing how real it all was for him as he jumped to his feet and began running victory laps around the chairs, unable to contain his glee. He still inhabited a world where good children were rewarded, where magic lived amongst the mundane, where little brothers could be plucked from shelves like teddy bears. 'It's Zwarte Piet!'

'Or it might just be old Pabe having locked himself out again,' Lee shrugged, by way of a bluff. 'We'd better answer it quickly, just in case he's getting cold out there.'

'I'll do it!' Jasper knew he wasn't normally allowed to open the front door onto the street by himself, but – as with Sinterklaas's visit – she let him run ahead down the stairs. It gave her enough time to remove the carrot and drawing from his shoe and hide both in a high cupboard he couldn't reach. She downed the milk too in three gulps, much to Gisele's amusement.

'Who is it?' she asked, as the two of them joined him a few moments later on the doorstep.

'It *was* Zwarte Piet!' he cried, almost overcome with joy.

'No, it couldn't have been,' she pooh-poohed.

'It was!'

'Well, did you see him? Which way did he go? Are you sure it was him?'

'Look!' He hoisted in a sack that had been left against the wall. It contained just one very large box.

Lee popped her head outside, pretending to look for him, and saw her neighbours Lenka and Gus letting themselves back into their basement apartment next door. 'Oh, hi guys,' she said in feigned surprise. 'You didn't see Zwarte Piet running past here a moment ago, did you?'

'No, sorry,' Gus said with a grin. 'We just got here.'

Lenka looked up at her with her large round eyes – shy to the point of apology, she was nonetheless strikingly pretty – and Lee had to suppress a squeal of her own. Jasper's excitement was contagious.

'Oh well, never mind, maybe next year,' she said, mouthing 'thank you' to them as she closed the door. She had asked Gus to help her out, when she'd been taking the bins out earlier, and he had timed the knock perfectly; being a single parent was never harder than on an evening like this when she needed to be in two places at once.

She and Gisele followed Jasper back upstairs to the large open-plan living area, where he was kneeling on the floor, his empty clog in his hand and a look of disbelief on his face.

'My God, he is *quick*, that Zwarte Piet!' Gisele exclaimed with a shake of her head, coming to join him. 'He must have been on the roof when we were downstairs.'

Lee smiled, ruffling his dark hair. 'So, what have we got here? That's a very big box to have just one present in it.'

'I know what it is! I know what it is!'

'How can you know? The box is wrapped. Did I accidentally build you with X-ray vision eyes?'

'It's the Nerf gun, I put it on my letter,' he said, tearing at the wrapping paper so that it came away in scraps. 'The Elite Alpha Trooper blaster with darts.'

'Yes but Jasper' – Lee frowned, her stomach lurching as she heard the joyous anticipation in his voice, saw it in his beautiful chocolatey eyes – 'do you remember what we talked about? Sinterklaas doesn't believe in guns and rifles and crossbows. He doesn't want children playing with toys that glorify violence—'

She put her hand on his arm to get his attention, but it was too late. The paper was off and the contents lay revealed. He looked down in bafflement. 'What's Scal . . .'

'Scalextric Extreme Speed? Oh *wow*!' she gasped, trying to rescue the situation. 'It's a race track with remote-control cars. And look – there are four track options! I always wanted one of these. These are the coolest.'

He looked back at her, tears shining in his eyes; they didn't fall, but that was almost worse. 'But I don't want a race track. I want the gun. Me and Sander and Espen were going to have battles.'

'But Jazzy . . .' Lee felt crushed. Had she got it all wrong? Imposing her views over his wants? 'We've talked about this.' Jasper pushed the box away. He didn't throw it, but that, too, was almost worse. 'Why don't we open another . . . ?' But there wasn't another. She had wanted the 'wow factor' of one big present; she didn't subscribe to the overt commercialization of giving dozens of gifts.

She wondered desperately how to rescue the situation, catching sight of the gift Gisele had brought with her. It was wrapped with snowman-printed paper and topped with a red velvet ribbon and bow. It never occurred to her to buy ribbons and bows. 'Why don't we open the one Gisele brought for you?' she suggested.

Gisele handed it over with a nervous smile, and Jasper took it with big, sad eyes. 'Um . . . Lee, I just happened to have this already for my nephew. He's eight. I was planning on getting another when the shops reopen; I won't be seeing them till they get back from skiing anyway. If I'd known—' Gisele whispered to Lee as he began opening it.

'I'm sure it'll be fantastic.'

'Well, the thing is, I—'

There was a shriek of joy. 'A Nerf gun!'

Gisele looked back at Lee apologetically. It wasn't as big and fancy as the one he'd wanted, but it was still a Nerf gun. 'I'm so sorry,' she grimaced. 'If I'd known about the "no guns" thing . . .'

Lee gave her best attempt at a dismissive shrug. It wasn't Gisele's fault. She didn't know what it was like to have a rifle pointed at her; she didn't know what it was like to run from a spray of bullets. She didn't know. That was why Cunningham loved her.

'I should have thought it through.'

'Of course not,' Lee whispered back, forcing a smile. 'How could you possibly have known? I'm just an overprotective mother with an irrational hatred of guns. Honestly, I'm glad you got it. He loves it. You've saved my bacon.'

Gisele regarded her, knowing her hatred of guns wasn't irrational. 'You know, Harry always says you are the bravest person he knows. He says you would keep snapping right until the last moment; whenever any of the men he'd worked with would have stopped and run, he said you'd stay there to get the shot.'

Lee was taken aback by the sudden compliment, the unexpected foray back into her past. 'Hmm, it's called insanity.'

'No. He said you were so determined to show the world the real horror of what innocent people were going through, you'd risk your own life.' She smiled, remembering something. 'He said one time he had to rugby-tackle you out of the way of a tank?'

Lee remembered the moment instantly. Kabul, 2012.

Gisele shook her head in wonderment. 'You just look so . . . normal. And yet you've done these incredible things.'

Lee turned away, wanting neither the compliments nor the reminders. 'Well, I was young, impetuous. I had all these high ideals. I wouldn't do them now.'

'Because of Jasper?'

Lee nodded. 'He needs me to stay safe for him.'

Gisele looked down, cradling her bump. 'Yeah. We said that to this one's papa too.' She looked up with sad eyes.

'He'll be back. He loves you.'

'Yeah – but does he love us *enough*? I thought we were his reason to stay.'

Lee swallowed, her face hot as she felt a rush of guilt. This wasn't her fault. She wasn't his reason to go. She'd never asked him to go. She would have told him not to if . . . if she'd just heard him out, just opened the goddam door.

All she'd had to do was open the door.

She got up from the sofa with a tight smile. 'I'll just check on the salmon. I think we must be nearly ready to eat.'

Chapter Fourteen

'Good morning!' Bart said, swivelling round in his chair as Lee strode in. 'Have we recovered?'

'I don't know, have we?' she replied tartly, swinging her bag over her head and dangling it over her chair. She unbuttoned her coat, finding it surprisingly hard to meet his eyes. She had never let her guard down at work before and she hated that her assistant had unequivocally and absolutely seen her kissing Matt Hofhuis, his suspicions about them confirmed. She was never going to hear the end of it.

'How was your St Nicholas weekend?' he asked benignly.

'. . . Mixed. A quiet day yesterday with Jasper but we ended up hosting last-minute on Pakjesavond.'

'Oh! That's not like you. Was it fun?'

'It was . . . interesting. I've certainly never worked so hard on a meal for three.'

'For three . . . Hmm,' Bart mused, his eyes narrowing interestedly. She knew exactly what he was thinking and decided it was easier to let him keep thinking that. The truth was far harder to explain. 'And did Jasper like his presents?'

'Eventually. But let's just say victory was snatched from the jaws of disaster.' She had spent most of yesterday setting up 'targets' around the house for Jasper to hit with his foam darts. She looked at Bart coolly, batting the ball back to his side of the court. 'Yours?'

He deflated like a balloon on a blackthorn bush. '*Total* nightmare. We went back to Katrin's parents' in Utrecht where, in no particular order' – he held up one hand and began counting off his fingers – 'their cat died, our car got a flat, the Christmas tree caught fire and my mother-in-law slipped on ice and broke her ankle.'

'Oh God!' Lee said, shocked and trying not to laugh.

'Honestly? I'm just glad to be back here in one piece. I was beginning to think I was in an episode of *Final Destination*.'

She did laugh out loud at that, relaxing into his company again. She knew Bart was always far more interested in tales of chase than conquest anyway. 'And has everything been okay here? No disasters on Friday?'

'Not unless you consider the taxidermy shipment getting caught in customs a disaster.'

She stopped and thought for a moment. The stuffed animals were props for a *Marie Claire* shoot in the new year. 'No. I don't,' she said, shrugging off the coat; she had far bigger matters on her mind than worrying about a stuffed hawk sitting in a crate for a few extra days. She wandered over to the coffee machine. 'Want one?'

'Can't. I'm on a detox,' Bart said, proudly holding up a bright turquoise-coloured juice.

'*You*?' she scoffed. 'Oh my God, that looks rank.'

'I'll have you know it's spirulina, kale, parsley, apple and lime.' He brought the cup to his face and dry-heaved as the smell hit him again. 'Oh God. You get used to it. Apparently.'

'I give it an hour before you break,' she laughed, making herself an espresso and sinking into her chair, swinging side to side as she waited for her emails to download.

'So, come on then. Put me out of my misery – *am I fired?*' he asked, his eyes gleaming confidently. They both knew perfectly well he wasn't. He just wanted to hear her say it, to admit the exhibition launch had been an unmitigated success. The reviews had been glowing, social media was alight with buzz about it, there had even been a report on it on the evening news . . . He'd outdone himself.

She looked straight at him. 'Only if you mention the "new Bond".'

A wicked smile made his face shine. Her instruction was also a confirmation of his greatest suspicion. 'I wouldn't dream of it,' he replied solemnly. 'My attention is solely on these fantastic contacts from the "new Eckhart Tolle" shoot.' He held up a folder and waggled it at her, walking over.

'Oh . . . Any good?' she asked casually, even though her heart rate had spiked at the mere mention of Sam.

'See for yourself,' he sighed, sitting against her desk and folding his arms as she took the file. 'There's not a bad shot in there. He's a photogenic fella.'

'Or I'm a photographer who knows how to get the best out of her subjects,' she jibed, steeling herself as she flipped back the cover to look. She reminded herself she and Sam were, if not friends exactly, then at least not sworn enemies any more, either. She could look at the pictures of him with a professional eye; she could do her job . . .

She fell still as she opened it up and he looked straight back at her off the page. Even one-dimensional and inanimate, he made her catch her breath. That gaze, so unflinching, so steady . . .

She stared back at him, not having to look away for once, and as she stared and studied and examined him, she realized what it was about him that drew her; there was a familiarity to him she had sensed but not understood, but she saw now it was because he looked at her exactly the same way as her previous subjects – not the glossy, starry types she shot here in Amsterdam, but the refugees, the victims, the women and children living in bombed-out shelters, the men carrying their wounded comrades to safety. There was honesty in their gazes, 'Why?' in their eyes, 'Help us' on their lips. There was no time for pretence when bombs were falling; no one posed or worried about angles when the ground was shaking beneath their feet. And that was what she saw in him. He was a man without a mask. No game, no propaganda, no agenda. She hadn't needed to shoot multiple variations; he had given her the story with just one look and she knew exactly what he wanted—

'Hello?'

'Oh my God, that's so meta!' Bart exclaimed.

Lee looked up at him, hearing the excitement in his voice and following his gaze to find Sam, the man himself, coming through the doors.

'Hi!' she exclaimed. This was his second surprise appearance in forty-eight hours, practically bordering on a habit. She had been expecting an email or a call from him – not a personal visit.

'How crazy is that?' Bart trilled. 'We're *literally* just looking at your pictures.'

Sam jammed his hands into his jeans pocket, his eyebrows hitched up but his gaze returning to her. Still wary. Still against his better judgement. And yet, despite that, still here. 'Can I see?'

'Sure!'

'No!' Lee said at the same time, shooting Bart a warning look. 'We have to let the client see them first. It can lead to all sorts of issues otherwise.' She shrugged apologetically.

'Like me insisting on having my jaw retouched or only having images showing my best side?' he deadpanned. She remembered his amusement when she'd asked whether he'd wanted hair and make-up artists on her set. He didn't really care how he looked, this shoot hadn't been important to him.

'Okay, fine,' she relented. 'Just a quick look. But I'm not indulging any requests. The client has editorial control.'

'Mm-hmm.' He walked over and bent down beside her, his gaze raking over the images on her desk. His sudden proximity felt disconcerting and, though he wasn't looking at her, she somehow felt that he had nonetheless ensnared her in his peripheral vision, their mutual gazes crossing over one another like the shadows of swords.

He studied the black-and-white images in silence. At a glance, there was almost nothing between them – she hadn't used any props; he'd barely even sat down. He had simply tipped his chin fractionally in some, looked from the corner of his eye in others as she prowled around him, crossed his arms in yet others. But without exception, he had not broken eye contact with the camera from the moment of her first click and it was his gaze – pinpoint-focused – that made the picture. The simplicity and honesty in his eyes was arresting, mesmeric. She felt his soul was there for everyone to see, but *she* hadn't drawn it out of him; she wasn't the genius who had tapped a hidden core – rather, he had given it freely. These images were about his power, not hers.

He nodded, straightening up again. 'I see.'

'You see?' Bart laughed. 'That's it?'

'They're very nice.'

'Ni—?' Bart's jaw dropped to the floor.

'Well, I'm no expert on what makes a good photo. And even less on what makes a good photo of me.'

'The photographer. The photographer is what makes it a good photo. I mean, you know who she is, right? Lee Fitchett?'

'Of course. She won the Pulitzer Prize for Breaking News Photography in 2015 with Harry Cunningham.' Sam's gaze slid back to her meaningfully as he said the name. *Who is Harry?* he had asked at the party. Well, he knew now.

Lee swallowed. 'Bart, I'll, uh . . .' Words had fled her mind. She felt thrown. 'Get some coffee, will you.'

With a groan, Bart wandered off. Lee watched him walk over to the coffee machine. 'Did you make the call? Have you heard anything?' she asked in a low voice, although she wasn't quite sure why; it wasn't like what she had asked him to do for her was a secret.

He nodded. 'I've just come from there. You were right. They did have a map, so they could be sure the dispersion around the city was even.'

'Oh my God.' She couldn't believe it. It had been a wild, desperate guess. 'So where was it left, then?'

'Well, if you're free now, I'll take you there myself.'

'*You*? But . . . why can't you just tell me?'

'Because those are my terms.'

She looked back at him in astonishment. '. . . You have terms? Since when?'

'Since I went to the great trouble of visiting my publishers and haranguing my marketing team till I got the information *you* wanted.'

Lee stared back at him. He wasn't smiling, but nonetheless she detected a hint of a tease in his words. She also sincerely doubted the women in his marketing team felt harangued by him; they had probably been delighted to be bothered by him. 'Okay, fine. Show me, then. I can spare an hour or so.' She reached for her coat. 'Bart, I'm going out.'

'*What?*' He turned, holding two cups in his hands. 'But what about your coffees?'

'You have them.'

'But I'm detoxing.'

'Just drink them, Bart.'

'Where are you going?'

'On a mission. I'm on my mobile if you need me.'

'Are you coming back? What should I say if *De Telegraaf* ring again? Will you do the interview? *Lee?*'

But the door was already swinging on its hinges.

They stood in Spui Square, although 'square' was a misnomer: it was rectangular, being on the site of a filled-in canal. The streets were cobbled and the trees all had flat-tops that Lee knew gave a neat, decorative effect in full leaf but which, bare-armed in the depth of winter, had a distinctly military feel.

She had been here a thousand times over the past five years, but today she stared around with a zealous, hungry newcomer's gaze. The stall-holders for the weekly Monday morning flea market were packing away the remnants of their wares, a tour group of Japanese tourists walking through with matching orange baseball caps towards the gate to the not-so-hidden Begijnhof courtyard. A row of mopeds stood lopsided on their stands, a rack of bikes behind them. She started scanning for recognizable faces, but even just at a glance, she guessed there must be over seventy people in the vicinity. And that was just the people outside. The square was encircled by coffee shops and bookshops – this was book-lovers' central – and at the far end stood a Christmas tree. Not huge, but it had been prettily decorated with lights and Lee's heart automatically lifted at the sight of it; she was always grateful for these little mementos of her own cultural festivities.

But Sam was already heading towards the large bronze statue in the centre of the cobbles. It was of an urchin boy – *Het Lieverdje*. He wore a cloth cap and tattered clothes, with rags wound around his legs and feet. His hands were positioned on his hips in a mildly insolent pose, a raffish smile on his open face. He was supposed to represent the mischievous street children – pranksters but with hearts of gold; supposedly it was modelled after one who had jumped into a canal to save a drowning dog – that was the legend, anyway.

'So, she said she put it there,' Sam said, stopping at the statue and pointing to the narrow gap between the bronze boy's skinny calves. 'A week last Thursday.'

'Right,' Lee murmured, turning on the spot, feeling her conviction begin to fade. This square was right beside Singel; it was a huge cut-through, probably used by tens of thousands of people a day. What were the chances of ever being able to identify the one person who had chanced upon a single left-behind book? She looked back at him and she could see the bemused 'What now?' look in his eyes. She felt a burst of frustration; she didn't appreciate failing. 'You know this is all your fault?' she said irritably.

'*How* is it my fault?'

'Because you started this, leaving your little gifts lying around the place. If you hadn't done that, I might actually be able to sleep at night instead of wondering who it is that so desperately needs my help.'

'Whoever needs your help could have asked for it without defacing my book.' He watched her. 'Besides, I was doing a nice thing.'

'It's glorified littering.'

'It's generosity,' he insisted with a bemused laugh, his light mood only serving to darken hers. 'What's so wrong with wanting to do something good? To improve someone's day?'

She rolled her eyes. 'What are you? A saint?'

'No. I'm just a guy who thinks that sometimes it's nice to get something for nothing, to be in the right place at the right time. That's all.'

Well, wrong place, wrong time was the story of *her* life; but in spite of her sangfroid demeanour, she still felt the twitch of shock fire up in her muscles at his words. She had never met anyone like him before. She was used to angry men – commandos and marines, rebel fighters, dictators, fundamentalists, bigots, misogynists. Everyone out with something to prove. Generosity of spirit wasn't something she'd encountered much before. His was the very opposite of a war-zone mentality.

'. . . So what now, then?' he asked.

'Ugh . . . I'm not sure.' She repositioned her kitten hat, fidgeting, feeling completely at a loss. She'd been so sure she had a new purpose, so sure she could deliver on it. But standing here . . . She could stand here 24/7 for a month and still not see anyone she recognized; and even if she did, they still might be entirely unconnected to the book and the message.

His brow furrowed. 'Well, how did you envision this going?'

'I didn't. I thought I'd just . . . know when I got here.' She bit her lip.

'And that's worked for you before, has it?'

'I like to work off my instincts, yes.' She ignored his sarcasm as she looked around the square again. 'But I'll admit I was hoping the book had been left somewhere . . . smaller.'

'Yes. That would have been helpful.'

They stood on the cobbles together, watching people cycle past, a woman struggling with a bag of shopping, everyone bundled up in heavy coats, hats and scarves, going on to somewhere else. She looked up sharply, wondering if there were CCTV cameras, but she knew she had no power to access the footage, regardless.

'Well, do you want to just . . . wait it out, then?' he asked. 'See who goes by?'

'I suppose so, but—' She shivered. 'It's just so cold. I can't believe it's not snowing.'

'It is in Friesland.' He looked around, blowing on his own hands to keep warm. 'Let's get a coffee. We can watch from over there, surely?'

He led her towards a cafe. It was tiny and unprepossessing, with a brown awning and only two windows facing onto the square; but it did give directly onto the statue. There was plenty of seating outside, but the wind was far too bitter for anyone to endure today, and there were a few bar stools by a bench along the windows to sit at indoors.

'How do you like your coffee?' he asked as she shrugged off her tartan coat.

'Strong and black,' she said absently, throwing her coat over some stools. She looked around for the loos and saw the ladies signposted behind the corner. 'I'll be right back. Just keep an eye on my coat?' she added as she passed, even though there was only one other customer in there. She rounded the wall – and collided headlong with a man rushing towards her. For a moment it seemed as though nothing happened at all; time itself seemed suspended. But then she heard something crash to the floor, she felt hands on her arms, brown eyes on hers – and the cafe receded . . .

Brown eyes. White teeth.

'Right, it's looking good,' Cunningham said in a low voice, coming back over, his shades back down again. Lee straightened up. She had

188

been sitting in a crouch, capturing the boys as they began playing football again, the mothers sitting as still as chess pieces in the narrow strip of shade, protecting, feeding the babies. None of them seemed to mind the intrusion of her camera now. They were Moussef's friends.

'He says the girls are in an abandoned building on the fringes of the village. They're intending on pushing for the border tonight, so we don't have the luxury of time. It's now or never.'

He looked at her and she nodded, knowing what he was asking. They both knew this story would be huge, global . . . and he had to be the one to break it. He'd made his career on just such scoops as this. But might he finish on it too? Nothing would ever top this, and with sixty beginning to loom on his horizon, even he couldn't keep doing this forever. They both knew a time was coming when he would have to hang up his boots and retire to a life of feathered luxury and lie-ins, daunting and unwelcome though that might be. Had he faced up to there being another world to this one they knew? Had she?

A shadow fell over them both. They looked up.

'My friends,' Moussef said in heavily accented English, coming to stand by them, and Lee had to force herself not to react to his powerful body odour. Running water and soap, air conditioning in bombed-out buildings . . . These were luxuries denied to all out here. 'You must be hungry.'

'We're fine thank you, we can get some food afterwards,' Lee replied without thinking. She just wanted to shoot and be gone.

Moussef looked at her, seeming surprised she could speak – then laughed. 'Nonsense. They are starving inside the city lines. But we country peasants' – his voice was inflected with irony – 'we have vine leaves, baba ghanoush, halloumi, goat . . . Come, eat with us.'

'But the girls—?' Lee queried.

Moussef's dark eyes burned into her, though his smile never faded, and she sensed he didn't like that she spoke to him directly, *unbidden. Her eyes met Cunningham's and she saw the wariness in his expression too. Almost imperceptibly, Moussef shook his head. 'They can only move under cover of darkness. We have time.' He waved an arm towards the low building. 'Please. I must insist.'*

'Your hospitality is much appreciated, my friend,' Harry said, taking the attention off her and walking in with him. 'Mmm, what is that smell?'

'Saj bread. It is good, no?' Moussef said proudly.

Lee closed her eyes as she followed them in too, savouring the aroma. A middle-aged woman in a hijab was sitting on a low stool, a flat wheel of dough spread over a domed black surface set on bricks; a red-hot fire was blazing beneath, stoked by the straw that was strewn over the floor and fed in. At the window, a flat-pile rug was nailed up to act as a curtain and screen, mattresses on the floor in the corners.

Immediately, Lee began clicking. The impulse was as automatic as breathing.

'Come through, come through,' Moussef said, ushering them into the next room where food had been laid out, meze style, on low tables.

'This is incredible, thank you, Moussef,' Cunningham said, smiling broadly as they stood at the doorway, admiring the feast, before passing through. 'You honour your cousin.'

Moussef bowed his head at the compliment.

Lee passed by, nodding her thanks too and feeling her mouth water at the aromatic smells—

She gasped, loudly, reflexively. Moussef's hand had slid between her thighs and ridden up and he was openly grabbing her crotch, as though she was a brood mare being assessed for suitability. It wasn't just the action that was so shocking but his matter-of-factness about it too. As though this was his right.

Cunningham heard the gasp and turned back in one fluid

movement to find Lee's hand on Moussef's arm, unsuccessfully trying to detach it, the two of them caught in a push–pull freeze.

'My apologies, Moussef,' he said, rushing back but still calm, a smile upon his mouth. 'I should have explained – Lee is my photographer. I apologize, the mistake is mine.' He pressed his hand to his chest. 'I should have made it clear. She is my photographer, that is all.'

Lee felt her breath coming hard – anger, fear, indignation at Cunningham's words boiling her blood. But by allowing Moussef to save face, he was saving her; she knew this was a game they had to play. It wasn't the first time such an altercation had happened and it wouldn't be the last. It was why all the female journalists she knew out here wore swimsuits beneath their clothes – anything to buy time should the worst happen. All women were vulnerable here – refugees were raped at border checkpoints, women brought into jails and raped in front of their husbands – but western women in particular were seen as fair game. Infidel meat.

Moussef smiled again, his white teeth like piano keys, as he removed his hand easily from her grasp, from her crotch. 'I did not realize, my friend. I thank you for explaining, it is not always clear, you understand.'

'Of course,' Cunningham agreed, the ball of his jaw pulsing only once.

Moussef's smile broadened. He looked back at Lee too. 'Then it is all good between us! Come. Let us eat.'

'Lee?'

She blinked.

Sam was standing in front of her, holding her arms, holding her up, a look of utter panic on his face. She realized she was shaking, sweating, gasping for air.

'Lee, are you okay?' He looked stricken.

She stared back at him, feeling her mind begin to clear, the sounds, the smells, the colours of her past begin to fade away, those sharp-toothed creatures disappearing back into the night again. She was in a coffee house, in Amsterdam. She was safe.

She felt his hand smooth her hair back from her face; she saw sadness in his eyes. 'Lee.'

She took a breath, stepping back, feeling her legs take the weight again. 'I'm okay.'

'What just happened?'

She took another step back. She needed air, to get away. Everyone was staring at her. Sam. The girl behind the counter. A man in a brown uniform with just a tray and no cups. A man with brown eyes.

Brown eyes.

She looked away and did what she should have done back then.

She ran.

Chapter Fifteen

The morning light was soft in her room, diffuse, as though she was looking at it through a veil. For a few rare moments she had a feeling of utter peace, as though nothing bad ever could happen, and never had. But the sound of breathing beside her intruded on her consciousness and she turned her head to find Jasper fast asleep next to her. She sighed, anxiety pinching at her; she didn't remember him coming in, which was a sure sign the nightmares must have been bad. They were getting steadily worse again; more often than not now, she was waking to find him beside her, his tiny hand in hers.

She felt her heart break. This was all wrong. She should be protecting him.

He was lying on his side and curled up like a shrimp, his thumb in his mouth as he clutched Ducky; she wriggled over and kissed his temple tenderly, loving that he still had his baby smell. She always used to tell him that, even blindfolded, she would be able to travel the world and find him by the smell of his head alone.

She watched him as he slept, untroubled. Unbroken. Somehow, in spite of everything, in spite of her, he was perfect—

Her phone buzzed with a text and she reached for it. *'Are you awake?'*

The number wasn't logged in her phone, and yet she knew exactly who it was from.

'Why?' she replied.

'I'm on your doorstep.'

She stared at the words, feeling her muscles clench in unwelcome surprise as the full reality of her wholly imperfect world crashed back into her consciousness. Yesterday's panic attack – he'd come for an explanation. She had run out on him when all he'd done was help.

She slid out of bed and pulled the duvet over Jasper's shoulders. She kissed him on the temple again and slipped from the room, tying her dressing gown – a vintage kimono – over her pyjamas. She quickly brushed her teeth and ran some drops of serum over her face. It was as far as her efforts towards early morning acceptability went.

She unlocked the various bolts, locks and chains, and Sam got up from sitting on her top step. He looked at her carefully, as though searching for signs of bruises. 'You left this.' He held out her tartan coat, carefully bundled in a roll.

'Oh!' She had forgotten all about it yesterday; she hadn't felt the cold as she'd raced through the streets, back home, onto the sofa where she had slept dreamlessly, heavily, until it had been time to collect Jasper; the flashbacks always drained her. She had been steeling herself to go back to the coffee house today to collect it. 'Thank you.'

She clutched it to her, unable to meet his gaze. '. . . Do you want to come in?'

He shook his head. 'No. I just wanted to catch you before you left for the day.'

'Oh.' She shifted her weight, knowing she had to explain herself. Give him something to understand. 'Look, Sam—'

But he stepped forward and silenced her with a kiss.

Nothing dramatic. It wasn't like the urgent first kiss in the kitchen that had left her feeling so confused, wanting more; this was gentle, soft. Complete. It said what words couldn't. It told her that words weren't needed.

He stepped back again. 'Goodbye, Lee.'

Mute, floored, she watched him go down the steps. Was that it? No one had ever kissed her before without it leading to something. A kiss had never been just a kiss, in her experience.

His bike was propped against the lamp post and he cocked a leg over the top frame, glancing back at her before he pedalled off. No wink, no smile, no intimacy to hint at the moment they'd just shared. Like she might almost have imagined the whole thing.

Heart still booming, she watched him pedal out of sight, turning onto the next bridge and heading towards the grand Prinsengracht canal. He had his head tucked low, keeping out of the wind, looking like an ordinary person when really she was beginning to suspect he was anything but.

She might have expected many reactions to her behaviour yesterday, but tenderness hadn't been one of them. The ground kept moving beneath their feet and she never quite knew where things were between them. They weren't lovers but nor were they strangers or friends; not colleagues and yet they'd worked together; they weren't dating but they were jealous; they kept saying goodbye and yet walking back into each other's lives. For something that was supposed to have been fleetingly simple, it was already so complicated.

He had gone again and she turned to go back in, but her gaze sharpened into focus on a couple walking briskly over the bridge, their heads dipped too. Something in their gait caught her eye, familiar. It took her a moment to register that it was Gus from next door – but the woman he was with wasn't Lenka.

'Oh no,' she sighed, feeling a pang of sorrow for her shy, pretty neighbour. She was unable to see from this distance whether they were holding hands, unable to make out anything except that the woman had short, bleached blonde hair. It could all be perfectly innocent, of course. But in her experience, it usually wasn't.

'Lee? It's me.' Dita's signature husky voice was crystal clear down the line; she could have been talking from the other side of the desk, not the other side of the world.

Lee hadn't even got her coat off as she'd lunged for the phone. Bart was coming in late this morning, stopping off first to get the *stroopwafels* for today's shoot.

'Dita! How was Pyongyang?'

'About as enjoyable as eating my own leg.'

'Huh. Powerful image.' Lee sank into her chair and swung back on it, letting her own legs go floppy. She had felt in an unaccountably good mood since Sam's visit yesterday morning; she told herself that if nothing else it had broken the monotony of her morning routine, but she was still quietly fizzing with the anticipation of his next surprise visit, waiting for some kind of follow-up text or call . . . 'Where are you now?'

'Hong Kong. Listen, can you talk? Is anyone with you?'

'No, I'm on my own. Why? What's up?' She hadn't yet had her constitutional coffee, but Lee's mind was already sharpening up. There was only one reason why Dita would be calling. Her old friend didn't do social calls.

'Cunningham's in Kobanî.' Straight to the point.

Lee dropped her head into her hands. 'Right.' She'd known

it; her every instinct had told her as much as soon as she'd heard he'd crossed the border at Jarabulus. 'Are you sure?'

'Yes. Derek Blasenberg thinks he saw him.'

'Thinks?'

'Said he would have been 100 per cent certain it was Cunningham except the guy didn't react when he called his name. Didn't look over, nothing. Acted like he hadn't heard anything. Like he didn't even speak English.'

'That's weird.' She bit her lip, thinking hard. That wasn't like Cunningham; he knew everyone and everyone knew him; he loved the fraternity out there. 'Could he be injured, do you think? Head injury? Amnesia?'

'Always possible.'

Lee winced, trying not to think of the possible ramifications of that – Harry wandering disoriented in a war zone. There was no one to help out there. No doctors, no UN, no MSF. 'So where is he now? Did Blasenberg see where he went?'

'No, the shelling's bad there at the moment, he only saw him momentarily. But he said he heard later that an American had been asking for a ride to one of the villages.'

She felt her heart stutter at the last word. 'Which one?' she murmured, willing Dita not to say it. Don't say it. Don't say it. Don't say it. There was still a chance . . .

'Khrah Eshek.'

Lee dropped her head into her hands.

'. . . Lee, are you there?'

It was several moments before she could speak again. 'Yeah, I'm here.'

'You know I know what that place is to you.'

'I know.'

'So what's he doing back there?'

'I don't know.'

197

KAREN SWAN

'You haven't heard from him?'

'Not meaningfully.'

'What does that mean, Lee?'

She groaned, frustrated. 'He called, but it was a bad line. He's written a letter but seemingly not sent it. Clearly there's something he wants to tell me, but I don't know what it is.'

There was a puzzled pause. 'It's not like Cunningham to write a *letter*. He's hardly the sentimental type.'

'Tell me about it.'

'Suggesting, again, that this is somehow personal.'

'Perhaps. Or perhaps he just wants to follow up on . . . what happened next. Get the sequel. You know Cunningham, always got to tell the story.'

'But there is no story. ISIL is dead. The international coalition regained control of the Kobanî canton almost immediately.'

'There are still smaller cells operating out there, though, isolated pockets of fighters still battling for the caliphate cause,' she said, desperately reaching.

'Precisely. And if any one of them gets hold of him . . . He's got no mandate, no official papers, no sanction, no protection. ISIL will kill him on the spot – or worse, they *won't* – they'll keep him alive, torture him, film it, make a spectacle of it, use him for propaganda—'

'Dita, stop!'

Dita sighed. 'Look, Lee, you and I both know there's no protection for journalists out there, even with the right passes. In this war, everyone's a target – civilians, press, doctors, kids – but he would be their dream catch. The headlines they would garner . . . If ISIL get hold of him, they won't give a damn if he's got paperwork, I know that. But I also know that if anything happens to him and it comes out that he was out there *without* it, on a personal agenda . . . we can't let that happen.'

'Cunningham won't get caught, Dita.'

'How can you say that? You did.'

The words were like an uppercut, sending her reeling, pushing her back and making her head ring and her chest tight. She could feel the shadows reach for her.

Dita's voice was low – apologetic but not repentant – when she spoke again. 'I'm sorry, but it's not happening on my watch. Not again. I'm not taking the risk.'

Lee frowned. 'What do you mean? Dita, what have you done?'

There was a short silence. 'I've reported it.'

'No! You can't, he'll go nuts!'

'It's for his own protection. I don't know what happened between you two back then and I don't need to know; it's your business, I respect that. All I know is that he's gone back out to the last place the two of you worked together before you threw it all in. As far as I can make out, he's risking his life and his legacy, and our reputation and our integrity – for you.' Lee heard Dita take a deep inhale at the other end of the line, the other side of the world. 'You say you don't know what this is about but you're holding something over him, Lee, and I think he's trying to make it right.'

Lee couldn't speak, couldn't deny it; tears were shining in her eyes.

'So the next time he surfaces, the Americans have authority to arrest him on sight and send him back on the next plane. I'm sorry, Lee, but whatever this is – it's over.'

It was a full moon, the street bathed in a pale lunar glow. Somewhere a cat was mewling, but other than that, there was an unfamiliar silence. The canal was now thickly iced – the tour boats had stopped running several days ago on the bigger waterways – so that the gentle hush of sluiced water and the low chug of passing boats had come to an abrupt stop. Everything felt held in abeyance, habits disrupted, behaviours modified. The ducks were waddling on ice, and so were they, the cobbles becoming treacherously silky in the endless frosts.

Lee struggled down the steps with the bin bags, in her socks and sheepskin-lined Birkenstocks. It wasn't a good look.

'Ah Lee! Good evening.'

She looked up to see Pabe, her elderly neighbour, standing at the door, holding onto the frame.

'Oh hi, Pabe, long time no see.' She saw a bin bag by his feet and his walking stick in one hand. 'Here, let me put that in the bin for you,' she said, replacing the lid on hers and jogging quickly up his steps. She took the bin bag from him and carried it back down again, dropping it in his bin. A twenty-second job for her; a five-minute job and potential hip-replacement for him. 'These steps are so slippery, you need to be really careful. Have you got good treads on your shoes?'

He chuckled. 'You sound just like my daughter.'

Lee grinned, hoping not. His daughter was a senior school teacher with a voice that could *project*. 'How is Marta? I haven't seen her lately.'

'No, you wouldn't have. She's moved to Antwerp with her husband. His job.'

'Oh.' Lee was surprised. 'Well, that's great news, for them. But how about you? She was here several times a week, wasn't she?'

'Yes, she's a good daughter.'

He hadn't answered her question, she noticed. 'Is anyone . . . helping you?' He had to be ninety if a day and his walking was so weak he didn't so much lift his feet off the floor as sweep it with a soft shuffle.

'Oh yes, I've got a new helper coming after Christmas.'

'Christmas? But that's two weeks away yet. Who's doing your shopping and cleaning till then?'

He waved a hand weakly. 'Marta stocked up for me before she left, so I can manage until they get here.'

Lee stared at him. 'Pabe, forgive me if I'm speaking out of turn, but that's not right. You are . . . a man of a certain age. You can't be doing that on your own.' It was a wonder to Lee that he still lived here, alone, at all. The stairs in all these canalhouses were so steep.

'Oh, you're kind, but I assure you I'm fine.'

Lee was not at all convinced he was. He'd never been a big man, but he looked to her like he'd lost some weight; his clothes were hanging and looked grubby, stains on his jumper.

'How was your Pakjesavond?' she asked instead, shivering, trying to stay warm. She had only intended to nip out to the bins, not stand chatting in the street.

'It was just a quiet one for me. I don't need too much excitement at my age. I thought I heard merriment on your side, though?'

'Yes, that would have been Jasper trying to shoot us with his Nerf gun . . . They're only foam darts, but you still want to get away,' she said, smiling at the memory. From a wobbly start, it had become a surprisingly fun evening and she had miraculously managed not to marmalize the salmon. 'I hope we didn't disturb you?'

'Not at all. It's wonderful to hear laughter.'

Lee smiled, seeing how his hand tremored, blue-tinged. She was cold but he looked frozen. Her brow puckered again. 'Listen Pabe, I'm going to be going to the shops tomorrow.

We're out of almost everything after this weekend; Jasper's eating me out of house and home. Can I pick anything up for you while I'm there?'

'Oh no, no. You're very kind, but I've got everything I need.'

'Really? How about some fresh fruit?' she pressed. 'The pears are particularly good at the moment.'

He hesitated, possibly sensing she wasn't going to give up. '. . . Well, some pears would be lovely, I have to say.'

'Great. I'll pop over when I'm back then. It'll be about three-ish?'

'You're really too kind.'

'It's my pleasure.' She blew on her hands and rubbed them together vigorously. 'Now let's get back into the warmth before we both get hypothermia. I'll see you tomorrow, Pabe.'

'Tomorrow, then. Thank you, Lee.'

She watched him go back in, and the irony wasn't lost on her that while her door closed to the symphony of bolts and chains, his shut with a simple click.

Chapter Sixteen

'. . . keep going.'

Dr Hansje was wearing the orange silk scarf with blue bridle motifs on it, her favourite one. It was from Hermès. Lee had looked up what they cost after one of their early sessions and had been so stunned that anyone would spend that on a *scarf* that she had supposed her therapist was either very good or very stupid. She had crossed her fingers and hoped for very good.

She shifted position again, feeling the memories stir. They seemed to creep through her, inside her veins, up her bones, agitating her blood.

'You said he was helping you?'

'They are in there.' Lee followed the direction of Moussef's stubby finger pointed towards a tiny, mostly destroyed building, set several metres back from the road, in the scrub. Scarcely bigger than an English bus shelter, almost all of the roof had collapsed and there were no windows or door that she could see. They were really in there? Even by war zone standards, there was hardly any 'there' to be in.

Lee lifted the camera to her eye and, from the back seat of the truck, began snapping just as a stray dog – thin and black, with a scar on its muzzle – trotted into the frame. It cocked its leg against the ruins of a rough wall set a few metres in front of the building and began sniffing interestedly, its tail going up, ears alert. It began barking, hesitantly at first but then more insistently, prowling forward a few paces and then jumping back again. Moussef threw a full Coke can at it, hitting it hard on the flank. It yelped and whimpered, then scuttled off, head low, ribs visible beneath its shorn pelt.

'We cannot allow it to draw attention,' he said simply.

Lee knew he was right, even though she winced as the dog limped off. If the dog had been allowed to carry on, people would have come to check on the nuisance, noticing them and, worse, the two young French women hiding within. The nearest buildings were just a hundred metres away, the sounds of the market still audible over the low walls. In the distance the bombardment of Kobanî continued, the booms a background soundtrack as ISIL tried to lay claim to that concrete wasteland.

Lee looked up and down the dirt track they were parked on. A buzzard was sitting in the branches of a dead tree a few metres away, throwing down a few scrappy shadows on the hard-baked earth. There was no one walking by, no cars, no soldiers . . . But there was also no privacy; if anyone did pass here, they would be able to look straight in and see the young women huddled there. It was no wonder they were moving on tonight. They were as vulnerable here as sleeping in the open and if any of the villagers were to know that two jihadi brides were taking refuge within their borders, it would be a lynching.

'You okay?' Lee murmured to Cunningham, sitting in the front seat.

He was staring ahead intently, his lips moving as he rehearsed his questions in Arabic. He had Moussef to translate for him, of course, but she knew he liked to receive the material at source. His notepad and pen were on his lap, his phone set to voice record. They were almost ready to move . . .

He inhaled sharply, as though only just hearing her question. 'Yeah. Just working out how to get trust going. I don't want them to spook.'

'Sure.' Two young French nationals trying to get their governments to take them back, trying to outrun the very organization they had run to in the first place . . . tensions would be high. They wouldn't trust anyone.

She looked at Moussef. 'How did you know they were here, Moussef?' she asked.

His head turned in her direction but she was seated behind him and he could only present his profile. 'I have eyes in these hills,' he said. 'There are many unwelcome intruders here.'

'You mean ISIL?'

'Among others.' He nodded. 'There is a time to fight and a time to run, no?'

'Yes.'

Cunningham clicked his tongue against the roof of his mouth. It was the subtle mark he was ready. If he could read her, she could also read him. 'Okay, let's do this,' he said quietly.

Lee pulled her hijab higher, making sure it was secure and covering her hair. She opened her door.

Moussef seemed startled by her action and put a hand on Cunningham's arm as he went to open his. 'I am sorry, friend, but it would be better if only you go, at least to begin. I did not know about her when this was set up. They will not be expecting two of you.'

Cunningham took his hand off the handle. 'But I need Lee. This will be only half a story without pictures. People back home need to see these girls, see what they've become.'

'Then she comes after, when all is good. She can wait here until you are ready.' Moussef gave a shrug but his eyes were steady. He wasn't going to back down on this; he was the facilitator, he could call the shots.

Cunningham looked back at her, knowing he had no leverage. '. . . Moussef's right, Fitch,' he said finally. 'If they're not expecting you, it could start us off on the wrong foot. Stay here, I'll give a signal when you can come in.'

She looked at him with concern. They never split up. It was their golden rule – the Two Musketeers, they called themselves: one for both and both for one. They were a team. 'And what if someone sees me here and wants to know why I'm sitting in this truck on my own? Those women are surely more likely to be rumbled if there's a western woman with a camera sitting opposite their shelter?'

'Hmm, this is true.' Moussef thought for a moment. '. . . Okay, you see there?' He pointed to a large-ish, squat building fifty metres away. 'The old school. It is abandoned now. No one will see you in there. Wait for Mr Harry's signal and then come over.'

'Harry?' Lee looked at Cunningham, willing him to disagree. She still didn't like this. She couldn't openly contradict Moussef – that wasn't how things worked out here – but he could. Homs had shown them both why they stuck together, no matter what, and right now, she wanted that security. She needed it. There was a low vibration in her bones, a feeling she couldn't quite explain. She was used to uneasy situations but she felt vulnerable now in a way she usually didn't and she needed Harry, as her partner, to see that, recognize it and step up.

Cunningham looked away from her as he swallowed. 'Moussef's is a good plan,' was all he said. 'Wait for my signal, Fitch. Then we can lock this story down.'

Lee sat at the table watching the strangers pass, not one of them with an iota of familiarity to her – not the toss of a head, the turn of an ankle, the pitch of a laugh. Every few minutes her gaze would return to the statue in the middle of the square.

'And so this is your great plan, is it?' Mila asked, sitting beside her, quietly shivering now that their lunch was eaten.

'Yep.'

'You're just going to sit here every day and wait for someone you recognize to walk past?'

'Humans are creatures of habit, Mila. The person who picked up the book from that spot right there the other Thursday could well walk past again this Thursday. Today.'

'Or not.'

Lee shot her a look. 'I know that,' she murmured, her eyes still automatically scanning the square – but not, she was beginning to realize, for just her unknown stranger. She was looking for Sam too, wondering whether he might chance to join her again in waiting. After all, he'd been interested enough to wait with her on Monday when he could have just emailed her the address. Of course, that was before he'd seen what a freak she was – she had deliberately avoided going back into the same coffee house today for that very reason – but they had kissed on her doorstep since then, and now her mind kept returning to him like some sort of homing pigeon. She was regularly checking her texts, emails, making sure she had no missed calls, but there had been nothing from him since. She was growing increasingly confused. Why had he kissed her, only to do a disappearing act on her?

Unless . . . She remembered his last words. *Goodbye, Lee . . .* Unless it had been an *actual* goodbye kiss? Oh God, had he meant it that time? Had he just been returning her coat and he'd . . . he'd pitied her?

She slumped down in the chair.

'What's wrong with you today?'

Lee glanced at her. 'Nothing.'

'You look like you just got hit with a tranquilizer dart.'

Lee pulled a face and began fiddling with her camera as a distraction. It was her small vintage Nikon F2, a discreet point-and-click that she liked to use when she was out and about. She held it up to her eye and scanned the square through the lens. It made more sense to her that way for some reason. She played with the focus, zooming in and out. Bored. Cold. Restless. Hating that she hated that he hadn't called. That his kiss goodbye had left her wanting another hello.

What a bloody idiot she was! She'd spent the past few days in a buoyant good mood – driving Bart crazy with curiosity – all because of one pitying goodbye kiss, and all the while she'd been completely oblivious that he had just stepped out of her life as quickly as he'd stepped into it. And she'd waved him off! She'd watched him till he'd glided out of sight, a smile and his kiss still on her lips.

She dropped the camera down again, fidgeting with her fingers, feeling inexplicably upset. 'It's useless.'

'Of course it's useless,' Mila groaned, stretching out on the cafe table and laying her head on her arm. 'But you are very sweet to have wanted to try to help this person. Only you would even have tried.'

'Mmm.' Lee exhaled, not wanting compliments or platitudes. She wanted him to call.

'Hang on.' Mila lifted her head again, an idea striking her. 'You said the book with the message in it was left in your bike basket, yes?'

Lee's eyes slid right to her friend's pretty face. 'Yes. So?'

'Well, why don't you put the book back in your bike basket, with another message in it from you, telling them how to get in touch directly?'

Lee looked back at her friend. That was actually a pretty good idea. 'That's actually a pretty good idea, Mils.'

Mila grinned. 'Thank you. I have my moments.'

Lee sat motionless for another few minutes, thinking it through. It surely made sense to try to communicate in the same way contact had originally been made . . . But her mind kept wandering back to Sam. He was part of this, interlocked with it. It was his book that had been used, after all; and it was because it was his book that she'd gone against all her instincts and re-established contact with him, sought him out. If it had only been anyone's book but his—

She jumped up, clapping her gloved hands together, as if trying to physically throw him from her thoughts.

'What now?' Mila asked, looking bewildered.

'Well, it's bloody freezing and there's no point still sitting here. He's not coming. I need to move.'

Mila frowned, getting up too. 'How do you know it's a he?'

'Huh?'

'You said *he's* not coming.'

'Oh . . .' Had she? She swallowed at the inadvertent slip. Her conscious and subconscious thoughts were too closely aligned. 'They. I meant they.'

'Yeah,' Mila sighed. 'I mean, I'm a feminist with the best of them but I can't help but assume the person you're looking for is a woman. "Help me" just doesn't seem like the kind of thing a man would write, does it?' She bit her lip, looking pained. 'Or am I being a terrible traitor to the cause?'

'No, I'd assumed it was a woman too. You're right though, there's a chance it isn't. It could be a guy,' she added disconsolately.

They retrieved their bikes from the stands, Mila pulling on her beanie and curling the little ends of her crop into Louise Brooks curls. 'Are you going back to the studio now?'

'No, I've got some paperwork to catch up on but I'll do it at home. I need to do some shopping for my neighbour on the way back, too. He's in his nineties and all on his own.'

Mila pulled a face. 'That's sad. Hasn't he got any family?'

'Yeah. A daughter, but she's just moved away for her husband's job.'

'And she didn't take him with them?'

Lee shrugged. 'I don't know the ins and outs. He seems sweet enough, but you know what old people can be like; he's probably not that easy. The young couple who rent the apartment from him in the basement say he's a nightmare landlord – apparently they had a leak in their bathroom for two months, mould growing inside the walls and everything. It was a real health hazard. Then again, the poor guy's in his nineties; what's he going to do about finding a plumber? He's at that age where he doesn't buy green bananas, you know what I mean?'

Mila laughed, clutching Lee's arm as they walked, expertly pushing their bikes with their free arms. 'You're outrageous.'

'It's true though.'

They wheeled their bikes side by side in the crisp, biting air, bundled up and looking in at the small window displays.

'Ooooh! Now you would look incredible in that,' Mila said, stabbing a finger against the glass of a boutique and pointing out a drapey olive-green silk dress on a mannequin. 'It would look great against your hair.'

'I don't wear dresses.'

'Yes, you're right,' Mila deadpanned. 'It was such a disaster for you wearing that one at the party last week. Matteo Hofhuis wasn't drooling *at all*.' She laughed, incredulous. 'I mean, Matteo Hofhuis, for crying out loud!'

'I don't want him drooling on me, thanks.'

'Drooling over you, not on you! He's not a dog!'

Lee stared at the dress. She did like the colour.

'Go on. Just try it.'

'No.' She turned away dismissively.

'Why not?'

'Because . . . you can't wear a bra with those straps.'

'Oh, like you need one!' Mila pooh-poohed, joshing her with her elbow.

'Well, I don't have anywhere to wear something like that.' They both knew Lee would never buy something just because she liked it. Everything had to have purpose in her life, in her home and in her wardrobe. '*You* try it.'

'I'm on sabbatical, remember? There's no point in me looking sexy. That is exactly the kind of dress that makes men come running. Or, in my case, married men.'

Lee gave a groan. 'This self-imposed sabbatical is nonsense. You're thirty, not twenty. I hate to break it to you, Mils, but you don't have the luxury of being able to take six months out of your life at this stage, not if you want the pitter-patter of tiny feet in your future.'

'Now that's totally breaking the feminist code!'

Lee shook her head. 'No, I can be a feminist and still acknowledge the very pressing reality of a biological clock ticking. Don't waste time unnecessarily just because of a few married jerks.'

Mila looked sulky. 'Well, it's not like *you're* out there dating.'

'I've got Jasper, Mils. I don't need to date.'

'So you're saying you only need a man for a baby? What about love, laughter, companionship? Someone to share the hard times with?'

Again, yet again, Sam's face swam in front of her – dressed as Sinter and trying not to laugh as she offered him a glass of milk; his anger in the gallery courtyard as Matt came looking for her; his concern in the coffee shop as the flashback faded; his air of sadness as he'd kissed her for the second and last time . . .

Mila suddenly jabbed a finger in Lee's direction. 'Hey, wait, you *do* have somewhere to wear it to.'

'No I don't.'

'You've got that dinner coming up, the *Black Dot* one.'

'Huh?' Lee felt a tremor of panic.

'Yes, you told me about it when you were trying to wriggle out of wearing the velvet dress to the gallery party.'

Slowly realization dawned. Bart had already booked the car. She had completely forgotten about it. When even was it? . . . Friday? *This* Friday? Tomorrow? She hadn't booked the babysitter! Brigit was the only student in the city who didn't smoke weed, it seemed, and therefore the only person outside of 'family' that she'd trust with her son. She'd never get her now. 'Oh, fuck.'

Mila looked delighted. 'Yes, fuck! And you don't have anything to wear.' She prised Lee's hands off the handlebars and pushed her towards the door. 'Try it on. I'll wait here and hold the bikes.'

'But you need to get back to work!' Lee spluttered, desperately trying to stall as she realized another reason why she couldn't possibly go to that dinner tomorrow night. It wasn't just that she had nothing to wear; it wasn't just that she didn't have a babysitter booked . . .

'I know, so you'd better hurry up before they fire me. Come out of the changing room so I can look through the window.'

'But—'

'No buts. Do as you're told.' She saw Lee's mutinous

expression. 'Unless you don't want me to babysit my godson for you?'

'You'll babysit for me?' Lee's eyes widened hopefully. It was one problem solved at a stroke.

'Only if you try on the dress.' Mila shrugged. 'Those are my terms.'

Because those are my terms. Sam . . . That was the other problem – he was going to be there too. Her stomach gave a pitch and dive in silent reply. She looked back through the window again. *That is exactly the kind of dress that makes men come running.*

'Fine,' she said, pushing open the door and hurrying in. 'If you're going to blackmail me, I'll try the damn dress.'

Chapter Seventeen

It was at least four minutes before the door was opened. Lee smiled, holding up the bulging shopping bags as her neighbour's pale, thin, baggy face appeared.

'Hi Pabe. I got those pears for you.'

He opened the door wider. 'That looks like a lot of pears.'

She laughed; she had indeed bought him a lot more besides those. 'They are a bit heavy. Mind if I come in? I'll put them away for you.'

'Oh . . . oh yes . . . thank you,' he stuttered, struggling to shuffle backwards out of the door's way.

She stepped in, instantly feeling the chill in the house. 'Gosh, are you warm enough in here?' she asked, only seeing after the words had left her mouth that he was wearing an overcoat over his clothes. 'Oh.'

'You get quite used to it,' he said, shuffling down the long, dark hall towards the kitchen at the back. 'I don't like a hot house.'

She closed the front door, able to see from this elevated vantage point the new copy of Sam's book sticking out of her bike basket. She had had to buy another copy on her way home, on account of Sam taking hers to hide it from Jasper at the bookshop, and there was no way she could give away the personalized copy he'd given her son. She had written her mobile number on the same page as *Help Me* had been written in the original copy, and had added: *Please call. Let me help you.* But how could she ever know that the book would end up back with the same person again? What if some bored kids found it and prank-called her? It was just a shot in the dark.

'No, I don't like a hot house either.' She frowned, seeing some towels stuffed against the window ledges. And as she walked past the sitting room, she glimpsed a small electric two-bar fire glowing a vivid orange, set on the hearth.

'Here we go,' she said, lifting the bags onto the counter. The place was tidy and ordered but there was a scarcity to Pabe's modest belongings that made her feel sad – a single hard chair by the small table, a faded and threadbare rug by the back door, no curtain at the window. His touch upon his own life seemed pitifully light, as though he floated around the building, scarcely making an impression. There was an upturned cup, saucer and a side plate on the draining board, a cat litter tray and feeding bowl in the corner of the room, a stack of empty tin cans beside the sink, rinsed out and ready to recycle. But other than that, there were no signs of a life being lived here. The air felt stale and thick and she felt an overwhelming urge to open a window. Through the back window she saw the small lawn was covered with leaves that had fallen from the sycamore tree. Everything felt neglected and gently decaying.

'So,' Lee said, her eyes scanning the room but trying not to stare. 'I hope you don't mind but I got you a few more things than just pears. These oranges were on special too – so important to keep your immunity up in this cold weather – and I didn't know if you liked tomatoes?' She pulled everything out – fresh seeded bread, a steak, some lettuce, two pints of milk, yoghurt, a *tompouce* pastry, today's newspaper. 'I'll just put them away for you, shall I? Save you the bother.'

Pabe stared at the produce, his mouth hanging slackly, looking overwhelmed, as she found the fridge, larder and fruit bowl. She also refilled the kettle, turning it on.

'Why don't you sit down while I do this and you can tell me about your daughter's move. Antwerp, was it?' she asked, hoping to distract him from her over-generous help. 'I've always wanted to go there. Have you been?'

Pabe shuffled to the chair, looking grateful for the order to sit.

'Not yet. We had talked about me going for Pakjesavond but they hadn't finished setting up the house; some of their furniture was still in storage, and I didn't want to be a burden for them, trying to find somewhere for me to sleep. But I may go for Christmas.'

'That sounds great. You must miss them.'

'I do.'

She poured the hot water from the kettle. 'Do you take sugar?'

'No thank you. I have to watch my waistline. For my lady admirers, you know.'

Lee threw her head back and laughed, surprised by the unexpected joke. 'Well, quite.'

She handed him his coffee and leaned against the worktop with her own, hands wrapped around the mug for warmth, and she resolved to bring some flowers next time to brighten the place up, as well as a mop; the floor looked filthy. 'So do you think this move is permanent for them? Or will they be back?'

'My son-in-law is an engineer so they've got him heading up some research laboratory project. Five years, they're saying, but I'll be long gone by then.' She looked up to find him pulling a face, crossing his eyes and sticking his tongue out of the side of his mouth. It was feeble but still funny.

'Pabe, don't say such a thing,' Lee scolded, laughing. 'You are clearly in your prime.'

'Thank you, my dear, as are you. I keep hoping we'll see a handsome man standing on your doorstep with flowers one day.'

'So do I,' she laughed, wanting no such thing. 'Let me know if you see him, won't you?'

He chuckled so that his shoulders shook.

But a sudden thud beneath their feet made them both startle. 'Oh, what was that?'

Pabe rolled his eyes as a male voice drifted through the floor. Gus? 'Always arguing,' he tutted. 'He shouts, she cries.'

'Oh no, that's such a shame,' Lee said, immediately re-membering Gus on the bridge on Tuesday morning, walking with that other woman. It seemed like confirmation of her suspicions that he was having an affair. 'Lenka seems so lovely. Quiet but very . . . sweet.'

'I never see her, just him. He does all the dirty work, complaining at me.' Pabe sighed, looking away, his mouth drawing into a thin line.

Lee gave an awkward smile, hoping he wasn't going to start bad-mouthing Gus, the way Gus had bad-mouthed him; their tenant–landlord relationship was none of her business. She checked her phone, hoping to move the conversation along. 'Sorry, I'm just keeping an eye on the time. I need to collect Jasper shortly,' she said, feeling bad for leaving him. 'But listen, while I'm here, why don't I put a fire on for you? A proper one. It'll warm the house through more thoroughly than an electric fire.'

'I couldn't ask you to do that. You've done so much already.'

'Nonsense. It'll only take a few minutes and I'll feel a lot better to know you're not freezing over here.'

'Well,' he blustered. 'I don't know what to say.'

'Are your logs in the bin out the back, like ours?'

He nodded. 'I can't get down the steps to them, that's the problem.'

'Yes, I can see it would be,' she said, peering out through the window and seeing moss growing on the stone steps. 'Listen, why don't you get settled next door? Let's take your coffee and this newspaper through and then I'll bring up the logs, enough to keep you going for the rest of the day.'

She went ahead into the living room and quickly disconnected the electric fire. It had to be at least thirty years old and would never pass fire regulations now – if a blanket or towel was to accidentally cover it, they would go up in flames within minutes. Moving it out of the way, she picked up the log bag. 'I'll only be a minute.'

She unlocked the back door, leaving it ajar so that some fresh air could enter the kitchen. She picked her way carefully down the steps and pulled up the lid for the log bin. It was set against the back wall of the house and positioned by the edge of the concrete well that allowed light – and garden access – to the basement apartment. Not that Gus or Lenka ever got to come out here; Gus had told her the key to the door had been lost ages ago. It looked from here like a black bin bag had been taped against the glass in lieu of a curtain.

Lee filled the log bag with as many logs as she could carry, staggering up the stairs and depositing them in the basket. She did that twice more, then knelt on the floor and got a fire going for him. Again, he was in his nineties; he couldn't be getting up and down on his knees any more, but she knew one of those combustible fire starters that burned for twenty minutes and allowed a fire to get going easily would make all the difference for him.

Her mental shopping list grew longer.

'There,' she said, setting the fire mesh in front of the flames, lest there should be any sparks, and bringing the TV remote to the arm of his chair. The room flickered with a warm glow, the crackle of the wood as comforting and companionable as a pet. Talking of which, it might help bring his errant cat back too; she had a penchant for scratching and wandering off – Pabe could often be heard calling for her from the back step at night – and now Lee knew why. Cats liked comfort.

'I don't know what to say, my dear,' he said, looking back at her with an expression of genuine amazement as she shrugged her coat back on, preparing to fly. She had eight minutes to collect Jasper. 'I never expected any of this.'

'It's no big deal, but if it's all right with you, I'll pop over before I go to work in the mornings, just to get the fire going for you and replenish the logs.'

'I can't ask that of you.'

'You're not asking, I'm offering.'

'No, I can't,' he protested.

She looked back at him, wondering how to convince him to let her help. 'Let me at least do it until your new carer comes in a couple of weeks? You need to stay warm enough, especially with this cold snap we're having. You know they're forecasting snow?'

'I heard. There's even talk of the Elfstedentocht happening this year.'

'Of course there is,' she smiled, giving a roll of her eyes. Any time the thermometers dropped below zero for more than three days running, talk would start up and down the country about this being the year the iconic cross-country ice-skating race would finally be held again. But the odds were firmly against them; linking eleven cities over 120 miles, it hadn't been held in over twenty years. The last had been in 1997 when she'd been eight and still living in the UK, but she had understood by her first winter here, a few years later, just what a huge deal it was for her adopted country. For the race to go ahead, the ice needed to be six inches thick all the way around the course and it had only been held fifteen times, since the first one in 1909; the doomsayers were convinced global warming meant it would never happen again and Lee suspected they were probably right. She checked her watch again. 'Oh shoot, I'm late. I'll see myself out. See you tomorrow, Pabe.'

She closed the door behind her with a click and a feeling – the first in a while – that she had done something meaningful with her day. *We're going to do some good in this godforsaken hellhole today.* She paused as she felt Cunningham at her back, in her ear. Always there.

Just not when it mattered.

'You made it!' Liam's relief was evident as she slid onto the tall stool opposite him.

'Seems like it,' she smiled as he reached over and kissed her on both cheeks. She was warm, having cycled a few miles to get here. To her delight, the book had been gone by the time she'd unlocked her bike this morning, although she still had a niggle of concern that it had just been lifted by another passer-by, possibly even someone who knew about the distribution marketing campaign – apparently it had a hashtag on social media now – and assumed it was there for the taking. If it was fair game by the bronze feet of a boy statue, why not a bike basket too?

Still, what else could she try? She had no idea from what or from whom this person even needed saving; to go public, to put it on social media or the local press, to go to the police even . . . she could well do more harm than good. It was an impossible predicament.

She pulled off her hat and smoothed her hair of static, having a quick glance around the seafood bar. It was always a dazzling experience – rough, pale-pink brick walls highlighted by tall backlit mirrors, glossy white surfaces and a counter of seafood nestled on shaved ice.

'Ooh,' she said, looking down at the platter he had ordered for them both – smoked mackerel, shrimps, crab salad and smoked salmon. 'Boy done good.'

'I remembered you like the salmon with the avocado,' he said proudly, pouring her a glass of wine and looking irritatingly handsome in his suit, a grey padded Loro Piana jacket slung over the back of his stool. Lee was pleased Mila wasn't here to see him looking so good.

'You've got an eye for the details, I'll give you that,' she said, picking up her glass and toasting with his. 'Cheers, chap,' she said in English.

'Cheers,' he replied in kind.

'So how was your Pakjesavond?' she asked him, spearing a morsel of mackerel.

'It was fine,' he shrugged, digging in too. 'Just family time, you know.'

'Oh dear. It sounds rather underwhelming.'

He shot her a weary look. 'It just got a little repetitive having my father go on and on about why I haven't settled down with a nice girl yet, that's all.'

Lee spluttered. 'Oh God. Does he have any idea about the reality of your social life?'

'Of course not. He wants grandchildren.'

Lee laughed. 'Well, he can have Jasper for the weekend if noise, mess and no food in his cupboards are what he wants!'

'I'll let him know,' he grinned. 'How was yours?'

'Mmm . . . yeah, fine.'

'Now who's being underwhelming?'

'We had Gisele Cunningham over.' She shrugged.

Liam's expression changed. 'Harry's wife?'

'Yeah, I mean she was there on her own. I couldn't just let her . . .' She sighed. 'The girl's pregnant. What you gonna do, you know?'

'No, I get it, it's a nice thing to do. I just didn't realize you were that close to her. I didn't think you and Harry were on good terms . . .'

Lee smiled. Liam had a way with understatement. 'We're not. But I didn't do it for him.' She dipped a prawn into the garlic butter, remembering why she'd called Gisele in the first place, hunting down the letter-that-wasn't. Dita's words floated back into her mind too. *The Americans have authority to arrest him on sight.* She felt another ripple of fear shimmy through her. That had been two days ago and there'd been no word since; she'd expected Cunningham to have been picked up by now. Unless he was on the move again?

'Anyway, what's up?' she asked him, determinedly pulling her thoughts back to lunch. 'I know you haven't called this emergency lunch so that you can find out about my riveting Pakjesavond with my five-year-old.'

'True that,' he sighed, dabbing a napkin to his mouth and taking another sip of wine. 'I need to ask a favour.'

'Oh yes?' She arched an eyebrow, looking at him over the rim of her glasses.

'It's about Haven.'

Lee paused for a moment. 'The singer?' Or specifically, the 'new Billie Eilish', as Lee knew her.

'Yes.'

'What about her?' she asked warily.

'I need to get hold of her.'

Lee sat back in her stool. 'Oh Liam, seriously? I am not hooking you up with Haven—'

'No, no, it's not for me,' he said quickly with a frown. 'Jesus, Lee, no, she's a teenager.'

'So who then?' she frowned, spearing a chunk of crab salad.

'It's for my boss's daughter. It's her eighteenth birthday coming up and he's doing this huge party for her. They've taken over De School, got van Buuren on the decks, but all she wants is Haven singing there.'

Lee stared at him. 'You know that everything you've just said to me is abhorrent, right? I want, I want, poor little rich girl.'

He put his hands up in surrender, agreeing with her. 'I know, you're absolutely right. It's disgusting. She's already ruined. They've got too much money.' He didn't mean a word of it. Money was his god. 'But that's not *my* lookout. I just need to make this happen and secure myself the fat promotion I've been trying and failing to nail for the past three years.'

'It's the only thing you've failed to nail for the past three years,' Lee quipped, munching on a slice of avocado.

He mouthed a silent ha-ha, looking around and checking no one had overheard. 'Seriously though. If I could just pull this off, it could be the break I've needed.'

Lee looked at him. Liam was a cryptocurrency broker, although no one really seemed to know what that meant (including Liam). 'It's pretty sad you've got to arrange your boss's daughter's birthday party in order to move up in your job, isn't it?'

'I'll take whatever edge I can find.' He shrugged. 'Please Lee, I know you know her. Wasn't she at your party last week? If I'd known back then they wanted her, I'd have asked her myself; it only came up incidentally on our way over to a meeting this morning.'

Hence his last-minute text. She watched him as she sipped her wine. He looked desperate, and Liam was never usually jostled out of his elegant air of calm. 'When's the party?'

'Tomorrow night.'

'Tomor—!' Lee spluttered. 'Oh my God, Liam! Not a chance! You've got to be joking!'

'I know it's *highly*, highly unlikely. But can't you at least ask her? Where's the harm?' He spread his smooth hands wide. 'Her management won't even put the request through. Couldn't you just . . . text her direct?'

Lee groaned, slumping back in her chair. 'Ugh, that could be really awkward, Liam.'

'I would owe you. I would owe you *so hard!*'

'No, no, I'm really not sure—'

'He said they'll pay seven figures.'

Lee groaned louder. 'That's disgusting! Do you know what good that money could be put to, instead of a spoilt little rich girl's eighteenth?'

'I know, I know!' He cringed, hiding his face in his hands. 'We're monsters. Debauched pigs.' He peered through his fingers at her with his big blues. 'But can't you at least just ask her. For me?'

Lee stared back at his puppy-dog eyes. They were wholly resistable to her, but to most other women . . . To Mila . . .

Yet she already knew perfectly well she would be seeing Haven at the Hot dinner tonight. It would be far easier to drop it into conversation, face-to-face, than to have to send a text. 'Okay, look, I'll—'

'Yes, thank you!' he cheered, fist-pumping the air.

'Wait,' she said, shushing him. 'I have a condition.'

Liam's jubilation disappeared. 'What sort of condition?'

She considered for a moment – was this the best idea she'd ever had, or the worst? – then leaned in, resting on her elbows as she regarded him. 'I want you to take Mila on a date.'

He stared at her, baffled. '. . . Mila? *Our* Mila?'

She nodded.

'*Mils* Mila?'

'Yes, Liam. That Mila.'

'But she's my . . . friend. I can't take her on a date.'

'Well, that's my condition.'

He leaned in closer now too, pinning her with his extraordinary blue eyes again. She remained unmoved. 'Lee, I'm not sure you're quite aware of what happens on my dates.'

'I am. And I'm not asking you to do *that*.' She tucked her hair behind her ear. 'I just need you to take her out and flood her with attention. Whatever it is that you do with women that makes them go ga-ga for you, do that. Talk to her – I mean, really talk – make her laugh, give her a good time. She needs the ego boost.'

'But why me? It'll just be weird if I start . . . doing that, with her. She's my friend.'

Lee leaned into him. 'Liam, are you saying you're never friends with the women you date?'

'I'm saying I don't generally see women for long enough for them to become my friends. I'm like you. Hook-ups work fine for me. Work's too crazy to commit to anything more.'

She sighed, hardly able to dispute his logic. 'Okay, well, just pretend she's not your friend for one night. Make out she's doing you a favour going out with you, and then give her the best night of her life. Make her shine.'

'That's putting a lot of pressure on a guy,' he laughed.

Lee smiled, knowing all Liam had to do was turn up and breathe for Mila to have the best night of her life.

'I don't know why you're asking me to do this. Mils is stunning. There are loads of guys who would want to date her.'

'Yes, sadly all of them married. Look, she's just really down since her last break-up and she's lost her confidence. She thinks men only want her as their mistress. You are the flirt maestro. Just build up her ego again and show her that not all men are cheating bastards so that we can send her back out there.'

'There?'

Lee waved towards the city. 'Out there. She's threatening a six-month dating sabbatical and I for one don't think I'll survive her doing it.'

He stared back at her. 'And if I do that, you'll speak to Haven?'

'Sure,' she shrugged. 'I'm going to be seeing her for dinner tonight anyway.'

He spread his hands, palms up, on the table as he gave her an incredulous look. 'And you've just made me *beg*?'

'I can only ask her. There's no guarantee she'll say yes. It's not like we're friends.'

'But you're having dinner—?'

'Yes, just us and the other nine Hotties I shot for *Black Dot*.'

'Oh,' he shrugged. 'Oh wait, is that the one Sam's going to?' Liam pointed his fork at her questioningly. 'At the Waldorf Astoria?'

Lee felt her stomach clench at the sudden mention of his name. 'Yes. He'll be there.'

'You know, I had no idea you and he even knew each other,' he said, looking over at her interestedly. 'I couldn't believe it when he said you'd photographed him. I'd brought him to your gallery party just so that I could introduce him to you. Do you remember I told you about his book and that mad marketing campaign?'

'Mm-hmm.'

'Why didn't you say you knew him?'

'Well, I didn't know he was the guy you were talking about at the time,' she said in a tight voice.

'He's a good man, Sam,' Liam said, having another drink of wine, his glass almost empty. 'We were at uni together.'

'Yes, you said.'

'Both on the skating team. He was the prodigy, really into it. The rest of us were just trying to keep up.'

'Were you close?'

'Yeah, we were pretty tight for a while. I mean, we're totally different – he's a bit of a dark horse, quite quiet, understated, plays it cool . . .' He winked at her. 'But the women go mad for him. He was my partner in crime for a while.'

'Really?' Lee felt a stab of alarm. 'I didn't . . . I didn't get that.'

'No?' Liam considered it for a moment. 'Well, I guess he's not really your type.'

Lee's fork hovered mid-air, her heart racing into a gallop. 'You don't think so?'

'Well, don't get me wrong. He's always had a thing for blondes, but you like the rough and ready sort, the treat-'em-mean guys, and energetically you're just . . . on different paths.'

'Energetically?'

'Yeah, you know – you've seen his book; he's all peace and kindness and you're . . .' He ran out of words. 'You.'

She stared at him, open-mouthed. 'What does *that* mean?'

'Well, you're . . . you're like . . . warry.'

'*Warry?* That's not even a word.'

'You know what I mean, though. Combative. Aggressive, but in a good way.' He frowned. 'Or do I mean assertive? You don't suffer fools. Or romantics. You like a good battle to get your teeth into. You're never happier than when you're in a conflict.'

She stared back at him. 'That's what you think of me?'

Liam chuckled. 'Lee, it's no diss. I stand in awe of you, trust me. Where most people have walls, you've got barbed wire. Nobody is going to get close to you. A guy like Sam wouldn't even know where to start.'

Chapter Eighteen

'It is unacceptable that you look better in a suit than I do,' Bart muttered, pulling on his cuffs as they walked towards the bar's steel door. It still had the three-armed entry wheel from when this had actually been a bank vault and her heart was pounding as hard as if she was staging a break-in. The adrenaline was pumping and she had to fight the urge to turn on her ridiculous heels and high-tail it out of here.

'You didn't see the dress I nearly wore,' she murmured, checking her jacket was correctly positioned. Her ivory crepe blouse was plunging, with two neck ties dangling loose and providing minimal coverage should she twist slightly too far.

Bart arched an eyebrow. 'Hot?'

'Hotter than hell.'

His eyes widened. 'So why didn't you wear it then? This is the Hot List dinner.'

'Yes, but *I'm* not on that list.' She winked at him with a levity she didn't feel. 'We're just staff, darling.'

They were running late; Mila had been apoplectic with her when she'd answered the door in her tux and there'd been a lot of explaining (lying) to do. Lee had given her the exact same spiel – it wasn't 'appropriate' for her to dress as the femme fatale; tonight wasn't about her – but the truth was, she needed a suit that doubled as armour. Sam's yawning silence had left her in knots at the prospect of seeing him again tonight. With every passing day, every slow-turning hour that he didn't call, he steadily filled the spaces in her mind; he was all she could think about now that it was becoming clear he had turned and walked away from her again – not like the first time, when he'd wanted more, but precisely because now he didn't. He'd seen what lay at the heart of her; he'd glimpsed the ugliness and fear that hid beneath her tough, assertive demeanour and it had been enough. He didn't want her.

And it wasn't like she wanted to want him. This messy complication was exactly what she always tried so hard to avoid. She just had to get through tonight with some semblance of dignity.

Bart put his hand on the door and looked at her. 'Ready?'

Her pulse spiked again. 'Sure. Let's get this over with and then we can get out of this hellhole,' she quipped, sounding a lot more dry than she felt. It was what she and Cunningham always used to say to each other on assignment. Black humour definitely had its place.

Bart chuckled as he pushed the door open and they walked in, the babble of conversation rushing over them like warm water. Lee took in the cosy, rich interior in blinked snapshots – russet-toned rugs; low-slung, high-backed cream chairs; caramel-coloured wooden floors; intimate, flattering lighting. Almost every table was taken, women in silks and men in baratheas enjoying pre-show aperitifs before they went on to the opera or ballet or theatre; hotel guests relaxing before dinner. With the high prices the hotel charged, everybody had to be a somebody just to be here, but it was the group standing by the bar that was grabbing attention, discreet glances flittering on their stardust-sprinkled faces, as light and fleeting as butterflies.

She saw Alexander Visser, the acclaimed director being hailed as the 'new Tarantino', talking with Honor Mbeke, the Estee Lauder cover girl being called the 'new Naomi', and Armin de Vries, the rising politician and young father lauded as Trudeau's successor. Beside them, in a languid grouping, was Matt (she'd completely forgotten *he'd* be here too), engaged in a lively conversation with Virgil Van Den Berg (the 'new Ronaldo'), Martine Van Dijk (the 'new Ellen'), Ricky Lazell (the 'new Ed Sheeran') and Claudia Prins (the 'new Sylvie Guillem'). Haven, she saw, was standing slightly apart from them with her manager, her phone in her hand and looking as awkward as teenagers do; she had to be eight years younger than the next youngest person here and, with her nose ring and dressed in a to-her-knees T-shirt and hi-tops, looked like she should be clubbing. Not for the first time, Lee wondered how the hell she was supposed to propose Liam's request without compromising her own professional integrity. She and Haven didn't know each other anything like well enough to be calling in favours.

In spite of her best intentions, Lee scanned the room for Sam. She just wanted to know where he was – so she could avoid it. She found him in the far corner. He had his back to her, his head nodding slightly as he listened to something Rubens Dekker, the editor, was saying; a diminutive, sharply dressed blonde woman Lee didn't recognize stood to his right. Had he brought a date?

'What'll it be?' Bart asked her, placing a hand lightly on her arm, bringing her attention back to him.

'Huh? Oh . . . let's make it an Old Fashioned.' She looked at Sam again; he and the blonde were laughing. 'I'll go over to Haven. She looks a bit isolated,' she murmured.

'Sure, I'll bring it over.'

'Bart!' She heard his name being called in happy exclamation behind her as he moved through the starry crowd – everyone loved him, for his jokes, his easy-going manner, his love of a gossipy story – heads turning as they looked for her too.

'Hey,' Lee said brightly, going over to Haven and her manager. She kissed them both on the cheeks. 'How are you? I'm so glad you could make it. I thought I saw something earlier that said you were touring?'

'Don't mention the war,' Andrik, her manager, grimaced.

'Oh no,' Lee frowned. 'What's happened?'

'Backing singer troubles.'

Haven looked up from her phone. 'They dumped me for Lily Savant.'

Lee had vaguely heard the name. 'No way.'

'I can't go on without them, I just can't,' Haven said firmly, looking back at her manager as though he was about to push her on stage this very minute.

Andrik put a hand on her shoulder. 'Of course, I completely understand.' He looked back at Lee. 'I keep telling Haven, *she* is the talent. She is the one filling the stadia, not them. She doesn't need anyone on that stage but her. But . . .' He gave a hopeless shrug.

'Can't you just get other backing singers?' Lee asked.

'It's triggered a more general crisis of confidence, hasn't it?' Andrik asked his protégée, patting her shoulder lightly, before casting Lee a weary look.

Haven stared straight at her. 'The girls have been with me since I got my first contract. They're my sisters. I know it's only my name on the records and all the publicity is about me, but my entire experience in this industry has been as part of a team. It was me and them together, that's how I saw it.

232

We were a family on that stage.' Her bottom lip trembled. 'And now they've just left me.'

'I'm really sorry,' Lee said sympathetically. 'That sounds very upsetting.'

'We'll work it out,' Andrik sighed, sounding endlessly patient. 'We've postponed tomorrow's event and rescheduled for end of January . . .'

Tomorrow? Lee tipped her head interestedly. Surely it couldn't be that easy, could it? She gave a small, sympathetic smile, knowing this was her opportunity to suggest Liam's 'alternative' arrangement – it would be something else off her mind, if nothing else – but a tinkle of laughter and Sam's name uttered in exclamation across the room made her smile and mind freeze.

'. . . It's just a bump in the road,' Andrik said in a reassuring voice. 'It's more important we focus on getting Haven's confidence back. We're in this for the long haul, after all. Got to keep our girl feeling safe and happy.'

Lee nodded in agreement. 'So are you excited about seeing the shots?'

'We can't wait, can we?' Andrik said, looking at Haven again encouragingly.

'Yeah,' Haven nodded, but there was a slight shrug too; a truculent element of 'whatever'.

'I'm looking forward to seeing what they've gone with myself,' Lee said.

'Oh? Don't you know?' Andrik sounded surprised.

'No. I send them my edit, but after that it's up to them what they choose to run with. They have to see how the images work together in the entirety of the feature – the flow, the energy, whether it's cohesive or more differentiated.'

'I hadn't realized.'

'Yeah, I'm excited. It's never quite what I think it'll be.'

'How long have you been doing this gig for now?' Andrik asked.

'This is my fifth year. Last year we did it in colour, but I liked the black and whites this time – it's edgier, moodier. Everyone's personality seems more distinct somehow when you strip away the colours—'

'Here you go,' Bart said, intruding with her cocktail.

'Ooh,' she said, taking it appreciatively. 'Haven, Andrik, you remember Bart?'

'Of course,' Andrik said, fist-bumping him. 'We stuffed ourselves stupid on those pastries you brought in.'

Bart grinned. 'I remember! They're good, right?'

Lee glanced around the room, her eyes treacherously finding Sam again. He was still in conversation with the editor and the blonde, his back to her. Did he even know she was here? Would he care?

She let her eyes travel over the sweep of his shoulders. He was wearing a charcoal-grey velvet dinner jacket, black trousers and an open-necked shirt, his hair seeming wavier and more raffish than the last time she'd seen him.

When he had just kissed her and cycled away. Hadn't looked back. Hadn't called.

She didn't blame him. He had realized she was more trouble than she was worth; he'd seen just how broken she really was. Why would he want to hang around for that? He understood now that it was all an act, this – making small talk in a five-star hotel bar, sympathizing over first-world problems like losing backing singers, when she had spent ten years in hotels with bombed-out windows and entire floors missing. He understood that no one came out of that as the same person they'd gone in. No one escaped unscathed. Bad dreams were the least of it.

'Haven, hi!'

Lee looked back to find Matt sauntering over; his hair had grown back so that it looked like a very fine buzz-cut, highlighting the sharpness of his bone structure. He was looking fine in a midnight-blue dinner suit and wing-collar shirt, also no tie.

She tensed as he came and stood beside her, his physicality somehow dwarfing her, his shadow claiming her.

'I was hoping we'd meet. I'm a *huge* fan of yours.' He grinned at Haven, looking dazzling and clearly expecting that the teen sensation knew who he was too.

But she looked back at him blankly. 'Sorry—?'

'Apologies, my manners,' Lee stepped in quickly, already able to see how this was going to go. There were egos to manage tonight. 'Haven, this is Matteo Hofhuis. He was the lead in *Liar Liar*, on Netflix.'

'Oh. Sorry, I don't watch TV.'

Lee cringed. 'It's good, I think you'd like it,' she lied; she hadn't seen it either. 'Word is he's been shortlisted by Barbara Broccoli as the new Bond. Can you confirm or deny this, Matt?' she asked jokily, having to make eye contact.

'I can only confirm that I will deny anything I'm asked on the matter,' he replied wittily, looking very pleased with himself. And her. They both knew she'd saved his blushes. 'And how are you, Lee? You're looking sensational tonight,' he said, grabbing his opportunity and kissing her on both cheeks, placing his hands on her waist, before leaning back to drink her in. 'Only Lee could make a suit look that sexy,' he proclaimed to the group.

'As I said, he's a good actor,' Lee smiled, brushing off the compliment and seeing how Bart's eyes were glinting with sheer delight at this very friendly reunion. Matt's arm had pointedly remained around her waist for several seconds longer than it needed to.

'It's a really eclectic bunch they've pulled together,' Andrik said, his gaze bumping over the crowd. 'That's Virgil Van Den Berg, isn't it? He's just on fire at the moment.'

'I know, I was just talking to him,' Matt exclaimed. 'Did you see his goal against Eindhoven last weekend?' He gave an impressed laugh. 'Insane.'

Lee felt a hand on her shoulder and turned to see the hotel concierge smiling back at her. 'They're ready for you in the Maurer Room now, if you'd like to make your way through?'

Already? 'Oh right, sure, thanks.' This was what came of arriving late. She looked back at the others. 'I'd better say hi to the boss before we sit down. I'll catch up with you upstairs.' So what if he was talking still to Sam? She might be freelance, but 60 per cent of her work was for his magazine – she had to network.

'Sure.' Matt's eyes lingered on her as she walked over towards the man responsible for signing her pay cheques, and the other one responsible for her disrupted sleep patterns.

'Hi,' she said brightly, interrupting their flow and coming to stand beside Sam. It was a defiant gesture, to show him she wasn't cowed by his rejection, and he seemed startled by her sudden proximity, tensing in exactly the same way she just had with Matt. Did he feel the same antipathy, then? She fixed the smile on her lips. 'I thought I'd better come and say hello before we sit down to eat. Apparently they're ready for us upstairs.'

'Lee, great to see you,' Rubens said, leaning across to kiss her. 'You look impossibly chic as ever. The whole androgyny thing looks great on you.'

'Thanks, Rubens.' She looked at Sam – direct, quick, no hesitation, back on her game. 'Hi-Sam-how-are-you?' she asked with a faux cheeriness, as though he wasn't the man who'd helped her to stand in a cafe, who'd kissed her on her doorstep in her pyjamas three days earlier, who'd walked out of her house rather than get in her bed.

'Lee.' They air-kissed politely.

Politely. She felt the new distance between them, a contraction in her stomach as their eyes fleetingly met – but she couldn't read him. He was an enigma to her.

She turned to the blonde. 'I'm Lee. I don't think we've met?'

'Hi Lee, I'm Veronika,' the girl replied as they shook hands; she was slender as a reed in a strapless ivory crepe midi column dress. She couldn't be more than twenty-three but she had the cool, steady composure that young women have when they believe the world to be at their feet. 'I'm Rubens' new PA.'

'Ah right, yes, we've spoken on the phone.'

'Yes, I think so.'

There was a little pause; the power dynamic was completely tipped in Lee's favour, and yet Veronika's youth, beauty, flaxen blondeness, the way Sam had spent this entire early part of the evening talking to her . . . Lee adjusted her glasses.

'Lee, before I forget, my congratulations on the launch of your new exhibition the other week. I'm sorry I couldn't get there. I was in New York. I understand it was a triumph?' Rubens said.

'Well, it seemed to generate a conversation on the issue, which of course was always the point.'

'I saw the party shots, we're giving over a page to it. It looked great. Just like this – but wilder.' He chuckled.

'Well, give us time. The night is but young,' she quipped, her eyes darting towards Sam as she smiled.

'There's a wonderful one of you with . . . Matteo Hofhuis, I think it was, doing the flamenco.'

'The flamenco?' she repeated, completely surprised and mildly horrified as a vague, indistinct memory began to press into focus. The flounces on her sleeves, the swirl of the skirt on her dress as he twirled her . . . 'Well, you won't use that, I hope,' she said quickly.

'Why not? You look great in it.'

'It wouldn't sit well with the message we're trying to get across. I don't want to hijack my own work on account of . . . high spirits.'

'High spirits,' he repeated, sounding amused. 'Ah yes. Leave it with me. I'll take a look at it again. You might be right.'

She took a sip of her drink, aware of how silently and still Sam stood beside her. 'So tell me, are you pleased with how the feature's come together?' she asked into the silence. Did anyone else detect the tension between her and Sam? Did anyone else see that he'd fallen quiet after having been a convivial guest only moments before her arrival?

'Lee, it's the best yet,' Rubens enthused.

'Really?' She felt a thrill of disbelieving delight. 'I can't wait to see it.'

'You've surpassed yourself. What you achieved with Matteo and Sam here, particularly. Your vision for them was so singular.'

She didn't glance at Sam, but she could feel his stare, how he had heard that they'd been bracketed together . . .

'I was just telling Sam what a devil of a time we always have getting you to agree to do the feature in the first place.'

Rubens looked at him. 'It's a great coup for us, getting someone of Lee's stature to do the portraits. It would be so easy for it to come across as a puff piece, some pointless ego-fanning. Lee coming on board really reframes the whole concept of the idea, she gives it gravitas that these are the people – you, them – who are shaping our social and cultural and political landscape. There's nothing flighty or trivial about that.'

'Well, I feel incredibly honoured to have made the cut,' Sam said neutrally. 'Although I don't know how I did. I've got full-blown imposter syndrome. This time last year I was just a struggling artist having to paint people's *pets* to make a living. Now, somehow, I'm a bestselling author.' He shrugged, bewildered.

'That's the beauty of social media,' Veronika smiled. 'You don't need to find your audience; if you're good enough, they'll find you. And you're amazing, Sam. Everybody loves you. Your book is already a classic. Not just your beautiful drawings but the words too. They touch people.' She pressed her hand to her chest. 'You make a difference to their lives.'

Lee looked between the PA and Sam, her heart feeling raisin-sized by this clear love-in.

'. . . Thank you,' Sam smiled, maintaining eye contact with her. 'It's kind of you to say so.'

Rubens clapped his hands. 'Well, on that most eloquent note – thank you, Veronika – I think we should head upstairs and see exactly what it is that this exceptional group of people has achieved.' He broke away from their huddle, herding the others towards the door. 'Upstairs, everybody. It's time for the big reveal.'

'Sam, I'll show you where you're sitting,' Veronika said before Lee could even open her mouth. 'I was responsible for the table plan tonight.'

'Oh. Well, lead on, then,' he said, nodding fractionally at Lee as they departed, leaving her there.

She watched them go, feeling her heart crackle and splinter into crystal pieces as the stellar group exited the basement bar, taking their stardust with them.

'Lee. You good?' Bart was at the bar, putting back his glass. 'Yes.'

He came back over to her, a wrinkle puckering his brow. He put a hand on her arm. 'Sure?'

No. She forced a smile. 'Well, maybe just a little nervous. You know what it's like – I'd always prefer to see it first without an audience.'

'Ah, but then where would the drama be?' he said drily, taking her arm and linking it through his, squeezing it tight. 'As well we know, drama *is* life.'

They walked into the dining room several minutes later. Everyone had regrouped in the beautiful space, with its famous eighteenth-century pastoral scenes painted on the panelled walls, an empire chandelier hanging low above the table, peacock-blue velvet chairs. Veronika was leading everyone to their places, serene and confident in her host-essing role. Along the walls were the easels with her portraits printed to A1 size and covered with sheets – drama indeed. It was the same every year, but Lee was surprised to see a cinema screen set up too. She wasn't aware of any 'behind the scenes' filming that had taken place, no extra footage for social media.

She sat down in her usual place, not needing to be shown by the oh-so-capable Veronika; she already knew she would be seated at the head of the table, to Rubens' right, as she was every year. Haven was seated on Rubens' left side, on the corner, with Sam beside her. Lee had the director Alexander Visser to her right, and the ballerina Claudia Prins to his right. She was relieved to see Matt was at the far end of the table, near Bart; less so that Veronika appeared to be to Sam's left.

Haven was talking intently to Sam, using her hands to make her point, looking impassioned and distinctly unteenage. She watched him listen, nodding, making eye contact . . . *A dark horse*, Liam had said. *The women love him.*

The last few wine glasses were filled, the hum of conversation dying as Rubens stood and ting'd a fork to his glass for silence.

'Hot Ones,' he began, drawing the usual surprised laughter, 'thank you for being with us here today. We know how insane your schedules are, especially at this time of year betwixt St Nicholas' Eve and Christmas. But I hope you'll agree it was worth your while coming out in the cold and the dark, for this is no ordinary project. Every summer, we start with a longlist of over a hundred names, people who – like you – are excelling in their fields, bringing a spotlight to important issues, changing how we look at and think about things, proving that diversity and inclusion are not only a part of the Dutch landscape but in fact the Dutch character . . .'

Lee, sitting beside him, kept her eyes down, knowing this speech well. He repeated it every year.

'. . . whittle it down over the weeks until we are left with the very pinnacle of each of those peaks – film, TV, fashion, sport, politics, music, dance, fiction, art. And that brought us to *you*. You are the new game-changers, the ones we shall be looking to for hope, comfort, beauty, escape, guidance. You've probably already noticed the air is becoming thin where you now reside, you're already not part of the masses any more. Anonymity is already denied to you, you are standing on the threshold of new lives. But that is nothing to what is coming. Because thanks to this woman' – he put a hand on Lee's shoulder and she looked up at him with a bland smile – 'you are not going to step onto the international stage, so much as be jet-propelled onto it.'

A burst of laughter – excited, curious – rippled around the room, all eyes landing on her.

'For the past five years now, Lee has sat beside me here and listened as I make this speech, graciously using her talent to lift others—'

'Rubens, really,' she protested.

'I've had the privilege, many times, of standing on the sidelines and watching her work and I always come away asking myself the same question: *what* is it that sets her apart? What makes her so much better than her contemporaries? *How* does she get to the heart of someone and show us who they truly are? She's not the most organized photographer we work with, nor, frankly, the most interested in this world; she's not even the most expensive – she doesn't care about fancy locations and ornate props and backdrops. And yet, her portraits stand apart. Where most photographers try to capture the *magic* of celebrity, she captures the *humanity* within celebrity. And I think it's because of this.'

At his cue, the lights in the room dimmed, the cinema screen suddenly glowing a bright white as a projector was shone onto it. Alexander, Claudia, Andrik and Honor moved their chairs around to face the screen.

'What are you doing?' she hissed to Rubens, as images started to come up – larger than life-size, black and white and in colour, the images of her past: faces that would always haunt her, screams and laments that still echoed in her ears . . . She felt her throat close as she remembered the

Yazidi woman sitting by the roadside, too exhausted to walk another step; the children's blinded tears as Assad's chemical weapons attacked their immune systems; a building exploding in the very moment a mortar hit; a skeleton in a ditch, holding a much smaller one; a group of rebel soldiers huddled against a wall, faces and hair sifted with dust, exhaustion making their faces slack, limbs limp.

She could remember every single one of those moments; they sat within her like a pulse. She would not forget them; it was her personal pledge that even if she could not change their fates, she would remember them.

Still the images kept coming, each one distinct and fully formed, her heart pounding as her old life flashed in front of her eyes, the one that had belonged to Cunningham and not Jasper. But then the mood changed, the tenor of the images shifting from war and devastation and ruin to rare snapshots of joy too: children washing in a river in Afghanistan, droplets of water catching the light; an old bearded shepherd walking through a village, surrounded by his flock of goats; two little boys using the husk of a burnt-out car as a climbing frame; a group of girls laughing as they washed clothes in buckets; Cunningham driving, his face in profile, mouth open in amused speech, the dry red landscape reflected in his aviators.

She caught her breath at the unexpected sight of him. So familiar. Like he was part of her own reflection. A face she had probably looked upon as many times as her own.

'Where did you get these?' she whispered, but Rubens just winked. She already knew anyway.

Dita. It had to have been why she had stopped in the city on her way to Pyongyang; what she'd had to say to her, after all, could have been done by phone.

She watched the pictures flash past, less familiar to her

than the headline-grabbing ones. These images had only ever been taken as asides, out-takes on the way to an interview or a red zone or a scoop. They had never been published, they had just been stolen moments to keep her going when the shellings and bombardments and killings all became too much and she needed to be reminded that there was more to life than just survival; that joy could be found in hellholes, that there was always light, even in darkness. Especially in darkness.

And then it came – the first of those defining images – as perhaps she should have known it would. They were attached to her now like a shadow upon her shadow. The first one. One of four.

The skinny dog cocking its leg against a falling-down hut.

An old man carrying a basket down a narrow street.

His splayed feet, holey shoes, as a soldier crouched over the body with dribbles of juice on his chin.

Brown eyes, point blank to the lens.

She snatched her gaze away, but too late: they scorched her retinas, remaining in her mind's eye like sun spots, her chest tight and hurting. Hurting.

Everyone began to applaud as the last image faded into obsolescence and *Lee Fitchett, Pulitzer Prize for Breaking News Photography 2015* appeared on the white screen in stylish black type. Someone began whooping – Bart or Matt, she didn't look. She willed the applause to die down, eyes to move off her as she struggled to keep her face impassive. These weren't just pictures to her. They were scars. A map of her own journey.

Rubens stood again, clearing his throat, driving the evening onwards.

'So you see, Hot Ones . . .' Another ripple of amusement

shimmied through the small group. 'You have not simply had your photograph taken for a magazine article. You have been seen by someone who has *seen* humanity – the best and the very worst of it. She's not interested in flattering your egos, as I'm sure you became well aware on your shoots – consider yourself lucky if you got given *stroopwafels*. We're not all so privileged.'

Everyone laughed loudly and Matt and Alexander clapped their hands above their heads proudly.

'But when you find yourself on the other end of Lee Fitchett's lens, you'd better believe that she's coming after you. She doesn't want your good side or your best smoulder. She wants your *soul* and she's not going to stop till she gets it. She's going to tell the truth about you and put it out there for the whole world to see. Can you handle that? Are you ready?'

'Yaasss!' they cheered, even Haven, Matt the loudest.

'Then take it away, please,' Rubens said, indicating to the waiters standing beside the shrouded easels.

The sheets were whisked off and a rolling, jostling expectant silence filled the room as everyone saw themselves with a fresh gaze. Then the gasps came. The murmurs. The squeaks of delight, hands flying to mouths as they absorbed themselves, redrawn.

Claudia – her dark hair worn down, and manspreading, wearing a man's suit and unlaced trainers, no socks, no shirt. No pointe shoes, no tutu, no princess.

Matt – roughed-up and feral, his self-satisfied shine lost to the mud and boredom.

Haven – sitting in a giant log basket, bare arms and legs dangling out, laughing uproariously like she'd just been pushed in. (She had. Bart had been terrified.)

Sam – the gentle artist staring unafraid at the camera like it was the barrel of a gun. Daring her to do it, see him, capture him. *Goodbye, Lee.*

The room erupted again, everyone clapping and cheering. 'Brava!' was shouted out by someone. Sam was clapping too but he had his head angled towards Veronika as she was saying something in his ear.

'Three cheers for Lee!' Alexander said beside her, raising his glass and leading them all in a toast. 'Hip, hip—'

'Hooray!'

'Well, I certainly wasn't expecting that,' Lee said a few moments later to Rubens, as he sat down again and the waiters moved in to start pouring water.

'Of course not. You wouldn't have come if you'd known,' he said accurately. 'But these things need saying every now and again. We know how lucky we are to have you.'

'Well, it was very sweet and utterly mortifying.' She patted his arm, knowing exactly what he was alluding to. 'Just so long as you promise not to do it again next year.'

He arched a hopeful eyebrow. 'So there'll be a next year?'

She smiled enigmatically. 'Let's just say it's definitely a maybe,' she murmured, her eyes sliding over to Sam again. He, Veronika and Haven were locked in a three-way conversation and she watched him talk – understated, calm and yet still somehow pivotal, as though he was the sun and they were the stars spinning around him.

He was being polite, of course, a good dinner guest, but she also had the distinct impression he was avoiding her. Unless she'd been directly talking to him or the focus of attention in the entire room, he hadn't looked her way once.

She tried to listen to Rubens as he began telling her about their ongoing negotiations for an exclusive with DiCaprio he wanted her for – cover, possibly limited edition covers, eight-page spread . . . but she scarcely heard the words. The minutes were sliding past, the entrées already on the table, and still Sam's attention stayed on everyone but her.

She couldn't fail to get the point. He had moved on. Deep, deep down, she had been holding out hope that he had just been busy, giving her time and space, playing her at her own game, even – but it was patently clear now that the kiss really had been a goodbye, that their brief flirtation, their faltering emotional entanglement, would stay forever that.

The realization felt like a burn, deep inside her. She blinked hard, trying to crush the feeling flat, to rationalize it – she didn't want to want him. She just wanted him to want her. Yes, that was it. She just wanted him to want her. Her vanity demanded it. Her ego needed it. She hadn't let him walk out on her a second time, surely? Reject me once, shame on you; reject me twice, shame on me.

She took another sip of her drink, feeling her heart burst into flames as Veronika touched his arm again, getting ever closer.

Mila had been right. She should have worn the green dress.

Chapter Nineteen

'Lee, I'll be in touch about DiCaprio,' Rubens said as his coat was handed back to him. 'As soon as we get a confirmed date I'll let you know, but it's looking like sometime early Jan – probably around the BAFTAs in London – so keep your diary flexible. You're my first choice.'

'Sure, no problem,' she nodded, buttoning her own coat too and feeling relieved Bart had pre-booked her a car. There was a time and a place for cycling around this city and midnight, in minus three degrees, wasn't it. Her kitten hat was in the pocket and she pulled it out, smoothing it down over her hair and not caring any more if it didn't 'go' with her soignée look. The night was done, their fates firmly spelled out.

He patted her arm. 'Speak soon. And take some time off over Christmas. Relax with your boy.'

'I will,' she called after him as he trotted down the steps to his waiting car. 'Night, Rubens.'

Bart came to stand by her. He had a Missoni striped scarf tucked into the neck of his coat. 'Is it here yet?'

'Not yet.' She looked down the length of Herengracht. The grand canal – the grandest canal – was frozen solid and glittering with lacy white frost crystals.

'Hmm,' Bart tutted, vainly searching the street too. He looked at her. 'So, you must be pleased with how that went?'

'Yes, I think the—' Andrik came up to them, pumping their hands hard. 'Oh, good night, Andrik.'

'Yes, it has been,' he said earnestly. 'It's given Haven exactly the boost she needed.'

'Well, she's an incredibly talented singer, we were delighted she wanted to be a part of the feature.' Lee realized she hadn't asked about tomorrow night, after all, her mind on other things than her friend's promotion hopes. And it was too late now, of course; she couldn't just spring it on them as they stood on the hotel steps. She would simply have to pretend the answer had been a flat no; it wasn't like Liam was holding out any realistic hope of it being otherwise, anyway.

'She loves the image. She's already spoken to Rubens about buying a print of it.'

'Ha, I'm glad. That's very flattering.'

'She's so used to being dressed up and styled, but she says you get her. No one's ever pushed her into a log basket before.'

'What can I say? Everyone'll be wearing them next summer.'

Matt's face appeared over Andrik's shoulder. 'Lee, I'm passing your way on my route home. Need a lift?' He winked mischievously, so sure of his glittery-eyed charms.

'Thanks Matt, but Bart's booked me a car. *Supposedly.*' She rolled her eyes and shared a smile with Andrik, as though it was a private joke.

'Cancel it then,' he shrugged, undeterred, still not getting it – the fact that she ghosted his calls and texts, had managed to avoid him most of the night . . . 'It's no bother for me to drop you.'

The smile died in her eyes, her voice hardening. 'You're sweet to offer but we've got some things to discuss, now that we've seen the spread. You know, post-production stuff.'

She watched as the snub finally registered. 'Oh.'

'Thanks, though. And it was lovely seeing you again. Good luck with everything. Exciting times for you ahead.' The door wasn't just closed, but locked. He could see that now.

Andrik turned to the actor, offering him his hand. 'Good to meet you, Matt. Let me know if you want those tickets for Oslo.'

'Thanks, man,' Matt said, shaking his hand awkwardly before nodding at her and moving away down the steps, into the night and out of her orbit.

Lee felt the relief roll off her.

Andrik cleared his throat, turning around to check they were alone again. 'Actually, Lee, while I've got you, Haven's asked me to put some feelers out to see if you'd be interested in shooting the visuals for her next album?'

'Oh . . .'

'I don't know if you've done anything like that before.'

'Not really, no.'

'Perhaps you could think about it? She's desperate to work with you again. You can see she's not the most trusting sort. She said she'd do anything to make it happen.'

Lee hesitated for a moment, a small smile slowly curving her mouth. 'Really? . . . Anything?'

'Yes, bye! Bye.' Lee waved as Claudia got into her Uber. She turned back to Bart again. 'So much for an early getaway. I told Mila I'd be back twenty minutes ago. Where *is* he? I feel like the bloody doorman standing out here.'

Poor Bart sighed, looking stressed as well as cold. 'I don't know, I'm so sorry. Let me try again.' He pulled his phone from his pocket. 'Perhaps the concierge sent him off to park down the street. I'll go check – oh, hi, Veronika. Bye, Veronika. Great night. Well done.'

Lee turned to see La Blonde emerging through the hotel doors in an ivory cashmere belted coat.

She laughed at the sight of Lee's kitten-ears hat. 'Oh Lee, you are a riot!'

Lee stared back at her. '. . . Are you off?'

Veronika clasped the collar of her coat tightly around her neck. 'Yes. Sam's dropping me back.'

Lee felt her heart drop to her feet like a lead weight. 'Ah. That's . . . kind.'

'Yikes, it's *freezing* out here,' Veronika tittered, giving a girlish shiver.

The doors opened again and Bart came back through. 'Right, turns out he's been sitting three houses up this entire time. He thought we were coming out the Fifty-Two exit.' Given that the hotel was comprised of six neighbouring town-houses, it was perhaps an understandable mistake. But Lee was oblivious. Sam had been following immediately after Bart and she had seen his face change as he'd clocked her standing on the step with Veronika. She knew he knew she knew.

'We'd better get up there then,' she said stiffly, wrenching her gaze off him and onto Bart.

He frowned, taking in her sudden change of expression. 'You okay?'

She nodded, knowing tears were about to shine in her eyes any moment. 'Mmm. So cold.' She raised a hand to the others. 'Bye then. Great night. Happy Christmas,' she said abruptly and she jogged down the steps before anyone could say another word.

In the car, the warmth enveloped her like a hug, making her shivering body soften and the tears fall. She was like an ice sculpture melting, her hard angles becoming indistinct and blurry. Bart climbed into the back seat beside her with a contented sigh. 'Over and out. You slayed it, girl,' he sighed, buckling up his seatbelt.

'Mmm,' she murmured, closing her eyes, pretending to be sleepy. But a moment later she felt his hand over hers, patting it, and she knew he could see the tear tracks on her cheeks, shining under the street lights. He seemed to know when the mask was slipping and she was grateful for the silence as the car swept through the quiet, cobbled streets, his hand holding hers. He knew when words were like sledgehammers, when pictures were like razor blades.

'See you Monday,' she said, as they pulled up outside her house, the little street prettier than ever in its winter lace.

His eyes were sad. 'Yeah. See you, Lee. Have a good one.'

The car door closed behind her with a thunk and she climbed her steps, sliding the key into the lock and feeling a wave of exhaustion suffuse her. Her legs felt leaden, her heart like a weight. She hung her coat and hat on the rack of bent-wood hooks and tiptoed upstairs. Mila was asleep on the sofa, snoring lightly, the TV still on, the iPad splayed open across her stomach.

'Psst,' Lee whispered, sinking into the armchair opposite and beginning to untie the ankle straps on her high shoes.

'Huh?' Mila stirred with a jolt. 'What? Where am I?'

Lee smiled back at her, hoping – in vain – that her mascara hadn't run in the car. 'I'm back. Sorry it's late. We couldn't find our driver.'

'Oh . . .' Mila yawned and stretched. 'What time is it?'

'Nearly one, sorry,' she grimaced, seeing how Mila winced. 'But at least you get to have a lie-in in the morning and won't be woken by a five-year-old sitting on your head.'

Mila grinned sleepily. 'Oh yeah . . .' she mumbled, sitting

up and sliding her feet onto the floor. "Bout that. Just so you know, I had a slight emergency.'

Lee stopped what she was doing. 'What?'

'Not here, it's all fine,' Mila said quickly. 'But I realized I left my bath running.'

Lee blinked, staring at her. *'What?'*

'I know, it's mad. But I'd been planning on having a quick salt bath before I came over here. That spin class was evil—'

'The point, Mils!'

'Yeah. So anyway, I had an Amazon delivery, signed for it, then the phone went . . . Long story short, totally forgot about the bath. I mean, you know how long it takes to fill. The pressure's shocking. Came over here . . .' She shrugged as though the rest of the story was obvious.

'And so . . . ?' Lee prompted uneasily.

'And so I had to nip back there to turn it off. Luckily the overflow worked and it wasn't too bad. Just a bit of mopping up with some towels and it was f—'

'So, you took Jasper with you? That's what you're saying?' Lee demanded, feeling a rush of fear. 'Clearly you didn't leave him alone and sleeping in the house.'

'God, no!' she protested, looking aghast. 'It was only just after you'd gone, he was still up. I'd never leave him alone, obviously. But it was too cold to take him out on the bike *and* I didn't know the combination for your lock with his seat on—'

'Mila, what did you do?' Lee cried. 'Just tell me what you did with Jasper. If you didn't leave him here and you didn't take him with you . . . ?'

'I just dropped him in with your neighbour for a bit. I was only gone half an hour. I was as quick as a flash, promise.'

Lee's jaw dropped open. 'You dropped him in with Pabe? Mils, he's ninety-two years old!'

Mila laughed. 'Not him! The young couple downstairs. Gus and Lenka, yes?'

Lee's eyes widened. 'Mils, tell me you're joking.'

'Why?'

'Because I hardly know them! I don't just ask them to look after my five-year-old child at the drop of a hat!'

'But you said they're so nice. And they are. They didn't mind at all.' Mila stared at her, looking perplexed, as if she couldn't understand the reason for Lee's horror. 'Nothing bad happened. He just drew a picture while he was there. Look.' And she held up a picture of a house with a family inside, all drawn in felt tip and neatly coloured in.

Lee threw herself back in the chair. 'Oh my God,' she moaned, rubbing her hands down her face. 'I can't believe this. I can't believe you left my child with them.'

'But they're nice people.'

'I hardly know them, Mils! Yes, they're sweet. Does that mean I just give them my kid while I go to the shops? No!' Her eyes were blazing, her voice fierce – all her bitterness and disappointment and anger from earlier intermingling now with fear.

Mila looked upset. 'I'm . . . I'm sorry, I didn't realize that was the wrong thing to do. I thought I was doing the right thing by not taking him out in the cold.'

Lee sighed, hiding her face behind her fingers. There was no point in going on about it. Mila just didn't get it. She wasn't a mother; she didn't understand that danger existed in the everyday, the commonplace, that nothing and no one could be trusted. 'Ugh.'

There was a long, awkward silence.

She heard the rustle of clothes as Mila got up. 'Look, he's fast asleep. I read him a story as soon as I got back and he went straight off.' There was a pause. 'I'm really sorry, Lee. You know I'd never intentionally do anything to—' Her voice cracked, a small sob of her own escaping her as Lee continued to avoid looking at her. 'You get to bed. I'll see myself out.'

Lee heard her sniff, her footsteps receding on the floor, the creak of the stairs as she ran down. *Great!* She flung herself back in the chair in angry frustration now that her friend was upset too. She knew she should call after her and tell her it was okay, that she knew she'd acted in good faith even if it was a mistake, that she didn't want them to fall out over it. But the words wouldn't come. Was it not enough that her big night had ended not in glory but despair? To come home to the fright of finding her son had been left with near-strangers . . . Just the thought of it made her pulse spike, her chest tighten, her stomach dive . . . If anything should happen to him. He was all she had in this world.

She listened to the sound of Mila's footsteps in the hall, the click of the door, the gentle jangling of chains outside the window as she unlocked her bike . . .

She sighed, knowing this would be something else to have to deal with tomorrow, soothing Mila's hurt feelings. It wasn't like Lee didn't know her friend had done her best. She knew perfectly well Mila loved Jasper.

Tears were streaming down her face. 'Ugh – *fuck*!' she cried, railing against herself. She was tired and emotional. She just needed today to be over.

She went downstairs and put the chains and locks on. She was throwing over the last bolt when she heard the knock and she paused, knowing her best friend could never sleep on a fight, that she'd be sobbing too. She worked her way back through all the chains and bolts again, and opened the door—

Sam blinked back at her, seeing the sheets of tears skinning her cheeks, her mascara smudged, shoulders up by her ears. His eyes tracked over her face, seeing her despair, and he stepped in, wordlessly gathering her in his arms and kissing her. Hungry, sad, desperate kisses over her mouth, her cheeks, her neck, leaving her breathless. They staggered backwards, joined, into the hall, Sam kicking the door shut. She reached back with a flailing arm as he clasped her against him, trying to find the doorway for the spare room.

He pulled back and shook his head.

'But—' she gasped.

He shook his head again. And without a word, he grabbed her under her arms, hoisting her up, her legs instinctively wrapping around his waist. He kissed her again, walking her along the hall and up the stairs.

'In there,' she panted, kissing his neck and pointing towards the sofa as they passed by the kitchen/living room door.

'No.'

'But—'

He silenced her with another kiss, carrying her up the next flight. She pulled away as he neared Jasper's bedroom, worried he had heard the door slam, but the bedroom door was closed.

'You can't stay,' she whispered, still kissing his neck as he carried her into her bedroom. 'He comes in in the night.'

'I thought that was only when you had a nightmare,' he murmured, groaning slightly as she kissed behind his ear.

She looked back at him and blinked. 'Yes.'

His eyes locked hers, holding them fast. 'You won't be having any nightmares tonight.'

Chapter Twenty

They lay still, finally, their skin beaded with sweat, limbs intertwined and heavy. She rested her head against his chest, feeling the steady thump of his heart. Her hand brushed over his skin gently, tenderly.

'I thought . . .' she whispered, finding she was unable to finish the sentence. Unable to say Veronika's name.

'I know.' He swallowed, staying quiet for a moment. 'You were supposed to think that.' His hand brushed her long hair off her shoulder. 'My great masterplan for getting through tonight.' The words rang with a sardonic tone.

'But why? It was cruel.'

He took a deep breath, as though steadying himself. 'Lee, there's the notion of seeing you, and then there's the reality.'

She frowned, one hand plucking lightly at the hairs on his navel. 'I don't know what that means.'

'It means that resolve doesn't mean very much when you're standing three feet away. It means that you are impossible' – he looked back at her with burning eyes – 'to walk away from.'

She rested her cheek on his chest, watching him. 'I thought you didn't want to walk away from me. Wasn't that the whole problem? You wanted more and I didn't.'

'Yes. And then I didn't.'

'Because of what happened in the cafe?'

He hesitated. 'Yes.'

At least he was honest, but still, the admission felt like a punch. Her brokenness repelled him. Instinctively her body curled, becoming smaller, but she felt his body stretch against her, forcing her outwards, longer again. 'Look, I know you're carrying something, Lee. I don't know what it is but it's . . . heavy for you. I can see it.' He sighed. 'And I wanted to be the guy that makes it all okay for you again, I really did, but when I saw . . . when I saw how it really is for you . . . I just wasn't sure if I could do it.' He looked at her. 'You've got PTSD, right?'

The frankness of the question shocked her. This wasn't the kind of pillow-talk she was used to.

'I know you have,' he said, before she could deny it, beginning to stroke her arm gently. 'I know that eighty per cent of war correspondents come back with some form of trauma. That it's worse for photojournalists than reporters because you're looking, looking all the time at what's happening.'

She realized the pads of her fingertips were pressing against his chest in a rhythmic pattern, self-soothing. 'Well, *I* didn't know any of this. How come you're such an expert?'

'Because after your party at the gallery, I went home and Googled you.'

She stared back at him, amazed he would even admit that. 'I thought you were going on with Liam?'

He gave a bark of scorn. 'Right. Like I was in any fit state to go out.' He sighed, but she could feel the tension in his outward breath. 'I was a mess, knowing you were with him.' He was quiet for a moment and she splayed her hand over his chest in a silent token of apology. 'On the other hand, I was also weirdly *glad*. I knew it meant he wouldn't last.'

'Really? Were you certain he wouldn't be back here tonight?'

He pinned her with his eyes again. 'Yes. I knew you'd done to him what you tried to do to me. The quickest way out of your life is getting in that bed.'

She arched an eyebrow. '*That* bed? How do you know the same doesn't apply to this one?'

'Because I know you've never let anyone up here. I'm the only one.'

'You don't know that.'

He stared at her. Still. Certain. 'I do.'

She felt her heart accelerate, the butterflies still in her stomach even though he was here, beneath her. He seemed to see past her alibis and excuses. She looked away, unable to hold his gaze. 'So the other day, when you kissed me?'

'I hadn't planned it. I just came to return your coat,' he shrugged. 'But when I saw you trying to explain, when I saw how hard it was for you to put words to it . . . I didn't think I could be what you needed.'

'So why are you here now, then?'

He was quiet for a moment. 'Because I knew what you were thinking about me and Veronika. It was what you were supposed to be thinking.' His fingertips pressed against her shoulder. 'And I couldn't stand it.'

She didn't say anything for several moments, her heart pounding too fast, emotions surging up and threatening to burst free from her. 'I'm not used to feeling jealous,' she said quietly, laying her head down again, her cheek against his chest.

'Of course not. You don't let anyone hang around long enough for you to actually catch feelings for them – except perhaps Harry—'

'No, don't,' she whispered, stiffening against him. 'Please don't mention him. Not now.'

He was quiet beneath her, his hand stroking her back languidly. '. . . What have I got myself into with you?' he whispered. 'You've scrambled my brain, Lee. Why can't I just let you go?'

She turned to look up at him. 'I'm not that abnormal, I'm really not. I mean, apart from the odd nightmare . . . and stuff.'

He smiled. 'You're not exactly the girl next door either! It's hard to reconcile the person I read about with the woman I met in a hospital toilet, you know?'

She was quiet for a long moment, knowing he could feel how her heart was banging against his ribs. 'Well, *you* didn't exactly correspond to first impressions either,' she said, lightly. 'Hot Sinter's actually a multi-million-selling author?'

'Oh no. I'm not an author. Trust me, I'm just an impoverished artist who got lucky.' He reached down and kissed the top of her head. She turned up to face him, their eyes locking, and she felt it begin again, the electricity surge between them. She wriggled up him a little and they kissed, the kiss becoming deeper and more urgent, her leg wrapping around him.

'Well, guess what,' she whispered, her lips inches from his neck.

'What?' His voice was a croak as she rolled on top of him.

'. . . You're about to get lucky again.'

'You've got to go,' she whispered, nudging him, unused to her bed being dwarfed by masculine proportions. He was sleeping face down, his feet practically touching each of the bottom corners, his arm heavy across her stomach. Oh, but he looked so good though . . . 'It's almost seven. Jasper'll be getting up any minute.'

He opened one eye sleepily. 'No.' He closed it again.

Lee's mouth dropped open. 'What do you mean, *no*?' she hissed. 'He can't see you here.'

'Why not?' His words were almost obscured by the pillow.

'Because I don't want him . . . getting ideas. He's at a tricky age.'

He took a deep inhale and held it for several seconds, before shifting himself up onto his elbows and looking back at her. 'He likes me.'

'That doesn't mean he wants to see you naked in his mama's bed.'

He gave a rueful grin, dropping his head. Lee's gaze slid over to the soft bulge of muscles in his shoulders. 'Fair enough. But is it really such a disaster for him to see a man in his house cooking breakfast?'

'Who says you're cooking breakfast?'

He leaned over and kissed her lingeringly on the lips, silencing her arguments. 'I do.' And without another word, he threw back the duvet and walked, butt naked, into her bathroom. He stopped at the door. 'Just as well you have an en-suite,' he grinned, shutting the door behind him.

Lee gave an astonished laugh, not quite able to believe what was going on. She sank back into the pillows, one arm slung across her face as her mind ran a replay of last night's events. She could still feel the shock in her body at finding him standing there, on her doorstep, the explosion of butterflies in her stomach as he'd stepped into her, kissed her, carried her, thrown her onto the bed . . .

Oh God. She realized she must look a state; her mascara was probably halfway down her neck by now. She reached onto the bedside table and put her glasses on, checking her reflection in the phone camera. Hmm, could have been worse. She had definite panda eyes, but with her mussed hair, it all luckily lent her a sexy, smudged look. And it wasn't like he'd been complaining.

She heard the shower being turned on and listened to the sound of the water hitting the tray, then muffling as he stepped in, hitting his beautiful body instead. She imagined him in there, the water running over his skin. She could hardly believe he was behind that door. That she could just go in there . . .

'Mama?'

She gave a gasp, her hand pressing to her chest in alarm as Jasper's sleep-ruffled head peered around the door.

'You didn't have a nightmare?' He seemed bewildered by the fact, as though these interruptions defined his own nights as well as hers.

She gave a smile. 'No darling. No nightmares last night.'

He shuffled in, still sleepy, and climbed onto her bed. He curled up on his side, where Sam had been lying, and she leaned over, kissing his hair, his temple, his cheek, marvelling all over again at his utter perfection. Every day it floored her.

'Did *you* sleep well?' she whispered, resting her cheek against his.

'Mm-hmm.' He sounded like he could go back to sleep again – which wasn't an option, she realized with alarm. She did not want Sam coming back in here in all his truly magnificent naked glory.

'Are you excited about decorating Mr Kuiper's tree today?'

That woke him up. He sat up with a gasp, his eyes wide. 'We're decorating his Christmas tree?'

'Well, I thought it would be a nice thing to do, seeing as

he's all on his own and he's too old to do it himself. I've got to do some shopping for him anyway as he's getting low on milk, so I thought we could buy a tree too – just a little one, mind – and make it look all Christmassy for him. But obviously I'll need your help because you're the tree-decorating expert.'

'He can have the snowflakes we made yesterday!' Jasper said excitedly.

'Brilliant idea. Okay, well, why don't you get dressed – and *make your bed* – and I'll have my shower—'

He looked at the bathroom door, realizing the water was already running. 'It's on.'

'Yes. Yes, it is.' Her brain struggled to find an excuse. 'I'm just getting the water nice and hot. I felt a bit chilly this morning so I want it to be super-hot for when I get in.' Please God, she thought, don't let Sam start singing.

'. . . Okay,' Jasper shrugged, jumping off the bed and scampering towards his own room, oblivious to Sam's clothes discarded on the floor. He stopped at the door. 'Can I wear my Spider-Man outfit?'

'Only if you promise to put thermals on underneath. It's still cold out there.'

'Okay.' He disappeared from sight and Lee gave a sigh of relief. She heard the water turn off in the bathroom and several moments later Sam emerged, a towel wrapped around his hips.

'. . . What?' he asked, as she threw herself back on the pillows and laughed. 'What'd I do?'

'Sssh,' she whispered as they tiptoed down the hall towards Jasper's room, keeping him back with a hand against his chest. He picked up her hand instead and kissed it. She shot him a look but she couldn't get rid of her grin. 'Stop it,' she mouthed, eyes widening as he began sucking on her finger. 'You are outrageous,' she whispered, pulling her hand back, unable to stop laughing.

'Mama?'

'Hey Jazz,' she said, recovering and walking into his room, shutting the door behind her so that Sam could tiptoe past unseen. 'I've come to check you've made your bed. Oh! And you actually have!' Today was full of little surprises, it seemed.

He was rifling through his dressing-up box for the Spider-Man mask, it not being enough to be dressed shoulder-to-toe in blue and red webbing. She walked over to the window and opened his curtains. His room gave onto the garden at the back, the grass frosted and stiff like iced Christmas cake peaks. She saw a magpie cleaning its feathers in the sycamore tree. A cat – Pabe's elusive, haughty pet, Toetsen – was slinking along the back walls, unbothered by either the cold or the drop.

She turned back to face him, taking a deep breath. 'So, Jazz Man. Do you remember last weekend when we went to get that book signed by mama's friend, Sam? You remember Sam?'

Jasper found the mask. 'He drew me the koala.'

'Yes, that's right.' She had forgotten that already. 'He drew that lovely koala just for you.' She bit her lip, watching as he turned the mask the right way in again. It was in a rolled mess from the last time he'd taken it off. 'Well, anyway, he and I were talking and we thought, wouldn't it be fun if we all had breakfast together? He's a brilliant cook, apparently, which would make a nice change for you and me to eat something edible for once instead of my usual horrors.'

Jasper glanced up at her. 'Okay.' He was more interested in his mask than his stomach right now.

'Right.' She'd expected that to be harder. 'Okay, well, he's downstairs, just so you know. I didn't want you to be frightened or anything like that. He's our friend.'

'I'm not scared. I like him. He's got kind eyes, like Sinter.'

'. . . Has he?' she asked, feeling another bubble of hysterical laughter. 'Oh, well, I hadn't noticed that. I shall have to pay more attention in future.'

She watched as Jasper pulled on the mask so that only his eyes and mouth were exposed. He blinked back at her.

'Very cool,' she smiled. 'Best boy *and* best Spider-Man in the whole city.' She shrugged. 'Is there no end to your talents?'

Together they went downstairs, the smells and sounds emanating through the kitchen door telling them that breakfast was already underway.

'Sam, hi!' she said brightly, bracing her stomach for its usual flip as he turned back to face them, looking Saturday-morning incongruous in last night's dinner shirt and trousers, his velvet jacket draped across the kitchen chair. It was not helpful to have him looking so good.

'Spider-Man!' Sam pressed the spatula to his chest. 'It would be an honour to cook for you. Thank you for keeping our city safe.'

Lee laughed, looking down at Jasper. He looked back up at her with excited eyes. 'Do you think we should tell him?' she asked.

Jasper nodded solemnly. 'I'm not Spider-Man!' he cried, dramatically pulling off the mask and making his dark hair stand on end. 'I'm Jasper!'

'Jasper?! Oh my goodness, that is crazy! Is it really you?' He knelt down as Jasper ran over to prove it. Gently, Sam prodded his cheeks and inspected his hair. 'It really is, isn't it? That's amazing. I thought you were the real Spider-Man back there!' He held his hand up for a high five. 'It's good to see you again.'

'I've still got my koala picture.'

'Well, I'm glad about that, because it's the only one in the world.' He rose to standing again. 'Tell me, do you like pancakes?'

Jasper nodded.

'Do you like them with strawberries and cream, or banana and maple syrup?'

'I don't know. I've never had that before.'

'Well, given that I don't have any bananas or cream, it might have to be strawberries and maple syrup?' Lee suggested.

Sam stared at her for a moment. 'Interesting combination,' he quipped, before shrugging. 'Let's go with that.'

'Can I help?' asked Jasper.

'Sure you can. You can pull the tops off the strawberries for me if you like?'

Lee stood at the island, watching them both as Jasper climbed up onto the kitchen stool and Sam passed him the bowl of berries, the two of them chatting easily as though they did this every Saturday morning. It was almost too beautiful to watch, her son welcoming this man without hesitation. It was everything she had feared.

'Coffee. Strong and black, as I recall,' Sam said, handing her one, deliberately holding the cup a moment too long and drawing her gaze to his, showing her with a single look that he knew what she was thinking.

'Thanks.'

He winked, turning back to Jasper again. 'Those are perfect.'

Feeling surprisingly redundant, she wandered over to the window, pulling back the curtains and allowing the day to fall in.

'Oh my God!' she gasped. 'Jasper, look!'

He scrambled off the stool and shot over to her, looking out of the large square windows onto the scene outside. Sam came and joined them too, watching a few early birds skating on the canal. Several more people were sitting on the edge of the dock and tying their boots.

'Can we, mama? Oh please!'

She scanned the length of the canal she could see between the bridges at either end, looking for holes or thinner patches of ice, but it looked reassuringly opaque and strong. 'I think it should be okay,' she murmured.

'I'll go check, as soon as we've eaten breakfast,' Sam said, squeezing Jasper's shoulder and returning to the pancakes, pouring the first disc into the pan. 'But it looks good from here.'

'Do you skate?' Jasper asked, trotting after him like a foal.

'Oh yes. It's my favourite sport. I grew up doing it as often as I could. My father skated in the last Elfstedentocht.'

'No way!' Jasper gasped. Even at the tender age of five, he had been indoctrinated into Dutch folklore.

'Seriously?' Lee asked, equally amazed. It was the Dutch equivalent of being an Olympian, if not more so – plenty of the Olympic ice-skating team had announced they would prioritize an Elfstedentocht over a Games.

'Yes.' He took the first pancake off the heat and placed it on a plate, before pouring the next. He looked back at Jasper. 'I wasn't much older than you are now when he raced; I remember watching him with my brother, the weather was so bad . . . We had made a banner for him, and we cheered so hard when he passed us that my brother lost his voice for three days afterwards.'

Jasper looked rapt as he knelt on the stool.

'Do you think it'll happen this year?' Lee asked him, sinking onto the sill. Every night now, as the high pressure remained stuck over the country, the growing possibility of it being staged was on the news; the weather forecast had become a national obsession, everyone praying for that perfect balance – not so warm it might thaw, not so cold it might snow.

Sam raised his hands in prayer towards the ceiling. 'Please God! It is the event I've been waiting for my entire life.'

Jasper laughed excitedly at Sam's grown-up excitement.

Lee watched him, seeing his passion too. It had been more than twenty years since the last Elfstedentocht. 'Would you skate in it? Liam said you were the skating prodigy at uni.'

'Well, I've made a point of keeping up my membership with the Frisian Eleven Cities Association and I've got my KNSB licence so I'm eligible to compete, but I doubt I'd do that well. The guys in the competitive race are elite athletes, training for hours every day. But just to be part of the pack, even if it was right at the back . . .' He made the prayer sign again.

'Can we come and watch you?' Jasper asked, drumming his toes on the seat. 'I'll make a banner and I'll shout so loudly I'll lose my voice. I won't mind.'

Sam chuckled, bringing the last pancakes off the heat. 'You're sure? What would mama say?'

Lee rolled her eyes. 'Mama would be glad of some peace,' she quipped.

He placed the last pancake in the pan. Lee heard it sizzle but the sound had become background, for staring out the window she saw a familiar figure walking down the street. She was silhouetted against the strong, low light, but the neat figure and drum-tum – like a snake who'd swallowed a football – told her it could only be one person.

'I'll just be a sec,' Lee said, getting up and glancing over at the boys cooking. Sam was teaching Jasper how to shake the pancake free of the pan.

She was coming down the stairs as the letterbox was pushed open and a letter dropped through. Lee picked it up distractedly and opened the door, for once not having to deal with bolts and chains first; Sam's unexpected arrival last night had put paid to that.

'Gisele?' she called, having to shield her eyes against the blinding glare of the vanilla winter sun. 'Hi!' Why hadn't she knocked?

Gisele turned on the steps in surprise, looking less than happy to have been accosted. Over her shoulder, a few more people were coming out of their homes and standing by the canalside, looking down excitedly onto the ice. This was one of the smaller canals and she could only imagine how busy it would be soon on the big canals, Herengracht, Keizergracht and Prinsengracht. 'Oh Lee, you're up. I didn't want to disturb you.'

'We're always up; no such thing as a lie-in in this house,' Lee grinned. 'What a morning!'

'I know,' Gisele smiled wistfully. 'The entire city's going to be on the ice today. Well, almost the entire city.' She patted her belly gently.

'Jasper's beside himself with excitement, although God only knows where our skates are. I'm going to have to hunt high and low to find them.' She stepped back a little. 'Do you want to come in?'

'Oh, no, thank you – I can't stop.'

Lee's eyes narrowed. Why not? Where else could she possibly have to be at 8 a.m. on a Saturday morning? 'Are you sure? Is everything okay?' Her eyes fell to the bump. 'Are you all right?'

'Yes, I'm fine, the baby's fine.'

'Cunningham?'

Gisele gave that little laugh she did whenever she heard her husband called by his surname. 'Well, I haven't heard anything, but he told me no news is good news out there, so . . .' She shrugged.

'Yes, right. Sure,' Lee agreed, still sensing something was up. Gisele looked nervous, jumpy, and she seemed to be having difficulty holding Lee's gaze.

'I just wanted to drop that by to you.' She indicated the letter, limp, in Lee's hand and Lee almost started as she suddenly realized what it was she was holding. She had been distracted when it had fallen through the letterbox, more surprised by why Gisele hadn't knocked . . . The letter was in a bright white utilitarian envelope, the sort used in offices across the world. No thick stationery cards, no fountain-pen ink. Just Cunningham's biro scrawl spelling out her name on the front. 'I . . . found it. Yesterday.'

Lee's gaze flicked up to her, hearing the hesitation. Yesterday? Lee had been waiting for this for over a week. 'Oh.' She pressed her fingers against it. It felt thin between her fingers. Everything he had to say compressed onto one sheet of paper, it seemed. 'Well, thanks.'

Gisele licked her lips. 'I'm so sorry. I had no idea it was even in the house.'

'No, of course not . . . Where was it?'

Another pause. 'It had fallen down the side of the bed. Harry must have left it on his side table and forgotten to bring it downstairs to post.'

'Yes. Sounds like Cunningham,' Lee lied. He was the most organized person she knew. In the field, bombs could be raining down upon his head, but his phone would always be in his right-hand flak jacket pocket, his pen and notebook in his left one.

How long had Gisele known about it, she wondered? Had she read it? Had she spent every night since he'd left, on her own, staring at it, wanting to? What torments must she have gone through trying to guess its contents? It was bad enough for Lee and at least she knew something of the story.

'Anyway . . .' Gisele hesitated, looking uncomfortable. 'I thought I'd bring it over as soon as I could. I don't know if there's anything important in it, but . . .' Her voice trailed off.

Lee felt a shot of adrenaline. 'Oh, I doubt it,' she said. 'Knowing Cunningham it's some old IOU.'

They both gave forced laughs that fooled neither one.

Gisele turned to go. 'Oh, and I know I've said it before, but it really was so kind of you to have me over last weekend. I know I'd said I was fine about spending the holiday on my own, but the truth was, I'd been dreading it so much. So thank you.'

'We loved it too; we were so pleased to have you. I think for Jasper especially, it can get pretty boring when it's just him and me on our own all the time.'

Just then – as if on cue – a shout and some laughter escaped from upstairs. The shout had been very definitely male and adult.

Gisele looked back at Lee questioningly – it was early, still; too early for most breakfast dates. Only overnight guests would be in the house at this hour. '. . . Well, anyway, I should get on. I've got the interior designer coming over to look at the nursery today and the house is a *wreck*.'

Lee knew that it absolutely wasn't. 'Sure. Well, listen, thanks for bringing this over, I appreciate it.'

'No problem. Let's have coffee soon.'

'Yes definitely, I'd love that.' Lee waved, knowing they wouldn't. Whatever stilted rapprochement had formed between them in these odd few weeks since Cunningham's abrupt departure, she sensed it ending now. Their reason for contact had closed.

She gently shut the door and leaned it against it, staring at the letter. It was clear Gisele had lied about having it. Had the guilt of accepting their hospitality last weekend forced her into a fit of scruples?

She turned the letter over in her hand. It had only her name, not her surname or address, on the front and at a glance she knew this wasn't a letter that Cunningham had intended to post. It had clearly been left out for Gisele to distribute.

There was no sign of it having been opened that she could see. Lee stared at its unthreatening blankness, knowing that it was anything but. Cunningham didn't write letters. He wasn't moved to sentimentality or nostalgia. If he'd written, it was because he had something to say. To share. To confess.

She felt light-headed, cursing him all over again for whatever the damned hell it was he was doing. Just for a few hours, she'd forgotten all about him; she'd shut him out and let in a little happiness, someone she thought perhaps she might trust. Why did he have to take that away from her? Because he would. Whatever that letter said, she knew there was an earthquake inside that envelope – something that was going to shake the ground beneath her feet and send her flying, all over again.

'Everything okay?'

She looked up to see Sam standing at the top of the stairs, her blue gingham frilled apron on over his trousers and shirt, a whisk in his hand. Was this what had prompted their laughter? She wasn't sure she'd ever seen a man look sexier.

She forced herself to smile, putting the letter on the shelf of the coat rack. Whatever Cunningham wanted to say, he'd waited six years to tell her. She could wait a little longer. This morning was the happiest she'd been in years. Couldn't she have a few moments more of pretending that theirs really was a normal family, that she was just the girl next door after all?

'Yes,' she stammered, forcing Cunningham to the farthest reaches of her mind again, a long-standing habit of hers. 'It's all fine. I was just collecting the post.'

Chapter Twenty-One

'Okay, hold onto mama.' Lee held onto Jasper's hand as they took their first tentative glides along the ice. There was something especially thrilling about skating on natural ice, knowing there was a dark body of water beneath their feet and not the concrete dish of an ice rink.

Jasper's fingers gripped hers tightly, though he was a far better skater than her. She'd first put him on skates when he was three, like all the Dutch. She – having not skated till she was in her teens – would never be such a natural.

'Whoa,' she laughed, windmilling her arms as they pushed out towards the middle of the canal, trying to avoid all the other people doing the same, albeit with more grace than them. The whole street had come out, it seemed, people setting up chairs on the ice to either rest on or get their boots on. A few people – probably tourists – didn't have skates and were trying to glide in their shoes, with predictable results, whilst the locals swept up and down in easy, languid strokes. An older woman had set up a large urn on a table on the jetty and was serving up hot chocolate with marshmallows; some other people were coming over with tins of *koek* cake too and setting them down beside the cups for her. Lee was sure the lady lived about three buildings up on the left; she walked past most days with a small white dog.

'Jasper, look, there's Mr Kuiper,' she said, seeing Pabe standing at his living room window, watching them all. They waved, Jasper almost losing his balance in the process. Pabe waved back, laughing, but Lee felt a pang of sadness that he had to watch it from behind a pane of glass. Even just to come down to the water's edge and watch from there would be something, to be part of the crowd, the noise, the spectacle . . . The entire city was quite literally *at play*.

They traced a large oval, taking care to avoid twigs that had fallen onto the ice from overhanging trees, gradually becoming more confident as they went. They did a figure of eight, making their turns tighter each time, laughing when Jasper went to catch her hand as he skated up to her and missed, sailing on for another hundred metres.

It was odd skating alongside the moored boats, able to peer through the windows, their hulls gripped in solid clutches. The residents of the biggest houseboat had put speakers on their roof and were playing Christmas carols, no one minding as tired skaters stopped for a rest on the bows. One man skated past Lee with a pickaxe around his neck – to break the ice should he fall in – which did nothing for her nerves.

She wondered whether Sam was skating as well. His skates were back at his place, naturally, and he'd needed to go back and get changed out of his dinner suit at last. But she had resisted his suggestion of meeting up later. Even though her every instinct was wanting to set a time when she knew she could be with him again, she wouldn't do it; even though she knew they had gone beyond this being a one-night thing, she still couldn't risk Jasper becoming attached when they didn't know . . . when in all likelihood . . .

Still, her eyes naturally looked for him, trying to find him in the crowds and hoping maybe he was going to pull another one of his surprises and disregard her wishes and just turn up anyway. She did double-takes every time someone glided past who looked like they knew what they were doing.

'What do you think? Shall we try Prinsengracht?' she asked as they did another lap of Bloemgracht. 'It'll be a lot bigger over there, we'll have some more space.'

They skated under the bridge and took a right turn onto the main drag of one of the grandest canals in the city. It was vastly bigger – much longer and wider – but also a lot more crowded. There were fewer children, and the speed and skill levels were greater as teenagers raced each other, as club members sped past in the familiar pose of hands behind their backs, bent forward from the hips. Older people were generally skating in the genteel long gliding style – *schoonrijden* – of a bygone age.

'Whoa!' Lee laughed again as they moved into the flow of skating traffic. The surface of the ice was chopped up, sliced into piles of shavings, calling for more skill than perhaps they had. One audacious salesman had wheeled his coffee cart onto the ice and set up shop in the middle, with people standing around drinking and taking a rest. Someone else had dragged a Christmas tree into the middle of the ice and people were skating around that like it was a handbag on a dancefloor.

The Prinsengracht was long and she was tempted to turn left onto Keizergracht and Herengracht too, to glide around the city like it was a playground. But Jasper's legs were still only little, and they contented themselves with a few long loops before heading back to the cosy confines of Bloemgracht.

She felt her neighbourhood's arms close around them as they passed under the bridge again, back into the orbit of the Christmas carols and the slower, jerkier pace of the baby canal.

'What do you think?' she asked Jasper as they finally came to a stop by the jetty. 'Have we earned ourselves a hot chocolate?'

'Yes!' he cried, his cheeks pink between his scarf and bobble hat, his eyes burning like bright coals.

They sat on the jetty and Lee tugged off his boots, finding their shoes scattered at random in the pile that had built up since they'd left.

'Phew, I'm going to be stiff tomorrow!' she said, holding his snow boot upright so that he could jam his socked foot back into it. She started untying her own boots, getting one off, when she glanced up and saw Lenka coming out of her apartment. With a jolt, Lee realized she owed her a thank you – and Mils an apology.

She scrambled to stand up. 'Jazz, I'm just going to thank Lenka for looking after you last night. You stay by the bench there, where I can see you, okay?'

'But—'

'Lenka!' she said, calling over as she saw her start to head down the street.

Lenka turned, looking surprised – not to mention cold. She was woefully underdressed in a thin jacket and no hat or gloves, and there certainly wasn't any weight on her to keep her warm. Was she mad? Sad, certainly. She cut a forlorn figure, too stooped for such a young woman, as though she had the weight of the world on her shoulders.

'Hi!' Lee panted, hobbling over with an ice skate on one foot and just her sock on the other. 'Hey.'

'Hello, Lee,' Lenka said in her strong Eastern European accent; Lee had asked where she was from when they had first met, but to her shame she had forgotten.

'I'm so glad I caught you.' She gave an exhale, trying to

collect herself. 'I just wanted to say a massive thank you for looking after Jasper last night.'

'Oh—'

'I nearly died when my friend Mila told me what had happened. I really hope it didn't put you out too much?'

'Oh . . . no,' she said, but there was hesitation in her words.

'You know I would never just presume . . . I mean, Mila's a wonderful friend and she means well, but I don't think she appreciated what a big ask it was to burden you with Jasper on your Friday night. You didn't have plans, I hope?'

'No. It was all right. No problem for me.'

'Good. Thank God.' Lee smiled, pressing a hand to her chest. 'I was mortified when she told me. I was going to come over later with something to say thank you.'

'Oh, no,' Lenka said quickly. 'Is not necessary. He is lovely boy.'

'Gus didn't mind, did he?'

'. . . No. No problem.' Lenka glanced to her left.

'Well, I promise I will never impose on you again—'

'Hello, Lee.'

She looked right to see Gus standing by their front door, a cup in one hand, the other resting on the door frame. Talk of the devil!

'Gus, hi!' she said, realizing she was going to have to say it all over again. 'I was just thanking Lenka for you two looking after Jasper last night. I was so horrified when my friend told me what she'd done, imposing on you like that. She just doesn't *think* sometimes. I really hope it didn't put you out.'

Gus gave a casual shrug to match his casual smile. 'It didn't. We had a great time with the little guy. He's very cute.'

'Well, thank you. That's very kind.' She wasn't sure what more she could add to her apology and thanks, and a small silence bloomed.

Gus looked at his girlfriend. 'Aren't you late for work?'

Lenka looked at Lee apologetically. 'Yes, I am sorry. I must go.'

Lee winced, seeing the friction between them, remembering their overheard argument when she'd been over at Pabe's. 'Oh. I'm sorry, I didn't mean to keep you.' Lee heard herself and inwardly groaned – over-thanking, now over-apologizing. 'Don't let me make you late.'

Lenka gave a shy smile and Lee smiled sadly back, wondering if this poor girl – so timid, quiet, pretty – had any idea at all that her charming boyfriend was cheating on her.

A sudden whine made them all jump as the Christmas carols were abruptly switched off and several further whining sounds suggested a PA system was being switched on. Lee turned to see a portly man in a dark-green knitted jumper climbing onto the roof of the big houseboat, a microphone in his hand.

'Ladies and gentlemen of Bloemgracht,' he said, one arm in the air and turning a slow circle, ensuring everyone could see him. 'Can I have your attention please?' He completed another full turn, waiting for the skaters to stop skating, people to stop talking. 'We have some exciting news.' Slowly, the activity on the ice came to an expectant stop. 'It has just been announced that—'

A murmur rippled through the crowd, and in the near distance, just over the next row of canalhouses, coming from Prinsengracht, an almighty roar erupted.

'*IT! GIET! OAN!*'

Lee felt the hairs on her arms rise on end as every single person on the canal, on the cobbles and in the houses screamed with delight, their arms in the air, jumping up and down dementedly. Lee's hands flew to her mouth, as she looked over at Jasper fully throwing himself into the celebrations too, and she realized what this meant. It had been twenty years in the making, but Sam's dream was about to come true. The Elfstedentocht was on!

Chapter Twenty-Two

The doorbell went. Lee stopped chopping the onion and hesitated.

'This is getting to be a habit,' she said several moments later, as Sam stared back at her. On her doorstep again.

'Yes,' he agreed unapologetically, stepping into her and clasping her head with his hands, his eyes blazing. 'It is.' He kissed her, not caring who saw. And there were plenty to see. The entire neighbourhood was out on the ice, the excitement of canal-skating now having turned into an Elfstedentocht street party.

He pulled away. 'Damn, I missed you. Was that really only four hours?'

She laughed. 'Yes!' But she felt exactly the same. She closed the door behind him, seeing how his movements seemed charged with an electric current, more powerful, channelled. 'So, good morning?' she asked blandly. 'You got changed, I see.'

He looked back at her in disbelief. 'Have you heard the news?'

She laughed again, unable to keep up the charade in the face of his excitement. 'Sam, *of course* I've heard the news!' She motioned to the door and the party going on behind it. 'The entire country's heard the news!'

'Woo-hooooo!' he roared, picking up her suddenly and whirling her around the hallway, so many times she felt dizzy. He held her above his head, looking up at her. 'I can't believe it. My whole life I've been waiting for this. I didn't think it would ever come.'

'It's amazing,' she laughed, feeling lifted by his joy.

'My father's been in tears all day. My father! He's a goddam potato farmer!' he laughed. 'Almost *nothing* makes that man cry!'

'Sam?'

They both looked up and saw Jasper standing at the top of the stairs, his eyes shining brightly too.

Sam lowered her to the ground and held his arms out. 'Jasper, did you hear?'

'*It giet oan!*' Jasper hollered, tearing down the stairs and into Sam's arms, being spun around too, just like his mama.

Lee laughed as she watched them, her hands to her mouth as she saw her son's unbridled delight. There was no doubt this had come alive for him because of Sam. Had it just been the two of them, hearing the news on the TV, it would have been something theoretical, a notional excitement, like the national football team getting into the World Cup final – fun, but they ultimately couldn't care less either way.

But Sam was going to be competing in this. History was going to be made. This could very well be the last Elfstedentocht ever and he was going to be part of it.

They went upstairs into the kitchen, Jasper on Sam's hip, the two of them chanting '*It giet oan! It giet oan!*'

'So you do cook?' he mused, setting Jasper down and seeing the meal prepped on the worktop.

'This is for Pabe, next door,' she said, picking up the knife again. 'I'm just helping him out till his new carer comes in two weeks. The poor man was living on microwave meals. He needs better nutrition than that at his age.' She glanced up to find Sam was grinning at her. 'What?'

'You just can't help yourself, can you? You've always got to be helping people.'

'Most of my friends would consider this attempted manslaughter,' she said, crushing some garlic.

He leaned against the counter, brushing a hand against her cheek. 'You're extraordinary.'

She checked to make sure Jasper wasn't watching. He wasn't. He was trying – yet again – to get his Scalextric cars to connect with the track.

'Do you want a coffee?' she asked, moving away to fill the machine with water. She felt his eyes on her back.

'Sure.'

'So when are you leaving?' The race was set for Monday, with a predicted low front beginning to move in on Tuesday and, with it, slightly milder temperatures. It would be a race against time to get the event completed before any coming thaw, and the entire country was gripped by a simultaneous joy and terror.

'Now. Within the hour. I need to get back home, get on the ice, get my head in the right place, sharpen the blades . . .'

She opened the fridge. 'I still can't believe you're going to be in it. It's unreal.'

'I know.' His eyes were shining brightly, almost feverish.

'Jasper wants you to wear bright colours so he can always see you on the screen. We're going to be *screaming* at the television.'

'Well, actually – that's why I came over.' He reached for her hand, catching her as she passed by with the milk and drawing her closer to him. Their bodies pressed together as he looked down at her. 'I was wondering if you'd both come along and be there, to cheer me on in person.'

Her mouth opened. 'But—'

'It'd mean everything to me.'

She stared at him, excuses reflexively flooding her mind. 'But where would we stay? Every hotel and room in the region will be booked already. The country's gone nuts.'

'Stay with me. At my parents' farm. They live near Leeuwarden. And don't worry, you wouldn't be in a room with me,' he said quickly, anticipating her every protest. He glanced at Jasper, still engrossed on the floor. 'For one thing, *I* need to get the sleep.' He kissed her hand, locking eyes with her and making her stomach somersault, just like that. 'But there's plenty of room. You and Jasper could be in one together so he wouldn't be alone in a strange house.'

Lee stared at him, hardly able to believe he had nailed her primary objection on the head.

'Well . . . oh God . . .' Her mind raced, trying to think of logistics, obstacles . . . 'We can't come today,' she said. 'We're going over to see Pabe this afternoon and decorate his Christmas tree, and then my friend Mils is coming over later.' She didn't add that she was getting her ready for going on a date with his good friend Liam. Mila had rung her in a flutter when Liam had kept his end of the bargain and called her mid-morning, asking her to 'help him out' tonight.

'That's fine. Come tomorrow. But just be warned, the journey will be horrendous. The entire country's going to be on the roads.'

She bit her lip, hardly able to believe this was happening. This was practically a mini-break, she was going to be meeting his family. It was everything she should be running away from. And yet she wasn't. She didn't want to run.

'So do you want to tell him or shall I?' Sam asked, seeing the emotions running – unspoken – over her face.

'You can, seeing as you've become his hero overnight.'

Quite literally, she thought, watching as Sam went over to Jasper. God help them all if he found out Sam was also Sinterklaas. She felt another frisson of fear as she watched them together, heads bent, eye contact held. They were so easy together. So natural . . . But what if . . . ?

'Jasper, what would you say to you and your mama coming out to Friesland to support me in the Elfstedentocht? I think it would really make a big difference to my performance if I knew I had the two of you there, cheering me on. Then I could wave to you as I passed.'

Jasper's mouth opened like a drawbridge. He would be *waved* to? By an actual racer? He looked straight at her. 'Can we, mama?'

Lee smiled. 'Well, I think we can guarantee kindergarten will be closed on Monday' – along with every other business in the country; official or not, this was going to count as a national holiday – 'so I don't see why not.'

She watched as Jasper threw his arms around Sam's neck. 'I'm going to make you a banner so you can see where I am.'

'That sounds perfect. Then it really will be my dream come true.'

'Mine too!' Jasper cheered.

They both looked back at her and she smiled. Mine too, she said – but only in her head.

'Pabe, does that look straight to you?' she asked, standing on tiptoes as she held the top of the tree, its bristles tickling under her arm.

'A little more to the right,' he said from his spot in the armchair. 'Yes, that's better.'

'Right, Jazzy,' she said, peering down through the fronds at her son kneeling on the floor, ready for action. 'If you screw in the bolts, all the way until you feel them touch the tree trunk, okay?'

'You won't drop the tree on my head?'

She grinned. 'I promise I won't drop the tree on your head.'

She watched as Jasper shuffled in on his tummy, just his little legs and feet appearing from the tree's skirt at the bottom. 'So Pabe, what do you think of the news? Exciting, huh?'

'The whole country's gone mad,' he said with a watery-eyed smile. 'I never thought I'd live to see another one, that's for sure.'

'We're going to watch it,' Jasper shouted from under the tree. 'Sam's racing in it.'

'Sam?' Pabe looked at her.

'A friend of ours. He's been waiting his whole life for it to be put on. His father raced in the last one in '97.'

'Oh, what was his name? Perhaps I will remember?'

'Well, I don't know his first name, but their surname is Meyer.'

'Meyer?' Pabe repeated. 'Evert Meyer?'

Lee shrugged. 'Maybe. You remember him?'

'Of course, who could forget him? He was a bad-tempered loser. Some people, they care too much.'

Lee frowned.

'Done it!' Jasper's legs wriggled as he tummy-shuffled out from under the tree again and sat up triumphantly, a sprinkle of needles in his hair. He shook himself like a dog, making

Pabe laugh. 'Can we put the decorations on now?' he asked excitedly and Lee knew he would crash into bed tonight. Everything about today had been lived at a high pitch of frenzy – waking up to find Sam cooking them breakfast, finding the canals skate-ready, the announcement of the iconic Elfstedentocht, decorating yet another Christmas tree . . .

'In the cupboard under the stairs, did you say?' Lee asked Pabe, daring to let go of the tree, checking it didn't topple.

'Yes. In a cardboard box with red-and-white tape. The bottom shelf, I believe.'

'Okay. Jazz, if you squirt some water from my water bottle into the base of the tree, just to stop it drying out too quickly. Make sure you don't get any on the floor. I'll be right back.'

She went out into the hall and opened the door to the understairs cupboard. She had to duck as she went in, her hands reaching for the light switch. A bare bulb swung from a cable, illuminating gappy floorboards and the detritus of a long life lived within these walls. Leftover rolls of vintage wallpaper, pots of paint, old tins of screws, a papier-mâché pumpkin, a few gilded frames with no paintings in them, boxes, boxes, boxes . . . Her eyes fell to the largest one in the bottom corner, some scraps of 'fragile' red-and-white masking tape still on the corners. She squatted down and pulled it out carefully, the cardboard feeling papery and fragile in her grip.

She went to close the understairs door behind her but just then, something came to her ear. She ducked in again, straining to hear what it was. It was distant, and yet also clear. Weeping? Someone was weeping.

She peered down through the gappy floorboards. The insulation was seemingly non-existent and although she couldn't see any light from below, she could hear sounds really quite easily when she concentrated. Weeping. Whispering.

With a sad sigh, she retreated, not wanting to intrude further. It wasn't any of her business, the state of play between Gus and Lenka's relationship, but clearly it was floundering. The tension between them this morning had been evident.

'Ta-da,' she exclaimed, setting down the box. Immediately, Jasper pulled out a length of gold tinsel. He had never seen tinsel before. He wrapped it around his neck and pushed out his chest, hands on his hips, like it was a king's scarf. Lee and Pabe laughed. 'It suits you,' Pabe chuckled.

'Right, well, with Jasper making a start on the decorations – he's the maestro on that score – I'm going to put those extra meals in the freezer for you, Pabe,' Lee said. 'Just take out one each morning and it'll be defrosted for dinner. And then I'll bring the logs in. I'll carry in extra to keep you going while we're away.'

'Lee, I don't know what to say,' Pabe said, the fire crackling beside him, Toetsen purring on the arm of his chair.

'I keep telling you, there's nothing *to* say, Pabe,' she said, patting his shoulder gently as she went out.

She put the pies into the freezer, leaving one in the fridge, and noticed that the bin was full. She tied the bag handles quickly and lifted it out. 'I'm just putting the bins out,' she called through, opening the front door.

The canal scene greeted her again, the first lights beginning to twinkle on the bridges and along the tree branches as dusk began to fall, people still skating, carols still playing. She felt a rush of love for her adopted home as she jogged down the steps and lifted the bin lid, arm upraised to drop the bag straight in.

But she stopped mid-swing, frowning as she caught sight of something in there. It wasn't sitting loose, on top. But

peeking through the opening of the topmost black bin bag
– it had simply been scrunched closed rather than knotted
– was a passport. She stared at it, feeling perturbed. She knew
from her old line of work just how vital a document a passport
was. It couldn't just be tossed out like that. Pabe may well
feel his travelling days were behind him, but didn't he know,
at the very least, that it had to be cut in half and rendered
wholly unusable?

Her arm dropping down, she reached for it, having to flick
off some potato peelings first. She turned to the photo page
– and stared at the photograph of the slightly puffy-faced
young man who was her neighbour.

Gus?

His hair was longer and lighter in the photograph and he
had been heavier-set when this had been taken. He might be
older now but seemingly no wiser. Didn't he know what could
happen if this fell into the wrong hands? Identity theft was a
modern epidemic in the first world, and as for the places
where she used to work . . . it didn't bear thinking about if
a valid European passport ended up in the wrong hands.

Not that she was in that world now, she reminded herself.
This was Amsterdam, not Afghanistan. She knew she had to
stop leaping to worst-case scenarios; she was the girl next
door now. If this wasn't Pabe's bin, then this was none of her
business.

On the other hand, it was better to be safe than sorry. She
slipped the passport into her jeans pocket; at the very least
she would cut it up herself.

'Right, how are we doing?' she asked, coming back into
the living room a few moments later.

Pabe, Jasper and Toetsen all looked back at her. 'It's going
splendidly,' Pabe said, his eyes twinkling with unfettered joy.

Lee looked over at the stubby Christmas tree in the corner by the window, upright but fully loaded with baubles in its bottom left corner. Again. She burst out laughing.

'Do you like it, mama?' Jasper asked proudly, coming over to her for a hug.

'My darling,' she said, bending down to kiss the top of his head. 'It is absolutely perfect!'

Chapter Twenty-Three

Mila was sitting cross-legged on the bed, in her bra and knickers and with gold gel stickers stuck beneath her eyes. 'I can't believe you didn't tell me any of this!'

'I did, sort of. I told you he turned me down.'

'But you made out he was a loser! Not that he was The One!'

'Uh-uh!' Lee almost fell off the bed in protestation. 'I never said those words. Not once. I have not said he's The One.'

'No. But your eyes have!'

Lee quickly shut them. 'Oh for heaven's sake. You're getting carried away again. It's been a day. One *single* day, to be precise. Let's not start planning the bridesmaid dresses just yet, shall we?'

But when she opened her eyes again, Mila was grinning at her like a lunatic. Lee picked up a face wipe and chucked it at her.

'Lee, don't you see? The fact that you didn't have sex that first night didn't mean nothing had happened – it actually meant a shitload happened between you. Emotionally! It means *everything* that he walked out on you.'

Lee stared at her, trying to ignore the way her heart thumped at her friend's words.

'And then he made you want him by not letting you have him?' Mila pressed a hand to her heart and almost fell into a swoon. 'Oh my God, I love him myself.'

'You are a lost cause, you know that?' Lee tutted, topping up their champagne glasses; but she was grinning. She couldn't stop. Jasper was downstairs watching *Star Wars*, again, before bed.

'So when are you going to *meet the parents*?' Mila asked, taking a big sip.

'We are incidentally staying at his family home so that we can watch him race. He wouldn't otherwise be introducing me to his parents – At. This. Point.' Lee tried to hammer home her point that it was early days. 'We'll leave after lunch tomorrow, I guess.'

'The roads will be terrible.'

'I know, but that doesn't matter. We don't want to get there too early. I don't want us to be in the way.'

'Lee, however you want to spin it, he's introducing you to his family. I don't think they're going to be seeing it as you *getting in the way*.'

Lee bit her lip, feeling another rush of the panic that had been zipping into her mind intermittently all afternoon. 'But what if they . . .' She trailed off.

'What if they what?'

'What if they . . . you know . . . disapprove.'

There was a pause. 'You mean because of Jazzy?' Mila looked at her sternly.

Lee nodded. 'I mean, I'd understand their position. Would they choose for their son to get involved with a woman like me – someone messed up, and with a kid? It's not the straight-forward Happy Ever After ending, let's face it. I am not the sort of woman mothers envisage for their sons.'

'Let me tell you something,' Mila said emotionally, jabbing her finger towards Lee, champagne sploshing from the glass onto the bed. 'There is no such thing as the Happy Ever After ending, that is bullshit. *You* are a living freaking legend and that boy is the most lovable child on the planet. Don't you tell me that anything about the two of you is somehow . . . flawed. It sounds to me like this Sam knows perfectly well just what a bullseye he's hit finding you.'

Lee looked back at her friend, wondering how she could be so fierce in her loyalties and yet so ridiculous in her sentimentality. 'Aw, Mils . . .'

They hugged, both relieved that last night's tiff had been forgotten already. They were neither of them ones for grudges and Mila had been over here within the hour after her apologizing text – especially because Liam had called, asking her for a favour tonight.

'Right, well, anyway, back to you,' Lee said, leaning forward and gently peeling the gels from beneath Mila's eyes. 'Oh yes, much better.' She looked at the little squidgy sachets in her hands.

'Really?' Mila asked hopefully.

'No. Why do you waste your money on these things?'

Mila patted the skin beneath her eyes. '*I* think they feel less puffy.'

Lee grinned. 'Well, I'm sure Liam will be able to spot the difference. He's probably got a more involved grooming routine than me.' She watched Mila from lowered lashes. 'I still can't believe you're going on a date with him.'

'Well, it's not a date-date. I mean, we're just friends. I'm just doing him a favour,' Mila said earnestly, her eyes wide, biting down nervously on her lower lip.

Lee suppressed a grin as Mila clambered off the bed to

double-check her reflection in the bathroom mirror, before beginning to apply her make-up. Lee rolled onto her tummy at the foot of the bed, dangling her feet in the air. 'Well, he's lucky you agreed to go at such short notice.'

'Just as well I had my sabbatical going on really,' Mila said, glancing at her in the mirror. 'Or I'd definitely have been out.'

'Thank heavens.'

'He says I'm really getting him out of a bind. He's hoping he'll get a promotion off the back of this, so I'm going to go out there and charm *everyone*; be on my A-game and show everyone how amazing he is.' She applied some eyeshadow to her lids, blending it expertly. 'Not that he needs *me* to do that.'

Lee sighed as she watched on, knowing that a smoky eye would be forever beyond her capabilities. 'Well, take it as an opportunity for yourself too. You never know who *you* could meet there.'

'Yeah right – at his boss's daughter's eighteenth.' Mila pulled a face.

Lee laughed. 'Trust me, it's going to be better than you think.'

'How do you know?'

Lee shrugged. 'Just a feeling.' She checked the time. 'He'll be here any minute, you'd better get a move on. Which shoes did you decide on?'

'I can't decide between the black or the petrol blue. Which do you prefer? They're in the bag.'

Lee reached down over the end of the bed and brought out one of each. 'You know, I think I like the blue,' she said after a moment. 'A bit clashy, a bit funky.'

'Yeah, that was what I was thinking.' Mila came back from

the bathroom, unhooking her bra and pulling Lee's unworn olive-green silk dress off its hanger. She wrapped it around herself, adjusting the drapery at the cleavage, smoothing it over her flat tummy.

Lee tossed the petrol blue shoes over to her and watched her friend rise by four inches.

'So? What do you think?' Mila asked nervously, biting her lip again.

Lee shifted back onto her feet, clasping her hands to her chest. That dress had super-powers. 'Oh. My. God. You are a fricking *goddess*. All the men are going to be falling over themselves tonight.' Liam too? How could he fail to see how beautiful, how special, she was? Surely this dress would bring Mila out of the friend-zone, once and for all?

'Yeah, but they're all either going to be eighteen or dads! And I am off married men, remember? Never again.'

'Don't worry. I'm sure Liam will be your noble protector.' They both heard the doorbell ring two floors below. Lee scrambled off the bed before Mila could protest. 'I'll get it. We don't want you twisting an ankle in those heels. Take your time.'

She darted out of the room and was just getting to the front door when it rang again.

'Hey!' she said, smiling back at Liam. 'Just the man.' He looked so good it should be illegal – navy velvet jacket, black narrow trousers, polished shoes – and she had a sudden pang of regret that maybe this wasn't such a good idea after all. Perhaps making Mila's dream come true with a perfect date wasn't a kindness if it only made her fall harder for him?

'Lee.' He stepped into the warmth of the hall, wrapping his arms around her gratefully. 'I don't know how the hell I can ever thank you for arranging this. My boss now thinks I'm the messiah. He's already booked me in for a one-on-one meeting on Monday.'

'I'm glad.' She glanced behind her and lowered her voice. 'But just remember to keep your end of the bargain tonight as well. Look after our girl tonight, make sure she has a good time. Do *not* abandon her and under no circumstances is she to go near married men. They're like catnip to her.'

'Sure, absolutely, got that,' he said earnestly.

'Good.'

The delicate clip-clopping of heels sounded on the stairs and they both turned to find Mila coming into view, her lean legs gleaming with iridescent dry oil, the straps of her shoes hanging loose around tiny ankles.

'Hi Liam,' she beamed. 'Lee's made me promise not to embarrass you. Will this do? I'm not overdressed, am I?'

And she held out her arms to show off the dress as she descended, looking like a Hollywood siren on a film set.

Lee glanced back as a silence opened up. Liam was staring as Mila as she reached the bottom and did a twirl. 'No. It's . . . fine.' He cleared his throat.

Fine? Lee scowled at him. Mila looked crestfallen.

But a tiny smile began to play on Lee's lips as she watched Liam's eyes sweep up and down over Mila's silhouette while she put on her coat.

Mila tied the belt tightly around her waist. 'Okay, well then, I guess I'm all set.' She hugged Lee tightly. 'Have an amazing time in Friesland. Ring me when you're back.'

'*You* have an amazing time tonight. You look glorious. That dress is a *Man. Slayer.* Isn't it, Liam?' she demanded in a pointed tone.

'Huh?' He looked back at her. 'Oh yeah, right. It is. Man. Slayer.'

'Incredible night!'

The message pinged, lighting up the dark room with a blue light. Lee was in bed, staring at her ceiling and failing to sleep. To think that last night, only last night, Sam had been lying in these sheets with her; that only this morning he'd been in that shower; this afternoon, back in her kitchen . . . It all felt so natural, so very normal that he should be here, doing these things.

She turned her head and looked at the name on the WhatsApp. Mila.

She grinned, picking it up. *'Tell me everything,'* she typed.

She waited, the room glowing blue again several moments later. *'Laughed so hard. Danced for three hours straight. And Haven was playing, can you believe it?'*

'Three hours? You must be crippled now.' Lee grinned. *'Liam good?'*

'Amazing. And so loyal. Stopped at least 3 marrieds in their tracks. Sent them packing.'

'So a good man then, in spite of being appalling tart.'

'Ye, we talked about that acc. Got rlly deep. Did you know his mother died when he was young? Heartbreaking. So sad. Tears in his eyes. Scared to commit.'

'Aw bless. Never knew.'

'No. Guess what tho?'

'What.'

'Got number of a hot guy. Not married.'

Lee's eyebrows shot up. That was not what she'd expected to come next. *'*screaming* Deets please.'*

'Early 30s, events marketing, Alexander Skarsgård vibes. Going skating tomorrow. Got feels!'

Had her plan backfired – or worked? Had the reality of a date with Liam not matched the fantasy? Was Mila, at long last, finally over him and onto the next? *'Sabbatical off then?'*

'Totally. Brunch? We can debrief.'

'Tricky. Have switched my weekly Mon slot with Dr H for a Skype sesh tomorrow in the a.m.; she's going to Friesland too. Hitting the road after lunch.'

'Back when?'

'Tuesday.'

'Argh. Okay. Can wait. Sleep tight Mary Ellen.'

'Night John-Boy x'. It was their usual *The Waltons* sign-off, a childhood echo she'd brought over from England with her.

The room went dark again and Lee sank back into the pillows, feeling the unfamiliar glow of contentment; happiness sat cradled in her palm like a roosting robin. Mila was happy, Jasper was happy, she was happy . . . This was the first time since she'd left the war zone that she actually felt at peace, and it was an alien feeling; she could still feel a small vibration of resistance deep within her, as though waiting for the twist, the bad news story that was going to take it all away again.

But she knew she couldn't think like that. Wasn't this everything she'd never dared to want? She was being given a second chance at love. Life. She closed her eyes with a determinedly steady breath. She just had to trust. Lightning never struck twice. Things would be different this time.

Old wooden desks pushed together, chairs on their sides, a blackboard still with a poem on it, a sharp but broken pencil in one of the pen grooves. Most of the windows had long since been blown out, glass littering the floor like chicken feed. She looked out of the one nearest the door and gave the signal. Cunningham and Moussef were waiting in the truck, checking she got in safely. (Got in safely! The notion was almost laughable. As though she was a teenager with a curfew.) Cunningham signalled back and jumped out of the vehicle, ready to work. Restless to get on.

She turned back into the room. It was perhaps six metres by eight, a row of windows on the opposite side. She wandered over and looked out. The view gave onto the village, looking straight up a street that led to the market.

An old man was walking down, dressed in white tunic and trousers, his head covered by a tan kufi hat. His arm was outstretched to the side and holding a wide, shallow basket of figs that balanced on his hip. He had a thin, lined face but his eyes were velvety soft and he was talking, or perhaps singing to himself, quietly, his lips moving.

Lee, never one for a zoom lens – it felt like cheating to be so far from the subject – waited for him to draw closer, then lifted her camera, unseen at the old school-house window, and went to shoot—

The flash, in the next instant, was blinding, sending her flying backwards, pressure on her chest, as everything went quiet. She lay on her back, blinking up, stunned, at the ceiling. She couldn't hear anything, not a single thing, just a ringing silence.

For several long moments, she felt paralyzed, not sure if she was alive or dead. Hearing nothing, feeling nothing . . . but gradually awareness began to dawn, sound coming back in threads. She felt the glass beneath her back, the breeze on her face through the open window. She coughed as the dust swept into her lungs, her eyes watering as the metallic smell filled the room.

Gingerly she tried to move, rolling onto her side and pushing up, shards of glass pressing against the skin. Her head dropped down from the effort. Everything felt laboured and heavy, amplified and yet distant at the same time. Her ears were ringing but gradually sounds were permeating her brain – a car alarm wailing incessantly, someone screaming, the staccato of gunfire tripping off in rhythmic rounds, no more screaming . . .

Carefully standing, she instinctively checked her camera for damage; she had been shooting right until the moment of the explosion. She tried to walk, staggering back to the wall again, her fingers reflexively fumbling with the lens as she peered around the blown-out window. On the street, the remains of a car were ablaze and beside it lay most of the body of the man she had just been photographing, a river of his blood trickling into the dirt, the basket of figs he'd been carrying now on the ground beside him, strewn by his splayed feet as if in a grotesque still-life. Her finger clicked on the button instinctively, a startle reflex almost.

The man had lost his right arm, but she couldn't stop staring at the holes in the soles of his shoes, the leather worn so thin it must have been like walking in gloves.

She saw a jihadist in black fatigues come out of a house. His head was wrapped with a black and white keffiyeh and he had an automatic weapon slung casually over one shoulder like it was a handbag. There was no tension in his body as he scanned the deserted street. Had he put the bomb under the car? He seemed to know there were no soldiers here; so much of the surrounding area had already been captured by ISIL and most of the Kurdish fighters were now in Kobanî, fighting the siege there. Here, with no defence, it must be like shooting fish in a barrel.

He glanced over casually, disinterestedly, at the corpse. He seemed to hesitate for a moment, before walking over, bending down and picking up one of the figs. He inspected it, as if for bruising or dirt or blood, then took a bite, juice dribbling down his chin.

Her finger clicked on the shutter again – an instinct, a reflex –

as, through the lens, she watched the soldier squat by the dead man,
enjoying the ripe fig while still-warm blood pooled around his boots.
She watched as he sucked his fingers clean, one by one, and wiped
his chin with his sleeve. Disgust and revulsion shuddered through
her body, as strong as fear.

She jumped suddenly as she heard something close by and she
whipped round, heart pounding – but there was no one there. Her
mind was playing tricks on her, her eardrums damaged, adrenaline
making her jumpy.

She turned back to the fighter again. He was wiping the blood
off his boots on the dead man's body, leaving vivid streaks of red on
the white clothes like lurid gashes. Her stomach turned over, nausea
making her skin prickle with a cold sweat.

'In there.'

She froze. She'd definitely heard that, the words distinct even if
the voice did sound underwater to her. Everything seemed so
distorted, like the world had been pulled inside out. The voice had
come from the other side of the wall and she waited for another
sound, her heart pounding like a boxer's fist in her ribs. Tentatively,
she peered out through the window again, knowing she was in
shock but unable to free herself from its grip; the jihadist was
walking into one of the houses further up the street. Not him, then.

'Moussef?' she asked out loud, scarcely able to hear her own voice
over the still-ringing silence in her head, slowly gathering her wits
again. He and Cunningham must be bringing the girls over here,
she realized. The car bomb would have everyone running scared;
those girls would be better protected here. With ISIL already in the
village, that shack afforded no protection at all now. At least this
had a roof and a door. .

. . . This had a roof and a door.

The realization made her frown, the fog in her brain clearing
fractionally. If this building had a roof and a door, then why hadn't

the women come and hidden in here in the first place? Why hadn't Moussef helped them to hide better?

Her sense of unease morphed into something more tangible, her mouth becoming dry as fear acquired a shape. She felt something behind her, a stirring of the air, another presence filling the space—

She whipped around to look, to find an ISIL soldier – already in – closing the door behind him. He was dressed in black, his face almost entirely covered, and he calmly walked over to her, setting down the gun against one of the desks. Like he wasn't going to need that here. Like he'd known she was in here. Like he knew exactly what was going to happen next.

She could see nothing but his eyes as he advanced – a shadow leaked from her nightmares – and they told her he had already lived a lifetime. Death, savagery and barbarism was his daily routine. Peace wasn't a distant dream; it wasn't even a dream. All he knew was bombs and gunfire and shelling and screams. Loving touch, clean clothes, birdsong, running water . . . they didn't exist for him. He was a dead man walking, a human brutalized into one-dimensional ferity.

His arm lashed out, sending her flying across the desks and setting stars spinning. And as she jolted in violent recoil, her finger hit the shutter-button one last time and the one sight – out of all the multitudes of others – that she never wanted to see again, the image of his deadened brown eyes upon hers, was captured forever, in perfect posterity.

'Jazzy, where's your red scarf?' she called up the stairs. 'It's not in the box.' She rifled once more through their accessories basket – myriad single gloves, too-small mittens on strings, a fleece balaclava, a beanie with a dropped stitch and unravelling stripes . . . 'Can you check in your bedroom please? Has it been kicked under your bed?'

'I'm doing my banner!' his voice came back from the middle floor.

'Ugh.' Lee gave a groan of annoyance as she jogged up the stairs herself. She was irritable and tired after a bad night's sleep – nightmares clawing at her now that her bed was empty again – and she'd been drained by Dr Hansje going in hard in their session this morning, pushing her on details she just wanted to forget. 'Honestly Jasper, I've got quite enough to do, packing everything up. You could try to be helpful. Did you brush your teeth yet?'

No answer.

'Jasper?'

'When I've finished this, mama!' he said, equally as irritably as her. His sleep had been disturbed too, of course.

'If I ask you to do something . . .' She stomped over to where he had set up his craft-making activities on the floor in front of the fireplace, in the shadow of the Christmas tree. Newspapers were spread over the floorboards, a pillowcase laid flat with red paint – but he hurriedly threw his little body in the way, blocking her view. She had made sockets at each end, for a halved broom handle to be inserted, by folding it over and fastening with safety-pins – rudimentary, but it seemed to work – but she was allowed no further input. 'No, you can't look yet. It's a surprise!'

'Not for me though, surely?'

'It's a surprise for everyone.'

She dreaded to think what that might mean. 'Fine, but you still need to brush your teeth and I still need to find your scarf. It's going to be cold up there and we'll be outside, standing around, for a long time.'

'Okay,' he said, still not letting her see his masterpiece.

She obediently moved away. 'We'll leave in ten minutes,

okay?' she said. 'They're already saying the traffic is heavy so I want to get on. It wouldn't do to be late for dinner, that would be rude, wouldn't it?'

'I don't care. I just want to see Sam.'

'Yes, well, that too.' She sighed. If things were moving quickly between her and Sam, it appeared they were moving even more quickly with him and Jasper. 'I'm going up to your room to find that scarf.'

She went out and was halfway up the stairs when the doorbell went. 'Ugh,' she groaned again, turning and going back down both flights. Who needed a gym membership with Dutch staircases?

She opened the door with a less-than-hospitable expression. 'Liam!' She frowned, taking in the sight of him. 'Are you okay?'

His eyes fell to her packed bags in the hallway. 'Oh God, you're not going up to Friesland too, are you?'

'Yes.'

'You and the entire country!' He looked back at her with pleading eyes. 'When have you got to leave by?'

'Well, I've told Jasper ten minutes, but it'll be more like half an hour. Why? What's wrong? You look hellish. Overdo it last night?'

'Can I come in?'

'Sure.' She stepped back and let him come into the hallway. 'Coffee?'

He shook his head. 'I just need to talk to you.'

'What's happened? Did it all go okay with Haven? Andrik texted me this morning saying it went well. Wasn't your boss happy?'

'No, it's not that. I'm flavour of the month now, thanks to you.'

'So what then?'

'Have you heard from Mila?'

'Yes, of course, she texted me when she got in last night.'

'And what did she say exactly?'

Lee shrugged. 'Well, just that you had a great time – danced all night, laughed, talked. I think it was exactly the tonic she needed. She was absolutely buzzing.'

'Did she say anything about a tall guy, blonde, dodgy shoes?'

Lee grinned. 'Uh . . . she was telling me about a guy with Alexander Skarsgård vibes? Nothing about the shoes, though.'

'What did she say about him?'

'Just that they're meeting up today. They're going skating.'

'Oh God.' He ran his hands down his face. 'I knew it. He was looking over at her all night.'

'So? She said he's not married?'

'No, that's the problem!'

Lee frowned. 'Well, how's that a problem? It's precisely what we wanted for her – to find a guy who's actually available.'

'No. You don't understand, she can't date him.'

'Why not?' She tipped her head to the side questioningly. 'Liam, what's going on?'

He gripped his hair with his hands, pressing his elbows together in front of his face. 'Fuck, this is a disaster. It wasn't supposed to happen like this. You said take her out and make her feel great and boost her ego.'

'And you did all that.'

'Yes. And *I'm* the sucker who's ended up falling for her!'

Lee's eyes widened. '*What?*' Everything was topsy-turvy – Liam had fallen for Mila, just as she'd gotten over him?

'I never saw her like *that* before until last night. She was like my little sister, you know, always clucking around – cooking for us, organizing us. It just never crossed my mind that . . . But then that dress, and she was just so funny, and the way we talked. The connection between us. I mean, I told her things I've never told anyone!' He stared at her. 'Lee, what the fuck have you done?'

'*Me?*'

'Yes, this is all your fault! You made me take her out. You made me pay attention to her, treat her like a date. She can't start seeing that guy. You have to . . . do something.'

'Oh no! I am not doing a damn thing and neither are you. You are *not* turning your attentions to Mils. She's not like the girls you go for; she won't just pick herself up when you lose interest – as you invariably will – and move on.'

'But that's what I'm telling you. I've never felt like this before. It feels different.'

'Yes, because it's Mils – it's the novelty of seeing an old friend with new eyes. Believe me, I've been there. And sooner or later, the rose-tinted mist will clear again and you'll realize you've made a mistake, and there's no going back. Your friendship will be wrecked. Things would never be the same, not just for you two but the four of us.'

'But Lee—'

'No. No buts. Leave her alone, I mean it. She's happy. Let her go on her date with Alexander Skarsgård and you keep well out of it. Two weeks from now you'll thank me.'

'I won't.' Liam stared at her, his hands on his hips, frustration blazing from his eyes, his mouth set in a grim line of despair. But he knew he couldn't refute her claims. The hummus in her fridge lasted longer than his relationships.

'Liam, I guarantee that by Christmas you'll have turned your attentions to someone else. Leave. Mils. Alone.'

'You have so little faith in me? You think I'm that shallow?'

'I think you can lead a horse to water but you can't change its spots.'

He looked confused and she laughed, hugging him and patting his back lightly, like she was burping a baby. 'Be angry with me, that's fine. But just trust me on this. Let the spool run. It'll be better for everyone this way. You can thank me later.'

Chapter Twenty-Four

'Do you think that's it?' Lee asked, peering through the dirty windscreen at the long, brick gabled building. It was two rooms deep, with blackish-green painted shutters at the windows and a cat-slide roof. There was a row of oak trees just a metre from the front wall, and behind it stood a windmill and barns. Several small tractors were parked in a hard, rutted yard and, in the early evening moonlight, she could just make out reeds standing stiffly like needles, marking the edge of the frozen waterway. Sam had said to look for the windmill, but they had passed nine in the last two miles. 'Jazzy?'

She twisted back in her seat to find her child fast asleep, his head lolling against the sides of the headrest, his lightsaber on the back seat and a crust of sandwich curling slowly on his lap. The journey had been predictably torturous, miles and miles of tailbacks snaking along the roads heading north; whilst the capital had had only hard frosts, it had been snowing intermittently in the countryside for the past few weeks and a thin crust of white blanketed the landscape, though not softening it.

They had sung every song they knew, at least three times; they had played I Spy, Bridges, Yellow Car; but eventually they had run out of energy as the line of traffic crawled along at a glacial speed. Lee had put the radio on for traffic updates; it appeared that not only were several million people trying to get to Friesland in one day, but most of the world's press too. There wasn't an available plane seat into the country, nor a hire car to be had, nor a bed to sleep in. The capital city hadn't been this deserted since the fifteenth century.

'Well, let's give it a go,' she murmured to herself. She turned in off the lane and drove slowly into the yard, triggering an automatic light. Several cars were parked there but she had no idea if one of them was Sam's – she didn't know which car he drove; she didn't even know where he lived in the city! And yet here she was, coming to stay with his family. They were leapfrogging some milestones and hanging back on others and she felt another acrid burst of nerves.

Not wanting to wake Jasper unduly – lest she be at the wrong address – she got out of the car. The house was set not in a garden as such – there were no flowerbeds, no evidence of landscaping – but just an expanse of grass dotted with aged trees, and she began walking up the narrow path through the middle of it towards the door set in the gable end, her boots crunching in the hard-packed snow. She could see squares of light spilling onto the ground on the far side of the house, when she heard dogs bark suddenly.

She stopped automatically as three dogs bounded towards her, barking loudly, leaping about, tails aloft as they surrounded her. They didn't growl or snarl but she stood rooted to the spot; she had encountered enough wild and stray dogs to know not to intrude further on their territory or show any signs of dominance.

'You made it!'

She looked up to see Sam striding towards her, looking every inch the wholesome country boy in dark jeans, boots and a chunky cream jumper. Without saying another word, he clasped her face in his hands and kissed her. 'I thought you'd never get here.'

'Me too,' she murmured, looking back into his eyes. They had an intensity to them she hadn't seen before – just because he missed her? – and he kissed her again, seeming to draw the strength from her body.

The dogs stopped barking, seeing she was definitely friend and not foe, immediately trotting over to her and sniffing her shoes.

Sam pulled back finally, seeming sated by her presence. 'Don't mind them.'

'Are you going to tell me their bark's worse than their bite?'

'No, their bite's pretty bad, just ask the postman,' he grinned. 'But they'll be fine with you now they've seen we're friends.'

'Friends, huh?' She arched an eyebrow. 'I hope you don't use this technique to signify friendship to your dogs with everyone who comes here.'

His eyes were steady upon hers. 'No one comes here.'

'Oh.' She felt a small thrill at that. 'Well, that's okay then.'

He smiled. 'That's Solomon, Juno and Frida, but if you tap your thigh with your hand, they'll come running.'

'Well trained.'

He shrugged. 'Farm dogs.' He looked back at her again, drinking her in. 'I can't believe you've come.'

'I said I would, didn't I?' she said, patting his chest, but also feeling the enormity of her quest – it was Sunday evening and she had travelled across the country to be here for him, when it had only been Friday night that they had become a They. It was all happening so fast, she knew that; all her long-held rules, mottoes, codes, were being dismantled one by one.

Don't stay over. Don't see him again. Don't meet Jasper. Don't bond with Jasper . . . 'How are you feeling?'

He rolled his shoulders and stretched his neck. 'Stiff! I had a massive session yesterday afternoon and again this morning, working on my technique and speed; but I've taken it pretty easy this afternoon. Waiting, waiting, waiting for you. I managed to get a sports massage in town – suddenly the place is overrun with experts – got my paperwork sorted, sharpened my blades. They get blunt so quickly on the natural ice.'

'Yes, I can't believe how different it feels! Yesterday was my first experience of wild skating. I've only ever skated on rinks before.'

'And did you like it?' His eyes roamed over her as she spoke, as though she was somehow magical.

'I *loved* it. Jasper had us out there pretty much all day.'

'Where is he?' Sam asked, startling at the mention of his name.

'Asleep in the car,' she smiled, touched by his concern as he turned to check the car was (a) there, (b) not being broken into and (c) not on fire.

He exhaled again. 'My parents can't wait to meet you both.'

She swallowed, stiffening in his arms. 'Really?'

'Of course.' He took her hand and kissed it. 'Let's get Jasper inside, the car will be getting cold quickly now the engine's off. Careful on the snow here, it's icy.'

'Okay, Mr Health and Safety,' she ribbed as he led her back towards her sleeping child.

'Hey, Jazz Man,' Sam whispered, squeezing his knee lightly. 'You're here, buddy. You made it.'

Lee sighed, seeing how he didn't stir. 'Mmm. When he goes, he really goes.'

'Shall I carry him in?'

'Oh . . .' She hesitated. 'Won't that look . . . ?' She didn't want this to look like a show of Happy Families, for his parents to think she was lining him up as a surrogate father to her child.

'What?'

She shook her head. She was over-analysing everything. Nerves were getting the better of her. 'Nothing. You take Jazz, I'll bring the bags.'

Carefully, protecting his head as he lifted him out, Sam carried Jasper over the lawn and towards a door at the back of the house. Lee followed after him, glancing in as they passed the windows and catching vignettes – an elm dining table and ladderback chairs, bronze candlesticks, a dark oil of a pastoral scene similar to this one with big skies, an open horizon, the silver veins of waterways channelling through the land. A utility space – a boiler suit hanging limp from an overhead drying rack, white goods, racks of wooden crates with apples arranged neatly, dog beds on a terracotta tiled floor.

Sam pushed against a green door and walked into a large wooden kitchen. It couldn't have been touched up in forty years but it was warm and inviting, with a huge range on the back wall, rails with copper pans and utensils hanging from hooks, and a tiger-striped black cat curled up in the seat of one of two armchairs set either side of the fireplace.

Sam's mother was stirring something on the stove but she turned as they walked in – a lean, slender woman with graphite-grey short hair and strong, straight dark eyebrows. Immediately Lee could see Sam's face in hers, the delicate touch of their bone structure, deep-set eyes. She was wearing jeans and a colourful knitted jumper pushed up her arms, revealing strong, pink hands.

'You must be Lee,' she said, smiling with her eyes as she took in the sight of the three of them. 'I am Agnetha, but call me Aggie.'

'Hello, it's so lovely to meet you,' Lee said, walking over and shaking her hand. 'And this is Jasper. I'm afraid the journey became a bit too much,' she said as they looked back at Sam holding the unconscious child on his hip, Jasper's chubby cheek pressed against his shoulder and drooling slightly.

'He is *beautiful*,' Agnetha whispered, her eyes shining.

'He is heavy,' Sam grinned.

As if on cue, Jasper stirred, his little nose twitching as the cooking smells permeated his brain and reminded his stomach he hadn't had a proper meal in over five hours. He blinked several times, trying to wake up, disoriented to find himself in the bright, huge unfamiliar kitchen. '. . . Mama?'

'It's okay, darling, we're at Sam's house in Leeuwarden, remember? This lady here is Sam's mama, Mrs Meyer.'

'Oh, he must call me Aggie too, please. We are not formal here.' Agnetha went up to him and, gently, as though she was catching a bubble, touched his hair. 'I am pleased to meet you, Jasper. Sam has told me so much about you.'

Jasper smiled, liking the warm greeting and the cat on the chair and the food on the stove. 'I made him a banner.'

'Did you?' Sam asked, looking pleased.

'Sshhh!' Lee whispered, pressing a finger to her lips and laughing. 'It's supposed to be a surprise.'

'That's what the commotion was! Our guests have arrived.'

Commotion?

The rough voice made her turn to see a tall, well-built man coming in from the hallway. He had shoulders like scaffolding planks and had to duck as he came through the door. He stopped short a metre in front of her, staring down with an unreadable gaze. Frisians were known for being surly, but he seemed more than that. 'I am Evert, Sam's father.'

He held out a hand and it was like being gripped by a vice. 'I'm Lee Fitchett, and this is my son Jasper; it's a pleasure to meet you.'

Evert's eyes rolled over to Jasper but did not stay upon him, coming straight back to her again. He openly scrutinized her, as he might have assessed a prize potato. 'Sam says you are a war correspondent.' It was a strange opening gambit – straight into that, no pleasantries . . . ?

'Was. Not any more.' She inclined her head towards Jasper by way of explanation.

He blinked. 'You must have seen some things.'

'Yes, you could say that.'

Another moment passed and he frowned, seeming almost disappointed. 'I thought you would look . . . tougher.'

She gave a small surprised shrug. Had he expected muscles, camouflage gear and an AK-47 over her shoulder? 'Well, quite often it was an advantage to look weaker than the people I met out there. They wouldn't feel threatened in the same way if they felt they had that over me. They would drop their guard more. I've found it's often an advantage to be under-estimated.'

He looked back at her, his dark, dark eyes – Sam's eyes – beginning to shine with a tiny gleam. 'Indeed. I've always backed the underdog.'

Lee glanced back at Sam, as much to check on Jasper as to change the conversation, and was surprised by the expression she saw on his face. Not fear – it wasn't that – but apprehension. He looked so tense.

'Would you like to see your room?' Aggie asked, chucking

Jasper on the cheek. 'We put in some of Sam's old toys for you.'

Jasper was fully awake now. Toys and food and a curled-up cat were too much to miss. Lee picked up their bags and followed the three of them into the hall, seeing how Evert watched her son as he was carried past. *His* look was not one of apprehension, like his son's . . . but of fear, as though domesticity itself threatened him.

The hallway was narrow, with rough limed walls and beams strapping the ceilings overhead, honeycomb-shaped terracotta tiles on the floor. There was plenty of artwork on the walls, heavily wrought, densely coloured, and she began to sense they had been drawn by the same hand – a bunch of tulips drooping in a milk jug; the windmill at sunset; twisted winter trees . . . Sam's? She remembered what he'd said about trying to work in oils, his frustrations at not finding his style there . . . Were these his early efforts, kept and displayed by his proud parents?

Rooms led off on each side – from what she could see: a cloakroom, a WC, a sitting room, a study . . . All of them with whitewashed walls and rugged floors, sparsely decorated with dark country furniture and fringed table lamps.

They climbed a narrow, creaky staircase that fed off to the right two-thirds of the way down the building, turning back on itself as it wended up to the first floor. Agnetha led them left and into a large bedroom at the back. It had two windows, looking down – she imagined – towards the water. A metal bedstead was draped with old linen sheets and a crocheted blanket, deep fluffy pillows that Lee could tell would balloon around their heads when they lay down. An almost-black chest of drawers had a blue-and-white jug and bowl on the top, red-and-blue-striped ticking curtains hanging from a metal pole. A large sheepskin rug was deeply piled and softer underfoot. Some camel-coloured towels were folded neatly at the end of the bed and on the far side of the room was a small blackboard on an easel, some chalks, and a yellow-painted wooden toy chest.

'What a beautiful room,' Lee said warmly. She could feel the history of this house; it was like getting into a bed moments after another had left it, still warm with memories.

Sam walked to the far end of the room and opened up the yellow chest. 'What have we got in here then, Jasper? Anything you think you'll like to play with?'

Jasper scampered across the floor, his footsteps no doubt reverberating through the house and making Evert downstairs scowl as the floorboards rattled. Lee watched him peer in and then reach down for something.

'He spent at least an hour this afternoon up in the attic, finding all these old toys, choosing the right ones, cleaning them . . .' Aggie whispered, as they both watched.

Lee blinked, feeling another complicated rush of feelings – excitement and happiness, but also panic . . . Sam was running ahead and she couldn't let Jasper get too attached. She had to make sure there was some sort of boundary, a buffer zone for *his* heart. If anyone was going to end up with a broken heart, it had to be her and not her son. But as she watched Jasper hold up a wooden plane, spinning the propeller whilst Sam made Spitfire noises, she knew she might already be too late for buffer zones.

'The bathroom is just here,' Aggie said, leading her back to the door and pointing to the next room down the hall. 'It isn't an en-suite, I'm afraid, we don't have much call for that here, but only you two and Sam will use it. We have another one we use at our end down there.'

Lee wondered where Sam's room was. Not that there would be any corridor-creeping going on tonight; between her son and his parents, they were well and truly snookered.

She saw a large framed photograph on the wall opposite, of a man skating. He was in that familiar hunched pose, body bent forward, hands clasped behind his back. The colours were faded but still bright.

'Is that your husband?' she asked, peering at it more closely.

'Yes, 1997, the year he competed. He came second.'

'Second? It's an incredible achievement.'

Aggie made a funny low sound. 'To be honest, it was a curse in many ways, coming so close. It might have been better if he'd come last: at least then he wouldn't have tortured himself with all the If Onlys. For years afterwards, he told himself he'd get it at the next race, he'd prove himself then. He would train and train and train, no matter the weather. But of course, there never was another race. Not until now – and now he's too old.'

Lee bit her lip, remembering Pabe's words – *a bad-tempered loser* – and now well able to imagine the hardening effect on the abrasive man downstairs, his bitterness to have been denied the chance to rewrite history, fulfil his destiny. Lee couldn't imagine what it must have been like for Aggie, being married to him as his ambition and desperation finally ceded to the sour acceptance that there would not be a next time. All his efforts were in vain. He'd had one chance and he'd blown it.

'He must be so pleased then that Sam's got an opportunity to compete as well?' she said instead, trying to find a positive.

'Sam?' Aggie looked blank for a moment, as though her mind had momentarily been pulled elsewhere, into another room. 'Oh, yes. Once my husband had accepted it was over for him, that became his focus; Evert's waited their entire lives for this moment. In many way, *his* entire life has led up to this moment – especially as this truly might be the last one we ever see, given all the things they're saying about global warming. I don't think he can quite believe the opportunity has come – his son will get to win for him.'

Lee was surprised. 'He actually thinks Sam can *win* it?' That wasn't what Sam had told her. He was just happy to be in the pack, he'd said.

'Of course.'

'But . . . he's had almost no time to prepare for it.'

'But that is the case for everyone,' Aggie shrugged.

Not the pro athletes, Lee thought to herself. Two members of the national skating team, Emil Hoog and Ard Langen, were eligible to race and had confirmed their intentions.

'There's never much warning for the Elfstedentocht,' Aggie went on. 'You have to go into every winter assuming it will happen – regardless of the fact that it hasn't for the last twenty-plus – because when it is announced, there's only ever two days to get prepared. No one can commit to a full-time training schedule for something that has such a low chance of occurring. The winner of '97 was a Brussels sprout farmer.' She tutted. 'Poor Evert, beaten by a sprout farmer.' She sighed. 'Besides, Sam has taken care to keep himself fit – he ran the Berlin and London marathons this year. It's always been in the back of his mind to be ready.'

Lee was confused; this was a very different impression from the one Sam himself had left her with. He'd indicated he was just happy it was on, happy he would be involved. There'd been no mention at any point of trying to actually win it. She recalled the brightness in his eyes when she'd arrived. His tension around his father. *His son will get to win for him*, Aggie had said.

'It is not just a matter of stamina, of course. Evert says it will come down to a matter of will on the day. That's what he's spent all these years teaching him: mental resilience. Can Sam *mentally* beat the opposition? Can he find that extra gear to be a winner?' Aggie sighed as she stared at the photograph, the sound echoing as though it were an ancient, far-travelled wind. 'Can he finally be the one to make his father proud?'

Chapter Twenty-Five

Lee looked down at Jasper's perfect little face, his cheeks clasped between her hands so that his mouth squished into a rosy pout. She laughed and kissed him again on the lips. 'I love you. I just love you *too* much.'

'I love you too, mama.' He blinked back at her, the pillow inflated around his head, the sheets tucked in tightly at the sides to stop him from falling out.

'I'll be downstairs, okay? The grown-ups are going to have dinner and then I'll be climbing straight back into bed for cuddles with you.'

'Okay.'

'You're sure you feel okay?' Every floorboard in this house creaked.

He nodded. 'Sam gave me his best bear from when he was little. He said he never had bad dreams when he slept with Tink.' And he pulled his arms out from the sheets to show her the small but loved teddy bear with a stitched-on smile.

Lee nodded. It was another brick from the wall that was fast coming down. 'But you've still got Ducky though, right?'

'Of course.' His tone suggested mild outrage that she could even think otherwise, as he produced his beloved cloth toy above the sheets too.

'Great.' She reached down and kissed Ducky's threadbare head. 'Well, snuggle up with Tink and Ducky and make the bed all warm for me. I won't be long.'

'Night night, mama.'

She crossed the room and closed the door as quietly as she could; it had a latch fastening that tinkled lightly as it dropped.

Downstairs, Sam and his parents were in the kitchen. Evert was sitting in his armchair with a drink in his hand, Sam opposite, as Aggie was moving food in and out of the various ovens.

Sam's eyes rose to her as she came through – a smile lighting his face – but not before she'd seen the darkness in them first and she sensed she'd walked in on a tense discussion.

He jumped up. 'Lee, a drink?'

She looked at the glass in his own hand and saw he was drinking . . . milk.

Their eyes met as they both remembered her joke to him when he'd been disguised as Sinter, back on that first evening when they'd thought everything was going to be easy between them. When he'd thought she was the girl next door.

He grinned. 'It's prep for tomorrow. I promise, this isn't my usual pre-dinner drink.'

'Well, perhaps I'll have a—' She looked to see what Evert was drinking. 'Beerenberg?'

Evert nodded approvingly. Little did he know she could drink spirits the way most people could drink . . . well, milk. The big farmer might be surprised by what this not-tough-looking photographer could do.

'Did he settle down okay?' Aggie asked from the stove.

'Yes, he's snug as a bug in a rug up there. Thank you.'

Aggie looked pleased. 'I was listening to his footsteps as

321

he was running around up there. It's lovely having a child in the house again. I can't remember the last time we had such a little one here.'

Sam handed her the drink, his fingers brushing hers lightly. 'Cheers.'

'Cheers.' She chuckled as she watched Sam sip the milk. 'Now go easy on that. It's pretty powerful.'

Sam grinned, flashing her a private look. 'I'll have you know this is a tried and tested recipe for success.'

'It certainly is,' Evert said solemnly from his armchair. 'I drank two pints of milk every day from September in the run-up to the '97. And the night before, we ate *hutspot* with *hazenpeper*.'

'So that's what we'll also be having tonight,' Sam said, a bemused apology in his voice. 'I hope that's okay?'

Hare stew with potato, carrot and onion mash? It wasn't the most romantic first dinner together, nor the fanciest. It did smell good, though. 'Wonderful. I'm so ravenous I could eat the chair leg. That journey was *so* dull, but I didn't even dare turn off the highway for snacks in case we couldn't pull out again. The tailbacks were solid for miles.'

'Lee, take my seat – but don't eat it,' Sam joked, gesturing for her to sit in the armchair. 'I'll use this.' And he brought over a low footstool, his legs stretching long in front of him as he sat between her and his father in front of the fire. One of the dogs – Juno, she thought – came over and sank down beside him, his hand absently falling to her coat, stroking it.

Evert was staring at her. 'So, you have seen a lot of the world, Lee.'

Back to this again. She felt a familiar tension gather in her stomach at the introduction of this topic. People often wanted to know more about what she'd seen, the places she'd been. What that meant they really wanted was to hear the horror stories, the gory details, as though it hadn't been real people and real lives she had captured falling apart on film. 'Definitely. Just not the places with ATOL ratings.'

The joke appeared lost on him, even though Sam and Aggie both chuckled.

'Would you ever go back to it, the war reporting?'

'No.'

'Not even when the boy is older?'

She bristled that he hadn't used Jasper's name. 'Well, I'll still be his mother, even then. No matter his age, he'll need me. I wouldn't take those risks now.'

She saw his eyes narrow fractionally at her words. Did he see her maternal love as weakness? Pointless sentiment? Had *he* ever had a member of the Taliban point a rifle at him?

'My son said you won the Pulitzer Prize.'

'. . . Mmm, that's right.' She glanced uncomfortably at Sam.

'Sorry, I was boasting,' Sam held his hands up in surrender, before reaching over and squeezing her knee apologetically.

'I looked up the photographs. There are *four* images that won the prize? Not one?'

'Yes, that's right. For the Breaking News Photography segment. It can be one image or several; and sometimes even multiple photographers can win the same prize if the images are submitted as a single collection.'

'Who decides whether to submit a photograph? Do you nominate yourself?'

'No. It's the choice of the person, or organization, who owns the trademark for the images – so in my case Reuters. I never would have submitted them if it had been down to me.' She hadn't even known they'd been submitted until two weeks before the announcement; Dita had wanted it to be a 'surprise'.

'Why not? You don't think they're good enough?'

She shrugged, trying to keep her body loose, her face impassive, but inside she felt on fire. Burning up. 'I've taken others I thought were better, sure.'

He nodded. 'I will be honest, I didn't really understand why they should have won, they seemed . . . quite random.' He spread his hands. 'But then, I am just a humble farmer,' he said, disingenuously.

'Well, I agree, it's not immediately obvious what the images are telling you when you see them in isolation. They made more sense when accompanied by the report from my partner, Harry Cunningham.'

Evert's eyes narrowed to slits. '. . . The American?'

'Yes. The piece he wrote accompanying the images won the Pulitzer for Reporting on International Affairs.'

There was a pause whilst he digested this, as though needing to give it thought. 'I see. So then, what was it all about? I don't know what a dog pissing on a wall and a man carrying fruit, what that has to do with war?'

Lee tried to steady her heart. It felt wobbly in her chest, like a domino about to fall. 'On a macro level, the images bear witness to the insurgence of ISIL in the northern Syrian province of Aleppo. The siege had begun of the nearby city of Kobanî and Cunningham and I were in a rural village in the area, investigating a lead, when ISIL launched a surprise attack.'

'Goodness,' Aggie tutted, wiping her hands on her apron, and Lee saw she had stopped cooking and was listening to their conversation with a concerned expression etched on her brow, her hip against the cabinets.

'So what those images are actually showing is a span of the very moments this small village tipped from a fragile peace into war again. It was seen as a microcosm of the whole.'

'I see, I see. So the dog, the man walking . . . these were the last moments of peace.'

Lee bit her lip. 'Mm-hmm.'

'And then the soldier eating over the corpse, the bullets and blood on the walls, okay I see it. But the man's eyes . . . ?'

'He was a jihadist.'

Evert's eyebrows went up, as though impressed at last. 'You were that close to a jihadist?'

Lee felt her mouth go dry, her heart become a paper moth. '. . . No.'

'But the picture—'

'I shot it on zoom. Long-range lens.'

'Oh.'

'Thank *goodness*!' Aggie said, pressing a hand to her heart as if to quieten it. 'You surely could not get that close to one of those people and survive it. They're barbarians. The things they've done . . .'

'I know.' She cleared her throat, forcing herself to talk. To *chat*. 'The rules have changed out there. It used to be that press – like medics and aid workers – had a level of protection, but IS have changed all that. Anyone not on their side is on the wrong side. They're ruthless.'

'No wonder you wouldn't want to go back to all that again. It's behind you. You've got your lovely boy – and, it seems, mine too.' Aggie's eyes sparkled.

'Ma, you promised!' Sam groaned, hiding his face in his hands as his mother laughed mischievously, looking delighted by her indiscretion. Lee gave a small, surprised chuckle for sociability's sake, hoping no one could see how her hand shook as she went to drink, but only too aware of Evert looking on in silence with a watchful, disapproving gaze.

'Here.' Sam draped a heavy blanket over both their shoulders and she pulled it in tightly, shivering in the moonlight. She scooched in closer to him on the bench. The blanched garden, such as it was, shone in silvered shapes – the slender reeds, bosky shrubs, many-fingered trees – and she could glimpse the waterway in bright, dazzling flashes.

'So why exactly are we sitting outside in the depth of winter at night?' she asked him.

'For the Midwinterhoornblazen.' He grinned. 'As we speak, my father is positioning himself above the well with a giant horn, just waiting for the call.'

Lee considered this in silence – before they both burst out laughing.

'And, of course, we all really, really hope he doesn't fall into the well,' he joked, dropping his head to her shoulder in a sign of despair.

Lee smacked his arm in weak protest, but she couldn't help continuing to laugh.

'Oh God, I really am sorry about him,' Sam sighed, kissing her shoulder. 'He's such a miserable beggar. I didn't know whether forewarning you would stop you from coming altogether.'

'Ha, as if. I've met far scarier men than your father, believe me.'

She had just made it as an off-the-cuff comment but she saw the smile fade in his eyes as he looked at her.

'On the plus side, your mother's wonderful!' she said quickly.

He beamed again. 'I know. God knows how she does it, putting up with him.'

'Oh he's not *that* bad. Just a little dour, perhaps.'

'Hmm, you're kind,' he said blandly, looking out to the horizon again and squeezing his jaw.

She wriggled in closer again, linking her arm through his under the blanket, feeling how his leg kept jigging. In spite of his attentions to her, he was still nervous, distracted. 'So tell me – how are you *really* feeling about tomorrow?'

He considered for a moment. 'Nervous, sick, feverish, dizzy – basically all the feelings I get around you.'

'You make me sound like the norovirus!'

He laughed, squeezing her thigh. 'No, I'm okay. I feel fine.'

'Fine, but intensely focused?' she asked, deliberately leading him for more. 'Because the whole "milk and *hazenpeper* diet, going to bed at eight" thing is indicating you're more invested in this than you first suggested.' And when he didn't reply, she added, 'Your mother told me you ran *two* marathons this year. Fit boy.' She arched an eyebrow suggestively, running a hand over his abs under the blanket. He glanced over at her touch, that first flame already in his eyes, and he leaned over and kissed her, both of them feeling the immediate heat ignite between them. The house was at their backs and she hoped Aggie wasn't watching from a window, 'attaching a narrative', as she always scolded Mila for doing. This was just a kiss. A very longed-for kiss. That had been the longest dinner she had sat through in years, Evert dominating the conversation and not so much advising Sam as drilling him on tactics, the opposition, the course . . .

He pulled back, their eyes remaining locked even though their lips weren't. Frustration tugged. If they were only alone here . . .

A bird flapping its wings in a nearby tree intruded on the moment, breaking the spell. He would probably say he needed to conserve his energy anyway. She settled back down with her head on his shoulder.

'So come on, be honest with me,' she pressed. 'Two marathons in a year. Tomorrow isn't just a nice little Christmas bonus for you, is it? You've grown up seeing your father train for his next race and you've done the same. Liam told me how good you were at uni.' She jabbed him playfully with her finger. 'Are you actually racing to win?'

He was silent for several moments, staring deep into the evening light and she heard him swallow, gathering courage. 'I think there's a chance I could be in with a chance,' he said finally, as though just saying the words, acknowledging the possibility, was somehow tempting fate. 'But it would mean a lot of luck – I'd have to get the best start to get in with the lead pack, for one thing. It would be almost impossible to catch them once they broke away. Langen is a legendary starter.'

Ard Langen was the winner of the International Big Rideau Lake speed-skating marathon in Canada and gold medallist for the Team Pursuit in PyeongChang in 2018.

'Well, there's definitely no doubt you've got the sharpest blades; I saw them in the kitchen. You could cut cheese with those babies,' she teased.

'Yeah, I'm hoping to take out some shins behind me,' he grinned. 'And if someone could cause a pile-up behind me, that'd help too.'

But she could see the tension in his face, his muscles all slightly too tight, his breathing shallow and rapid. She watched him, feeling like she was soaking him up, her eyes soft upon this man who was rapidly becoming everything to her and her son. 'If you did win, do you think your father would finally be happy?'

A mocking bark escaped him. 'Probably not. The fight's all he knows. His entire life has been built around this. The Elfstedentocht is the classic fight for the underdog – a farmer can beat a king in this race,' he said, alluding to the '86 event when the then-prince Willem-Alexander had competed under a pseudonym.

'But Olympians?'

Sam shrugged. 'He says when it comes to endurance, the battle is mainly up here,' he said, tapping the side of his head. He was quiet for a moment, his profile having settled into a hard mask. 'He's probably right about that.'

'And how do you feel about effectively having inherited his dream? It's a huge amount of pressure on you, surely?'

Sam was quiet again for another moment, as though he had to choose his words carefully. 'I feel sorry for him, honestly. He always had ambition, but never the luck. He had talent but not the edge; on the day, there was someone just that little bit better. And even though he perfected *his* game, the weather never played ball.'

'So you're going to go out there and try to get his dream for him?'

'. . . Something like that.'

She watched him, sensing more. His relationship with his father was complicated – outright difficult, even. 'It must have been hard, growing up with someone so . . . obsessed.'

His jaw pulsed, just once. 'It would be hard to overstate what he was like.' He glanced at her. 'Especially because he never thought I'd amount to anything.'

She frowned. 'But surely he must be overjoyed about your success with the book?'

He shook his head. 'Art isn't a real profession as far as he's concerned. He believes in *doing* things.'

'You mean like pulling potatoes from the ground and skating a hundred and twenty miles on any given Monday?'

He smiled at her gentle irony and squeezed her interlinked arm against his. 'Exactly.'

In the distance, a gentle lowing could be heard starting up – strong, steady, continuous, growing . . .

'Is that it?' she whispered, feeling the hairs raise on her arms.

He nodded as they listened some more.

'It's sort of . . . ghostly. Like two ships passing in fog.'

'Aha. Just wait.'

Sure enough, several moments later, another lowing started; this one was much closer, strong and sonorous.

'God, it's a powerful image, isn't it?' he deadpanned, bringing to both their minds the image of Evert standing on the edge of the well and blowing the two-metre-long elder-wood horn.

They laughed again and she nestled her head on his shoulder as they pulled the blanket tighter and listened to the gentle back and forth between the horn-blows, passing from farm to farm across the region. Aggie had explained, in a brief pause between Evert's diktats, that the farmers would do this every Sunday from the start of Advent until Epiphany, that it was a rural tradition. Something from the past reaching into the present – much like this race.

'Tomorrow's going to be a really big day, then,' she murmured, returning to their previous conversation and clutching his arm tightly.

'Biggest of my life,' Sam said in a low voice, coming clean finally. 'Unlike my father, I know this will be it – my one and only shot to wipe the slate clean and put this thing to bed for our family, once and for all.' He looked at her, his eyes burning with an intensity she'd never seen in him before. 'There's not going to be anyone on that ice tomorrow who wants it more than me.'

She put her hand against his chest and felt the strong, rapid thump of his heart. 'Then it's already yours. All you've got to do is go get it.'

Chapter Twenty-Six

No one slept well – even Jasper was thrashing about for once, and Lee was too scared to drift off fully in case her nightmares came creeping upon her and she woke the household. She didn't think she'd slept more than forty minutes at a time, all night, and was lying blinking in the dark when she heard the creaks coming from Sam's room across the hall a little after half three, followed by the sound of retching and a toilet flushing.

Jasper stirred, his face flushed with what she called 'sleep heat'; she always said he was her little heat stone in bed, radiating warmth. She snuggled into him, scooping her body around his and smelling his hair. It was enough to begin to lift him from sleep and she felt the realization of which day it was enter his body, his muscles tensing fractionally as his mind began to shift into consciousness too. 'Is it morning?' he whispered in the dark room.

'For today it is,' she whispered back; any other day it would count as the middle of the night.

She was able to just make out the muffled sounds of a radio coming through the floorboards. Aggie was up now too, moving about in the kitchen, feeding the dogs it seemed. Jasper wriggled over to the side of the bed to check that his pillowcase banner was where he'd left it, neatly rolled on the floor. She still wasn't allowed to look at it. 'Can I see Sam?'

'Let him get ready first. He's probably going to be nervous and a bit . . . distracted, so don't bombard him with questions, okay? Let's get ready too. That way we won't be holding anyone up if we want to go in the car with them.'

They were downstairs twenty minutes later, the world outside the windows still shrouded in darkness, the farm-house kitchen a beacon of light in the sleeping landscape. There was no welcoming fire – there was no point, when they were all going to be out within the hour – but the homely smells more than made up for that: coffee, porridge and spiced buns, more milk for Sam. He was at the table, already piling into a large bowl of porridge as his father sat opposite him like a police officer, drilling him again on all the various technicalities of the course. In spite of a prohibition order which had been brought in several days earlier, stopping people from skating on the canals to preserve the ice, there were several *kulning* points where the ice was too thin to permit mass skating and the racers would have to walk the stretch until the next good patch of ice. There might be only three hundred skaters in the race pack, but the organizers were anticipating 16,000 amateurs following in their wake. Safety was paramount.

Sam looked waxy pale, with dark moons cradled under his eyes. Had he slept at all? 'Hey,' he said, looking cheered by their arrival, but there was no disguising his exhaustion, nor his nerves. It was clear he didn't want to be eating anything – he had to almost grimace with every swallow to force the food down – but he knew a six-hour-plus skating marathon couldn't be done on sheer will and nerves alone.

'Good morning,' Aggie said brightly. 'Did you sleep well?'

'Brilliantly,' Lee lied. 'I'd say I didn't move all night but I had to keep dodging Jasper's flailing arms and legs. It was like sleeping next to the spaghetti monster,' she said, ruffling his hair.

Aggie laughed. 'Coffee?'

'Yes please.'

'Jasper, some hot chocolate for you?' Aggie asked, already holding up the jug of hot milk.

He nodded happily.

'And porridge for you both? You'll need fuel to keep you warm standing out in the cold.'

'Great, thanks.'

Aggie brought over their bowls as Lee settled at the end of the table, Jasper pointedly going and sitting beside Sam.

'You'll see my banner today,' he said, clambering onto the chair.

'I can't wait,' Sam said tiredly, mussing his still-crazy bed hair.

'You can't see it before the race, though. It's got to be a surprise.'

'Then knowing I'm going to see your banner will make me skate faster.' He looked back at Lee. 'Where are you going to stand? So I know where to look.'

Lee saw Evert's head snap up at the comment; he had ceased with his drills and tactics in their presence and had been staring into his empty bowl of porridge. Clearly he didn't think Sam should either have time – or such inadequate focus – to be looking for them.

She dragged her gaze back to Sam. 'Well, you tell me. This is your neck of the woods. I imagine the crowds are going to be horrendous in the towns.'

He groaned. 'And Leeuwarden in particular will be the worst, as the start and finish point. I doubt you'd see anything there either – nice though it would be to have you there; you'd probably be better off watching on TV here.' He thought for a moment, an idea coming to him suddenly. 'Hey.' He looked back at Jasper. 'You could stand in the exact same spot where I cheered on *my* papa.'

'Yes!' Jasper hissed excitedly. 'Can we, mama?'

'Sure. Just tell us where to go.'

'It's an ideal spot,' Sam said. 'You can walk it from here, but it's about two miles from the finish, on a particularly isolated stretch, so you won't get the crowds there.' He looked down at Jasper again. 'Which means I'll be able to really see and hear you.'

Jasper drummed his heels excitedly against the chair leg, make Aggie laugh and Evert scowl.

'Okay. So go out of the back door and down the grass to the water's edge. You can go on the ice there, of course; turn right and keep going until you pass under the little bridge. Keep going about another five minutes after that and you'll see the junction to the Bonkevaart canal. It is much wider there, like a highway. You will be able to see us coming for hundreds of metres. Bear right and when you see three windmills in a row, with a single one opposite, right on the water's edge, that is the spot. There's a small jetty on the left where you can stand. The grasses are really long, higher than your head. And it's far from the roads at that section, which is why it's quieter.'

'That's where we'll be,' Jasper said determinedly. 'And I'll have my banner so you can extra see me.'

Lee smiled as she ate her porridge. 'Hear that? You've got to *extra* see him, Sam.'

He managed to wink at her, something not missed by either of his parents and eliciting very different responses in both. Evert cleared his throat and placed his hands flat on the table.

It appeared to be a statement of intent – the time for chitter-chatter was over.

'The wind is westerly today – I've already been out and checked – and it's milder than they forecast. I know they said minus three, but it's minus one already and if that wind doesn't turn, then you mark my words, that thaw will be coming today, not tomorrow. You'll need to be fast. You remember '85.'

Sam nodded, looking grim.

'What happened in '85?' Lee asked.

'It was three degrees that day and the ice began to thaw. They had to stop the race prematurely,' Aggie said, with a roll of her eyes as she set down a plate of hot spiced buns.

'Oh.'

Evert looked at Jasper, staring at him with stony eyes. 'Do you know what they called the '63 race, boy?'

'His name's Jasper,' Sam said quietly, pausing eating.

Evert's eyes slid from his son's back to Jasper's again. 'Well? Do you?'

Jasper timidly shook his head.

'The Hell. Only sixty-nine out of *ten thousand* competitors finished it. They had to deal with temperatures of minus eighteen, drifting snow, an east wind. Reinier Paping, the man who won it, could not even *see* the finish line because he was snow blind! He became a national hero. That's what it takes.'

Jasper looked terrified and Lee knew he had visions of a blinded, wildly flailing man in a snowstorm.

Sam saw his expression too and pushed his porridge bowl away. 'Hey Jasper, I've got a better story than that. Do you know what happened in the '56 race?'

He shook his head warily.

'There was a lead pack of five skaters and they made a

pact, and all skated over the line with their arms linked. The organizers were so furious, they disqualified them and awarded the prize to the man who came sixth. But then *he* refused to accept it! So that year they ended up with *no* winner being declared at all.' Sam widened his eyes. 'What do you think of that?'

Jasper considered for a moment. 'I think it sounds nice they were friends.'

Sam beamed. 'It does, doesn't it? All of them skating across the line together . . .' He looked back at him. 'I wish I could take you across the line with me.'

Jasper gasped, ready to say he could – he absolutely could – but Evert's hand slammed down on the table as he leapt up so roughly his chair toppled back on the floor.

'This is no time for sentiment! Do you think this chance will ever come again? Do you think this is just an ordinary day?'

The briefly bright, light moment disappeared like a bubble on a blackthorn. Sam sat back and eyed his father, history a current that flickered and flared between them. 'No,' he said evenly. 'I do not think it is that.'

Neither man spoke for several moments, the air dark with a storm about to break. Confrontation could turn into conflict in one stroke, one wrong word . . .

Then Evert turned and looked straight at Lee, cold fury in his eyes. 'This was a mistake. You should not have come.' And before anyone could react, he strode out of the room, slamming the door behind him.

Sam threw his chair back too, scraping it so loudly against the floor that even the dogs flinched. But Lee put her hand on his, stopping Sam from going after him. 'No, don't,' she said quickly, soothing him with her low voice, steady nerve. 'I'm fine. Focus on you.'

She had seen last night what this race meant to him. He couldn't go into it distracted by events here. She didn't need him to defend her and risk triggering something bigger between him and his father. She squeezed his hand, encouraging him to let it go.

Slowly, reluctantly, seeing the determination in her eyes, Sam sat back down again. Lee picked up her spoon and began eating her porridge, outwardly calm. But her heart was pounding like a monkey's drum. She already knew that when today was done, she never wanted to see that bloody man ever again.

Lee stared in amazement – bright stadium lights had been set up alongside this initial stretch of the canal, drenching the crowds in a glaring, alien light. Dawn was still several hours away yet. Banks of television cameras from broadcasters all over the world were trained on the start line, a crowd five deep along either side of the waterway for as far as anyone could see. The noise level was deafening, people shouting and cheering and laughing as they waited impatiently for the impossible to happen; an entire generation had grown up hearing about the iconic event, whilst being told it couldn't possibly happen again in this rapidly heating world. The ice needed to be six inches thick all the way along the 120-mile course, and since 1997 there had been a couple of almost-rans – most notably the crashing disappointment of 2012, when the ice grew to a depth of almost ten inches in most places, but was only a dangerous one inch in the westernmost point of Stavoren. Lee was bemused to find she was fast becoming an expert on the subject.

'Oh my God,' she said, as Sam held the car door open for her and she climbed out. She and Jasper had sat in the back with Aggie, while Sam and Evert were up front. She slowly turned a full circle, taking in the sight.

'I know. You can imagine what it would have been like here last night,' Sam said, looking drawn.

'What happened here last night?'

'Nacht van Leeuwarden. One massive street party. You've heard the saying? Frisians only thaw when it freezes.'

She smiled. 'Funny.' She looked around at the vast crowds again. 'This is even madder than I thought it'd be.'

'Yeah.'

She looked back at him, hearing the slant in his voice. 'Feeling okay?' She reached for his hand.

'Mm-hmm.' But he looked tense, the fibres in his body coiled. He kept stretching out his neck, rolling his shoulders back. She saw him glance back at his father, who was already talking animatedly with some officials, receiving some back slaps and handshakes as he was recognized not as an 'also-ran' or 'sore loser', but as a silver medallist; his chest was puffed, his chin held high. Sam looked away again, jaw pulsing, and she knew their argument in the kitchen was sitting within him still; as it was her. But this wasn't the time. For his family's sake, he had to put this ghost to rest, and that meant staying focused.

She put a hand to his cheek. 'You're ready. Don't think about anything else. Just remember why you're doing this.'

He looked back at her, his eyes swimming with emotion far closer to the surface than she had expected, his raw relationship with his father like a festering wound.

Jasper bum-shuffled out of the car, looking tired. It was five fifteen in the morning and no matter how bright the lights, no matter how large the crowd, it was still the middle of the night to his little body.

Sam squeezed his shoulder. 'Jasper, got the banner, buddy?'

He held it up proudly as Sam dropped down onto his heels to be at eye level with him.

'Great. I'm going to be looking out for that when I get to Bonkevaart, so wave it like mad, okay?'

'I will.'

Sam held his hand up for a high five and they slapped palms, before Jasper threw his arms around his neck. 'Please win.'

'. . . I'll do my best.' He winked and rose to standing again, looking back at the registration area. The competitive racers had their own private registration tent, but with 16,000 amateurs following on behind them, the spectacle was just like a road marathon, with countless nervous, restless, warming-up bodies everywhere.

A cheer went up and they all turned to see Ard Langen, the favourite for the title, being interviewed, his lean, pinched face filling the screen. Sam sighed, watching on impassively as the interviewer asked about his Olympic Games success in PyeongChang.

Lee touched Sam's arm and he looked back.

He blinked. 'Right, well, I guess I'd better get over there and get my bib on.'

'Can't wait to see you in your skating suit,' she teased in a low voice, one eyebrow arched provocatively.

'Oh, it's a real treat,' he laughed, his nervous tension slackening momentarily, leaning over and kissing her on the lips. She remembered only as they pulled apart that Jasper was standing there, watching. It was yet another rule broken – no PDAs in front of her child – but when she looked down, he was smiling up at them.

'Okay, go, go,' she said quickly. 'We'll watch you set off,

then head back home with your mother. Your father's definitely staying here all day, yes?' The last thing she needed
was to be around him any longer than was strictly necessary.

Sam gave a weary sigh. 'I'm half-expecting him to run
alongside me, shouting instructions the whole way round.'

Lee laughed again. Frankly it wouldn't surprise her either.
'And we'll get in position where you told us, in about five
and a half hours from now?'

He nodded. 'No one's going to be passing sooner than that.'

She smiled, seeing the nervousness in his eyes. 'You're
going to be great. I can feel it.' He nodded, his hand slipping
from hers as he stepped into the crowd, looking just like
another spectator in his thick layers. She watched him go –
her own heart pounding at the sight of his nerves – until he
was out of sight, then looked back at Jasper.

It was just the two of them again. Funny how that felt . . .
diminished now. Like something was missing. 'Okay. Well,
let's see if we can find somewhere to stand where you can
see *something*.' He would barely come to waist-height of most
of the people in the crowd. 'Just keep holding my hand. These
are big crowds and we don't want to become separated,' she
said, gripping his mittened hand more tightly in hers as they
left the competitors' car park and became a part of the human
swell. News forecasters had estimated three million people
had travelled to Friesland in the past two days and surely a
third, if not half that number, were right here; the race started
and finished in this town and right now it felt like the epicentre
of the universe.

Because of the ban prohibiting spectators on the ice at all,
the crowds were forced back towards the streets and shuffling
along the banks, everyone restless and wanting a ringside
view. Lee gripped Jasper's hand tightly as they walked

through the compacted snow. It was slow-going, progress sometimes limited to a shuffle, and she quickly realized they could walk five miles and still not get to the ice's edge; but a mile or so along, she chanced upon a spot that opened up, one back from the ice, behind a particularly short woman. 'Here,' she said, bending down and lifting Jasper onto her shoulders. He was getting heavy, but she could manage it for a short time at least. They had been walking for over half an hour – the race was surely due to start soon.

Giant screens had been set up at intervals, the cameras panning over the racers as they stood, herded like cattle, all of them jostling for a few more inches towards the front, all of them trying to stay warm.

'There he is, I see Sam!' Jasper cried, drumming his heels against her arms as he pointed towards the beautiful, dark-eyed man on the screen who wielded an unheard-of power over her. He had a bib on, with the number 111 – Lee liked it, it felt auspicious. He was wearing navy skating skins, gloves, a hat with a headlamp and goggles too, in case it snowed. She felt another pitch of nerves for him, but also excitement too. She had never seen him skate before, but she remembered Liam's awe; he had to be good. A banner appeared on the bottom of the screen, showing his name and then: *Son of Evert Meyer, runner-up 1997.*

Would it anger him to be referred to in relation to his father?

The racers all looked towards the left, as though someone was talking to them, and they seemed to suddenly move as one, a concentrated hush descending upon them as physical agitation gave way to sudden focus. They collectively assumed a hunched pose, one hand for counterbalancing in front, hands pulled into fists.

Lee held her breath and the crowd fell quiet as the racers

kept the position, poised and ready for the ultimate endurance event . . . And then the starter's gun went and they were off in a messy clatter of metal on ice as the pack surged forward, everyone trying to get some momentum and find some space, find a rhythm.

The crowd erupted, cheering like it was a football World Cup final as the skaters' blades quickly found purchase. She could hear the strength of Jasper's cheers vibrating through his body onto hers as they watched the action on the giant screen, waiting for the moment – any minute now – when the skaters would be passing in front of them. It was impossible to see down the straight without standing on the ice, but they could hear the crowd's roars steadily rolling towards them like a wave, and within a few minutes the pack was right there, blades flashing, arms locked behind their backs, heads down but eyes up, like panthers on the hunt.

She saw Sam flash past, one of many and yet distinct to her. He was at the back of the front third, gone again in the next moment, too many other bodies behind him to keep him in frame. But she had seen the set of his jaw in profile, the quiet grit. This was exactly the start he'd wanted.

Stage one of making his father proud was complete.

Chapter Twenty-Seven

They had arrived back at the farmhouse, still before first light, and set up camp in the kitchen, Aggie setting a match to the pre-set fire as Lee carried a small tub chair through from the sitting room. They'd made more rounds of breakfast – coffee, hot chocolate, spiced buns – in an effort to rally their beleaguered bodies from the brutally early start, and Jasper had soldiered on for several hours, cheering enthusiastically at the small television and kissing the screen every time there was a close-up of Sam; Lee felt like doing much the same herself, and Aggie too, no doubt. They were all so proud of him, all in disbelief that he was out there, right now, skating through the dark and the cold, gliding further from them with every stroke as he toured the Friesland region of the country while they sat in the farmhouse kitchen.

Jasper was asleep now though, his body clock scrambled by the pre-dawn excursion, curled up in the chair, his thumb in his mouth. Aggie had draped a blanket over him and positioned a cushion under his head to keep him from getting a stiff neck. The curtains were still drawn even though it was now mid-morning, adding to their cloistered, feverish sequester, the farm dogs stretched out on the tiled floor beside them in rare blissful languor. The house was womb-like and warm, and Lee felt relaxed now that Evert's stern, disapproving presence wasn't lurking around corners. Aggie kept getting up at regular intervals to throw another log on the fire or make hot chocolate or cut some *boterkoek*. Lee sensed she was enjoying spoiling them. Mothering them, even.

'Where's he now?' Aggie asked, coming back from having put a load of washing in the dryer. She was excited, but also jittery, biting down on already-short nails; she perhaps, more than anyone, would benefit from Sam winning this and her husband finding some peace at last. But if Sam didn't win . . . ?

'Ninth, it looks like. Hoog is in first, Langen's in eighth.'

'Hmm, eighth means nothing,' Aggie muttered, watching the screen with laser-focus. 'Langen's just biding his time. He won't go too early. He's not got the tank to lead from here. Not when there's another sixty miles to go.'

Sam was right on his tail, his right skate only inches from the back of Langen's, matching his stroke as perfectly as a sculling crew. Lee sensed it was Langen Sam was mentally battling out there, that it didn't matter if Langen was currently placed eighth and not first. Langen was the favourite and Sam wasn't going to let him get away; Langen would have his game plan and Sam's was to be his shadow; where Langen went, so would he.

'Hoog will regret breaking away first,' Aggie continued knowledgeably, her eyes never leaving the screen. It was clear she was as much an expert as her husband, having been exposed to precious little else all these years. She sank back into her armchair, the seat cushion saggy and faded, a few feather tips peeking out through the fabric. 'He's doing all the hard work up there on his own. He'll be burnt out by Bolsward, mark my words. He'll be lucky to be in the front ten by the end.'

'Sam's looking steady,' Lee said hopefully.

Aggie squinted as the cameras switched to an overhead shot. 'Does it look to you like he's twisting there, do you think? Would you say he's dragging his right leg a little? Your eyes are better than mine.'

Lee wasn't sure about that; where her son was concerned, Aggie had the vision of a hawk, it seemed. She peered closer too. 'Ummm . . .' She scrutinized his form. 'Yeah, maybe a tiny bit.'

Aggie's mouth set in a grim line as she sat forward and she settled her elbows on her knees, her chin resting in her hands. 'He had a hip injury after the Berlin marathon. I told him to get physio on it, but he became so busy with promoting his book . . .' She bit her lip, shaking her head as she watched the tiny screen.

Lee looked back at the race, feeling apprehensive now. Sam had two Olympians in front of him – he couldn't possibly take them on with an injury.

They sat in tense, but also easy, silence, both of them glued to the action. Jasper was fast off, his cheeks growing ever rosier as he slept in front of the fire.

Aggie gasped suddenly, making Lee startle too as they both saw the collision happen as if in slow motion – the clash of a blade against a knee, knocking both racers off balance and sending them sprawling in an ungainly heap. It was Krol and Verheul, the skaters in second and third. Aggie gave another horrified gasp as the chasing pack, including Langen and Sam, immediately behind, were forced to leap over them. Lee's hands flew to her mouth as she saw Sam reflexively spring up to miss skating into them, his arms windmilling wildly. Langen, slightly to his right, didn't have to jump quite so high but Krol's arm swung up as Sam was mid-leap, knocking him off balance too. Momentum carried him over but he landed heavily and awkwardly on his left foot, struggling to remain upright and not go over too. Langen was already recovering and pulling away again, and Hoog had a clear lead now that the loss of Krol and Verheul right behind him opened up the gap between him and the rest.

'Come on, my boy,' Aggie whispered, biting frantically on her nails. 'Come on.'

Lee felt like she couldn't breathe as she watched Sam recover his balance and reset himself again. But Langen was now several paces ahead, with clear water between the two of them as he fought to convert his automatic jump to sixth place to fifth instead.

'Come on, Sam,' Lee murmured, hardly able to bear it. Had he hurt his left leg now? Was his right leg still looking fatigued? Would he be able to catch up with Langen?

Lee's leg was jigging, her hands wound tightly in her hair as she and his mother watched him dig in. The camera was tight upon his face now and she could see every muscle taut and firing.

'. . . My God, I think he's doing it,' she whispered, as somehow he began to close the gap on Langen again.

'Come on Sam, come on!' Aggie willed as he lengthened his stride, steadily, surely, getting to within two strides of Langen again. She looked back at Lee with a delighted smile. 'His father was right, the fight is up here,' she said, tapping her head. 'Hoog will be gone by the next stop. This race is between these two now.'

Lee blinked, adjusting to the brightness, as she and Jasper carefully crunched across the snow, the farmhouse at their backs and Aggie waving at the door. Night had been cast off to reveal a sky that was a soaring pale blue, just a few threads of cloud gauze streaming like gymnasts' ribbons. The landscape all around them felt vast, frozen and empty, the air as clean as a flute with only a few songbirds singing in the bare branches of the splayed trees.

They turned and waved to Aggie a final time as they got to the water's edge and stepped carefully onto the ice. It was a thick, opaque frosted white, but she could see shavings of slush on the surface; the thaw had definitely begun. It was helping the racers, of course, that the weather was being so kind – there were no side-winds blowing snow onto the ice as in '63, no arctic temperatures to make limbs sluggish and heavy, but it was clear the forecast had been fractionally, crucially, out. Evert had been right – those amateur racers for whom the midnight finish was a target might well find themselves off the ice earlier than that.

Not Sam, though. He was going to be done within the hour. She had left it as long as she dared, wanting to stay glued to the television and to see him as long as she could, but they couldn't risk not being there when he passed. They had promised he would *extra* see them.

'Stop at the bridge,' Lee called as Jasper immediately settled into an easy glide, his little arms swinging side to side as he set off. The banner was rolled up in his hand – she wasn't even allowed to carry it.

She looked around at the countryside as they passed in a gentle *schoonrijden*, trying to see Sam's boyhood self playing in these fields, skating on these frozen channels. Had he had a happy childhood, playing here on these very waterways, or had his father's demons robbed it of joy and made it a trial to endure?

They got to the little bridge within minutes, having to duck to pass under the low bricked hump, arriving at the Bonkevaart shortly after. It was four times the size of the one they had arrived by; a wide, white motorway, flat and glistening under the gentle December sun.

They looked left and right but there was no one on the ice as far as they could see. There was no one anywhere. It was splendid isolation indeed, a beautifully delicate and pale watercolour of just sky, ice and the bleached blonde grasses on the banks, three metres high and toppling over themselves in vast hummocks.

'Come on, this way, I'll drag you,' she said, taking Jasper's hand in hers and skating fast for a few steps, then swinging her arm forward and letting him go so that he continued past her, his arms out to the sides, wide and stable as he felt the wind on his face. She could see he felt free, joyously happy, and they continued the game for perhaps half a mile, laughing, playing on the ice, enjoying the day's brightness.

Soon enough, they came upon the triple windmills, and opposite, the lone one with the small loading dock Sam had told them about.

'Right, over here,' she said, leading the way, just as a distant sound came to her ear. 'Wait – what's that?' She looked around and up. There was nothing to see on the ice, but in the sky she glimpsed a small dark speck. 'Oh God, I think that's the helicopter!' she said excitedly, clapping her hands together. Sam was going to be passing right in front of them? They had timed it to perfection. She couldn't imagine how exhausted he must be. Whilst they had been sitting (and sleeping) on feather-filled chairs and munching on cakes, warm in front of a fire, he had been out here, in the dark and the cold, and now the brightness and the cold; he hadn't stopped moving once since he'd left them five and three-quarter hours earlier.

'Yes!' Jasper hollered, punching his arms up.

'Okay, let's get off the ice and into position. No, don't rush, if we can't see the racers then they're not that close. We've got a good few minutes yet.'

The dock was set above the water's edge, but the steps were narrow tread, and the wooden slats – and, more pertinently, the gaps between them – were not conducive to skating blades.

'Careful here,' she warned, pointing to the gaps. 'Keep your blades at right angles to these, like this,' she said, demonstrating with her own foot. 'We don't want your blade slotting down there, now, do we? You could end up twisting your ankle. Let me go up first and I'll help you up.' She held her hands out and balanced him as he trod onto the wooden steps. 'Okay, now, be really careful here, avoid the gaps. Mind the gap,' she said with a smile, as though he had any idea of the famous London tube slogan.

He put his hands on the handrail and they both leaned over, looking for the skaters. They were easy to spot now, dark, fast-moving shapes, growing ever larger. Lee felt her heart rate increase as she wondered how Sam was doing, where he was in the race now. He'd been in a tightly held third position when they'd left the house but, if Aggie was correct, then Hoog should have dropped back by now, unable to keep up the too-fast pace he had set early.

'Oh my goodness, they're so close,' Lee exclaimed, looking back at Jasper. 'Open up the banner, get it ready.'

The safety-pinned pillowcase was suspended between two poles like a scroll, and carefully – the pink tip of his tongue sticking out between his milk teeth – he unravelled it against his legs. It was upside down and back to front from here, but when he held it up . . .

The drone of the helicopter was loud now, the cameraman clearly visible from the open sides, the camera pointing out and towards the ice like a giant black eye. Lee could feel the vibrations through the air, making her bones hum, and for a moment, she was back there, in a different landscape, a different time: hot and red, brown faces and black hair, huge Chinooks and Apaches buzzing up and down the airspace, helmeted soldiers in the backs, anti-tank missiles pointed towards the ground, the buildings, the people . . .

The helicopter was all but overhead, the sound of the blades clashing and sluicing, so close now.

'Mama!' Jasper's voice brought her back and she turned to see him pointing to the ice. Exactly as Aggie had predicted, Hoog had fallen back, his bright orange skins not what came to the eye first, nor even Langen's red-and-black suit.

'Oh my God, he's winning!' Lee screamed in disbelief, throwing her arms in the air and wishing she could jump. Sam's cheeks were flooded with a deep port-coloured stain, his head dipped, his mouth open as he tried to breathe, but she could see a small smile at the very edges as his eyes met hers – theirs – telling them he was going to do this. He had the reserves, she could see it in the way he moved. He had the belief and the mental strength to outgun Langen on the final sprint.

'Yes, Sam! Go on! Go on! You're doing it! Keep going!' she yelled, so hard her voice was immediately hoarse.

But something was wrong. Something else was already in motion, her head was already turning back, as she realized Jasper wasn't cheering, the smile fading from her face as she realized what Jasper was pointing to. Not the skaters but—

She saw it in the last moment, same as Sam, as his eyes lifted off her and he saw – too late – the banner pole on the ice, right where his left foot was about to go. It had slid out from its precarious safety-pinned hold . . .

There wasn't even time to scream, as the pole rolled beneath the blade and his leg shot out in front of him, sending him down hard on the ice and setting Langen free as he shot past without missing a beat. Everything went silent to Lee – the helicopter, Jasper's cries – as she saw Sam roll to a stop across the ice, his body in an awkward position.

'Sam!' Jasper was clattering down the steps and onto the ice, skating over to him, crying. 'Please don't be dead! Please don't be dead!'

'Jasper, come back!' she yelled, running awkwardly over the deck too. The chasing pack was only metres away now, sensing an opportunity. Second place was still up for grabs.

The helicopter was hovering, leaving Langen to lengthen his lead as Sam groaned, struggling to get up.

'Sam, I'm sorry!' Jasper sobbed, falling to his knees and clutching his arm. 'I'm sorry, Sam!'

Lee was just stepping onto the ice as she saw Sam's head whip up. 'You idiot! What the fuck have you done?'

She stopped, stunned by the vitriol, as Jasper fell back onto his bottom, scrabbling to get away like a frightened rabbit. Sam's eyes were bulging, his face puce with rage. Suddenly, he looked just like his father. 'Look what you've done!' he spat as the chasing pack of racers sped past, blades glinting like knives in the afternoon sun. Leaving him behind. He pulled his legs in and got up to his feet again, wincing with pain. And with a dip of his head and a furious yell of frustration, he set off again without another word.

'Jasper,' Lee cried, getting to him and falling to her knees, hugging him to her closely as they sat on the edge of the ice, Jasper sobbing and shaking uncontrollably as the skaters came past in a never-ending stream. And all the while, the helicopter hovered overhead like a mosquito in the sky, biting them both.

She saw the banner where Jasper had dropped it as Sam had turned on him; a deflated pillowcase on the ice, all but invisible until metres away. She reached for it and pulled it out of the way of the other skaters, turning it over and only able to read the vivid red letters for a second before the tears blinded her.

We Love You Sam!

Oh God. What had she done?

Chapter Twenty-Eight

'I'm sorry,' Lee said.

Aggie stared back at her as Lee pushed the bag strap further up her shoulder. Jasper was already in the car, still sobbing, his face swollen and pale. They had arrived back at the house within ten minutes, a journey which had taken over twenty on the way out, rushing in through the back door to find Aggie pacing the kitchen, her hands pressed to her mouth in a steeple as though she was in prayer.

The small television set was still showing the race, the leaders over the line already, the very helicopter that had hovered over her and her child – no less terrifying than an Apache, it had transpired – framing the dramatic shots and showing the jubilant scenes in town.

She and Lee had just looked at each other for a moment but words had failed them both, the consequences mutually devastating, and Lee had rushed upstairs to stuff their overnight clothes into their bags. Jasper wouldn't even come into the house, cowering by the far side of the car.

She stood on the step now, knowing there was nothing she could say, no way to explain the disaster that had befallen Aggie's family because of them. *Accident* wouldn't cut it. Aggie had spent over twenty years enduring her husband's wretched bitterness; now she was destined to listen to her son's too?

She had been nothing but kind to them, a mother hen who had done everything to make them feel welcome, and sitting cocooned in the curtained kitchen this morning, Lee had felt a sense of home such as she hadn't experienced since she was a child.

But that belonged to another world now. She had strayed from her own path. It never should have gone this far. She should never have come here, never involved her child . . .

'I'm sorry,' was all she could offer. And she turned and hurried away, the dogs trotting amiably alongside her, sniffing the cold air, tails aloft. She was friend, not foe. Or so they thought.

She secured Jasper into his seat and turned the car on. It took several turns of the key to get the ignition to fire, and the windscreen was covered in a thick frost. She had no option but to sit there until it cleared, her and her son enclosed in the cold car, screened by the backlit opaque windows. This was no quick getaway. Evert could be on his way back even now, screaming down the lanes to vent his spleen. His son denied! Him denied the Meyer name in the history books!

It took several agonizing minutes but eventually the frost cracked, split and marbled, and she could get the wipers going. She reversed and swung round, taking in a final look at the farmhouse: the dogs wagging their tails at her in the yard, the bench where she and Sam had sat yesterday evening listening to the midwinter horns, the back door that looked down to the water. It was still open but Aggie was not there. Was she in front of the old television set, watching their dreams die?

In the back seat, Jasper's sobs had turned into silent streams, his breath still coming occasionally in hiccupping gulps, a sudden grab of breath, his little shoulders hitching up to his ears.

'It's okay, my darling,' she hushed him as they turned onto the lane, reaching back for his knee and squeezing it with as much love as she could. 'We're going home now.'

She was half an hour from the city when her phone rang.

Mila.

She switched on the Bluetooth. 'Oh my G . . . Lee, I've just seen it on the news. Are you okay?' Her friend's voice was suffused with concern – and static. The reception was poor.

It was on the news? Jesus. Lee glanced back in the rear-view mirror but Jasper was fast asleep again, exhausted by his tears. 'Not really,' she said quietly. 'We're just on our way back now.'

'I just can't believe this . . . ppened. You must be . . . pieces. Are you sur . . . kay to drive?'

'Well, what other choice do I have? We just need to get back home.'

'Sure . . . ure.' Her voice crackled in and out of reception. '. . . you be back?'

'Google Maps is saying half an hour. We left before the end of the race, clearly. It's meant we're ahead of the traffic.'

'. . . hat's something.'

'Yeah.' The only positive in this god-awful mess – a decent car journey.

'Listen, I'm co . . . o matter what you say . . . n't try to fob me off . . . ring dinner with me.'

'Okay, thanks Mils,' she said flatly. It hadn't even crossed her mind to think about food yet.

'Don't be alarm . . . use my . . . ey . . .'

'Yes, that's fine.' She had given both Mila and Noah keys to the house. They were her alarm holders, Jasper's god-parents, his guardians in the event of her death—

'Hav . . . ung . . . sele?'

Lee frowned. 'Sorry Mils, you're really breaking up. What was that?'

'. . . said have you . . . ken to Gisele?'

Lee frowned harder. '. . . *Gisele?* Why would I speak to her? . . . Mils? . . . Mils are you there?'

She glanced down at her phone. No reception bars. Call disconnected.

Her grip tightened around the wheel. Why the fuck would she call Gisele at a time like this? They weren't best friends. Spending St Nicholas' Eve together didn't mean they were now obliged to keep each other informed of their comings and goings. She bit her lip, staring dead ahead as the signposts for the city told her she was drawing nearer and nearer, back to life as it always had been, this long weekend nothing more than a slipstream they had fallen into.

Her body felt rigid and she wanted to scream, to kick something, to hurt something instead of always, always being the one to be hurt. She felt possessed by a white-hot fury – shame, frustration, but most of all, worst of all, guilt. Because this was her fault. It had been entirely avoidable, wholly within her power to make sure her son was never exposed to something like this. She had seen the signs he was becoming too attached and she had chosen to ignore them. She had let herself believe there might be another version to their story and because *she* had wanted that, she had put herself first. And now there were two broken hearts to deal with.

He was a little boy who wanted a daddy, of course he did. He wanted to be just like his friends whose fathers let them ride on their shoulders on the way to the park, who would play football with them for hours in the garden and knew how to make Scalextric cars stay on the track. He wanted a little brother. He wanted a family more than just the two of them. Of course he had wanted Sam. And she had let him believe, let him start to love him . . .

Her mind stalled, her thoughts catching like a balloon held in a tree. Something heavy shifted inside her, something buried deep, a creature that had been dormant and hidden away in dark folds, beginning to stir and creep, to impress itself.

Fear. Her old friend, her truest instinct. She knew it only too well. She knew when it was on the march. When something was deeply, badly wrong.

Her mind cleared, the clouds of high emotion peeling away to the one true fact, the only one that really mattered: why had Mila asked if she'd spoken to Gisele?

Mila wasn't irrational. She wasn't mad. *I've just seen it on the news . . . You must be in pieces . . . I'm coming over . . .*

With a shaking hand, she reached for the power button – and switched the radio on.

Mila was at the first-floor window as they parked, by the door as they tore up the steps. 'Oh God, you poor thing!' Mila gasped as Lee stared up at her, sheer terror in her eyes.

'It's not true, is it, Mils?' she demanded, clutching her arms. 'They got it wrong. It's all wrong. A mistake. The Americans got him. They were going to get him.'

Mila's gaze slid back to Jasper, standing on the lower step, his eyes swollen from all his tears. He looked exhausted, drained, overwhelmed. Confused.

'Why don't . . . why don't we go in and talk about this inside?' Mila said, clasping her hand and tugging her gently up the last step, a cautious look in her eyes.

Lee tried to catch her breath. To breathe. She had to breathe. It was okay. This was all a mistake. They meant the Americans. Her feet moved as Mila led her in to her own hallway. Her tartan coat – not warm enough for the countryside – was hanging limply on its hook, Jasper's red scarf – the one she hadn't been able to find on Sunday afternoon, a whole lifetime ago – peeking out from underneath.

'I've run you a bath, Jazz Man,' Mila said, shutting the door behind them and crouching down, opening her arms wide. Jasper stepped into them with the shell-shocked look of anyone in trauma; his cheeks grubby with tear stains. She rubbed his back, hugging him tightly. 'Come on, let's get some bubbles going for you.' She took off his jacket and hat. 'You'll feel a bit better when you're all clean and in your pyjamas.'

It was barely five but it was dark outside again and today had been so topsy-turvy . . .

Mila put a hand on her arm. 'I've got the fire going and left a tot on the table for you. You just sit down, take a few moments and try to relax, I'll look after Jazzy, okay?'

Lee nodded dumbly as Mila took Jasper's hand and together they walked up the stairs. She unzipped her padded jacket and hung it up, pushing off her boots with her feet. She pulled off her hat and tossed it onto the shelf above, turning away, just as she caught sight of a tiny white triangle.

She turned back, staring at it, her heart almost leaping from her chest with shock.

Cunningham's letter. The one Gisele had brought over on Saturday morning, the one she had refused to open because, for that brief, brief moment, she'd been happy and she'd wanted to stay that way. She hadn't wanted Cunningham stealing it from her by stealth, words on a page ruining her rare, fragile peace. He'd done her enough damage.

She pulled it down, staring at his bold, fluid handwriting, her name in his hand. A fine skein of dust had already begun to collect and she wiped it clean, an automatic motion, a stalling tactic. But she already knew what it said: in her heart, she'd always known – she knew the guilt he carried. Still, it sat in her hands like an unexploded bomb.

She walked up the stairs and into her living room, the fire crackling away quietly, a nugget of liquid amber glistening in a shot glass on the table. It wasn't her usual eggcup, but still . . . The lights on the lop-sided Christmas tree had been switched on, a single wrapped present beneath it.

She sank onto the sofa and immediately downed the whisky, letting it burn. Hurting . . . it was all she knew. Living with pain. Memories that wouldn't die. Nightmares that wouldn't cease . . . She looked at the blank TV screen. Five times the size of the one in the farmhouse.

She blinked, immediately banishing the thought. She would not think about the scenes in that kitchen. Not now, not ever again.

Picking up the remote, she switched it on, going straight to the menu and news channels. She didn't want domestic news; she didn't want to see the rest of the country's celebrations, to know who'd won – and who hadn't. She found CNN, which was showing the weather forecast for America's southern states . . .

She looked back at the letter, still there, not going anywhere. She could toss it in the flames, she supposed. That would be one answer, one way not to hear the words he'd been trying to say to her these past six years, the ones she'd refused to hear – her only power over him – and which now sat within those precise folds. To read them, to let them be said, would be to let him off the hook. She knew he thought an apology would be enough. It would be sincere and heartfelt because he *was* sorry, she knew that. But sorry didn't change a damn thing. It didn't mean she hadn't gone through what she'd gone through.

The sound of his name caught her ear, leaping out of her head and into the room. She looked up at the screen and suddenly there he was – looking thin, bloodied, bruised, two black eyes and his head hanging down as two men, their faces covered so that only their eyes could be seen, held him up under the arms. They were speaking in Arabic, some of the words familiar enough to register in her brain: America. Infidel. Millions. Brotherhood. Revenge. Death.

A black-shrouded man came and stood in front of the screen, blocking Cunningham from sight. He held up a newspaper. Today's date on the top right corner. She knew what that meant. Proof of life. For now.

The man stepped back, moving so that Cunningham came into shot again. He said something she couldn't pick up and the two men holding him up released their grips. Cunningham fell to his knees as heavily as a bag of potatoes, his hands splayed on the ground. The guards took their rifles and lifted their guns above their heads, discharging ammunition into the sky in a single-arm display. Then everything went black.

Lee gasped, her hands going to her mouth as she waited for the next scene to cue, a dread the like of which she had known only once before chilling her blood.

She waited and waited – but it did not come. Instead, they cut back to the network's correspondent in the area – Sylvia Raven – in Raqqa. Lee had never worked with her although they had met once at some press awards ceremony in Washington. She was standing downtown, wearing her flak jacket and helmet.

'. . . *latest is that IS are demanding the release of all their commanders and fighters currently being held in detention centres in northeast Syria, in exchange for Harry Cunningham's release. Now, Washington's official policy is that it does not negotiate with terrorists so that, clearly, is not going to happen, but there will be a concerted effort going on behind the scenes to try to get him out. Harry Cunningham is of course known to many of our viewers, having filed reports to this television network, as well as in his role as chief Middle East correspondent for the* Washington Post. *He is a seasoned and highly regarded war reporter, and he received the Pulitzer Prize in 2015, alongside his long-time partner, the photographer Lee Fitchett. There is no doubt he is exactly the kind of high-profile target IS would want to take captive and this will work in his favour, for the short term at least. For the moment, he is more valuable to them alive than dead, but as we have seen with Islamic State in the past, that will not stay the case for long and the clock is quickly ticking down for the security services to locate him and try to extract him – if indeed they can. He may deliberately be kept with women and children, in order to maximize risk to civilians and impede any rescue efforts.'*

The news anchor – a fake-tanned man in an expensive suit – nodded sombrely. '*And what of the reports emerging that Cunningham was not in Syria under official press sanction? We understand the* Washington Post *were caught off guard when news of his capture became known and that they didn't know he was even in the country.'*

Sylvia shifted her weight. '*Yes, there are a lot of unanswered questions about what he was actually doing out here. Clearly he wasn't reporting for the* Washington Post, *with whom he is still officially contracted, although that alliance is now understood to be more of a roaming role as he had moved into semi-retirement. There have been suggestions from some sources that he was out here working on an undisclosed book project; Reuters were aware he was in the area and I understand it had come to the attention of the US* units in the region too. But the specifics are still sketchy and the priority at the moment has to be on a successful extraction.'

Anchor man nodded again, his cup of coffee steaming in front of him. '*Sylvia Raven, speaking to us from Raqqa, in Syria, thank you very much—*'

Lee turned the TV onto mute, staring down again at the envelope in her hands. She had been wringing it, she realized, and tears were blanketing her cheeks.

He was alive. For now, he was still alive. That was all that mattered now. She tore open the envelope. Accept his damned apology, she told herself furiously. Let him wriggle off the hook. Let the past . . . slip away. She had survived it, after all. He must too.

She read the words, black smudges on white as her eyes tried to focus past the tears.

Fitch,

I don't blame you for not wanting me in your life. I know why you can't forgive me and believe me when I say you can't hate me more than I already hate myself. I know that my following you here didn't give you the sense of safety that I hoped it would; you're far stronger than me anyway, and I was fooling myself to think that trying to 'protect' you now could make up for not protecting you then.

I've tried doing what you want and just letting you go but I'm going to be a father soon and I can't bring a child into this world knowing what kind of man I am. You've been so brave but I have to make this right. I have to be able to live with myself and I can't, knowing that he's still out there, getting away with it.

I know what I'm getting into and that's why I've asked

Gisele not to give you this letter until I've gone. Don't try to stop me, we both need this to be resolved, one way or the other. I pray I can do this and give us both the happy endings we deserve – we always did want to do some good together, didn't we? – but if I fuck it up, know I wanted it this way. I'd rather have died trying, than lived any longer with the shame of what my choices meant for you.

You're the best friend I ever had, Fitch, and I've missed you.

I'll see you again soon, I hope,
Cunningham x

The letter fell from her hand, a dove's feather lilting softly to the ground. Not an apology then, but vengeance?

She felt the world stop spinning, felt herself become light, unanchored. She had wanted him to suffer, yes; she had punished him over and over because his quest for glory had come at the ultimate cost to her. There was no doubt she had dreamt of the revenges she would take if she found herself back in that schoolroom again, but for Cunningham to actually go back out there, looking for him . . . It would be 'kill or be killed', he knew that as well as she did.

She began to shake, the tears falling in sheets.

If she'd only opened the door . . .

If she'd only read the letter . . .

If she'd only told him – that he only knew half the story.

Chapter Twenty-Nine

'I know they'll kill him.'

Dr Hansje let the words hang in the air, making no effort to catch them. 'How do you know that?'

Lee stared into space, seeing nothing. There seemed to be a time lapse between the doctor's mouth moving and the words reaching her ears. She hadn't slept, lying on the sofa all night and watching the same images run on a loop, coloured banners running along the bottom of the screen with other headlines, none of them telling her what she needed to know. Mila had got hold of Dr Hansje for her and set up this appointment, but what was the point, when there was only one thing that could make her feel better? 'Because it's personal. Because it's a game. They know Washington will never meet their demands, but they've got themselves a nice poster boy to attract the world's attention. And when they think they've hit peak viewing figures . . .' She looked back at the doctor, her eyes glassy and cold. 'A Christmas Day slaughter, striking at the heart of the infidel calendar, would send out a big message, don't you think?'

Even Dr Hansje – unflappable, inscrutable, the person whose phrase 'I see' could cover everything from 'Good heavens,' all the way up to 'Holy shit!' – looked taken aback. 'You think they would do that?'

'Of course,' she shrugged. 'They call for increased attacks against their own during Ramadan. They even call it the "holy month of jihad".'

The pen in the therapist's hand twitched as she considered her words. '. . . How do you know it's personal?'

'Because he sent me a letter, explaining everything. He's gone there for revenge. After what happened to me.'

'Did you ask him to go?'

Lee's eyes flashed. 'Of course not.'

'So why has he taken it upon himself to avenge you?'

'Guilt.' There were many things she could have said: Honour. Principle. Justice. But it was guilt that had made him get on the plane.

'You think he feels responsible?'

'He knows he's responsible.'

There was a pause. 'And how does that make you feel, knowing he felt that level of guilt?'

'Pleased.' The word glittered like a chandelier, attracting attention, demanding to be noticed. The therapist's head tilted, her scrutiny dialling up a notch as her eyes narrowed. Lee looked back, defiant. Making sure he suffered the guilt of his actions had always been her intention and she wasn't going to deny it now, water it down into something more palatable. The very least she owed him was the honesty that she had wanted him to suffer.

'And how does it make you feel knowing he'll soon die because of that guilt?'

How does it make you feel . . . how does it make you feel . . . The question drifted to her like a cloud, but knives were hidden within it, cutting her. Because words couldn't answer this question and she sank back into herself again, hiding in a screaming silence, her face shining with hot tears.

Dr Hansje let the silence expand, filling the room. '. . . Lee, it's time now. It's time you tell me everything.'

Lee nodded, resisting it no more, though her heart fluttered in her chest like a frightened bird.

'Close your eyes for me,' Dr Hansje said, putting down the pen. 'We're going to go back there, back to the end . . .'

. . . On her stomach, on the desk, she watched him walk out, casually picking up the gun as he passed. He was sideways, the world tipped on its side, the world gone to shit. A bright rectangle of light flashed on the floor as he opened the door and passed through it. As though nothing untoward had just happened.

She didn't know how long she lay there for. Maybe only a few minutes, possibly days, but she cried out in pain as she tried to move, immediately retching, heaving over and over. She clutched her shirt, trying to close it, but the buttons were ripped off, and as she tried to step into her trousers, she saw they were inside out from when he had wrenched them off her. Her hands went to her chest, aware of a dull pain, and she saw a dark bruise already forming on her sternum from the camera that had been trapped beneath her, trapped beneath him.

'Fitch??'

Her head lifted, slowly, painfully, ears still ringing from the bomb, his fists, and she realized she could only see out of one eye, the other one closing up and reducing one side of the world to a narrow slit.

Cunningham gave out a sound as he saw her, his legs buckling at the knees, and he had to grab the door to keep from falling to the floor, a shout that became a wail escaping from him. 'No!'

He had been beaten too; there was a wound to his head, blood trickling down, a split lip. Limping, he staggered over to her, shaking off his jacket and wrapping it around her shoulders, trying to cover her up, his hands smoothing her hair and taking in the battered sight of her as tears flowed down his cheeks. 'My God Fitch, what . . . who . . . who . . . ?'

She couldn't speak; only a tiny shake of her head could convey that she didn't know who. He had been covered whilst she had not. He had walked out of here. Sauntered. Strolled. Having a good day . . .

Cunningham held her so tightly to him she thought her ribs might crack, his sobs convulsing his body in rolling waves. She felt his anger. Felt his love. She felt safe again.

He kissed the top of her head, pulling back. 'We can't stay here. They're everywhere, taking the town. We've got to get back to the car.'

She closed her eyes in defeat. It was too much to ask. She couldn't run, she couldn't even walk. Her body had turned against her – leaden and helpless. But he didn't ask her to; with a strength that seemed improbable given his own injuries, he scooped her up in his arms and carried her like a baby, past the overturned desks and toppled chairs, past the poem on the blackboard, out through the golden rectangle and into the light, running past clumps of dead grass, over red earth, plumes of smoke still drifting into the skies above Kobanî. She saw the Coke can Moussef had thrown, rolled to a stop outside the walls of the destroyed shack, caught a glimpse of the walls inside saturated with the deep, dark red of arterial blood.

Carefully, like she was made of china, he put her down on the passenger seat, covering her with a rough, patched blanket and fastening the seat belt for her, his teary eyes travelling over her face, seeing her blank stare and distorted, swollen features. He limped into the driver's seat and turned the ignition on, wheel-spinning as he pulled away and sending a shower of earth high up in a spray behind them, the village at their backs.

They drove for miles, over roads that could scarcely be called tracks, only a few wild goats watching their progress, the car bouncing erratically on old springs, throwing her about and making *her battered body burn harder. He kept looking over at her, resting his hand upon hers and squeezing it, checking she was still there, still with him and not sinking into some deep, dark place inside where he wouldn't be able to reach her.*

'They were dead, Lee,' he said eventually, his voice choked. 'Raped, mutilated. Murdered. The baby too. There was blood everywhere . . .' Another sob escaped him and he smacked his hands hard against the steering wheel, shaking himself against it, like he was trying to rattle the memories free.

He stared at the horizon, his breathing heavy and laboured.

'. . . One of the girls, Virginie, was still alive. Just. As soon as Moussef saw the scene, he ran to find you and I tried to get from her what I could. It was the only . . .' He sobbed again. 'It was the only thing I could do for her.'

What?

His words sounded far away but they still registered. If he had come to find her instead of Moussef, if he hadn't hung back trying to get the girl's dying words, her final testimony for his story . . . He could have helped her, saved her. They never should have separated in the first place; they always went in everywhere as a team, both for the sake of the story and their safety.

He looked over at her again, oblivious, angry tears shining in his eyes. 'It was a set-up, Lee. Someone knew we were coming. They wanted us to find them like that. They were waiting for me. For both of us.'

She turned her head slowly to him, even that making her feel dizzy. She stared at him, feeling a pressure begin to build inside her, something uncomfortable. Painful. Wasn't it obvious? Didn't he get it? '. . . Moussef.'

He looked confused, glancing over at her like she was raving. 'No, Moussef was with me. He came to find you, to make sure you were okay.'

Lee blinked, hating him suddenly for his stupidity, his ambition. How could he not see it? 'Moussef told Him I was in there. He sent him in to me.'

Harry looked back at her, confusion and denial flickering over him in a dance. 'No . . . That's not . . . He's Abbad's cousin . . . He owes me . . . He's our friend.'

Friend? This was a war. Moussef was a stranger, the cousin of another stranger. He had already physically assaulted her. Was Harry really questioning her, taking that man's side over hers? Could his pride not accept that he'd been played? Could he not admit that his mistake had meant such a high price for her?

She saw the way his head shook side to side, refuting her words as he drove, and she felt something break deep inside her, a dam collapsing, a tide of bile rushing into her blood. Dismay. Despair . . . Betrayal.

Slowly, swinging her legs to the other side, she turned her body away from him in disgust.

'. . . Lee?' His hand could no longer reach her knee.

She tuned him out, resting her head against the seat and closing her eyes, sinking into her mind and drifting far away from here. It was all too late now anyway – those girls were dead, the village had fallen, she was broken – all in the space of an hour. What did it matter what he believed? It wouldn't change anything. Moussef was still the informer. Moussef was still IS, no matter what Harry tried to tell himself.

'Coffee?' Mila asked, already filling up the water in the coffee machine. She was wearing the frilly apron, succulent smells of roast lamb drifting over to the sofa area.

Lee was lying curled up on her side, seeing and hearing nothing as *Aladdin* played on the TV, Noah and Liam sitting cross-legged on the floor playing Ludo with Jasper. They were

370

taking it in turns to stay with her during the days, all convening here in the evenings and trying to keep things steady for Jasper whilst she silently fell apart. It had been eight days since news of Harry's capture had broken across the globe, and no matter how many times news networks discussed and analysed the story, nothing had been heard since.

It had been three days before she'd noticed Mila had disconnected her landline, keeping the house in a state of relative quiet as reporters scrambled to try and get hold of her mobile number, wanting an interview, a comment, a line. Her photographs had been reproduced in almost every newspaper in the world as Harry's capture drew international attention, but it was the Pulitzer images, the perceived high point of his career, which were reissued again and again. No one realized those very images were the reason he'd gone back out there, why he'd risked this predicament; no one, not even Cunningham, understood what it did to her every time she glimpsed those brown eyes. Dita certainly hadn't known when she'd submitted them for the Pulitzer jury's consideration.

Dita was a fierce gate-keeper, mostly managing to keep the press at bay and ringing in regularly with updates, even though there was nothing meaningful to tell – reports came and went that he might be being held in Sarrin, or he'd been moved to Idlib, that he was as close as Mistanour Hill or had been smuggled over the border to Iraq. In truth, no one seemed to have a clue. In spite of the order that had gone to US units to arrest him on sight, he hadn't been spotted since Blasenberg's sighting. He had spent too many years running from artillery fire, trekking over mountain passes, hitching rides on tank and aid convoys, not to know how to avoid capture. He'd stayed below the radar for weeks and although he had started his search in Khrah Eshek – beginning with their ending – she could only imagine where his investigations would have led him by now. He could be on the opposite side of the country. Had Moussef finally blown his cover to fellow villagers? Did he too ride openly on vehicles dressed all in black, with the caliphate's flag flying and a rifle slung over his shoulder? Or was he still a wolf in sheep's clothing, hiding behind his big friendly giant smile? Six years had passed, IS had lost almost ten thousand fighters. Was he even still alive?

She had given Dita Moussef's name. Literally just that. *He's called Moussef, his cousin, called Abbad, lives in Raqqa.* That was the sum total of what she knew about the man who had destroyed her life. Dita had passed it on to American Intelligence but they both knew it was like searching for a grain of salt in a sea of sand.

She closed her eyes, hearing the fire crackle. Harry might be dead already, Gisele a pregnant widow, and her left without the one person in the world who had truly and completely known her. She had only hated him because she'd loved him so much; he knew that, right?

She felt a hand on her shoulder and saw Mila setting down a coffee in front of her, a sandwich on a plate. 'Eat.' She jerked her head fractionally in Jasper's direction, and Lee nodded, knowing what she was saying – she had to stay strong for him. If her friend only knew just how very strong she'd actually had to be these past five years, that he'd been born through trauma. It was almost part of his DNA.

She pushed herself up to sitting, beginning to tune in to her son's chatter with his godfathers, blankly noticing how Liam's gaze followed Mila as she walked back to the kitchen and checked her phone; a small smile spread on her mouth as she read something, biting her lip as she wrote something back. He sighed, looking away again.

Lee dropped her head in her hands, numb to such domestic dramas, raking her blonde hair through her fingers and wishing there was just *something* she could do. She had never been good with sitting around, much less waiting to hear whether her best friend and soulmate was dead or alive. She got up, needing to move, beginning to pace. She went and stood by the window. The canal was still frozen – the dreaded thaw had lasted only a day in the end – and there were still a few skaters out there, but it didn't have the carnival atmosphere of that first weekend. She watched as a young woman practised double axels, an elderly couple gliding arm-in-arm, *schoonrijden* style, some teenagers having a race—

—Sam exploded in her mind's eye again: his eyes bulging, his lips retracted in a sneer as he gathered his legs back in, Jasper's terror, scurrying like a rabbit . . . She shook her head, throwing the images out. She would not think about him. Never again. She had blocked him on her phone, email . . .

She turned back into the room, noticing for the first time that there was now a multitude of beribboned presents behind the tree, and she felt a rush of love for these friends who had put their arms around her and her child in this moment of need. She felt desperate and besieged on all sides, but even in the midst of this despair, she knew she was not alone.

Liam was over in the kitchen now, holding his coffee and chatting to Mila, making her laugh. They looked good together, Mils relaxed and at ease now that her attention was with someone else, clearly oblivious to Liam's interest. Wasn't it the most ironic thing? The moment she'd stopped trying to become the woman of his dreams, she became the woman of his dreams.

'I'm going to get some air.'

Everyone looked back at her as she set her half-full mug down.

'Okay, shall we all go for a walk?' Noah asked with worried eyes.

She walked over and crouched beside Jasper. 'No. Don't worry. I can see Jasper is about to thrash you. I wouldn't want to deprive him of that joy.' She managed a weak smile, ruffling her son's dark hair and kissing the top of his head. He had been sleeping in her bed every night since they'd come back, wriggling in close to her, subdued and downcast. They had left Ducky behind in their haste to escape the farmhouse but he hadn't even asked her to get him back and she hadn't offered, both seeming to understand it was easier to lose him than resume any sort of contact with Sam.

'Damn,' Noah sighed. 'I guess it was worth a try.'

Jasper gave a little smile that didn't quite reach his eyes.

'We can come with you,' Liam offered, 'we' meaning him and Mila.

'Thanks, but I'd rather be alone; I just need to clear my head a bit.' She looked at Mila. 'Are you still happy to take Pabe's dinner over for him and get tomorrow's logs in?'

'Of course.'

'I can help you with that,' Liam said to her.

'Sure,' Mila shrugged.

Lee kissed Jasper again. 'I won't be long, okay? I'll just stretch my legs a bit and then we'll run the bath.'

He nodded, watching her as she rose and walked away, still watching as she disappeared into the hall and down the stairs. She pulled on her tartan coat and her kitten hat and, pulling back the deadbolts, locks and chains, stepped outside.

The chill was immediate, nipping at her cheeks, and she set off at a brisk walk past the gingerbread houses with

Christmas trees in the amber-glowing windows, over the little humped bridges stacked with bikes, below the trees sparkling with threaded lights. This was her town, the place she had chosen to call home when she'd fled her old life in search of a second chance, needing a new start and safety. Knowing Jasper was coming had been the motivation she'd needed to carve out a new world. She'd done it for him, but in doing it, *he* had saved *her*. He'd been her reason to keep going, to keep trying, when the memories crowded in on her, and the flashbacks and the panic attacks and the nightmares threatened to overwhelm her. Jasper needed her, he was the innocent in all this. If he was never going to have a father, then he'd need twice the mother.

She walked without looking, moved without thinking, but it was no surprise when her feet stepped up some steps and stopped outside the glossy greenish-black door. At some level, she had known she was going to come here. She hadn't been able to pick up the phone to her, or even message her before now, because she knew when she did, she would have to say the words she had never told anyone. Not even Dr Hansje. Yet. She would have to admit her culpability in this.

She knocked and waited.

Knocked and waited.

Knocked and waited again.

She knew Gisele was in there – the lights were on and she had seen a shadow on the first-floor wall. She went back down the steps and crossed the cobbles, looking up from across the street, looking into the first-floor drawing room. She was about to call up – like Harry that last time on her doorstep, she really didn't care who heard or looked or watched – but the door was already opening, a narrow shaft of light falling onto the steps.

Lee ran over – very nearly colliding with a cyclist who,

rightly, yelled at her. She bounded up the steps, seeing how, curiously, the door hadn't opened further.

'Gisele?' she enquired, pushing on it gently and peering into the marble-floored hall. Gisele was standing behind the door, her hands on the walls and her arms outstretched, head hanging down between them as she panted.

Lee took one look at her. 'Oh fuck.'

She walked the corridor, up and down, up and down . . . it was more waiting, more than she could bear. The baby was five weeks early. Viable, yes, but this was too soon. This was all wrong. This was her fault.

The ambulance had arrived quickly, Gisele's bag already packed and by the door, just as she'd told her the day they'd had coffee. They'd not spoken on the way to the hospital, not in the conversational sense, Lee instead just telling her how well she was doing, not to panic, holding her hand when the contractions hit, rubbing her back . . . just getting her through it. The doctors had been waiting for her when they'd arrived, whisking her off in a wheelchair and, minutes after that, wheeling her on a trolley into theatre, an oxygen mask over her face.

Lee had rung home, explaining the situation to the others. Mila was going to stay over with Jasper; there was no question of leaving Gisele here alone – her parents were still trying to get back from their distant, exotic holiday; apparently it had been several days before word had even got to them about their son-in-law.

Gisele had been utterly alone.

Lee moaned, wanting to cry but unable to. She knew she should have made contact before now – rung, texted, visited . . . but she'd been so pole-axed by the double whammy of Sam's betrayal and Harry's capture that she'd been unable to see beyond her own pain. She'd been so immersed in the miasma of *her* story, *her* past, she had failed to see it was also Gisele's present and Gisele's future. The woman was pregnant, she was alone and she was completely, wholly ignorant of what was going on and why.

Whatever Lee was going through, she realized now it had to have been worse for Gisele. She was in the dark about everything – she didn't have Harry's letter, Dita's contacts, Lee's history. She had no idea about why her husband had left her to go to one of the most hostile places on earth, weeks before their baby was due. Wouldn't it have been better – kinder – for her to know he'd gone to right a wrong and try to become a good man, in his own eyes at least, before he became a father? It would have given her something to hold on to.

One of Gisele's neighbours had come out as they'd waited for the ambulance; she'd described how Gisele had practically been under siege for the past week, reporters camped outside her door. No one had seen hide nor hair of her in that time, the lights remaining off day and night, so that eventually the press had moved off, believing her to be hiding out somewhere else. Lee couldn't bear to think of her sitting, heavily pregnant, in the house in the dark like that, night after night, not daring to switch on a light, the television. The stress she must have been under . . .

A doctor in scrubs came through the swing doors, pulling off her cap. 'Next of kin to Gisele Cunningham?'

Lee's heart froze, forgetting to beat, as she watched the doctor cast her gaze around the waiting area. Next of kin? Slowly she raised a hand. 'I'm her friend,' she said quietly. 'But not her next of kin.'

The doctor came over. 'You brought her in?'

Lee nodded, panic beginning to rush. Surely—

'Well, I'm happy to report Mrs Cunningham is out of theatre now.'

Lee exhaled like she'd been smacked on the back, pitching forward slightly. 'You mean she's okay?'

'Yes, she's going to be fine.'

'Oh God,' Lee breathed. 'I thought, when you said . . .'

'I'm sorry, it wasn't on the notes who had brought her in. You're a friend of hers?'

'Yes. I dropped by to check on her and she was already in labour.'

'It was as well you visited when you did. The cord had become wrapped around the baby's neck. If her waters had broken, there may not have been a happy outcome.'

'So the baby's okay too?'

'Yes. The paediatricians had some work to do after delivery, with him being so small, but he's stable now. He's in an incubator in the Prem unit and Mrs Cunningham is coming around from her sedation. You can sit with her if you like, but she'll be groggy for a few hours yet.'

Lee nodded but her attention had snagged. *Him*. They'd had a boy? Harry had a son? Gisele had told her they were expecting a daughter. '. . . Then can I see the baby first?'

'Yes, but you can't hold him, I'm afraid.'

'That's fine.'

'This way then, I'll show you where he is.'

Lee grabbed her coat from the chair and followed the doctor back through the swing doors, stepping out of the way as some other medics rushed past, pushing a trolley and another patient towards the theatre lifts. They were on the front line too, these people, saving lives every day, helping others . . .

They must see things that invaded their dreams as well, surely?

They walked down a long corridor, the doctor stopping finally at an internal window. 'Baby Cunningham, third from the left here.'

Lee pressed a hand to the glass, staring in at the improbably tiny human – wrinkled skin, sealed-shut eyes, hairless head warmed by a skull cap and a thin body swaddled in a utilitarian, no doubt hospital-issue white sleepsuit; Lee realized the clothes Gisele would have bought would be for a full-term baby, far too big for this little thing. He was lying on his back in the Superman position, tubes smaller than drinking straws poking out of his body.

'I'll leave you here. Mrs Cunningham is in the maternity wing when you're ready.'

'Thank you, doctor,' Lee said, her voice thick with emotion. 'For everything you've done. You don't know how important this baby is to them.'

'All babies are important to their parents,' the doctor smiled, before heading off.

Lee looked back through the glass again, searching for something of Harry in that barely formed face, but it was impossible to say; he'd been born too soon.

She felt a tear roll down her cheek, followed by another. Then more. He was safe, but everything was a mess, nothing was as it should be. And it was all her fault.

Harry was a father and he didn't even know it.

He didn't know.

Worse – would he ever?

Chapter Thirty

'Hi Lenka.' Lee slotted her key into the lock, glancing down at her neighbour with a tired smile. She just wanted to go to bed, regardless of whether or not she actually slept.

'Oh. Hello.' Lenka nodded as she stepped out of her doorway. She looked pale and even more tired than Lee, her eyes seeming swollen, as though she'd just been crying again.

Lee felt another, distant shot of sympathy for her as she remembered her predicament; with everything that had been going on with Sam and Harry, and now Gisele, she had forgotten all about it. She'd forgotten about lots of things. Did Lenka know about Gus's affair? Was it Lee's place to say, when she didn't have proof?

'Nearly ready for Christmas?' she asked instead, bewilderingly unable to fully cast off her British manners, even in the face of adversity and exhaustion.

'Oh.' Lenka looked down and Lee saw her legs were bare under the coat too; it had to be a couple of degrees below freezing out here. 'No, I forgot.' She looked back at Lee. 'It is soon?'

Lee gave a small bark of disbelief. Was she serious? 'Uh, yeah – three days.'

'Oh.' She shivered, looking upset and embarrassed.

She actually was serious? The poor girl really did have other things on her mind. 'Don't worry, there's still plenty of time,' Lee said limply. 'I haven't made a start on my presents either. I'll just go to HEMA, that's my one-stop for emergency presents.'

'HEMA?' Lenka repeated blankly.

Lee was surprised she hadn't heard of it. It was the biggest department store in the city. 'Yes, on Kalverstraat.'

'Kalverstraat.' Lenka looked blank.

Lee frowned. Kalverstraat was the main shopping thoroughfare. How could she not know it? It was like a Londoner not knowing Oxford Street.

The door behind Lenka opened again and Gus peered out. 'Oh, hi, Lee,' he said, breaking into a friendly smile. 'I thought I heard voices! How are you?'

She ignored the question – it demanded either an outright lie or an answer so detailed they'd be here till breakfast. 'We're just talking about Christmas shopping. Or lack thereof.'

'Oh. Yes. Same here. We're so behind.'

She tried not to sigh out loud – they didn't have a five-year-old boy and a Christmas stocking to shop for. 'Have you got any plans?' Lee pushed the door open and retracted the key from the lock again.

'No, just a quiet one for us,' he shrugged. 'You?'

'Yes, same.' She gave a small smile, but she was too tired, too worn down for further small talk today. 'Well, see you around. Bye.'

'Yes, bye.'

She stepped in and closed the door, catching sight of Lenka stepping onto the cobbles and walking away, looking like the loneliest woman in the world. She paused for a moment, watching her pityingly through the crack and wondering where she was going at this time of night. The young woman looked so desolate; there were dark circles under her eyes and her hair looked unwashed. She was neglecting herself, and Lee felt she was clearly depressed—

'. . . You okay?'

She turned to find Mila standing on the stairs. 'Yes, I'm fine . . . Tired.' She was so bone-achingly tired. Everything felt wrong, rattled, jarred out of position.

'I'm not surprised. How is she?'

'Sleeping. They had to give her a general anaesthetic so she's pretty out of it, in and out of consciousness. There wasn't much point in staying, in the end. And the baby's in an incubator so . . .' Lee tried to give a shrug, but to her shock, a sob escaped her instead, the tears flowing – as surprising as they were unstoppable.

'Oh Lee!' Mila flew down the stairs and wrapped her arms around her, rubbing her back. 'What a fright you must have had, finding her like that. It's been one thing after another for you lately.'

But Lee pulled away again, refusing to accept kindness or sympathy when she knew she was the architect behind all this. '*I'm* fine. I'm not the one this has happened to!' she protested, her breath coming in ragged gulps. 'Gisele's the one lying drugged up in a hospital bed with no idea she's become a mother!'

'And how is the baby?' Mila's hand rested comfortingly on her shoulder, nonetheless.

'A little boy. Three pounds four. Absolutely titchy. He's in an incubator in the Prem unit.' She dabbed at her still-leaking eyes.

'Oh, the poor darling.'

'I know. I'll go back tomorrow and see how they're doing.'

She sniffed loudly. 'I stopped at some shops on the way home and bought some extra-tiny sleepsuits for him. Everything she bought will be far too big.' She limply held up the shopping bags in her hands and Mila took them from her, setting them down carefully by the coats so she'd see them on her way out again in the morning.

'That's so sweet of you.' Mila squeezed her shoulder affectionately. 'Listen, Jasper's in bed but not quite asleep. I said I'd send you straight up.'

'. . . Okay. Are the boys still here?'

'No, they had to go. But I've put your dinner in the oven, it's just on a low simmer so have it when you're ready. But make sure you have some. You must eat.'

Lee nodded obediently, already knowing she was too tired to eat. She also sensed her friend was restless. 'You should go. You've been here for hours.'

'I can stay if you need me to.'

'No, really, I'm just going to eat and then go straight to bed.' She'd had enough of this world for one day.

Mila reached across her for her coat.

Lee watched her, seeing energy in her friend's movements. 'Have you got plans?'

'Maybe. They were only provisional. Obviously everything's been dependent on things here, but seeing as it's early still . . . I've got another date with Joost.'

'Who?'

'You know – Alexander Skarsgård?'

'Oh.' Dodgy shoes, she remembered Liam saying as her friend pulled on her coat.

'He's been messaging me all week, wanting to meet up again, but I've been putting him off to be here with you. But I don't want him to give up on me altogether.'

'No, of course not.'

Mila gave a bemused smile as she tied her scarf. 'Honestly, it seems the more I tell him I'm unavailable, the more the guy seems to want me.'

'Classic,' Lee said flatly, unable to muster enthusiasm. The world of dating seemed so far from her emotional landscape right now.

Mila pulled her in for another hug. 'Go see your boy and have a good night's sleep. You look wrecked.'

'Okay,' Lee said obediently, too worn down to argue.

'Oh – and before I forget, Liam said to tell you he's throwing a Christmas Eve party at his. Nothing wild: carols, mince pies . . . he says it'll be *family-friendly*, can you believe it? I thought he was terrified of children? Anyway, that could be something to look forward to?'

Lee took a step back. She couldn't think about celebrations, festivities, songs, happiness, a world existing several days in the future. She couldn't see past right now. 'Maybe. Let's see.'

'There's no pressure, of course. Just if you feel up to it.' Mila smiled at her. 'I'll be back in the morning.'

'Mils, you can't keep taking all this time off work.'

'Oh, trust me, they owe me holiday.'

They walked to the door together.

'Have fun tonight,' Lee said wanly. 'Don't do anything I wouldn't do.'

'Hmm. That widens the scope for what I *can* do quite considerably.' Mila winked at her.

Lee raised a reluctant smile at that, waving her friend off and closing the door behind her, fastening all the bolts, the chain and the Chubb lock. She pressed her hands against the door and stood there for several moments, as though making sure the world wasn't pushing against the other side, trying to ram-raid its way in. It was just them again, her and her boy.

She climbed the stairs, turning off the lights as she went, putting the mesh guard in front of the fire, turning off the fairy lights on the tree – there were yet more presents under it, his over-indulgent godparents seemingly on shopping steroids. She picked up the remote to turn off the TV – it was on mute and set to Sky News, Harry's story now relegated to the ticker tape that ran along the bottom of the screen. No news meant no news coverage. It had been eight days; public interest and private hope was fading . . .

She went upstairs to Jasper's room. Shrouded in a fuzzy, not-quite-complete darkness, she could smell his scent as she walked in, see the dark shapes of his clothes strewn on the beanbag.

'Hey,' she whispered, curling around him on the bed. He was in his tightly balled shrimp position, thumb in. No Ducky. Getting off to sleep without him had been difficult this past week, but he was almost off now, stirring fractionally and giving a tiny moan as she leaned over and kissed his temple. 'I'm back,' she whispered. 'I missed you.'

'. . . Missed . . . you.'

She listened to the sound of his breathing, steady and strong. She reminded herself, as she had the day he was born, that every breath *he* took, was a step *she* took further away from the horrors of her past. He was her benchmark, her getaway car. An AA member's sobriety token.

She lay her head down beside him on the pillow, feeling it was damp. She touched his hair but that was dry; he'd been crying again. Broken-hearted, his trust betrayed.

She stroked his cheek. 'You okay?' she whispered.

There was a long silence and she thought he'd dropped

fully into sleep when his words finally drifted into the darkness. 'I miss . . . Sam.'

'You're not sleeping,' Pabe said, watching her as she carefully unloaded the logs into the log basket.

'Oh dear, do I look that bad?'

'Well, put it this way – I'm almost blind and even *I* can see how exhausted you are.'

She smiled. 'Face mask tonight then.'

He watched her. 'No one could tell it was you, you know – on the telly, I mean. Only those who actually know you both. The cameraman missed the worst of it, luckily. He had switched to Langen and I think by the time he caught on there was an accident, you had turned in the other direction. I just happened to recognize your coats.'

'I hope that's true,' Lee sighed, though in truth, her horror at their highly public pile-up had rapidly paled into insignificance compared to what had happened to Harry. For several days after the race, the Dutch press had been at pains to uncover the identity of the mother and child 'on the ice' on the final stretch to the Elfstedentocht finish, but the aerial footage hadn't captured their faces and no one had offered any information. 'The last thing Jasper needs is some fanatical idiot yelling at him.' Or some *other* fanatical idiot, rather.

They both looked over towards the little boy sitting cross-legged on the floor and watching *Ben 10* cartoons.

'Hmm,' Pabe sighed sadly. 'He's not himself, is he?'

'Hopefully he'll perk up in a couple of days when he gets to open the mountain of presents under our Christmas tree.' She had already ordered the outlandish super-blaster megatron Nerf gun of his dreams. To hell with her principles;

she just needed her son to smile again. 'I'll go and get another load of logs in and that should keep you going till tomorrow evening. Have you got any Christmas Eve plans?'

'Dinner for thirty. I was thinking haunch of venison.' His eyes twinkled and she chuckled as she went through to the kitchen and outside again.

She jogged down the steps, taking care on the slippy moss, and walked over to the covered log store against the back of the house. It was over half empty now; he would need to place another order soon. She loaded the logs into the sack carefully and replaced the felted lid, her eyes catching on something bright in the long grass as she walked back to the house. She walked over and picked it up – a key. Not a Yale, not a front door one, but smaller, finely toothed, with a red dot on it, like nail varnish.

She frowned as she pocketed it.

'Pabe,' she said as she re-entered the living room a few moments later, he and Jasper watching the cartoons in companionable silence together. 'I just found this on your lawn.' She held out the key for him.

'Mine? In the garden?' Pabe examined it as best he could without his glasses. 'But how did it get down there?'

'No idea,' she shrugged. 'Could it have fallen out of one of your pockets perhaps?'

'I haven't been down there for months. Certainly not since summer.'

'I guess it could have been there since then. It looks tarnished and it wouldn't rust easily.'

He reached for his glasses on the side table and turned the key between his fingers. 'Oh. No. Look.' He pointed to the red dot. 'It's from downstairs. All the apartment keys have a red dot on them. My granddaughter let me use her nail polish to identify them so I wouldn't get confused. I did once spend forty-five minutes trying to get in here with one of the downstairs keys.'

'Oh, okay.' Lee began unloading the final rounds of logs. She gave a small gasp as she suddenly remembered something. 'Wait – it's not for the back door, is it?'

'I couldn't say,' Pabe shrugged. 'One key looks much like all the rest to me.'

'Because Gus was saying a while back that their back-door key had been lost and he was worried because it could constitute a fire hazard.'

Pabe jerked agitatedly. '*Why* does he keep saying that? I must have replaced that key five times already. He makes me feel like I'm going dotty. If *they're* going to keep losing them, it is hardly *my* fault.'

'Don't worry about it, Pabe,' she soothed, feeling bad for having upset him. 'Jazz and I will stop and hand it back to them on our way past.'

'No!'

Lee looked up at Jasper's pinched face. 'What?'

'I'm not going back there! I didn't like it!' he protested forcefully, angrily almost.

Lee frowned. When had he been—? 'Oh, you mean when they babysat you?' She had all but forgotten about that.

'I didn't like it.'

'Well, I know it may not have been . . . like home,' she said diplomatically, remembering the black bin bag in lieu of a curtain. 'But Lenka and Gus were kind to you, weren't they?' Her heart had begun to pound at the mere thought they hadn't been.

'She wasn't Lenka.'

Lee felt a little chill ripple down her back. '. . . She wasn't?'

'Her name's Natalia.'

Natalia? Could that be the woman Lee had seen with Gus on the bridge?

'She was mean.'

Lee thought her heart was just going to stop beating and fall into her boots. 'Mean how?'

'She thought I didn't hear but I did. I heard her shouting at the others.'

'. . . *Others?*' Lee looked at Jasper's downturned mouth; at Pabe, who was looking bewildered, as though Jasper was suddenly talking in another language. 'Just wait there.' She got up and went back through the kitchen, leaving the door open as she ran down the steps. She went and stood in the spot where she'd found the key and looked back at the house.

The concrete well down to the basement apartment was damp and covered in lichen, a crisp packet and a crumpled packet of cigarettes in the corner at the bottom of the steps. The black bin bags were still crudely taped up to the windows – a poor man's curtains option, she'd assumed, but looking closer now, she saw they were commercial grade plastic, and that there were thin rows of baggy ripples in the plastic.

There was a small frosted window to the left, with a narrow opening aperture at the top. It was situated below Pabe's downstairs bathroom so she guessed it was the basement bathroom too. The opening was far too small for anyone to climb through, but an arm could certainly extend through, certainly far enough to throw something out – something like a key . . .

She caught her breath as the questions began coming, one after the other, the answers stacking up behind one another in a rush.

Why throw away a key – if not to stop anyone using the door?

Why throw away the key to ensure the door could *never* be opened?

And why pretend it had been lost?

She stood staring at the window, at the black bin bags, thinking back on her past interactions with the people who lived there. Gus, a friendly, charming, safety-conscious tenant dealing with an elderly landlord: a man in his nineties, a man he portrayed as set in his ways, embittered even, always complaining about noise, losing things, failing on upkeep. And yet that wasn't her experience of Pabe. He was frail, yes, but neither dotty nor cantankerous. So why discredit him like that? Was the discord between Gus and Pabe a simple clash of personalities – or something more deliberate? If accusations were to start to fly, who would be the more reliable? Who would believe the man in his nineties making wild claims about the friendly, safety-conscious tenant? An unreliable landlord made for an unreliable witness, surely?

Her heart was beating faster and faster as she tried to remain calm, to still her racing thoughts, to apply logic over emotion. She stared again at those ripples in the plastic; claw marks that hadn't quite broken through.

And she saw it: the painful, hidden truth. *The others*, the people on the other side of those bags weren't supposed to see out. Get out. Be out.

She remembered Lenka's withdrawn demeanour, her inadequate clothing, her lack of familiarity with her own city. She remembered how every single time she tried to talk to her, Gus would suddenly appear: chatty, friendly and yet watchful too, always taking over the conversation, always quickly bringing it to a close with a smile. She remembered his passport still in her jeans pocket on her bedroom floor – she had forgotten to cut it up and throw it away properly. She remembered too the drawing Jasper had drawn for her in there – a house with a family (she had thought). In purple felt tip pen.

Purple felt tip. Just like the message in the book, found in the bicycle basket, right outside this building. Two words she could never turn away from. *Help Me.*

She ran back up the steps and into the house, wide-eyed. 'Pabe, where's your phone?'

'Why?'

'We need to call the police. Right now.'

Chapter Thirty-One

The lift doors opened with a pretty 'ping' and Lee stepped out, shopping bags hitting her knees as she walked. She went straight to the ward she had left last night, Gisele laughing in surprise at the sight of her coming through the door, a yellow helium balloon attached to her wrist.

Gisele was pale, her face puffy and hair scraped back in a bun, still wearing the unsightly surgical pressure stockings, a butterfly cannula in the back of her hand. It was the most dishevelled and imperfect Lee had ever seen her look – and also the most radiant. She was sitting up and holding her newborn son to her chest, skin upon skin. He was so tiny, it was like clutching a bag of marshmallows – only less squidgy.

'Hey, you're up.' Lee kissed her lightly on the cheek and quickly sank into the chair beside the bed to preserve her modesty. 'Thought I'd pop in and see how your night was. It's great to see the two of you together.'

Gisele looked down at her son with the universal look of the Madonna, but Lee could see her lashes were wet and that she'd been crying. 'He's doing so well,' she smiled, almost as though surprised by it. 'He's had a feed already and I've changed two nappies.'

Lee grinned. 'Oh, well, *that* will become infinitely less

charming by the end of the day, believe me.' She pointed to the bags by her feet. 'I stopped at some shops on my way home last night and got some things that will hopefully fit him, until he's in his proper clothes.'

Tears filled Gisele's eyes again, her bottom lip wobbling. 'Oh God, I mustn't cry again. I can't stop crying!' she laughed, but not really, as a sheet of tears raced down her cheeks.

'It's completely normal,' Lee said, grabbing a tissue from the side table and dabbing them for her. 'I was the same. Cried buckets the first five days after Jasper was born. The doctors were worried I was going to get dehydrated.'

Gisele laughed again, more sincerely this time. She tipped her head as she looked back at her. 'I just don't know how to thank you, Lee. Everything you've done for me . . .'

'Oh it's just some sleepsuits and nappies,' she pooh-poohed.

'Not just that. There was St Nicholas' Eve. And if you hadn't come over yesterday when you did . . . he might not be here right now.' Her voice caught on the very idea of it, fresh tears falling as she gazed down again at the tiny bundle in her arms, as though to reassure herself he really was there.

But Lee knew she was no Florence Nightingale figure. 'Don't thank me. I should have come over a lot sooner than I did,' she said ashamedly. 'I knew you must be struggling, but I just . . . I just didn't take the news about Harry as well as I might have thought I would.'

Gisele squeezed her hand. 'I could have come over to you too. It's been rough on you, I know that.'

'*I* didn't have the world's press camped out on my doorstep.'

'Maybe not, but Harry going out there has raked up skeletons for you.'

Lee watched her as she tucked the blanket under her son's

tiny pointed chin, knowing it was time. '. . . Gisele, what do you actually know about Harry and me?' she asked. 'Has he told you why we . . . fell out?'

Gisele's shoulders slumped. 'No – he said it was your story to tell and that only you could tell it.'

'Oh.' Lee swallowed, feeling a lump of emotion that he had protected her privacy at least.

'Believe me, though, I tried everything to get it out of him. When we first got together and I realized there was this . . . rift in the middle of his life; when we'd end up walking past your house, when I found out the only reason he was in Amsterdam at all was because he'd followed *you* here . . .' She closed her eyes for a moment, the corners of her mouth pulled downwards. 'I was convinced he must be in love with you – even though things were so good between us, all I ever heard was how brave you were, how talented, how kind . . .'

Lee looked down at her feet, knowing she was all those things – and much worse besides.

'He would try to reassure me. He said you were his best friend but that he'd betrayed you. He didn't say how, but I knew it was bad. He'd wake up in the morning with a look of peace on his face, and then I would see the memory of whatever it was literally climb into his mind and he would change. I used to find him just standing in the garden at dawn, pacing the kitchen in the middle of the night. His spirit was so . . . restless, it was eating him up inside. But I couldn't help him, he wouldn't let me in.' She sighed. 'So when he left for Syria, and asked me to give you the letter, I knew it was bullshit that he was going for a news story.'

Lee looked down at her words. This was everything she had wanted – wasn't it? To hear of his torment, his ongoing anguish and guilt for what he'd done and, more crucially, what he hadn't? But there was no victory here, no jubilation in her bones. Her suffering wasn't diminished for knowing that he'd suffered too. 'Did you read the letter?'

Gisele hesitated, then shook her head. 'But I wanted to. I spent days just staring at it, knowing the answer to the questions I'd been asking for years was right there. Several times, I so nearly did it, I'd boiled the kettle . . . But then when you came over to check on me, and then had me over for Pakjesavond . . . You were so kind to me. Suddenly it wouldn't just be his trust I was betraying but yours . . . I realized that if this thing between you was so bad he had to go back out there to make things right, then I had to let it happen and trust that he'd tell me when he got back.'

If he got back. He'd been held for nine days now.

'You must hate me,' Lee said simply.

'No. Well, not any more.' She gave a rueful grin. 'I'm just sad for you both. I think you've both been grieving for a long time.'

Lee bit her lip, feeling her heart gallop and tears threaten, but she knew she had to be brave now, to do the thing she had sworn never to do. '. . . Gisele, the reason I came over to see you yesterday was because I wanted to tell you everything. You should know what happened; you're Harry's wife and the very least you deserve is to know why your husband is missing.' She stared at the tiny child, fast asleep against her, deprived of his father. She looked at Gisele again. '. . . But I don't want to upset you either. I don't want to ruin this for you – it's your first morning of being a mother. These are special moments. It can wait for another time if that's what you'd prefer. I promise I'll tell you everything whenever you're ready.'

Gisele swallowed, looking nervous. 'Is it bad?'

Lee nodded. 'Yes. It is.' She had to be honest. There was no sugar-coating what she had to say.

'But it will explain why Harry's gone?'

Lee nodded. 'Only – he doesn't know everything. I've never told anyone the full story.' She blinked. 'It will be hard for you to hear. Probably you more than anyone. I'm sorry.'

Gisele was quiet for a long time, staring down at her sleeping child. Harry's son. He might never come back. He might never meet him. Surely she had to know why? She looked back at Lee with tears shining in her eyes again as she reached for her hand and squeezed it tightly. 'Well,' she said, taking a deep, steadying breath. 'I'm ready if you are.'

Lee cycled home slowly, shopping bags balanced carefully on her handlebars and the turkey wedged in her basket, prompting laughs as she cycled past. She didn't care. Tomorrow was Christmas Eve and she was going to make sure her son had the best Christmas ever. She was quietly hopeful that she'd got him the best present.

She pedalled past the frozen canals, the spectacle of ice-skaters gliding up and down now almost routine, the city's newly restored old habit. The windows of the coffee shops were all steamed up with gentle warmth as it tried to snow outside, but just a few flakes dusted the cobbles, not settling. She passed by elaborate shop windows, beneath the exuberant light displays that lit up the entire city, feeling her heart swell. But for the crack through the very middle of it, she might have said she felt happy; but 'at peace' would do too. She would gladly take that. Gisele had been remarkable – stoic, kind, understanding, even though what Lee had done deserved none of those responses and they had both cried and hugged and cried some more. She no longer had a rock in her stomach. She no longer had a secret to carry.

She passed through Spui Square on autopilot, lost in her thoughts and only clocking where she was as she saw the bronze statue of the urchin boy on his plinth. She stopped pedalling and stared at it, remembering that day with Sam when everything between them had started to shift, the gears beginning to move – only to crunch to a halt again as her past tapped her on the shoulder and eyeballed her. Everything between them had been stop-start, effortless and yet turgid – one-on-one, the energy flowed, but life seemed to keep getting in the way, pulling them apart again. Keeping them apart.

Kicking her leg over the bike, she walked over the cobbles and put a hand to the boy's feet. The questions that had been thrown up by the message in the book – his book – had brought her back into his orbit; but now, she had the answer and it was another lock turning on their brief interlude in each other's lives. At the time, a part of her had wanted to believe that the book – and the message in it – had brought Sam into her life because he was her happy ending; but she understood now it was quite the reverse. Sam's book and the message in it had been the means by which Lee stumbled into Lenka's life and found for *her* a happy ending.

Somehow, against the odds, she had found the stranger in a city of almost a million, the prisoner – *prisoners* – living in plain sight, right under her nose the whole time: young women smuggled into the country illegally and forced to work without pay, for inhumane hours, to live in cramped and squalid conditions, their families back home threatened should they speak out or try to escape . . . She didn't think she would ever forget the image of those young women being led up the steps by the police officers – their pale, malnourished faces, blank eyes, thin legs . . . Lenka turning to stare up at her window and mouthing 'thank you' as the police car took her away for her witness statement. Natalia, the blonde woman she'd seen with Gus on the bridge, had been one of the traffickers – the woman who would meet the girls off their flights into Schiphol airport and extend for a few minutes more, until they were in the van, the illusion that this was the start of an exciting new life.

Lee had handed over the passport she had found in the bin. She hadn't even clocked the different name in it at the time, too distracted by Gus's longer hair and altered appearance; according to the police, it was just one of his many aliases. He was but one part of a wider web and his arrest was expected to have a domino effect – there would be others in the coming days.

It was neither the story nor the ending she'd expected when she'd made that first phone call to Olander Books' marketing department, but it had a glistening silver lining and she'd take that. She was determined to find them from now on; for Jasper's sake, as well as her own, she had to believe there was goodness and happiness in this world. It was time to stop looking for wars.

She looked over at the coffee shop where she'd run out on Sam, almost able to see her own ghost trembling – rooted to the spot, tethered to the past – through the window. She saw him watch her run out, stare into the space of where she'd been, pick up and fold her coat, sniffing it for a moment, his eyes closed.

The ghosts faded. Gone now. But she saw, serving behind the counter, the man who had bumped into her as she'd headed for the loos last time . . . He was wiping the counter and was seemingly singing along to something. He was no villain.

Perhaps it was time to start laying all her ghosts to rest.

She wheeled the bike over and locked it outside the cafe, taking care to lift the turkey from the basket and bring it in, along with the bags of presents. Only a few customers were in there, two absorbed on their phones, another staring sightlessly out the window. With a slow, steady exhale, watchful for any first signs of a repeat episode, she went up to the counter. The man looked up and smiled – brown-eyed, kind-looking if a little tired, slightly stooped, older than she'd recalled. She thought she saw him recognize her too, but as he took in the sight of her cradling the turkey like it was a baby, he looked like he had far more to be worried about from her than she did him.

'Hi, an espresso please,' she said quietly. 'And don't worry, I won't put this on the counter.'

'Thank you.' He nodded. 'One espresso coming up.' He glanced at the turkey again in her arms before heading to the machine and beginning to pull on the levers, sending hissing plumes of steam into the cafe. Settling the turkey on her hip, she reached a hand down into her cross-body bag and pulled out her purse, noticing his iPad on the ledge in front of her. It was almost out of sight from her vantage behind the raised serving counter but she recognized the distinctive red banner streaming across the bottom of the screen.

She stood on tiptoe, leaning in and angling herself to get a better view of it. The Sky News logo could be read easily, even upside down. *Breaking News* in bright white words, catching in her brain.

The man looked over, frowning as he saw her evident interest in his iPad. 'Uh—' He stepped over and moved it away.

Lee stared at him, embarrassed. Did he think she was going to snatch it?

'No, I wasn't . . . Could I just see that news feature? I'm just trying to hear what it's saying. Please?'

Her phone rang and she reached for it in her coat pocket. 'Hello?' she asked absently, as with her finger she pointed to the iPad again. 'I just want to see that news item,' she whispered.

'Lee, it's me.'

'Dita!' She straightened up, feeling a jolt of pure fear shoot through her limbs. Her bones became liquid, her brain a vat of static.

'Have you heard?'

Her mouth was dry, her heart beatless.

She watched the man moving the iPad onto the back counter but set up on its stand so she could see the screen. See Harry. They were showing an old photograph of him standing in a desert somewhere, wearing tan camouflage and a baseball cap, his aviators stuck in the neck of his jacket. He was grinning, squinting slightly, looking tanned, quite dusty, lighter build than of late. They ran a sequence of his old reports filed from when he'd worked at CNN – Harry crouched outside the drain where Gaddafi was cornered; Harry in the mobs in Tahrir Square; Harry sitting with refugees in the Dadaab camp in Kenya; Harry with her . . .

The man looked back at her in surprise, recognizing her in the same instant as Lee recognized herself.

Harry with her, hiding behind a sandbag as sniper bullets whistled in Sirte.

'. . . then you know?'

She realized Dita was still speaking. 'Sorry – what?' Her voice kept fading in and out of recognition as she competed with the images on the screen.

'. . . special ops . . . midnight . . . drone strike.' Dita paused. '. . . Are you hearing me? He's dead.'

He was dead?

The world tuned out again, noise fading to silence, colours bleaching to white as she saw only the images of her friend on the screen, the composites of a glittering career, a homage to a man who had lived and died for the noble cause of always trying to do the right thing. He had been trying to do the right thing that dreadful day too, when her own fate had collided with a jihadi's – and she had punished him for it, every day for six years.

The man behind the counter slid her coffee in front of her, watching her curiously. She was in his coffee shop and on the news. She was holding a turkey like it was a baby. She had tears streaming down her face.

She jolted as another image came up – not Harry. But *Him.*

Moussef, wearing the all-black uniform, gun pointing to the sky. An out-and-out leader now. Grainy footage of a cavalcade of jeeps sweeping through a rural village. Then a quick camera sweep over an image of . . . his corpse? He was dead too? Bloated and pale, a dried head wound, there was no sign now of those white domino teeth that had haunted her dreams.

'Moussef's dead?' she whispered.

'Are you not hearing a damn word I'm saying?' Dita demanded. 'Of course the fucker's dead. They got him!'

Lee gasped, the world's volume dial suddenly ratcheting up again. 'They got Moussef?'

'Jesus damn Christ, it's like talking to a chihuahua,' Dita muttered to someone in the background. 'Yes, they got Moussef.'

'. . . And Harry?'

'Is on a military plane as we speak! Jesus, he'll have freaking landed by the time you start paying attention!'

'Oh my God!' A gurgle of laughter escaped her, big fat bubbles of joy and relief rising in repetitive waves as she watched the footage on the screen, green-tinted night images of a pale, thin, very tired-looking, beaten-up man being helped to a car by soldiers. 'He's alive?!'

The man behind the counter looked at her.

'He's alive!' she cried, laughing and crying all at once as she pointed to the screen. 'He's actually alive!'

'Yes, I know, it is all over the news. You know him?' he asked.

'Know him? I'm his best bloody friend!' Her tears overflowed at the words, at the simple truth. She was his best friend.

She wanted to wipe her tears but with the phone in one hand and a six-kilogram bird in the other . . .

'Come, madam, let me take the turkey.' He held out his hands to take it from her. 'It is okay. I will hold the turkey.'

'You're sure? Because it's really heavy,' she said, struggling to pass it over the counter, laughing again, crying still, covering her eyes with her newly free hand now as the tears just flowed and Dita tutted affectionately down the line, two hundred and twenty miles away. Her best friend was alive. Harry Cunningham was coming home.

Chapter Thirty-Two

'Liam, a mince pie doesn't *actually* have mince in it.' Mila was holding out the offending article, as though asking him to sniff it.

'But then why is it called a mince pie?'

'Mince*meat*, man. Mince*meat*.'

'Precisely.' He shrugged. 'Mince meat.'

'Ugh!' she groaned. 'Mincemeat is different to minced meat.'

'Well, how am I supposed to know that?' he called after her as she set it back down again and went to pull the next lot of festive surprises out of the oven.

'I'm *really* intrigued to see the pigs in blankets now,' Lee quipped.

'The English are crazy!' Liam called after Mila. He glanced back at her. 'No offence.'

'None taken,' she said, having another sip of her mulled wine as Noah laughed beside her.

'They're actually not bad,' he shrugged, helping himself to another.

'They're just not *mince pies*,' Lee demurred as he offered her one too. She winked at Liam. 'It's very sweet of you to have an English-themed Christmas party just for me, though.'

She looked around the room, oh-so-tastefully decorated

with flickering candles, beautiful, very tall people standing in clusters, looking chic in black.

'Well, seeing as Christmas is back on and all is happy again in Fitch World—'

'Well, *nearly* all,' Noah interrupted, throwing an arm around her shoulders and hugging her protectively, looking over at Liam accusingly as though Sam's behaviour was his responsibility.

'Hey, I didn't even know they had a thing going!' Liam protested. 'They deliberately kept it from me.'

She batted a hand casually. 'Nothing was kept from you. There was honestly nothing to tell. It was a weekend fling, nothing more. Just how I like it.' She shrugged, inwardly amazed at how something that had felt so seminal could be traduced so easily with just a few choice words. She took another long sip of her mulled wine, wishing it was whisky in an eggcup.

She looked around for a sighting of Jasper; he was playing with some other kids, mainly the children of Liam's work colleagues. They were slightly older than him and, much to his delight, were playing Hide and Seek in the bed and bathrooms. Liam had thought this was a great idea to keep hyperactive, overexcited kids away from the adults; as a non-parent and dedicated bachelor, he couldn't possibly imagine the destruction awaiting him later when everyone had left – duvets on the floors, loo paper off the roll, crushed crisps in the carpet, avocado dip on his Hermès silk ties, one of his shoes missing – probably lobbed behind a wardrobe and not to be found till his next house move . . .

'I still can't believe you never heard from him though – after the race I mean,' Noah pressed on, clearly believing her act that it meant nothing and feeling that this was safe ground to tread. 'To not even try to apologize.'

'Well, he clearly thinks *we* owe *him* the apology,' she said briskly.

Noah tutted and shook his head with a dark look. 'If I ever see him again, after the way he talked to my godson . . .'

Liam looked away, seeming distinctly uncomfortable.

'Hey Liam, it's not your fault,' she said quietly. 'Really. It's all fine.'

He nodded but still looked unhappy and for a brief moment Lee wondered what he'd heard from Sam, his version of events. But she brushed the query aside. She'd been there, she'd seen it all happen; there wasn't another side to tell. An accident had happened and he'd terrified a little boy, that was all. He was just like his father and why would she want to be around someone like that? She was just relieved she and Jasper had both seen his true nature before they'd become any more involved.

'So – any more on Harry?' Liam asked, changing the subject.

'Gisele texted me. He was landing this afternoon so, with any luck, he'll be at the hospital right about now.'

'You haven't heard from him yet?'

'No, not yet.' Lee felt her heart speed up. 'He's got his wife and baby to see first. That's only right, don't you think?'

'Of course. I just wondered—'

'He'll be in touch when he's ready,' she said lightly, but privately she wondered how long that might take. *Could* he forgive her for what she'd put him through? What had he been through out there? Were they 'even' now?

'How is the baby?'

'Seems to be a right little fighter. He's tiny, but feeding well, which is always a good sign.'

'Do we have a name?' Noah asked, reaching for another

minced-meat pie. Seeing as no one else was going to be having one . . .

'She's not decided yet, but I put in my bid and told her I always liked Sebastian.' She gave a casual shrug.

'Sebastian? No. Tell her to go for Noah. Good name. Strong name. Biblically masculine.' He stroked his beard in an ironic way.

She grinned. 'Well, I can pass it on, but I reckon as godmother my choice will get dibs over yours.'

Noah looked surprised. 'Gisele asked *you* to be godmother?'

'Yup. Thanks for sounding so stunned.' She shot him a sarcastic smile.

Noah laughed. 'Sorry, but you've got to admit it's a surprise.'

'Well, when you think about it, it actually makes perfect sense. I am Harry's best friend and the only person who will call that man out on his bullshittery. That baby needs me in his life.'

She caught Liam glancing over as Mila walked past with another tray of hot canapes. She jogged him with her elbow. 'Behave.'

Noah looked at them both, squinting with suspicion. '. . . What's going on?'

'Liam's got a crush on Mila,' Lee whispered, when Liam didn't reply.

'It's not a crush,' Liam protested.

'It's a crush,' she mouthed to Noah.

'I'm a thirty-one-year-old man, not a fourteen-year-old Belieber,' he said hotly. 'I do not get crushes. If I like a woman, then I take her to bed.'

Lee leaned in to Noah and spoke in stage whispers. 'Only

I won't let him do that with Mila because she is our friend and she has a boyfriend and she is *not* going to be one of the legion on his list.'

Liam looked across at her, unimpressed and actually quite angry. '. . . And what if I told you I think I'm in love with her?'

Lee burst out laughing. 'I'd say you were being wildly melodramatic because for once you didn't get to have your own way. Or . . . have your way.' She smiled at the pun.

'I find that offensive. Don't you think I'd *like* to fall in love with someone?'

'Liam, we've discussed this before. You're like me,' she said, patting his arm. 'A realist. Love is a fool's game.' She glanced at Noah. 'No offence.'

'None taken,' he murmured automatically, then looking taken aback that the comment should be directed to him.

Liam's scowl deepened. 'I'm going to refresh drinks.'

They watched him wander off, so sleek and elegant, his environment carefully curated as a reflection of his personality – the apartment minimally but stylishly furnished with walnut cabinetry, navy linen-lined walls, leather mid-century sofas and arched sweeping floor lamps. Even the Christmas tree was a design statement – a perfectly symmetrical fir decorated with only a single cream velvet bow on the top and lit from below by a light set into the floor. No fairy lights, no angel, no presents, no decorations and definitely no tinsel. Jasper had looked at it pityingly – particularly the bottom left corner – when they'd first walked in. Christmas songs were playing on the state-of-the-art sound system but they were of the tasteful sort – Eartha Kitt and Nat King Cole, not the Slade variety she and Jasper rocked out to. Except for the mince pie fiasco, this was the most stylish

Christmas party she'd ever been to. It had justified making the effort of putting on a dress and heels.

'I've never seen him like that before. Does Mila know?' Noah asked.

'Not a clue.'

'I thought she was seeing someone? An actor?'

Lee chuckled. 'He's not, but yeah, she is.'

'Is it serious?'

'No, they've been trying to meet up, but thanks to the shit-show that's passed as my life lately, they've struggled to get any real traction. But don't tell Liam that.' She finished her drink.

'Why not?'

'Because the longer he has to wait for Mila, the better the chance of his feelings actually growing into something real.'

Noah looked at her in surprise, his eyes beginning to twinkle as he sensed a conspiracy. 'Lee Fitchett, what are you up to?'

She was quiet for a moment, her eyes shining with mischief. 'Haven't you ever noticed that nothing makes you want something more than being told you can't have it? Go on a diet and don't eat that cake? Play with the puppy but don't touch it? It's no bad thing for Liam to pine for a bit. Mila's distracted by this new guy for the moment but you know as well as I do that she's always had a thing for Liam. Sooner or later she's going to notice the change in his behaviour and when she does . . . well, I don't want her getting hurt. Liam needs to know what it's like to want someone and not just be able to get them.'

'Lee, Lee, you are wicked,' he tutted. 'That man is *agitated*.' He leaned in closer. 'Hey, you couldn't do some of the same for me too, could you?'

In the other room, they heard a loud cheer, a sudden uproar of celebration from the children. The parents all shared bemused looks, none in any hurry to put down their drinks and check on the cause for joy – cheers meant they *weren't* needed, tears meant they were. Instead, someone turned the music up, a few people beginning to dance, the evening beginning to loosen . . .

Not so long ago, Lee knew she would have darted through to the bedroom, to double-check everything really was okay. Instead, she linked her arm through Noah's and turned them both towards the rest of the room. 'Well, let's see. Is there no one here who catches your eye?'

'It's not them catching my eye that's the problem. It's me catching theirs – and keeping it.' He sighed. 'I'm not asking for much, I don't think – just a nice smile and kind eyes.'

'A nice smile and kind eyes are exactly what you deserve.' She leaned into him affectionately. 'Don't worry, she's out there somewhere. And you know what they say – you'll probably find her when you're least expecting it.'

'Ha, I won't hold my breath.'

She looked at him sadly. Poor Noah. He was a big-hearted man, gentle, sweet and loyal – and always firmly in the friend-zone.

'And you? When are you going to find someone?'

She glanced at him quizzically. 'I'm not looking, Noah.'

'For the record, I'm not buying what you're saying about this Sam guy. I don't believe it was nothing to you – he got under your skin. You *want* the happy ending, Lee.'

She smiled determinedly back at him. 'Yes. And I've already got it. Jasper *is* my happy ending.'

Noah looked back at her sceptically. 'And what about when

he grows up and – I hate to break it to you – he leaves you? You know all boys leave their mothers in the end.'

'Uh-uh,' she smiled, waggling a finger at him. 'That's why *you're* his godfather. The second he turns eighteen, you're going to sit on him for me and stop that from happening.'

'Oh, I see!' he laughed. 'Okay. Well, slight expansion of my godfatherly duties – but anything for y—' He stopped talking, a small frown on his face.

'What?' She looked back, following his line of sight towards the hallway.

He looked confused. '. . . Nothing. I think it's just the kids mucking about.' He turned back to her, refilling her drink from a bottle on the table. 'So when are you going back to work?'

'Oh, not till the new year now. With everything that happened with Harry, I told Bart to cancel everything in my diary and shut up shop for the holidays. He's gone to Morocco with his partner for ten days—'

'Mama!' She turned to find Jasper tearing through the doorway. 'Mama!' He raced towards her, holding a present in his hand. It was a small box, wrapped in pale-blue paper and tied with a green ribbon. 'Father Christmas came and he gave me this!'

Lee looked over towards Liam, chatting closely with Mila. It was just like him – Uncle Smooth – to arrange for Father Christmas to come and dole out gifts to the kids.

'He said it was especially for me! Can I open it?'

She hesitated, preferring he waited till the morning, *comme les Anglais*. But several of the other kids came tearing through with theirs too, ripping off the paper. It would hardly be fair to make him be the exception to the rule. And he was having such a fun time. 'Okay fine, just this one though.'

Jasper pulled off the ribbon – which thankfully hadn't been

double-knotted, the cause of so much frustration and tears in their house – and let it waft to the floor. He tore at the paper and looked at the plain card box. It had its own lid on, like a hat.

'Look inside then, silly; he didn't just give you a box,' Lee prompted as he stalled.

But he kept on staring at it, suddenly reluctant to see what was inside.

'. . . Jasper? What is it?'

He looked up at her and she sank down to her heels in one movement, eye level with him, knowing something had happened. He cupped his hand around his mouth and said something into her ear.

'. . . What?' she asked, her voice sounding hollow. She looked back at him, feeling strangely weightless. 'No, darling, they're different.'

She rose to standing again, but Jasper just kept on nodding slowly, contradicting her.

'What did he say?' Noah asked, seeing the way their eyes had locked in silent communication.

'He said Santa Claus and Sinterklaas are the same person,' she murmured.

'Oh no,' Noah smiled. 'That's a common mistake for the non-Dutch, but I can assure you, Jazz Man, they are very definitely different people.'

But as Jasper pulled off the lid and they looked in to find a very old, loved, bedraggled Ducky curled up on tissue paper inside, Lee knew they were one and the same.

She ran through the apartment, rushing to the front door and staring out into the communal hall, looking up and down for a sign of him. But no one was to be seen on the winding stairs, just a large potted olive tree at the bottom and expensive fresh wreaths decorating the doors, Liam's own embellished with real pine cones and holly berries.

Where the hell was he? There were no footsteps on the stairs that she could hear, no drafts from an external door opening. Confused, she stepped back into the apartment and closed the door behind her, feeling her breath coming heavily, her emotions running high. Had she overreacted, jumped to the wrong conclusion?

'Lee?' Noah peered around the doorway, Jasper beside him. 'Everything okay?'

She nodded. 'Sorry, I . . . I just . . . wanted to see for myself.' She looked at Jasper and forced a shrug. 'I've never seen Santa Claus before, so . . .' She couldn't understand it. She'd been so sure.

Noah frowned, seeing straight through her bluff, but he didn't press her on it in front of Jasper.

She put a shaking hand to her head, trying to pull herself together. 'Look, I'm . . . uh, just popping to the loo but I think then we should start saying our goodbyes, Jazzy – it's getting late.' Just like that, her good mood had gone, her bright evening of determined celebration soured by the blots on her soul – invisible to the naked eye, perhaps, but like shadows on an X-ray, they attacked her from within.

'But I don't want to,' Jasper whined.

'Oh. Don't you want Santa Claus to bring you presents?'

'He already did. He brought Ducky back.'

'Well, you must want other presents too, I'm sure? And wouldn't it be awful if he came down our chimney and you weren't even there?'

He shrugged, looking sulky but also perturbed by that prospect.

'Come on, bud, let's have one last mince pie before you go, they're delicious.' Noah put a hand on Jasper's shoulder and led him back into the sitting room, as Lee walked into Liam's bedroom and over to the bathroom door. It was locked.

'Great,' she muttered to herself, sinking onto the bed and waiting, leaning on her arms splayed behind her, her head tipped back as she stared up at the ceiling, trying to bring her heart rate back down. She'd been so sure when she'd seen Ducky . . . there was only one person who could have given him back. She supposed Sam must have given it to Liam to return to her and he'd given it to Santa Claus?

. . . But no – Jasper had recognized him as Sinterklaas; he *knew* they were the same person.

She heard the bolt slide back and lifted her head.

'Sorry, I was just—'

Silence thundered as they stared at each other, Sam looking so very normal – and not like someone who could destroy two lives, just like that – in jeans and a shirt.

'Lee—'

But she was already charging towards him, her arms outstretched and palms flat against his chest, pushing him back into the bathroom again. He staggered backwards against the marble vanity unit, dropping the bag he was carrying, one red velvet arm flopping limply over the side. She stared at it contemptuously. 'How dare you!' she shouted. 'How dare you go anywhere near my son!'

Sam put his hands up in surrender. 'I'm sorry—'

'I don't want your goddam sorry! I just want you to stay the fuck away from my son, do you understand me?'

He stared back at her, visibly drawn since their last meeting – that kiss in the car park, the altercation on the ice . . .

'You have no right to go anywhere near him! You don't speak to him, you don't give him things, you don't even *look* at him!'

'I know. You're right. I just—'

'No! No justs! No buts!' She glowered at him, hating him, hating what he'd done to them. '. . . Don't you think there was a reason why we didn't ask for the toy back? His most beloved, precious belonging? Because *that's* how much we wanted never to have anything to do with you ever again!'

He looked away, swallowing hard. 'I'm sorry—'

'*Stuff* your sorry! Just stay away from us!' she cried, her voice breaking on the last word, tears threatening as all her frustration and all her anger disgorged in a single furious stream. He'd ruined it, something that could have been good – more than good. Their few days together – not just the two of them but the three of them – they'd been the best she'd ever known. They'd felt like a family, even though their time together could be counted in mere hours, and now she and her son felt the diminution of going back to what they'd been before, just the two of them . . . He'd spoilt that now – they knew what they were missing. They weren't enough any more. Didn't he see that?

A sob escaped her for what he'd done. 'You broke his heart! A little five-year-old boy who put his trust in you and looked up to you, and you just tore him apart.' Hot tears fell, only making her angrier because it wasn't just for herself that she was crying, but her son, heartbreak rising in her like a bear coming out of hibernation. She shook her head, hating the pity she saw in his face. 'Don't look at me like that! You disgust me! I've seen angry men in my life and you're as bad as the worst of them. You're a monster, just like your father.'

'No!' His voice, so placatory before, growled in protest. 'I'm nothing like him.'

'I saw what you are,' she sneered, staring back at him, hoping he could see the pity in *her* face. She – they – would move on, eventually; but he would always be this man.

She turned to leave. She had said everything she had to say to him, her hand already on the door-knob—

And then his hand on hers, stopping her.

'Get off me,' she shouted, whipping her hand away and squaring up to him, threat in her eyes.

He lifted his hands up like a soldier in surrender, removing any semblance of physical threat.

They stared at one another.

'Lee, I know what you think of me,' he said slowly, carefully, and she knew he was trying to de-escalate things, to calm her down. 'You hate me and I . . . I accept that. I don't blame you—'

'Big of you.'

His eyes flashed at her sarcasm. He took another breath. '. . . But there was more going on than you knew about, and Jasper, he got caught in it for just that one moment.' His voice wavered slightly. 'You know I would *never* deliberately do anything to hurt him. Never.' He pressed a hand to his heart. 'It's crushed me, knowing what I did. I'll never forgive myself for it.'

'Good. I hope you suffer.'

He stared back at her with a devastated gaze, seeing her anger, her walls, knowing she would never let him back in.

Her hand was back on the doorknob again. This time, *she* was the one doing the leaving—

'I had a brother.'

Her feet stopped at the past tense, remembering something

415

Aggie had said to her, something that had jarred at the back of her mind. *Evert's waited their entire lives for this moment.*

'He killed himself seven years ago. He was fifteen months older and he was . . . everything, to me.' His voice wavered again as he spoke to her back. 'He was called Pim, named after the man who put together the first Elfstedentocht, which, alone, tells you pretty much all you need to know about what it was like for him, growing up. My father put all his hopes and all his dreams onto him, burying him with pressure – he had to be the smartest, the fastest, the strongest boy in school.

'*I* wasn't strong like him. I was dyslexic, school was a nightmare; I was a dreamer, with no idea of what I was good at or what I was going to do with my life. Pim took the brunt of our father's attentions so that I wouldn't have to.'

Lee turned and looked back at him, hearing the tension quaver in his voice, seeing the strain in his muscles as he held himself still, all but his finger which tapped anxiously on the counter.

'By the time Pim was fifteen, my father had finally accepted his chance had passed and Pim winning it for him became his obsession instead – diet, training schedule, social life . . . Pim went along with it for years. But when the winters were so warm, year after year . . . he wanted to have some fun.'

He was quiet for a long moment, staring at his feet, his jaw sliding slowly back and forth. 'I don't know what happened exactly but they got into an argument; I think it got physical, because Pim left. Just went. He didn't come home for nine months.' His eyes narrowed, like he was trying to see something in the bathroom tile. 'Everything was different after that. *He* was different, like something had broken inside him. He'd laugh and joke and go through the motions of being happy but there was a sort of . . . flatness to him. His smiles never reached his eyes any more. I thought he'd snap out of it, that it was just a phase.'

His silences grew longer, his breathing becoming heavier and deeper as something big, something traumatic rolled through him.

'I don't think it was coincidence that he used Dad's shotgun.' The statement hung like cordite in the air. 'And I don't think he'd—' He looked down, sliding his jaw forward slightly, like it was a brake. 'I don't think he'd intended for me to be the one to find him . . .'

Lee's hand went to her mouth. She knew exactly what he'd seen that day. She knew too well what weapons did to flesh and blood . . . *wanted to be the guy that makes it all okay . . . wasn't sure if I could . . .* Suddenly she understood. She wasn't the only one living with trauma.

He dropped his head down, leaning against the vanity unit and taking several deep breaths before he looked back at her. 'I'm not telling you this because I want your sympathy. I'm just trying to explain that . . . I wanted to win for Pim and I lost sight . . . I lost sight of what really mattered. Winning that race was never *my* dream. You and Jasper are.' He looked straight at her but she couldn't speak, not a word.

'I was determined to get you back, to try to explain it all to you then and make you understand and forgive me – until I heard about Harry. And that was it; I knew you had bigger things to deal with than my *apology*.' He closed his eyes, the ball in his jaw pulsing. 'I told myself I just had to wait, but as the days went by and he still wasn't released, I realized the moment had gone. You don't trust easily and what I'd done, to the most treasured person in your life . . .' His voice broke and he coughed into his fist, pressing it to his lips for a few moments, steadying himself. 'You hated me. Of course you did. I did too. And I know it's too late now, too much has happened.'

She stared at him, feeling like she was being held in a vacuum. It was hard to breathe, to move . . .

He cleared his throat again. 'But when Liam said he wanted to surprise the kids with a visit from Santa, and asked if I could lend him the costume I've worn on the hospital visits . . . I saw an opportunity to try to make it up to Jasper, that was all. I knew he'd be missing Ducky and I thought perhaps I could "send" a message through Santa saying how sorry I was. I thought he needed to hear that, even if you didn't.' He blinked, staring back at her with burning eyes. 'That was all I came to do tonight, I swear.'

She nodded, believing him. '. . . Okay.' It didn't excuse what he'd done, but it did explain it at least. She'd seen enough of his father to understand the negative impact on both sons' lives. She couldn't hate him now.

She stared back at him, her heart beating erratically, her mind racing but finding no clear path to follow. She felt on the edge of a precipice – one word, one step forward and she knew she would fall. Headlong in love with him. Into his arms. But there would be no turning back and that terrified her. She needed an escape route. She had always needed that. She couldn't move.

He looked like he wanted to say something else but he closed his mouth again and stood up. 'I should go. It's better if Jasper doesn't see me.'

She felt the fibres in her muscles flinch, defensively. He was going? Already?

She watched in silence as he picked up the bag again, taking away the Santa disguise and walking past her to the door.

Her heart thudded harder with his every step. She knew she had to say it but she couldn't.

He didn't look at her again as he crossed into the bedroom, didn't turn back as he stepped into the hall, almost gone—

'I lied to your father.'

He stopped and she could read the puzzlement in his hesitation. He turned back to her. '. . . What?'

She stared into the silence, her mouth hanging open, scarcely able to believe she'd done it. Said the first words, taken the first step.

She felt the blood rush in her head. 'Yes, I . . .' Could she do it? Go on? Could she be brave like him, and put it all out there? 'I've never . . . used a zoom lens . . . It's . . . it's cheating.' Her voice was wavering and she knew she was growing pale as she willed him to make the connections, make sense of the clues she was giving him so that she wouldn't have to say the actual words.

'. . . Zoom lens . . . ?'

'Yes.' Her breathing was rapid. Shallow. '. . . That jihadi in the picture was never . . . three hundred metres away from me.' She swallowed, feeling almost faint. '. . . He wasn't even three metres—'

Silence exploded like a fireball, engulfing them both and rooting them to the spot. Then the bag dropped from his hand and he strode back to her, a look of such sorrow on his face it knocked her backwards. 'Lee.'

'It's okay,' she said quickly as his hands were upon her arms, tears spilling onto her lashes. 'I'm okay. I've got Jasper. He made it all okay.'

'But . . .' He frowned, pain a spasm across his face. 'He's . . . he's . . . ?'

'No.'

'. . . *No?*'

She swallowed, knowing she had to say the words at last. Name it. 'Jasper wasn't conceived from the rape.'

Sam's face slackened, relief interwoven with bewilderment, fear, pain, dismay . . . 'But . . . ?'

'When I went out to Syria that last time, I already knew that it was going to be my last time out there. Because I already knew I was pregnant.'

He stared at her, processing, catching up, understanding finally. 'Harry.'

She nodded.

'You love him?'

'Yes.'

He exhaled and looked down, then back at her again. He looked broken. Exhausted. Her hand went up to his face. 'But I'm not *in* love with him. I never was. Never will be. He's my best friend, Sam, he was my safety. But it was a mistake, we both knew it. We'd just come out of a particularly bad shelling – three days, four nights in Raqqa, constant bombardment. Barrel bombs. We were out of our minds with fear, we had to drink whisky from the bottle to stop shaking. It only happened the one time.' She looked up at him. 'Things happen out there, when you're living minute to minute. They don't mean anything. Sometimes it's just proof you're still alive.'

His face was so marbled with emotion she couldn't tell if he was about to laugh, cry or shout. '. . . Does he know? About Jasper?'

She shook her head, feeling a wave of shame. 'No,' she swallowed. 'I'd gone back out there to tell him. I knew he didn't want kids, and frankly I wasn't ready to become a parent either. I was pretty sure I was going to terminate but

I felt we should . . . talk about it. It was his baby too. I wanted him to have a say.'

She pressed her tongue behind her teeth as the memories rose up again; they would always be horrific but now – in her third telling of them – they were a little quieter than before, less vivid in colour.

'But before I could tell him, the ISIL attack happened and . . . it changed everything between us.' She exhaled slowly. 'I blamed him for what happened to me. I felt he had made choices that put me at risk. I was deeply traumatized and, for a long time afterwards, I couldn't pull myself back from it. I never spoke to him after that day.'

Sam's hands tightened around her arms. 'He must have understood though.'

'Yes. But also no. I don't think he fully realized how his actions felt like a betrayal to me – how he'd endangered me – until he finally accepted that we'd been ambushed. He denied it for a long time and that just made it so much worse. I think it was easier for him to believe it had been bad luck – wrong time, wrong place; just one of those things that happen in a war zone. He couldn't accept that his ambitions had played a part.'

She shook her head, feeling the familiar pressure in her chest. 'So I never told him about the baby. I'm not proud of it now, but at the time, it felt . . . it felt like the only thing I could control, the only part of me that was pure. I needed that baby; he was the only thing that gave me the strength to keep going.'

She swallowed. 'I came to live here, tried to build a new life and put all of that world – and him – behind me. But when Harry heard I was pregnant, he followed me here. He assumed, like you, the rapist was the father and I let him believe that, because I didn't want him back in our lives; every time I looked at him or thought about him, it brought it all back. Jasper felt like my second chance at life and I didn't want to share him, not even with his own father.' Her face fell as she said the words out loud for the first time, the enormity of what she'd done, not just to Harry but to Jasper, hitting her finally. 'I deprived my child of knowing his father, because of *my* selfishness.'

'Lee, no, you were traumatized.'

'But Harry moved back here to try to protect me, he wanted to make things right. And I wouldn't let him. I was terrified he would take one look at him and know . . .'

'That wouldn't have happened.'

'But it did. His wife knew. She saw it.'

He frowned. '. . . Really?'

'I went to tell her everything – I felt I owed her the truth about why her husband had gone – but she had already guessed it. She had spent Pakjesavond with us, and although she didn't fully process it at the time, she had a gradual realization back home that they shared certain mannerisms, a particular look. And once she'd had the thought, she could just . . . see he was Harry's son.'

It was why Gisele had brought the letter over several days later, why she hadn't had to read it. Much of it she had been able to guess.

Sam grazed the back of his hand down her cheek sadly. 'And now Harry's back . . . are you going to tell him?'

'I don't know if he'll even want to see me. But he deserves to know the truth.'

He swallowed. '. . . And Jasper?'

She was quiet for a moment, feeling another pitch of nerves. 'I'm going to sit him down tonight and tell him. An edited version, clearly. But it's the right time – before anything gets out. He just wants to be like all his friends, he wants a father.'

Sam looked down. 'Well, that's . . . yes.'

She watched him swallow, saw the tension in his face. He had no claims here. He wasn't Jasper's father, he'd got it wrong and made one terrible, awful mistake. And yet fathers were made, not born – and didn't she make mistakes too? She couldn't deny the bond between them was natural, instinctive, close. If she deserved a second chance with Harry, didn't Sam deserve one too? 'So, as for letting *you* back in his life . . .' she murmured.

He looked back at her.

'I can't make any promises; the cut might be too deep,' she said quickly, before he dared to hope too much. 'We'll have to take it slow. Jasper gets to decide. It's going to be a lot for him to take in, finding out about his biological father. There may not be space for you too. Not yet.'

Sam nodded, drawing back. 'Yes.'

She saw the apprehension in his eyes and wished she could kiss him. She could see the longing in his eyes too and she wished it could be as easy as that. But she would not fall further than this point, not unless Jasper fell with her.

'. . . So how do we do this, then? I just wait . . . give you space?'

She stared at him, thinking, desperately trying to think of how they could stitch themselves back together again. '. . . Well, what are you doing tomorrow?'

'Tomorrow?'

'Yes. Do you have plans?'

'No – it's Christmas Day. My father would never let us go in for it. He said it wasn't Dutch so we never celebrated it.' He shrugged.

'Even better, then,' she quipped, her smile broadening and a dark gleam in her eyes. 'I think I've got an idea.'

Chapter Thirty-Three

'Ah! I see you got the memo!' Liam exclaimed as Sam stood in the doorway.

Sam looked down at his bottle-green reindeer jumper, complete with red pom-pom nose. 'This was an *emergency* purchase.'

'Was it, though?' Lee teased, stepping forward from her spot at the island with Mila, drying her hands on a dishcloth. She saw the light in his eyes turn up at her voice, knew that he wanted to step forward to kiss her, but he didn't dare – Jasper was on the floor across the room, doing a puzzle with Noah. 'Are you sure you didn't really have that lurking in your wardrobe, just waiting – hoping – for the right occasion?'

Liam pulled at his own jumper, raising an eyebrow. His had an almost-tasteful intarsia polar bear, Jasper's a snowman with a sewn-on scarf, Noah's a jolly Santa stretched over his own round stomach; even Pabe had been game for wearing the reindeer cardigan she had presented him with when he arrived, complete with jingle bells on the shoulders. 'Apparently it's an English thing.'

'It's not really,' Lee whispered with a grin, patting Liam's chest. 'I just thought it would be amusing to put you in acrylic for the day.'

Liam showed her the bird.

She laughed, throwing the dishcloth over her shoulder. 'Everyone, this is Sam.'

'Hi Sam!' they responded in unison, with friendly waves. Sam waved back to the room but his eyes caught on Jasper, who pushed back on his heels, looking over but not moving.

'Hi. I'm Mila,' Mila said, darting over in the frilled pinny and offering one clean hand; her other was covered in flour.

'Hi, Mila,' Sam smiled. 'Heard lots about you.'

'And I you,' Mila replied with an enigmatic smile before running back to stir the gravy.

Sam swapped a questioning look with Lee, who could only roll her eyes. The news of their last-minute guest had been greeted with high spirits by her friends, to say the least. 'Liam, get Sam a drink, would you?' she asked as she wandered back to help Mila. The turkey was already out and resting, covered like a marathon runner in tinfoil sheets. She peeked a look at the juices running clear.

'What'll it be?' Liam asked as they wandered towards the bar by the window. 'Champagne or a glass of Noah's lethal – sorry, I mean legendary – punch?'

'Oh,' Mila said under her breath, watching them go. 'He's so gorgeous. He even makes that jumper look good.'

'I know,' Lee murmured, feeling her heart beat thirteen to the dozen. Had this been a good idea after all? Was she just fooling herself? How could she possibly stop herself from falling? She felt she was clinging to a ledge by her fingernails. 'Wait – we are talking about Sam, right?'

Mila gave her an innocent look. 'Of course.'

Lee narrowed her eyes, unconvinced. 'Hmm.' Liam had turned up with a suspiciously large bunch of mistletoe and had been in the process of trying to find somewhere to hang it when Sam had arrived. It was left on the table now.

Mila moved the roast potatoes into the warmed tureen. 'You know, you've got quite a large gathering here today, for someone who three days ago couldn't get off the sofa and hadn't bought a single present.'

Lee agreed, baffled herself. 'I know. It's all just sort of . . . developed,' she said, looking around her home with fresh eyes – the asymmetrically but beautifully decorated, squat Christmas tree in the window, Pabe sitting in front of the fire and talking with Lenka, Jasper and Noah playing on the floor, a bulging bag of shredded and torn wrapping paper by the window – not that the present mountain was depleted yet. The table had been laid with crackers across the plates; the colourful paper-chain links Jasper had made yesterday afternoon were now looped across the ceiling, courtesy of Noah's long-armed reach and a half-ton of blu-tack . . . The house looked colourful, bright and full of life.

'Drinks for the chefs,' Sam said, as he and Liam came back with fresh glasses for them too.

'Thank you, Sam,' Mila said bouncily. 'Guys, could one of you give me a hand with the turkey? I want to collect the juices in the gravy pan.'

Liam almost broke into a sprint towards the carving board.

Sam came over to Lee's side. 'Did you talk to him?' he asked in a whisper, looking suddenly serious. Nervous.

'Yes.'

'What did you say?'

'That I'd asked you to come for Christmas lunch.'

'And? What did he say to that?'

'. . . To be honest, not much – but he didn't burst into tears either. So just take it slowly with him.'

'Can I hug him?'

'No, let him lead. And don't overcomplicate things. He doesn't need the backstory. Just tell him how you feel.'

'Okay, right,' Sam nodded, looking anxious.

She put her hand on his. It was the only touch that had passed between them since the Elfstedentocht and she felt the current zip between them. 'You'll be fine. I'll call Noah over here and you can speak to him now.'

'Shouldn't we go somewhere more private?'

'No, he'll feel more secure in here. But it's best to clear the air quickly. You'll both feel better for it.'

He nodded, looking sick. She wished so much she could kiss him.

'Hey Noah,' she called instead. 'Come here a sec, would you?'

'I'll be right back, Jazzy,' she heard Noah say, ruffling Jasper's hair as he clambered up from the floor. 'What is it, Lee?'

'Can you, uh, check on drinks for Lenka and Pabe for me?'

'Oh, okay. On it,' he shrugged.

'Go,' Lee whispered, pushing Sam towards her son, playing alone now in the middle of the floor.

Noah returned a moment later. 'They're on lemon sodas,' he said, reaching into the fridge instead. He leaned in closer to Lee as he poured. '. . . That Lenka's got a lovely smile, don't you think?'

Lee's mouth opened in surprise, looking over at Lenka and then back at him again. '. . . Yes.' Unlike the men in their acrylic finery, the women had been freed from the dress code. Ritual humiliation for the men, Lee had explained, was an integral part of the English Christmas, but in truth, she had just wanted Lenka to feel comfortable, and to Lee's delight, she had arrived wearing jeans and a striped sweater with shearling boots. She looked *warm*. And like she'd slept.

'But she's got such sad eyes.'

'Yes, she does,' Lee agreed as they both watched her talk quietly to Pabe. The old man was holding her hand, patting it kindly, and Lee could guess what they were discussing. Pabe had been deeply distressed at the revelations about his tenants. Lee had tried to console him that she'd not seen the signs either, that she'd been taken in by Gus's friendly-enough demeanour, but he had taken it to heart; Pabe had already told her he intended to offer Lenka the apartment rent-free for the next year as some way to say sorry.

Lee looked back at Noah. 'All the more reason why she needs a friendly face. Why don't you go and talk to her? Tell her your priest and nun story.'

'You think so?'

'Noah, if ever there was a moment for the priest and nun story, this may well be it.'

Noah rolled his shoulders back and stretched his neck side to side. 'Then I'm her man.'

Lee watched as he made his way over, folding with laughter as he accidentally trod on a stray Lego brick so that he concertina'd in height and hobbled like a goblin for several paces. Lenka was laughing before he'd even got to her.

'Good start,' Mila grinned, joining her again at the island.

But Lee was watching Sam, standing by the Christmas tree with Jasper. He was kneeling, sitting back on his heels, so they were at eye level, Jasper's chin tucked in as Sam spoke quietly, Sam keeping his hands in his lap and keeping himself small.

Lee felt her heart hitch at the sight of them talking; her every instinct told her to run to her son and wrap him in her arms, keep him safe from everyone who wasn't her, who couldn't *guarantee* his happiness and safety. But then she saw

Sam stop talking and the two of them stared at one another for a long, long moment, before Jasper hesitantly put out his hand for a handshake.

Sam's mouth curved upwards as he shook it, the two of them beginning to smile a little now. Hands still clasped solemnly, still shaking, Sam reached over with his free hand and suddenly tickled Jasper under the arm. Her son collapsed in wriggling giggles against him, and then, just like that, they were hugging – Jasper's arms wrapped around Sam's neck, Sam giving him a kiss in his hair.

'Oh my God,' Mila whispered at the sight of them, one hand slapped on Lee's arm and holding it there as man and boy continued to hug – until Sam tickled him again, sending Jasper off into more wriggling snorts of laughter.

Lee felt herself breathe again. It was going to be okay.

No; Sam glanced over at her with shining eyes and she knew it was going to be *better* than okay. Having utterly convinced herself she would truly never see him again – there had been no way back that she could see, no way she could forgive what he'd done to her child – it felt unreal that he should be here now, looking like he always had been. He just seemed to slot into her and Jasper's lives somehow, unforced, unselfconscious.

She heard the doorbell ring downstairs.

'Oh my God, who *else* is coming?' Mila asked incredulously. 'We're going to be short on potatoes.'

'Relax, it's just a delivery for Jasper. I got him his own bike. He's been begging for one for months. He wants to be a big boy.'

'They're delivering on Christmas Day?'

'Amazing what can be done if you offer to pay double the asking price,' Lee shrugged. 'I only ordered it on Wednesday, so they did well to even get it in for last night. They've put on all the bells and whistles for me and promised to wrap it in ribbons and bows so it's ready to give.'

'Mama!' Jasper ran over to her, his eyes brighter even than when he'd opened his super-mega Nerf gun. She lifted him up onto her hip, but he was almost too heavy for her these days.

'Did I just see you and Sam make up?' she asked, stroking his cheek.

He nodded. 'He asked if we could have a man-to-man talk. He's really sorry. It made him really sad. He's missed me a lot.'

Lee tried to keep her smile from being too wide. 'Ah. And so how do you feel about him now?'

'Happy. I missed him too.'

Lee let her smile be what it was. 'Great. Because so did I.'

The doorbell rang again. 'Oh damn!' she said, jolting in surprise, realizing she'd been distracted again. 'Jazzy, let me get that. I'll be right back.'

Sam, still at the window, looked over at her as she ran from the room. She winked at him on her way down the stairs.

She swung open the door. 'I'm sorry, so sorry, it's a madhouse up th—'

The words died on her lips as Harry blinked back at her. He had lost a dramatic amount of weight, his hair was significantly greyer and longer, and his eyes had finally lost their laughter. A veil of tears shone in them instead.

Without another thought, without even another breath, she threw her arms around his neck, instantly sobbing as the past few weeks' fear, and the past six years' pain, poured out of her in a rush. A sound she didn't recognize came from deep inside her, a wail of the type she'd seen from other women in other lands – mournful and ancient.

'. . . Are you okay?' she sobbed and hiccupped into his hair, easily feeling his bones beneath his overcoat. She felt him nod but she'd felt the hesitation too. 'Are you all right? . . . Oh God, what did they do?'

'I'm okay, Fitch.'

But she tightened her grip on him, hardly able to believe it. 'Oh Harry, I was so frightened,' she wept into his neck.

'I know. I know you were.' His voice was the same as it had always been. Solid. Steady. Safe. And she knew they weren't just talking about his capture.

She pulled back to look at him, tears streaming down both their cheeks. He opened his mouth to say something else but she silenced him with a finger to his lips. 'No. Don't say it,' she said quickly, knowing him too well. 'You have nothing to be sorry for.' Her voice was thick and choked. 'You were trying to do good . . . and sometimes it just goes that way . . . Bad things happen.' She nodded, feeling the tears surge again, but she let them fall. Fall away from her. 'The risk was always there and I knew that. It wasn't your fault . . . And I . . . I shouldn't have punished you the way I did.'

He put his hands on her shoulders and looked her straight in the eye. His were bloodshot still, the faint traces of a bruise still around the socket of his left eye, a small scab on his lip. 'I don't blame you for a single thing, Fitch, you hear me?'

She stared back at him, hiccupping more gently as she heard the subtext. '. . . Oh God, you know.'

He inhaled slowly and nodded. 'Gisele told me.'

'. . . Yes.' Lee felt a slow deflation in her lungs. Perhaps that was only right, for this was part of her story too now. Her family. They were all connected forever. 'Harry—'

'It's okay.'

'No, let me say this. I have to say it,' she pleaded. 'You have to know why.'

He nodded then, letting her speak, and she looked back at him with shining eyes.

'After it happened, I was so . . . broken, and so angry, I needed someone I could blame. I couldn't forgive you because if I did, who would I have to hate?' The tears overflowed again, her shoulders pressed up to her ears as her voice broke. '. . . I never even saw his face.'

Tears shone in his eyes too. 'I know, Fitch, I know.' That had been one of the hardest things. Never knowing who had done this to her. 'And if it makes any difference at all, he's probably dead, and probably has been for a long time. But that's why I went for Moussef. Because he engineered it. And he's paid for it.' His arms wrapped around her again. 'He's gone now, Fitch,' he whispered into her hair. 'You're safe again.'

She was safe. It was over. The past belonged to another land.

She closed her eyes as he kissed her hard on the cheek, forgiveness and love in one movement.

'Do you want to come in?' she asked as they finally pulled apart. 'I'm afraid there's a crowd up there—'

He grinned and she saw a flash of her old friend still lingering behind the cuts and bruises and thin skin. He'd come back from this, she already knew it. He shook his head. 'I need to get back to the hospital. I only went home to change but I couldn't go another hour without seeing you. I needed to know we're good again.'

Good again. She smiled at his typical understatement, wondering when he'd last slept. 'We're better than good, Cunningham,' she replied, punching him softly on the arm. 'We're best friends.'

He gave a relieved smile. 'I'm glad to know it was worth it, then.'

'Yes,' she chuckled, sensing their black humour resurfacing. 'I don't ask for much.'

They both grinned, feeling their bond come back to life as they stared at one another with the deep affection of old friends.

But his smiled faded and he became more serious again. 'Does . . . does Jasper know about me?'

She nodded. 'I told him last night. He took it very well. I had always told him you lived very far away. So now I've told him your name, and that you're back.'

'And . . .' He looked nervous, just like Sam had. 'Does he want to know me?'

'Harry, you're his father,' she said gently. 'Whenever you're ready, he'd like to meet you.' She qualified that. 'I mean, perhaps *right now* isn't the best time, with all these people . . .'

'No, no.' A light flickered in his eyes. 'But . . . how about tomorrow then?'

'Tomorrow? That's not too soon for you?'

'What would we be waiting for?' he shrugged. 'You could come to the hospital and he could meet his little brother.'

'Is Gisele okay with that?'

'It was her idea.'

Lee smiled, feeling something in her loosen. 'Then we'll do that. Although I should warn you, you'll probably come a distant second on the "interesting new people" scale when Jasper finds out he's got a little brother to play with.'

Harry smiled. 'Second's fine.' He nodded as his eyes began welling up with tears again and she knew exactly what he was thinking. He had thought he was coming home to a baby daughter and instead found himself with two sons. It would be a lot for anyone to absorb. 'Oh God.'

She put her arms around him again. 'We're all going to be okay, you know?'

'I know,' he laughed, roughly wiping away the tears. 'I'm just not used to feeling this happy. It's going to be the death of me.'

'Yeah, right,' she laughed. 'It's the happiness that'll get you.'

They both the heard the echo from their old life, the day everything had changed.

'Go!' she said, shooing him away affectionately before she started off crying again too. 'Go be with your wife and baby. We'll come over during visiting hours tomorrow morning.'

He turned and went back down the steps and she noticed for the first time the cab idling on the cobbles.

'Hey, Cunningham!' she called as he opened the car door. 'Have you decided on a name for the baby yet?'

'Gisele likes Sebastian!' He shrugged. 'So I guess that's what we're going with.'

Sebastian. So she'd gone for it after all? She grinned, biting her lip, delightedly. 'Tell her I love it!' she called back as he got into the car.

She waved as the taxi glided away, her gaze falling for a few moments on the frozen canal, a few of her neighbours gliding up and down the ice. Life was idling at a slow, quiet pace this Christmas Day.

She closed the door behind her with a gentle click – completely forgetting all about the bolts and chains – and slowly climbed the stairs, growing more aware again of the noise coming from her living room. Everyone seemed to be cheering. What on earth—?

She walked through the doorway to find Jasper standing on a chair, holding up the bunch of mistletoe, and Liam and Mila standing beneath it, kissing.

'Oh honestly! I leave you lot alone for two minutes!' she laughed, seeing how Liam's arms were wrapped tightly around Mila, like he never wanted to let her go.

Noah, Lenka and Pabe were all cheering – but where was Sam?

'Hey.' His voice was low.

She turned to find him behind her. He looked down at her wet lashes and tear-tracked cheeks; he seemed apprehensive. 'I saw from the window . . . All okay?'

She nodded, walking into his arms and resting her head on his shoulder, hearing his heart beat faster. 'Yes,' she whispered. 'Everything's perfect.'

She wished they were alone, but she had a house full of guests, and as she heard the cheers start up again, she turned to see Noah whisking Jasper off the chair and holding him up under the arms; together, they came running over and carefully, Jasper dangling in mid-air, he positioned the bunch of mistletoe above *their* heads.

Lee laughed, blushing, as the cheers grew louder, Sam's hand encircling her waist.

'You have to kiss him, mama! It's Christmas good luck!'

Sam turned her to face him, his hand upon her cheek. 'What do you say, Lee? Don't you think it's about time we had a little luck?'

She felt the butterflies in her stomach take wing, and with them, her hopes too. 'Oh yes,' she smiled as he bent towards her. 'I really do.'

Epilogue

The fire crackled, the three of them variously stretched out and curled up on the sofa. She and Sam were lying in spoons, Jasper sitting atop Sam as *Return of the Jedi* played on the TV. His toys old and new – Nerf guns and Scalextric cars and Lego bricks and lightsabers, all played with at different times today – were discarded in various parts of the room; but Ducky was threaded between his fingers, his thumb in his mouth.

Their guests now departed, only the lights on the Christmas tree were on, the living room feeling almost Dickensian in its dimly lit glow. Sam stroked her hair, taking in her profile by the firelight, gazing at her like she was made from the stars.

The credits rolled and she looked back at him with glowing eyes, knowing the beginning of their time – alone, at last – was almost upon them.

But not quite yet. There was still one last thing to do. A final piece to be slotted into the puzzle.

'Jazzy,' she said, pulling herself up the sofa as he stirred and yawned, knowing without needing to be told that it was time to go to bed. He was worn out. Playing with all the grown-ups had been exhausting. 'There's one more thing I wanted to talk to you about.'

He looked at her sleepily.

'I know you've had a lot of news to take in these past few days – but it's all been good news, hasn't it?'

'Yes.' He looked back at Sam again, smiling shyly.

Sam's arm rose, ruffling his hair affectionately.

'Well, this is good news too. I think – I hope – it will make you very happy.' Jasper tipped his head to the side, his brown eyes resting upon her. She knew she was his safety, his place of refuge.

'You know how we talked last night about your father, Harry – about how he's been far away but now he's back? Well, he wondered whether you'd like to see him tomorrow?'

Jasper's eyes widened. 'Tomorrow?'

'I know, it's soon, isn't it? What do you think? Would you like that?'

Jasper hesitated, glancing at Sam.

Sam smiled back, squeezing his leg. '*I* think it sounds exciting.'

Jasper's mouth spread into a small smile, his relief evident that he didn't have to somehow choose. 'Yes, it's exciting.'

'The thing is, Harry's wife Gisele – do you remember she came for Pakjesavond?'

Jasper nodded. 'She bought me a gun and had a baby in her tummy.'

'That's right, she did!' Lee chuckled. 'But you see, the baby has been born now. She had a little boy. And because that little boy is Harry's son, that means he is also . . .' She swallowed, feeling suddenly nervous. 'He's also *your* baby brother.'

Jasper blinked, his mouth opened to a perfect 'o' as her words settled in his young brain. '. . . I've got a baby brother?' he repeated.

Lee nodded, feeling her heart lurch, not sure on which side of the fence this news might fall.

'That means, you're a *big* brother,' Sam said quietly, his eyes glowing with an inner, checked emotion. 'And take it from me, brothers always grow up to be best friends.'

'I'm a big brother,' Jasper repeated excitedly.

'You are. His name is Sebastian, but I think it will probably get shortened to Bas.'

Jasper gasped as he heard the echo. 'Bas and Jazz!'

'Exactly!' Lee laughed, clapping her hands together at the spectacle of his delight. 'You even sound like brothers!'

'Does he look like me?'

'I don't know,' she shrugged. 'We'll just have to see tomorrow, won't we?'

The excitement was too much for him now and Jasper clambered off Sam like he was a hunk of rock – almost winding him in the process – and jumped onto the floor. Picking up his lightsaber, he did a dramatic flash and turn. 'I'm a big brother!'

Sam and Lee laughed as he ran a lap around the room, roaring, lightsaber held aloft.

He did a full circuit and, as he got back to them again, his eyes were shining like coals. 'It's just like in my poem for Sinterklaas.'

'Huh?' For a moment Lee was confused. But as she thought back, dredging through the memories, she remembered again . . . 'Oh my goodness, yes!'

'Santa brought me my baby brother on Christmas Day!'

Lee laughed. 'Sort of, yes.'

His mouth opened wide, eyes so full of wonder she thought he was hallucinating. He gasped. 'Mama, I *told* you Sinterklaas and Santa Claus are the same!'

Sam, confused, looked between them both, just as Jasper took off for another roaring lap of the room. 'What?'

'Long story,' she grinned, squirrelling back into him and reaching towards him for another kiss. 'But I'd say your days in fancy dress are well and truly numbered.'

Acknowledgements

This was the most difficult book I've written to date. Deciding to set a Christmas story in a country for whom Christmas is a footnote to St Nicholas' Day – several weeks earlier and actually beginning in mid-November – posed logistical challenges that meant my timing and pacing were completely out in the first draft, and required a significant rewrite. With three weeks until my deadline, I effectively only had half a story, couldn't see a way forward and my confidence really deserted me, to the point where, for several very long weeks, I thought I wouldn't have a book on the shelves for you this Christmas. The person who dug me out of the hole was my agent, Amanda. Somehow sensing through the ether that I was in trouble, she called at precisely the right time and we talked it through; her suggestions unplugged the plot block and I was able to get back on track. Amanda, if the agenting doesn't work out, you'd make a fortune in plumbing! Thank you, thank you.

Caroline, my editor, also helped restore my confidence, greeting the book with an enthusiasm I never would have predicted. There was scar tissue left from this writing experience, and even though I'd managed to push through to an ending, I was concerned the fault lines would still be visible. Of course, every book needs a damned good edit (or ten!) so

I knew we could finesse the bare bones, but would it be enough? Caroline's energy upon reading even the first draft lifted me up when I needed it most and persuaded me that perhaps the writing genie hadn't abandoned me completely, so thank you Caroline for those well-chosen words; they meant more than perhaps you realized.

My Pan Mac gang – all of you – thank you for being the best bunch. You're so good at what you do, you make it look easy, even though it really isn't. And it never feels like work, putting these stories together and the books out. I love every step of the process, and even though this book has been produced under the difficult circumstances posed by Covid-19, we still feel like a team. Thank you.

Finally, a shout-out to my Dutch friends who gave me crucial advice about their native customs and national character – Martine, who makes a cameo appearance in the story; and Nicole, whose two sons are in fact called Sebastian and Jasper – Bas and Jazz – and ended up inadvertently giving the book such a lovely note to finish on. Little did you know, Nix, sixteen and fourteen years ago, that you'd be doing me such a favour! I owe you one (that 'one' probably being bottle-shaped and ending in -ollinger!)